I0610386

Spore Press

SEASON
OF THE
DEAD

By

Lucia Adams, Paul Freeman,
Gerald Johnston,
& Sharon Van Orman

SPORE PRESS LLC
LITTLE ROCK

SEASON OF THE DEAD

Lucia Adams, Paul Freeman, Gerald Johnston, Sharon Van Orman

Published by Spore Press

ISBN : 978-0-9881923-7-9

SPORE PRESS LLC
6916 Incas Drive, North Little Rock, AR 72116, USA

PRINTING HISTORY
Spore Press eBook/ July 2013
Spore Press Paperback / July 2013

For information, address: Spore Press Marketing,
6916 Incas Drive, North Little Rock, AR 72116.

http://www.sporepress.com

Spore Press Books are published by Spore Press LLC
SPORE PRESS and the "Spore" design are trademarks of Spore Press

Edited by Allen Brady / Cover design by Alan Davidson

DEDICATION

For our families

ACKNOWLEDGMENT

We would like to thank everyone who contributed to, encouraged, and inspired Season of The Dead.

SEASON OF THE DEAD

Centers for Disease Control and Prevention

CDC 24/7: Saving Lives, Protecting People, Saving Money through Prevention

*****Press Release*****

Effective Immediately:

The Center for Disease Control has issued a nationwide rabies warning. A particularly virulent strain has been discovered along the U.S.-Canada border. Should you encounter an animal that you believe is infected, exercise extreme caution. Do not approach the animal. Instead, contact your local law enforcement agency.

In the event of a bite, please seek medical treatment immediately. Do not return to your home. Symptoms include: extreme headache, increased salivation, and aggressive behavior.

Repeat: Seek treatment immediately in the event of bite.

We are working towards containing the issue. This release is purely cautionary in nature.

Contact Information
Centers for Disease Control and Prevention
1600 Clifton Rd. Atlanta, GA 30333, USA
800-CDC-INFO (800-232-4636)
New Hours of Operation:
8AM-8PM ET, Monday-Friday, Closed Holidays
cdcinfo@cdc.gov

CHAPTER 1

Omaha, Nebraska, USA
Sharon

My grandmother, with her thick Kentucky accent, used to say things like, "Don't stand there blinking at me like a toad in a hail storm." Now, as I lay on the floor of my bedroom with blood streaming down my face, I had to admit that I was feeling very toad versus hail-like.

After a long day, I had finally fallen into bed around midnight; sleep claimed me before my head hit the pillow. About six hours later, I was woken by an explosion that rocked my building and startled me to the point where I fell out of bed and smacked my face on the hardwood of the floor.

I grabbed a box of tissues off the nightstand, held one to my bleeding nose, and swallowed—the taste of iron thick in my mouth. Rising on shaking legs, I padded into the living room.

My apartment was ultra-modern, very minimalist. To my left was a fireplace, clad in limestone, and flanked by windows. Directly in front of me was a line of windows that stretched from my living room to my high-tech kitchen. I had paid extra to have a view of the Bob Kerry Pedestrian bridge that linked downtown Omaha to Iowa.

A small giggle escaped me when I realized that the city had only just paid the bridge off last month. Now it had about a ten to fifteen foot gap right in the middle of it. The windows were closed, but I imagined I could hear the metal groan as the tension cables began to snap free.

I looked up; a pale blue sky unmarred by even a single cloud was the perfect backdrop for the black wedge that was quickly disappearing over the horizon. I lived near Offutt Air Force base. My father had been stationed there. I had attended many an air show. I knew a Stealth when I saw one. I also knew there were several types. I couldn't tell you which one this was, but I had a sinking feeling about what was going on.

Walking back into my room, I slid open the patio doors and looked north. The I-80 bridge over the Missouri River had been similarly damaged. I blinked, my stomach clenched, and my heart rate increased.

They were disabling the bridges over the river. The analytical part of my mind registered that they did not destroy them, which meant that they hoped to rebuild someday, but the more vocal side was screaming that a line in the sand was being drawn and I was about to toe that line. I breathed in the late fall air and tried to calm myself. I would not panic.

Stepping back inside, I tossed the bloody tissue into the basket, walked into the bathroom, and washed my face, squinting at my reflection in the mirror. I looked tired. My pale skin highlighted faint purple smudges under my eyes; my hair, long and red, was still in a ponytail with the hair band hopelessly tangled. I took a pair of cuticle scissors, snipped it out, and let the unruly mess fall about my shoulders.

I grimaced at the mirror, ran my fingers through my hair—it was good as it was going to get until I showered—and grabbed my robe. I decided to go check on my neighbor.

Each floor of my building had three apartments. Rob, who was a major in the Air Force, was gone and had been for several days. His flight crew was on standby, so he was staying at the field house on base. Jenny, my best friend since the eighth grade, lived in the other apartment with her husband, Jameson, and their son, Parker. Jameson was also stationed at Offutt, but part of Global Weather, or AFWA.

I opened my door and was immediately greeted by screaming—Parker's terrified screaming.

I ran to their apartment and pounded on the door. "Jenny!" I yelled. "Open the door!" I slammed my fist on the hard steel, frantic for an answer, but all I heard was Parker.

Rob, Jenny, and I had exchanged keys on the off chance that one of us lost ours. So far, I was the only one that managed to lock myself out—more than once, if I was honest. I ran to my apartment and grabbed my purse, emptying its contents all over my kitchen counter in search of my keys.

They clinked against the granite. I scooped them up, the metal cool in my hand, and ran back towards the door. As I passed my hall closet, I paused.

A few years ago, I had dated a cop. For our anniversary, he bought me a hand gun. To say that I was less than impressed was the understatement of the year. But once I was at the shooting range, firing that weapon and putting neat little holes in my target, I began to see the appeal.

The boyfriend had long since gone, but the gun was still around. On impulse, I grabbed the hard plastic case off the top shelf, keyed in the code, and opened it, revealing a small Glock 27. I quickly loaded it and ran back to Jenny's apartment, praying that whatever was going on in there was something I could stop.

Parker's screams had reached a new level of terror, sending tendrils of fear dancing down my spine. With shaking hands, I unlocked the door and turned the knob. The security chain kept me from opening it all the way. I screamed in frustration.

"Jenny!" I shouted, pressing my face to the opening. "What is going on?" When there was no answer from her, I shouted for her son. "Parker, can you hear me?" He screamed louder.

I took a step back, intending to try to kick the door and hopefully break the chain. Suddenly, Jenny's face appeared in the door, only it wasn't the face that I knew and loved. Milky white eyes glared back at me, and an arm that had been flayed of skin reached towards me. I screamed in fright, tripped on my own feet, and fell. I scuttled backwards like a crab towards the wall where I braced myself against Rob's door.

I had dropped the keys, but still held the gun in my shaking hands. A Glock doesn't have a safety, just a tight trigger. If you fired it, it was because you meant to. I swallowed as I looked at her. She snarled and grabbed at the door with both hands, yanking on it until the small screws holding the security chain to the door frame began to work their way out.

Her groaning, drooling countenance glared at me in hatred, anger, and hunger. I blinked again, stunned for the second time in less than an hour. My grandmother's words came back to haunt me; this was not the time to be slow.

I raised the gun, just as she flung the door open. "Jenny," I whispered her name like a benediction. She paused and cocked her head like a dog that didn't understand what I was saying. As tears streamed down my face, I looked at the sister of my heart, and fired.

She fell to the floor, dead—again—and I threw-up.

CHAPTER 2

Sarnia, Ontario, Canada
Gerry

On the heels of the outbreak of the Hauksson virus, airport security footage of an unidentified, infected man savagely attacking several of his fellow travelers was leaked to the Internet. The mysterious upload, titled simply *Hauksson virus – insanity in Canuck airport – really fukken grose – check this out!!!* immediately went viral, racking up thousands of hits in the first hour. Due to the graphic subject matter, the video was pulled a short time later, but the damage had been done. The video had given the disease a face—an ugly one. Also, by then there had been copies made, and copies of those copies.

You can't stop the signal.

*

Everything is under control. The plague has been contained. No new cases have been reported outside known hot zones. Go on about your business.

Army vehicles, piece of shit beaters pulled from mothballs after fifty years of decorating a surplus dump, retrofitted with loudspeakers and squeaky clean soldiers, rolled through the streets like khaki-coated ice cream trucks, handing out "intel packets" to concerned adults, and balloons and suckers to their kids.

At the time, given the speed with which the local government took control of the situation, the majority of the populace was satisfied; all that could be done was being done. Daily town hall meetings were held, an ad hoc committee was created to oversee possible quarantine and evac facilities (an unneeded precaution, 'They' said), and liaisons liaised as the community did as they were told. Even when newscasts were blocked out and test patterns populated all but our local community station, we trusted them.

Yes, we had questions, and voiced them loudly, but their answers made sense to most. I thought—we all thought—things were going to work out and the world would keep spinning. Like any other scare we'd had over the past few years—the West Nile thing, that bird flu, SARS, the Mad Cow disease—this Hauksson virus was nothing more than some upper echelon government assholes making money from disease and misery. Nothing new under the sun.

Any day now, the Government would come charging up on its white steed, peddling the cure for this disease for the bargain basement price of $149.95. We believed in them because we had to. We'd even buy their cure and smile while we did, because we had to. The alternative was to admit the bogyman existed.

Believing did nothing to stop the rumours.

That was the first week. Week two began with frantic phone calls to 911, reporting the mysterious deaths of livestock and household pets. By early afternoon, the mayor had disappeared along with five members of the city council, leaving the town in the care of the local police and a tiny detachment of soldiers.

That night, the Army's loudspeakers belted out a new message: that the plague was spreading and warm bodies would be needed to help keep the peace during the difficult times to come. Local Army and Sea Cadets, and Law and Security students at the college were promised full credit for volunteering to fill out the thin Army presence. Doctors were rounded up, willing or not, and housed somewhere within the Army's temporary command center. In the days to come, the Army loudspeakers had said, doctors would be the salvation of us all.

Of course none of the cadet recruits were issued weapons. Not at first, anyway.

A city-wide curfew was enacted, and militia, armed and armoured, took to patrolling the streets in three-man details. Signs were posted on every corner: "Anyone caught on the street without a signed pass will be detained for the remainder of the occupation."

Petrochemical refinery workers (process and operations only) would remain under a plant-wide lockdown, but all other nonessential trades and maintenance crews would return to their homes until otherwise directed. Keeping the refinery workers locked in made sense to me. If a plague really was on its way and the men and women who run the refineries became sick, dying from a disease would be the least of Sarnia's problems. Without key refinery workers present, one minor mishap could spark a chain reaction that would decimate everything within a hundred kilometer radius, maybe more.

Side note (but relevant): Up until the early eighties, Sarnia, with a population of no more than fifty thousand, was among the top five targets of Russia's nuclear arsenal. For some ungodly reason, we simple folk wore this fact like a fucking badge. Any fame is good fame, I guess.

The day that a pack of American jet fighters vaporized the twin bridges connecting Sarnia to its U.S. sister city of Port Huron (effectively pulling up their welcome mat), was the day we-the-people started paying a little more attention to the conspiracy theory rumour mill. Everything wasn't under control. Contrary to the sugar-coated shit pie the Army had been feeding us, things began adding up for us. When questioned about the bridges, the Army's spokesman claimed the bombing had been an act of terrorism, and that the perpetrators had already been arrested by the American government. If not for the fact that most of the people attending the meeting had seen the bombing with their own eyes—seen the jets as they fired upon the bridges—the Army might have gotten away with their flimsy lie.

An angry protester threw a brick through the windshield of an Army Jeep, and a jumpy soldier fired a shot. Next thing I know, I'm on the front line of a full-scale riot, staring down the barrel of a shotgun.

What could I do? I raised my hands and the cop grunted and spat at my feet. "Fuckin' pussy. That's right, step off, bitch."

I'm no pussy, but I'm also not stupid. When I stepped back, he turned the gun and drove it into my gut, knocking the wind out of me. Then, in one fluid motion, he spun and fired a shot into the advancing crowd. The blast hit three people, but the poor woman in front took the worst of it. Her raised right arm exploded, and half of her face disappeared in a shower of bone and blood. Pieces of her sailed further out and rained down upon those behind her.

As the cop raised the shotgun to fire again, I stepped forward, grabbed the gun by the barrel, and drove my fist straight into the center of his face. He fell, and I fell with him, pounding and pounding at his face, deaf to the screams from the crowd, the sporadic gunfire, and answering wails. I hadn't known the woman he killed, but right then, she might as well have been my baby sister.

This cop, this random murderer of women, was my first confirmed kill.

As I rolled away from his lifeless body, I reached for his gun. I'd evened the score with the woman, but these motherfuckers had a lot to answer for. But before I could grab the shotgun, the crowd surged forward, pushing me before them, driving me head-first into a wall of riot shields and Taser guns.

I've gone over these events at least a thousand times since waking up in this cell, but still don't know how I didn't die that day. I'm told that of the crowd that rushed the stage, I was among four who lived. The other three survivors had also been locked up. None of us have been charged with a crime—and I'm certainly not going to offer myself up for killing that cop—but no one's sent us a lawyer either.

The ensuing violence the previous day claimed the lives of sixty-seven civilians and an undisclosed number of military and police personnel. The guard who brought my dinner told me that much, but said nothing about any sort of funeral service. For obvious reasons, I didn't press the issue. I was still reeling over the events of the previous day, and the guard, a guy I remembered from high school (but couldn't think of his name), looked even more spooked than I felt.

I thanked him and took my dinner over and sat on my bunk. I figured he'd leave, but he didn't. I felt his eyes upon me as I sipped tomato soup straight from the bowl. After setting aside the empty bowl, I lifted the lid from the Salisbury steak and cut it into chunks with the provided spork. I popped a piece of meat into my mouth and glanced up. His eyes remained fixed on me. For the first time since his arrival, I studied his face. He must've been crying recently; dark circles cradled his eyes, and dried snot coated one side of his tidy moustache.

Suddenly, his name came to me. Jack. Jack Anderson. I'd dated Leslie, his younger sister, in grade 11. "Something wrong, Jack?"

He stood there so long I began to think he hadn't heard me, then he blinked and leaned in close to the bars. "I saw one."

"Saw one what?"

He jumped back and clapped his hands over his ears. "Oh-my-god-my-head." He moaned and moved to the opposite wall, but kept his hands cupped over his ears. "I saw one of them. You know." He nodded; whether it was for my benefit or his would forever remain a mystery. "Last night while some of us were out on patrol, we saw something in the woods out off Number 7."

I'm not stupid. I knew what he meant. He'd seen one of the infected. "Is it as bad as they say? I mean, what it does to them?"

He giggled, then began to sob, sliding his hands around to cover his face. After a moment, he raised one arm and smeared snot from one cheek to the other. "Sorry. I picked up this cold yesterday and the meds are fucking me up some." Then he turned and started for the door.

The known symptoms of the virus flashed like a neon sign in my brain, and so far he was three for three. "Hey," I said, as evenly as I could muster, "I thought—"

Before I could blink, he was at the bars, snarling and reaching. "No," he growled. "No-no-no more yelling! I'll kill you, Gerry. I swear, I'll fucking do you if you yell one more time!"

I backed away, whispering as I did, "S'okay, buddy. I'm sorry. It won't happen again."

"You're right it won't... or I'll... I don't know what'll happen, but it won't end well for you."

All things considered, my dinner was finished. As hungry as I was, there was no way I was going to eat another bite. I wanted to know more about what he saw the night before, but feared upsetting him any more than I already had. He had keys for my cell, and I'd eventually need to sleep.

I breathed a silent sigh of relief when Jack walked over and sat in a chair near the door. Eventually, he fell into a fitful slumber. Sometime later—could've been an hour, maybe two—I, too, fell asleep.

I awoke to a familiar sound. Five short blasts followed by one long one, repeated—the Ceveco emergency alarm at Imperial Oil. Beneath IOL's alarm, I could make out at least two others: Nova and Suncor. That was bad... very bad. I stood on the stainless steel sink and jumped up to grab the bars covering the window overlooking the south parking lot. I pulled myself up and my face barely fit into the small space. Off in the distance the night sky glowed orange, lit up by every flare in the Valley, each no less than two-hundred feet. This was bad. If feed stock had been dumped to flare, something must have gone wrong. Given the fact that every plant was flaring meant only one thing. *We're fucked. If the hydrocarbons don't leak out or explode and kill us all, when the boilers go critical, we all die.*

As I was about to let myself drop back down to the sink, movement out in the parking lot caught my eye. A man, likely out on patrol, stepped into the glow of a streetlight. His head was tilted as though he was listening for something, and his exaggerated gait suggested he was drunk. Fucking idiot. There's a plague at our back door, every fucking siren that could possibly be screaming is going off, and this guy's got time to drink.

"Hey, asshole! Can't you hear those alarms?"

In answer (I'm guessing, but am pretty sure he heard me), the man jerked around, sniffed the air, and emitted a tortured, gurgling wail unlike anything I've ever heard. Screech after garbled screech, the man headed toward the building. As he reached the next closest lamppost, his features fell under the pooled light. Naked above the waist, pale flesh hung in slimy flaps from his chest, and chunks had been torn from his abdomen.

Every nerve in my body screamed in chorus for me to run, to hide, to curl up and allow insanity to wash over me like a spring rain, but his one remaining eye, milky yet penetrating, held me.

At the sound from somewhere in the room at my back—like a drain choking on the world's biggest turd—I screamed and fell from the window, missed the sink, then landed flat on my back beside the bunk.

Jack stood staring past me at the small barred window. "That's the noise they make when they're hungry."

As I lay there trying to understand what it was I'd seen, a rap at the outside door sent my heart into my throat. The knock was followed by a muffled voice: "Anderson, open up. It's me."

Jack opened the door and a uniformed cop pushed past him and closed the door. His face was grim and blood covered most of his body. He pulled a pistol from his belt and pushed it into Jack's hands. "For you. If shit goes south and they get past us, you know what to do."

Jack coughed and spit a clump of phlegm to the side. "Thanks," he said.

The cop had obviously not looked at Jack before this. Realization quickly dawned, and he skittered backward into the door. The cop's eyes dropped to the key-ring on Jack's belt, then our eyes met. That one look told me there was nothing he could do for me. He shot me an apologetic look, then slipped back out of the room. Seconds later, a succession of shots rang out from inside the building, followed by an inhuman scream, and another, and another. We were overrun.

My eyes remained glued to the gun in Jack's hand for quite some time. When I felt I had enough courage to look him in the eye, I did. "So… how ya feeling, Jack-o? You OK, buddy?"

Jack, who'd been lost in his own thoughts, hefted the six-shooter, turned it and gave it a once over, then slipped it into his belt. His eyes, more grey than his usual brown now, glowed with some inexplicable inner light. He didn't seem to be able to look me in the eye. "Truth be told, Gerry, I've been better."

CHAPTER 3

Pittsburgh, Pennsylvania, USA
Lucia

All of the large cities on the Eastern seaboard reported outbreaks...but the government said they were contained. The airports and trains had been shut down for weeks, so I didn't think the virus could come as far west as Pittsburgh. The propaganda shit the government posted ran in continuous banners on all television channels and across the top of all websites:

Contamination Alert: The Center for Disease Control has issued a RED ALERT for the following cities: New York, New York; Boston, Massachusetts; The District of Columbia...they trailed on. DO NOT PANIC.

So, we didn't.

We became acclimated to the warnings and ignored them like commercials—well, for the most part. People were buying things like bullets, bottled water, and batteries. But, in the beginning, we stayed calm—because that's what they told us to do. Pretending it wouldn't happen to us kept it at arm's length.

I decided to go to the furry convention anyway. Logic told me I was safer in the farmlands than the city and that I shouldn't gather in the same spot as people from across the nation. I was stupid.

I spent a lot of money and time on my costume and alterations. I was a realistic brown squirrel—not one of those cartoon-looking fucks. My plumed tail curved in a sighing 'S' shape and I'd sewn stuffed pleather claws. I wasn't a furry convention aficionado, but faked it because curiosity compelled me to experience something so bizarre. But, as with most costumed events, no one would smell my lie.

I might have left the convention sooner, but with all of the animal imitations going on, it was hard to differentiate between normal furry activity and infection. I knew it had hit when a costumed brown dog chewed off a woman's face until she stopped struggling. Two panda bears were enthralled in a bloody struggle. A zombie's mouth tore the ass flap off of a person's leopard costume and started feasting. The zombie at the leopard's back door looked up for a moment and I saw his face was covered in blood and shit.

I ran—not like a squirrel, but like a gimp in a squirrel costume with a stick joining my two knees.

The costume saved me. Zombies clawed at me and bit me, but none of their teeth could break through the material. My escape lacked stealth and finesse. I darted with outstretched arms and my screams were dulled inside of my foam squirrel head. My car wasn't an option—I couldn't get the costume off quick enough before zombies would be on me, and I couldn't fit inside of my car with the costume on.

A FedEx truck was parked just beyond the front doors to the convention center—its wide door was open to the driver's seat like an invitation to a good idea. I grabbed a metal chair and swung it as I ran with gimpy hops. I struck some zombies, but mostly the chair rebounded off of me as I vigorously waved it back and forth.

As I neared the truck, I tossed the chair behind me and jumped through the door. My paws slid off of the leather seat and I panicked to get inside without traction as the fur repelled my attempts. I felt a hand thrust up under my ass, and I was pushed further inside as I heard the door slam shut.

"Jesus fuck! Tell me you aren't a zombie under that squirrel costume."

"I'm not a zombie."

"I didn't think you were with the way you almost hit me with that chair."

I felt the truck lurch forward, sat up and removed my squirrel head. My face was covered in sweat and my own spit from screaming. My long, dark hair had worked its way out of my ponytail and was stuck to my cheeks and forehead. I looked at the twenty-something man driving. "Are you bit?"

"No. Are you?" He eyed me frantically.

"No. They couldn't bite through the costume."

A huge guffaw laugh erupted from his lungs as he looked at me. "You're one lucky girl."

"Where are we going?"

"I don't know. Word must not be out that we have an outbreak here—the traffic's too calm."

"Do you think the virus was brought into the city because of the convention?"

"No, it's been here for over a week."

"Over a week? But they haven't announced it."

"They were keeping it quiet. I made a delivery to the hospital today and one of the nurses told me."

"Then why the fuck were you continuing with your delivery route?"

"I wasn't. I stopped at the convention center to pick up my girlfriend so we could leave."

"Your girlfriend is at the furry convention?"

He rolled his eyes, "No, she worked at the front desk."

I prayed he wouldn't say we were going back for her. "Did you find her?"

"Yeah, she was the one trying to bite your left shoulder."

"Oh."

"We need to think. Where should we go?"

"My parents have a farm about an hour east of here. It's secluded—we could go there."

"No. Everything east of here is the red zone now. We'll never get through the blockades they'll be putting up."

I swallowed hard. My parents would surely be dead soon. "We just need to get out of the city as fast as possible."

"Do you know anyone here with a boat?"

"Um… yeah, why?"

"Because look at the traffic to the Fort Pitt Tunnel—it's already closed."

The traffic was deadlocked and army trucks blocked the entrance. "Can you get down to Carson Street over the West End Bridge?"

"Is that where the boat is?"

"Yeah." I was numb with terror. I wanted to call my parents, but my cell phone was in my car and I needed to stay focused.

"Where am I going, exactly?"

"Just head West down Carson Street. I'll tell you when we get close."

"My name is Fred, by the way."

"Fred the FedEx guy?"

"Yeah. Something wrong with that?"

"Nope." I sat back in my seat and gripped the upholstery.

I didn't tell him my name, and he didn't ask. I scoped the streets out as Fred drove. Nothing was unusual. An old man sat on a bench, reading a paper; a mother exited a store with her child in tow.

"Wait, shouldn't we warn these people?"

"No."

"Why not?"

"Our only chance of getting out of the city is if we aren't battling a stampede of people trying to jam up our exit."

Guilt panged in my chest. I knew he was right. "Up ahead, the brick house with the black iron fence. That's it."

It was my friend Jason's house. My best friend had been his father's hospice nurse a few years back, and he often invited us to party on his boat. After his father passed away, we all remained friends.

I knocked for a few minutes and even tried the knob before I heard someone shuffle to the door. Jason opened the door, his face was a swollen, and his eyes were red. For a second, I thought he might be infected, but he was just crying.

"Lucia..." he choked.

"Jason, what's wrong?"

He just shook his head, but did not speak. Fred and I pushed past him to get inside. "Where's Vanessa?" Vanessa was his wife. They had just married the previous year. She was nine months pregnant with twins and her due date was close.

"I had to take Vanessa to the hospital. She kept bleeding, but they sent her home and told her to rest. They said she'd be fine." He was crying and slobbering.

"Where is she?"

"She's in the bedroom. She's dead."

"She's dead?" I bound up the stairs, two at a time, and ran towards their bedroom. Thoughts raced through my head. She had a difficult pregnancy, but I never thought she would die from it.

No zombie movie could have prepared me for what I saw when I opened the door. Vanessa lay on the bed, now thoroughly soaked with blood. The babies were infected. They had clawed their way out of Vanessa's stomach and were chained to her by their umbilical cords, mindlessly squirming and biting, making gurgling sounds as they choked on the blood they tried to consume. Startled, I ran from the room and descended the stairs as quickly as I could.

"Jason, the infection has reached the city. We have to leave."

"I'm not leaving my children or Vanessa."

"Jason, they're dead. You have to come with us. We want to take your boat. It's the only way. They're starting to close the tunnels already."

"I can't go. I've already been bitten."

Jason held up his hand. A crescent moon shaped bite was on the side of his hand. Lightning strikes of red veins shattered around the perimeter of the wound. I realized that was what a zombie bite looked like.

"The change is quick, but mine was a shallow bite, so it's taking longer. Listen, take the boat—take everything you need, and go. There are extra gallons of fuel in the boat house. Take them as well, but hurry. Save yourselves."

I looked at him, grateful for the help. "I wish I could hug you."

"Don't—you shouldn't touch me." He smiled at me, "In the basement are my guns. The key to the gun cabinet is the small one on my key chain—there, on the counter. Now hurry."

We made four trips back inside the house—carrying all of the food, water, guns, and other items we could, as quickly as possible, down the dock to the boat. It was a luxury boat with couches that folded out into beds and Jason kept it well stocked.

Once on board, we untied the boat and headed up the Ohio River.

"I'm sorry about your friends."

"I think it's something we need to get used to."

"Yeah," he sighed. "I guess so."

"We won't get very far if the locks aren't running."

"Just so long as we can get out of the city, then we can make a run for a vehicle."

"Then what?"

"Just start packing stuff up better—a bag for each of us that we can carry as we run."

"We're going to leave all of this stuff behind? The boat would be our safest bet."

"I don't want to, but we might have to. Eventually we'll hit a place where we can't travel any further up the river. We can't just float, waiting for the apocalypse to end. Soon the infection will engulf this entire area and we'll be a floating snack, slowly starving to death."

"An apocalypse—that's what this is, isn't it?"

"Yes."

CHAPTER 4

Dublin, Ireland
Paul

I woke with a start as a loud knock first trespassed into my dream, and then tore it asunder. With a pounding heart and disoriented mind, I swung my legs from the warm embrace of my bed to stand unsteadily on unsure feet.

"What do you want?" I asked. I was on edge, seriously on edge, on the verge of going over if truth be told. We all were. It had been a tough couple of weeks… Tough? Ha! It was a living fucking nightmare.

Whoever it was knocked again without answering. Bastards were going to make me get up.

"For fuck sake!" I grumbled and marched to the front door of my apartment in my boxers. Mrs. Watson from down the corridor was standing in the hall. I could see she had been crying, and her hands were trembling. I bit back the nasty comment I was about to unleash on the person who disturbed my sleep.

"I need to go out," she said. Her voice quivered.

"That is not a good idea," I answered her. *Understatement of the century,* I silently added.

"I have no choice. Brian's medication is almost gone. I had hoped we would have been rescued by now. I thought it would be all over." She started to cry.

Brian was her nine year old son. He had some sort of breathing problem. To be honest, I wasn't really sure what it was, I hadn't paid that much attention to them before, well… before we all ended up in hell together.

"Come in," I said, and opened the door wider for her to enter. "Grab a seat while I get dressed." I quickly threw on a pair of jeans and tee-shirt before rejoining her in the living room.

"What do the others think?" I asked. The others were the surviving residents of my City Centre apartment block. About forty of us had barricaded ourselves into the building when hell was unleashed. I had hoped we would have been rescued before now too—I did not say that to Mrs. Watson though.

"I haven't said anything yet."

"Okay," I said. "We'll need to talk to everyone else. Fuck! None of us have been outside in what… three weeks?"

Why was she bringing this shit to me? I'd hardly ever spoken to the woman.

"I know," she said, her head bowed.

"Give me a minute," I said, and walked her to the door. Over her shoulder I could see her son standing in their open doorway. It tore at my heartstrings to see his small chest heave in and out as he tried to gulp down air.

I walked over to the window; I was three stories up and had a grandstand view of the city. The streets were eerily quiet. Overhead, the sky was covered by an iron grey mantle; hazy drizzle filled the air with moisture. I had a sudden urge to stand under the purifying drops and let the cool water wash over my face. Would it cleanse the dark, deserted avenues and laneways of the contagion? I wondered. I did not think so. I brushed back strands of, shoulder length, light brown hair from my face and massaged my temples. I could feel the coarse bristles of an unshaven chin, as my mind wandered with my gaze over the streets of Dublin.

It had not been too bad at first. Those of us who had survived the initial outbreak locked ourselves away in the building. I watched the world wide epidemic unfold as panic ensued globally. At first, the emergency services struggled to cope, and then they collapsed completely. Pictures came in from every corner of the Earth showing hellish scenes where riot police and the Army tried to contain the infected. The walking dead, some labeled them. But then the soldiers and policemen, everybody, became infected themselves.

Those of us left in the building got together and decided to stay put until a rescue came. Surely this would be all over in a couple of weeks, we thought. We broke into the other apartments and took whatever food and anything useful we could find. Some of the group gathered together, even sharing apartments, for comfort, for safety, or out of loneliness. Others, like me, preferred to stay alone.

Like I said, at first it was not too bad; we had pretty much everything we needed, but then the power was cut. Somehow the screams during the night sounded worse when there were no lights in the corridors. The pleas for help from unseen victims would wrench your soul. There was nothing any of us could do.

We quickly learned to stay away from the ground level windows and doors. The infected pretty much left us alone, apart from occasionally passing by the front of the building, pressing grotesque faces up to the glass before moving on. With their dark, sunken eyes and rotting flesh, they really did look like animated corpses. Needless to say, none of us had slept well for the previous couple of weeks. Every one of us bore a haunted look in our eyes, the mark of dark dreams and horrifying nightmares both real and imagined.

I knocked on Mrs. Watson's door, and we went to see Robbie from number twenty-nine. Robbie was a big burly fireman who had appointed himself as our leader, which was fine by me and everyone else.

"We have a problem," I said.

"You better come in then," Robbie answered, and we followed him into his apartment.

I got straight to the point. "Mrs. Watson's boy needs more medication."

He looked from me to her, stroking his chin. "Hmm, I've been thinking we would need to send out a foraging party soon. God knows how long we're likely to be here. Okay, we'll put a team together. There's a pharmacy on Talbot Street that's ten minutes away. While we're there, we'll grab what we can from the Spar and any other shops."

"Okay," I nodded.

"Have you got a weapon?" he asked. I shook my head dumbly. "Here," he said, handing me a hurley stick. I had played the Irish game of hurling at school and the weight of the ash stick, with an axe-shaped head, felt familiar in my hand. I hefted it and gave an exploratory swing.

Looks like I'm on the team, I thought.

Eight of us were chosen, all youngish males. The plan was simple: run like the clappers to the Spar on Talbot Street, then the pharmacy, and then get back. Simple.

"Mrs. Watson will have to come," I suggested, "to identify her son's medication."

"I'm a paramedic," Robbie answered. Some people just know how to make you feel six inches high.

We gathered in the lobby of the building, Robbie gave us a pep talk.

"Okay, let's do this quickly. Grab what we can in the Spar, on to the pharmacy for the kid's medicine and anything else you might think useful—painkillers, bandages, penicillin—and then straight back. At least it's bright out. God, I'd hate to be caught out there in the dark. Oh, and wear something over your nose and mouth. Best to be on the safe side."

If only we'd realised going out while it was bright was exactly the wrong thing to do. I found that out later.

We filed out onto the street. The building was right in the IFSC, Dublin's financial centre. We were all nervous. There was a weird atmosphere and a strange smell in the air, kind of sickly sweet, not overpowering, but lingering all the same. The rain felt good—cool and refreshing. We all had some kind of a weapon: golf clubs, baseball bats. I had the hurley, and Robbie had a whopping great axe. My face was covered by a bandana, and I had thrown on a leather jacket before we left.

None of us knew what to expect; we had all watched the infected from the lofty perch of our balconies or the building roof. They could move quickly when they needed to. Somehow I had expected them to be slow-moving lurchers. I hated to use the word—they were, after all, sick people—but "zombie" was constantly in the back of my mind.

Sleep deprivation and fear can kill as quickly as carelessness. Can you forgive these things? Not if you are dead.

We moved quickly in single file through deathly quiet streets. Abandoned cars and buses blocked the roads, many with dark stains on the seats and the ground around them. I thought it best not to dwell on it. We passed by Connolly Station. I could imagine idle trains lined up on tracks like the carcasses of enormous, stricken sea creatures stranded on a beach somewhere, only this beach was made of concrete, metal, and glass, built with the blood and sweat of a hundred and more generations of Irish men and women. People who lived, loved, and died in this city—their city, my city. I wondered, *would I be the last?*

I was not happy, not happy at all. To be honest, I was totally freaked. I didn't really understand what had happened; maybe I never will. I watched the events on the TV just like everybody else, but it made no sense to me. They said it was caused by global warming; when the icecaps started to melt it unleashed some sort of prehistoric superbug, dormant for millions of years. First it killed most of the bigger animals—nearly all of them! I'm not religious, never have been, but what that thing does to people is like God's vengeance on us. People are turned into mindless, barbaric cannibals. Zombies!

I've seen what they can do, and they scare the livin' shite out of me.

We agreed at the start: once we locked the front door of the building, that was it. No one goes in or out until we get rescued. It made sense. Sometimes it was not easy. A few days in and I heard a woman's scream coming from the street. I ran to the window to see what was going on and saw her running past the building. I was about to step out onto the small balcony and tell her to run to the front door, and I would let her in. And then I saw them.

There were about a dozen of them chasing her down. They could move. Not an all-out sprint, but over a distance I'd imagine they could wear you down. I'm not sure why—some inner sense maybe, perhaps it was just bad luck—she looked up and saw me at the window. Her eyes were full of terror and pleading, then she stumbled. It was enough. They were on her like a pack of rabid dogs.

I froze, paralysed with shock and fear. They dragged her down and ripped her to pieces like jackals feeding on some unfortunate beast. I watched, mesmerised by their savagery. And then one looked up; it had her decapitated head in its hands. I jumped back from the window, but could still look out. For as long as I live, I will never forget the sight of it gnawing at the woman's head, stripping flesh from the skull. Sometimes I think the ones who died at the beginning were the lucky ones, and the survivors were the truly cursed.

We made it to the Spar on Talbot Street, a once busy shopping street in the heart of Dublin. It was now deserted. Most of the shop fronts had their windows smashed. A lot of the merchandise lay sodden on the paths and road.

We all had shopping bags and sports bags, anything we could use. We stuffed them full of tinned food and bottles of water. I could not help but pause at the broken down freezers and fridges, looking at all the rotting food. What sort of future was there in a world with so few animals?

"Leave them to this, you come with me," Robbie instructed.

Something caught my eye.

"Hang on a sec." I leapfrogged the counter, grabbed a bottle of Jack Daniels, and jammed it into a bag. "Okay, let's go."

The pharmacy was only a couple of doors down. We both entered cautiously. I, for one, was shitting myself. I'd never been so afraid. All I kept thinking about was that woman and the horrific death I witnessed. Witnessed? Stood idly by and watched. Could I have done anything to help? Would it have made a difference?

"Grab anything you think we might need. I'll go in back to the dispensary and grab the kid's medicine," the big fireman said.

I was barely listening. "Jesus, what the fuck is that god awful smell?" I asked. It hit me the moment I stepped through the door. Robbie sniffed the air and shrugged.

"Probably the drains," he answered, before disappearing behind the counter.

I started loading anything I could: paracetamol, bandages, allergy tablets, even a few packets of Lemsip. All the strong drugs would be in the back, and Robbie knew what to look for. I wrapped the bandana tighter around my face—the smell was making me gag.

I noticed Robbie walking slowly backwards from the dispensary. A bottle of pills dropped from his hand. I scooped them up.

"We done?" I asked, relieved we could get the fuck out of there.

"R-r-r…" he said, like he had something stuck in his throat.

"What you sayin', man?" I asked.

"R-r-r-r-r…"

"You alright?" I asked, taking a step towards him.

Then I heard a snarl.

A hideous face of rotting flesh and dead eyes appeared. The fireman turned ever so slowly. Blood poured down the side of his head, a huge flap of skin hung from his cheek, exposing the bone.

"RUN!" he finally screamed, before falling to his knees.

"Jesus Christ!"

The zombie stepped forward, its black hands reaching for the fireman.

"Fuuuuuccckkkk!" I screamed and hit it in the face with the hurley. Jesus, it was like hitting a tree trunk. I hit it again and again and again, all the time roaring at the top of my voice. I kept hitting it until I felt something give way. Finally, the stick broke in two, and the head rolled off the zombie's shoulders onto the floor with a sickening squelch.

My breath came in greedy gulps as I steadied myself. Robbie was lying on the floor now, and I couldn't tell if he was alive or dead. As I bent to examine him, I heard another scream.

"Get the fuck outta here!" A voice said from out on the street. Another resident was grappled to the ground by more of the walking dead. I grabbed Robbie's axe and ran. Okay, I'm not proud of deserting my comrades, but—fuck it—I hardly knew them.

I ran the length of the street at a full sprint, out onto Amiens Street, and ran like fuck back towards the building. I glanced over my shoulder, but could only see three of the men who had started out. Thankfully, no zombies were following. Of course, that probably meant they were feasting on the other four lost souls.

As we neared the building, we slowed, all of us with heaving chests as we tried to catch our breath.

"Jesus! What the fuck is that?" One of the men said, pointing upwards. I looked up. A woman stood on top of a railing on a third floor balcony.

What the fuck?

Her arms were stretched out on either side of her, her head was held high. And then she jumped.

At that moment, I realised it was Mrs. Watson. She sailed through the air in a graceful arc, like a diver springing from the high board, or a ballerina leaping into the air. The world slowed down for me; words died in my throat.

Then her head exploded on the hard, cobbled ground.

CHAPTER 5

Omaha, Nebraska, USA
Sharon

2 months earlier…

I swiped my key-card over the small red light, granting me entrance into the protected rooms of the Cryopreservation department of the Henry Doorly Zoo. This was where we housed the frozen genomes of every species on the planet for the protection of the gene pool diversity of endangered species. "The Frozen Zoo", as it was commonly called, was a joint collaboration of several wildlife preservation societies, the Zoological Association, and over a dozen countries.

We even had the DNA strand of the extinct Tasmanian tiger. It was believed that within five or six generations of genetic engineering, we would be able to have a full blooded tiger. Unfortunately, with Australia's animal population under stress from all the introduced species, the government wasn't prepared to handle the reintroduction of an animal that had been extinct since 1936.

The doors shushed open, the hum of the cryo tanks greeted me. I did a tour of the room, making sure that all the lights were green and not red. This wasn't really my job—we had interns to monitor the tanks—but something about this room calmed me. The silence embraced me, the potential for so much life awed me.

Those of us who worked here called this room "The Ark", and the computer system that monitored it, "Noah". I logged into Noah and made a few notes, stating that I had checked the machines and found everything in working order. I then logged off, took one last look around, and left.

As the doors opened, I saw Dr. Jack Mecum leering at something on the computer with one of the interns—Sam, I think his name was. Jack whistled low and said, "Good thing no one that looks like her works here, or our frozen zoo would experience some melting." They both guffawed loudly. Sam looked up and made eye contact with me. At my raised eyebrow, he blanched and poked Jack.

Dr. Mecum looked up and smiled his best snake oil salesman smile. "Hey there, Red." I shook my head and walked on, but he followed after me. "C'mon, Red, don't be mad. It was just a joke."

"I'm not mad," I said.

"Then why are you ignoring me?"

"I'm not ignoring you. I'm paying you the same amount of attention I would to anyone who calls me 'Red'." Honestly, I really didn't mind the nickname. Several friends and family members have called me that. But when he said it, it just sounded so damn condescending that it set my teeth on edge. It reminded me of those men who call women "Blondie".

"Aww, Red." He moved in front of me, effectively blocking my path. He really was a handsome guy—if you liked overly manicured metrosexuals. I didn't. "I'm sorry. Forgive me?"

I raised an eyebrow and looked at him in exasperation. "That's some serious charm you are trying to work on me."

"I know," he laughed. "My mother always said if I could find a way to bottle it, I'd be rich."

I rolled my eyes and sidestepped him.

The outer room was lined with workstations and microscopes. A large first aid kit sat upon the counter next to the sink. I smiled wickedly and walked over to it.

"I think someone beat you to it, Jack. There is already a product on the market that has the same effect as your charm."

I opened the kit and grabbed a small brown bottle. He had followed after me. When I turned, I slapped the bottle into his open palm and walked away.

He read the label "Ipecac" out loud. Sam had evidently heard the last part of our conversation and howled in laughter.

"Dude, that stuff is used to induce vomiting!"

"I know what it's used for. Now get back to work!" he shouted as the door closed behind me.

*

I was seated in the lab, peering through a microscope at a tissue sample, when I heard the doors shush open, and then felt a presence behind me. I stopped, turned, and frowned in confusion at what I saw: Military Brass.

There were about a dozen of them in the room, with more filing though the door, decked out in all their uniformed splendor. My friend Jenny called the collection of medals and ribbons "fruit salad". Those standing before me wore an entire produce section on their chests.

"Dr. Pennington?" Having grown up in a military town with a father who was retired Air Force, I recognized a four-star general when I saw one. A full-bird colonel stood next to him, surrounded by more officers and a few enlisted men.

"Yes?" I said, drawing the syllable out into a question.

"I am General Daniels, and this is Colonel Marks," he said. I guess the others didn't need names.

"Hello. Is there something I can help you with?" I asked, resisting the urge to stand at attention. I rose from my chair, as it seemed rude to keep sitting, and I didn't like the way he was towering over me. The General was in his late fifties and had a full head of white hair, but I could tell that he was in good shape and wasn't someone I wanted to mess with.

"We need to talk. Is there somewhere we can go that is secure?"

I gestured to the room around us. The lab was as restricted as the Ark, which begged the question: how did they get in?

The men parted like the Red Sea, revealing a woman. She was about five feet tall and just as round. She appeared to be about the same age as the general. I met her faded blue eyes and was momentarily stunned by the intellect that stared back at me. It was almost divine.

"We have a bit of a situation, Doctor," General Daniels said. "We could really use your help. I understand that you are one of the best in your field."

I fidgeted nervously "I wouldn't say I was the best, General."

"I didn't. I said one of the best." The flush that crept up my neck exploded across my face, which had the unfortunate effect of making me look like a pomegranate.

I met the woman's gaze. She smiled back, not unkindly. "I'm Dr. Leslie Anders from the CDC." She didn't offer to shake hands. I guess when you deal with infectious diseases all day, you tended to shy away from such things. Instead, she indicated a steel table nearby. I followed and sank into a chair across from her. The soldiers remained standing.

"Lieutenant," she said, nodding to a young man in Navy whites who had a steel suitcase handcuffed to his wrist. Stepping forward, he laid the case on the table and unlocked the cuff.

"I did a lot of begging and pleading, and when that didn't work, I did a lot of yelling and cursing to get you this information," she said, clicking the lock on the case.

"I believe, as a scientist, that we need all of the facts, not just the convenient ones." And with that, the lid popped open. She reached in and took out an iPad.

"You will want to change the password on this," she said handing it to me. "I must remind you that what you are about to read is highly classified."

"Why me?" I asked, taking the tablet.

"We've had you checked out," the General said. "You passed the screening, and are very respected in your field. Why not you?"

"Passed the screening?" I said, bristling at the idea of them investigating me. He blinked, but said nothing. I wouldn't get any answers from him.

Dr. Anders unloaded the case. Inside were several paper files and a small temperature controlled case that had been nestled in a foam cut-out. "These are your samples. I suggest you use them carefully. It will be… difficult… to get you more."

She had brought up the files she wanted me to read on the iPad, and immediately I fell under the thrall of the unknown. Patient Zero was one Malik Hauksson. He had lived in Niaqornat, a small town in Northwestern Greenland. The rest of his personal information had been redacted. The file said that he'd participated in a seal harvest where via a bite, it was suspected he contracted a virus. He did not present symptoms at the time, stated one of the men he had worked with.

The Hauksson virus, as they dubbed it, was fatal. Within the first ten minutes, the infected person tended to exhibit symptoms of the disease. Symptoms included cold-like nasal discharge, increased aggression, profuse salivation, and a high pain tolerance akin to someone on PCP. Death usually occurred within four hours, and resurrection followed shortly after. I paused.

"Resurrection?" I asked, frowning. "How can that be?"

"Read on," she said. I did. Similar to AIDS, fluid exchange was the only means of transmission, which explained the copious salivation. It didn't appear to be airborne. That was good news. The report stated that the virus took control of the hypothalamus. Since that portion of the brain controlled body temperature, hunger, thirst, fatigue, sleep, and circadian cycles, it fit with the urge to bite. Make a body think it's hungry, take away its ability to reason, and you had yourself a biter.

The cerebellum was also targeted. That part of the brain controlled all the voluntary actions, making it possible for the virus to animate the body after death.

"Surely, you aren't suggesting that this virus…" I couldn't even bring myself to say it. It was too ridiculous.

She blinked at me and waited. I exhaled through my nose in frustration and wondered if I was the subject of an elaborate hoax. Touching the screen, I scrolled to the next page. The pictures that greeted me were so gruesome my stomach turned, and I nearly dropped the tablet.

Subject Zero had returned home, where he lived with his girlfriend and her two children. Complaining of a headache, he went into a spare room to sleep it off. Sometime during the night, he died and was resurrected. The woman and her two children—a boy aged seven and a girl aged eighteen months—had been reduced to bloody pulp. There was a photo with an evidence tag numbered nine, which showed a small hand clenched in a fist. There was no arm attached to the small fist.

My stomach finally made good on its threat. I managed to make it to the sink just in time. No one spoke. A hushed silence fell over the room, almost as if everyone knew how I felt and was content to give me the time I needed to collect myself.

After rinsing my mouth out and splashing some cool water over my face, I returned to the table. I sat back down, trying very hard not to look at the photos. I swallowed and met the sad eyes of the Doctor.

"Of the fifty-eight people who lived in that town, there are three survivors," she said quietly. "We have been trying our best to contain this, but it has proven… difficult. From what we know, the virus sticks strictly to mammals. We have several cases of animal to human contamination. The symptoms present the same in the animals as they do in humans, only there is no evidence of resurrection."

"We don't know if there is a possibility for human to animal contamination, as the animals that are attacked are… well, there isn't much left. And since there has been no resurrection with the lab animals, we feel it is safe to say that infection is a one way event. For some reason, reanimation requires a human brain. We don't know why," she said.

The puzzle that the virus presented was quickly working to overcome the horror of the photos. I picked the tablet up again and scanned through the rest, forcing myself to view the carnage that had once been a small coastal town. "You said you are having a difficult time containing it. Can you elaborate?"

"As I said, the animals are carriers."

"It has spread out from this initial location then?" I asked. At her nod, I continued. "How far has it spread?" I asked.

"We have had to quarantine all of Greenland. We are advising travelers it is purely cautionary."

"Which means…?"

"Greenland has..." she paused "*had* a population of just over fifty-six thousand."

"And now?" I asked, bracing myself for the final number.

"It's been reduced to less than fifty."

"Why hasn't an alert been sounded?" I asked. My mind was racing, imagining so many dead.

"What would you have us say, Doctor? Should we tell the general population that the zombie apocalypse has begun?"

Those words coming out of her mouth struck me as funny, and I giggled. It was a bad habit. I tamped it down quickly before they thought I was insane.

"There must be something we can tell them. A new strain of rabies perhaps, warn them to be leery of animals with certain symptoms. We have to tell them something. If we don't, this will quickly get out of control."

"I'm afraid it already has. We have confirmed cases on six continents." I blanched, but she didn't give me the chance to respond, she just kept talking. "But your PSA is a good idea, Dr. Pennington. And coming from you, that type of warning will carry a lot of weight. Write it up as a press release, and we will distribute it." She stood then, her metal chair scraping on the tile floor.

"We have to find a preventative measure. We are hoping you will be able to help us."

I rose as well. "We won't be looking for a cure?" I asked, thinking it odd.

"The subjects are dead, Doctor. So far as I know, there is no cure for that." And with that, she turned and walked through the gathering of uniforms who parted for her, just as they had before.

I stared in shock after her, trying to process what I had just learned.

"You will be assigned two guards," Colonel Marks said, speaking for the first time. "They will ensure that the information you have remains classified." I looked up and met a pair of fern-green eyes in a deeply tanned face lined with the echoes of countless smiles. Somehow, knowing that he had cause for happiness enough to leave such tangible reminders calmed me.

"We will station a guard at your building, not outside your door, but in the parking lot. We need to keep you safe."

I nodded, not sure what sort of response was required of me.

General Daniels nodded smartly, and he and his entourage left. Alone again, I sank back down on the chair and rested my forehead on the cool steel of the table. A single tear trailed down my cheek and puddled on the shiny surface. I swiped it away hastily.

With a deep exhale, I rose from my seat, and noticed the two uniformed men that flanked the door. "My own personal goon-squad," I grumbled. Opening the small case with the samples, I prepared the slides, settled them beneath the microscope lens, and sought out the virus that could resurrect the dead.

CHAPTER 6

Sarnia, Ontario, Canada
Gerry

It had been about an hour since the last of the gunshots fired from inside the building. I'd climbed up to gaze out my little window a few times since Jack had collapsed into the chair nearest to my cell. My window gave little view of the city, but the alarms and unchecked fires told me all I needed to know: Sarnia was burning. Beneath the car and fire alarms, sporadic gunfire and mingled screams sent my imagination into overdrive.

Jack wasn't sleeping; his current stupor seemed like there was some sort of internal struggle going on. If his pained expression was any indication, he was losing. When he finally stood and nodded to himself, I jumped. Before I could speak, he turned, swayed for a few seconds, and then walked to the door leading to the remaining three cells. I'd been so taken in by the happenings outside the jail that I'd forgotten there were three other people back there. I think Jack did too. With his hand on the doorknob, he spoke without turning to face me, his voice so soft I had to strain to hear him.

"Did you ever see *Lassie*?"

"Yeah," I said, even though I'd never seen the series.

"I remember crying my fool face off and having nightmares for weeks after seeing it. My dad said it was the humane thing to do—you know, shooting the dog. That way, it didn't have to suffer."

Old Yeller. He meant *Old Yeller*—the story about that rabid dog. I hadn't seen it either, but I sure as hell knew what happened to the dog. It was like he'd tossed a pitcher of ice water in my face. Every nerve in my body sang in time with my heart. He was going to kill us all. As much as I wanted to be as far away from him and the disease festering within him, I had to do something.

"Wait a minute. Why don't we talk for a little while? You can tell me about Lassie."

He shook his head. Mucus dripped freely from his chin and dribbled to the floor. "Talking time is done, Gerry. Only one thing left to do: the right thing. And I need to get it done while I still can. "

I couldn't pretend any more. "Why don't you let us decide that for ourselves? Let us go. We could find somewhere safe to ride this shit out. That's the fucking humane thing to do, Jack. What you're planning to do is murder, plain and simple. Let's talk about this."

"Can't," Jack croaked. "This isn't a sickness, it's a reckoning. The sooner we all see that, the sooner we can accept it. A few need to step up so that many don't suffer." He yanked the gun from his belt and thumbed the safety. "This is me, stepping up and doing my part while I still can. May God have mercy on us all."

"No, Jack. It doesn't have to be like this. Somebody'll come for us."

He tilted his head back and sniffed the air. A rueful smile died on his lips. "There's *somebody* coming, but you don't want them to find you—trust me."

With that, he bowed his head and opened the door. Even as it swung closed behind him, he aimed and fired. Muffled screams and calls for help mingled with the shots, with the chorus dwindling as each bullet silenced another prisoner. After a few minutes, there was only one person screaming: Jack.

He stumbled into the room, coughing, nearly fell, then came to stand in front of me, his face inches from the bars. Earlier, when the shooting had started, I'd backed up to the far wall, but had since resigned myself to whatever God had in mind for me.

Jack tilted his head and sniffed. "Say something, Gerry. I can't see you in the dark."

The lights were on and I could see him just fine. His face was pale and glistened with sweat, and blood ran in tiny rivulets from each ear. His eyes, still wide and darting wildly back and forth, had dulled to a milky grey.

"Like the song says, bud: just a little pin prick..."

I opened my mouth to speak, but as I took a breath, he fired two wild shots into my cell. One ricocheted off the bed frame, and the other embedded into the back wall. I dropped quickly to my hands and knees, but couldn't move. He screamed and groped further into the cell, swinging his arm back and forth, firing blind. Thinking fast—not something I'm generally known for—I crawled toward him, staying as close to the floor as I could. So far the shots had all been chest-level, but that could change. As he shot, he screamed in tandem. High pitched at first, it eventually became an inhuman growl, punctuated by sporadic coughing fits.

Closing to within a few feet of his outstretched hand, I gave a short mental prayer, and then lunged for the gun. My hand closed over the barrel and searing pain shot up my arm, but I held on long enough to find my balance and drive my fist into the middle of Jack's face. He let the gun go as he fell, but I grabbed his arm and pulled him close. In one quick move I tore the cluster of keys from his belt, and then let him fall.

Now able to make noise without the danger of being shot, I screamed out in pain and tossed the gun onto the bed. If I was lucky, I wouldn't lose any skin, but the burns from the heated gun barrel were already blistering. There would be a first aid kit out in one of the offices, and I could take care of the burns later. For the time being, I tore a sleeve from my shirt, soaked it in the toilet water, and wrapped my hand. I rinsed the blood from the hand I'd hit him with in toilet water and dried it on my shirt. Luckily, I hadn't broken the skin when I struck him.

Jack hadn't moved since our tussle, and I was worried I might've killed him. My fears were put to rest as his fingers curled into fists, relaxed, then curled again. He was alive. He looked like death warmed over, but at least he was moving and making noise.

I snatched the gun from the bed and strode over to the bars. "I'm gettin' outta here, Jack. It's up to you if you want to come, but you're not getting the gun back."

After going through half the keys, I found the one for my cell. As I pulled the door inward, I kept the gun trained on his chest. His eyes were open, but he seemed dazed. It was like he hadn't even heard me. I stepped over him and headed for the door. I tried it, but it was also locked. As I fumbled for the keys, Jack rolled to his feet and dove toward me. Without thinking, I raised the gun and fired.

The bullet hit him just above the hairline and cut a valley through the top of his head. The force whipped his head back even as his legs carried him forward. I sidestepped his body as it crashed into the wall and then crumpled to the floor.

"Noooo," I moaned. "You stupid prick! Why? Why'd you do that?" Tears stung my cheeks as I gasped for breath. "You're crazy—this whole world has gone fucking nuts."

I'd like to say that I left him there and bravely sought out others who hadn't been infected, but I'd be lying. I stood above his body for a long time, staring at the gun in my hand. Or maybe I was staring through the gun, looking back at all the people I'd known, and realizing right then that I'd probably never see them again. They were probably dead—just like Jack and the three people he murdered. Then I started thinking Jack might've been right—that we were done for and the easiest way to go would be to eat a bullet.

As I closed my eyes and raised the gun to my head, a crash followed by hurried footsteps came from the other side of the door, and then something struck the door hard enough to crack the frame. I backed away, gun trained on the Judas window.

"It was an accident," I yelled. "He was sick. Look for yourself. He killed the people back there in the other cells, and what I did was self-defense."

I waited for a response, but the pounding gained in force, rattling the door with each strike. I crept closer and peered out the shatterproof window, and a face, or what was left of one, slammed into the window. Its lipless mouth snapped and snarled as bloody mucous smeared the glass. Without thinking, I stepped back and fired the gun.

True to its name, the glass didn't shatter, but the small hole in it, along with the ensuing silence, told me that whoever—or whatever—attacked the door wasn't getting up again. I found the right key, unlocked the door, and whipped it open. There, lying in a widening pool of blood and chunks of brain matter, were the twitching remains of the police officer who'd arrested me. If not for the name tag on his uniform shirt, I wouldn't have known. Most of his face was missing, and one arm, ending in a crusted stump, looked as though it had been chewed through by a pack of crazed beavers. The virus turned people into superhuman cannibals? I was going to need guns—lots and lots of guns. In a flash, all the so-called crazy rumours flooded my head: Patient Zero, the attacks uploaded to YouTube, and the conspiracy nut jobs claim that the government had unknowingly unleashed a highly contagious superbug. If they were right, we were screwed. I had to get far away from Sarnia before Chemical Valley lost power.

I stripped the utility belt from the cop and buckled it around my waist. Aside from the bullets in his sidearm, a pair of pouches held six magazines. A gurgled moan from the darkness at the far end of the hall sent shivers down my back. I fought the urge to retreat to the relative safety of my cell and took off running in the other direction.

The hall ended in a T, so I stopped and peered both ways. Bodies littered the ground, but none moved. Cautiously, I sidestepped a pair of corpses locked in what looked like a lovers' embrace—one with a torn-out throat, the other with a crater blasted through the center of his face—and I proceeded down the hallway, heading toward the door marked EMERGENCY EXIT. I giggled nervously, pondering their definition of 'emergency'. *It fucking well couldn't get worse than this!* Still carrying Jack's gun, I edged forward, checking each open doorway as I went, mimicking how TV cops would 'clear' a room. Each instance that I began to think I was wasting my time, I'd imagine one of those crazy bastards creeping up on me. No way. I was gonna keep on keeping on how I was keeping alive.

At the second-to-last door, I swung the gun and entered the room. After a quick scan I turned to leave, but caught movement across the room out of the corner of my eye.

I snapped back around and aimed in the general direction of the desk. "I'm not sick. If you're OK, come out."

No answer. But something stirred. I waited, holding my breath. I took a step, and a young woman of about twenty pulled herself drunkenly to her feet, snarled, and ran at me. I backed out of the room, keeping her in my sights, praying she'd speak or stop coming, but she didn't. I shot her once in the neck, spinning her, but she quickly found her feet and kept coming. I raised the gun, aimed, and shot her through the eye. She fell and stayed down.

Back out in the hallway, I turned in time to see five more infected stumbling toward me. I shouldered past the door marked EMERGENCY EXIT and entered the stairwell. Upon spying a crowd of them lurching across the lawn outside, I opted to stay inside and head for the basement, to the garage used by the police for prison transport. With any luck, the transport would still be there.

The door at the bottom of the stairwell didn't lock, but opened up to a small ante room with one that did. Thankfully, this inner door wasn't locked. Not yet, anyway. Those… things…

had already found the stairs, and would soon be hammering at the locked door.

I paused and held my breath, listening for any movement or noise in the basement. I was met by silence, but decided not to celebrate until I was safe. Intuition seemed to be working well for me; the first door I checked was the garage, and yes, the keys hung from the ignition of the prison transport. I reached in, swung the lever to open the folding bus-style door on the passenger side, ran around, hopped into the driver's seat, and fired the engine. I wasn't out, not by any stretch of the imagination, but I had a way to get out. Then I thought: Guns. I'm gonna need guns. No better place than here. I checked the fuel gauge, saw it was full, then decided to leave it running while I checked the rest of the rooms.

In all, there were four doors to open. Stenciled across the first was Emergency Response Unit: STORAGE. A card reader panel was mounted to the left of the door. I gave it a longing glance, but moved on. The next was the firing range, and there I was in luck. A metal cabinet on the wall held three police-issue handguns, along with an unopened box of ammo. I tucked the three weapons into my belt and dumped the ammo into the front pocket of my pants.

The next door was a janitor's closet. I was no MacGyver, so there was nothing in there for me. The last door led to another locked door, but one of the keys on my stolen utility belt took care of it. The door might as well have opened to the sound of Beethoven's *Ode to Joy*. There, glowing like manna from Heaven, was the fabled regional stash of guns, drugs and other illegal substances and paraphernalia. I'd once heard my father speak of it in passing. He said the RCMP, local police, and OPP housed all confiscated items here until they'd been inventoried, had ballistics done, or their court date had passed, then they were taken away and destroyed. Blah blah blah. All I saw was guns, guns, and enough weed to last me a lifetime. A rolling cart had already been stacked with assorted ammo, so I checked the boxes and tried to match them to at least a few of the tagged guns located high on the shelves.

In all, I took two pump-action shotguns, a suitcase sniper rifle, a box marked GRENADES, and an AK-47 that looked to have seen better days, but seemed to work. On the way out, I couldn't resist grabbing a duffel bag with the word CANNABIS scrawled upon the ident tag. What the fuck, right? It's not like they were gonna miss it. Hell, there was no one left *to* miss it.

I loaded everything into the bus and walked over to the panel marked 'OPEN', but couldn't bring myself to push the button. Everything was about to change. There was no going back. The ship was about to sail. Fuck, if I could've thought of another cliché, I would've used it too, but instead, I pushed the button and took off back to the bus. Once inside, I slid the door shut, dropped the transmission into 'Get-The-Fuck-Going', and stomped down on the accelerator.

Then I hit the brakes. The door was slow, so I needed to wait. I nervously tapped the steering wheel, my head swinging, searching for movement, until the door was high enough for me to punch it. Outside, all along the ramp, more of the infected wandered. I closed my eyes and floored it. Picking up speed, I ploughed through the few in my way and rocketed out into the parking lot.

What I earlier thought was going to be 'freedom' turned out to be a nightmare. The streets were clogged with the slouching infected. I'd stopped thinking of them as human after seeing the cop with half his face gone, still moving despite suffering from a clear case of (in my amateur opinion) death. I didn't aim for them, but they sure aimed for me. More than once, I had to reverse back down a street because their sheer numbers and derelict cars rendered the street impassable. I soon saw that I was boxed in, and decided to retreat to the marina to find a boat to take me down river.

All around me, the city burned. Screams of the living mingled with the moans of… I don't know what… filled me with terror. There were others out there in the dark, fighting for their lives. Women, children, people I've known my whole life, dying, but I couldn't help them. This city belonged to the dead now.

The marina stood deserted and locked. I burst through the gate and cruised toward the slip reserved for the police boat, a twenty-one foot cabin cruiser modified to double as an amphibian assault vehicle. I knew it would be there; I'd found the keys on the peg board back at the station. In the rear-view, I spied a meandering cluster of shapes heading toward the water. The gurglers had already found me. I pulled up to the dock, loaded up my arms with weapons, and ran for the boat. Three trips took care of everything, and I loosened the mooring lines before jumping aboard.

Before bothering to try to start the engine, I used a ten-foot salvage pole to push off from the dock. If the engine didn't start, I'd rather it happen away from the dock. They were coming.

After a few panicked minutes, the boat fired up, and I smiled my first real smile in days. But elation turned quickly back to panic as my eyes flicked to the fuel gauge. It sat just below an eighth. Without fuel, I was fucked. I didn't have time for this. My time crunch had nothing to do with the infected, which were now stumbling off the side of the dock like lemmings off a cliff and disappearing beneath the water's surface. My time crunch had everything to do with Chemical Valley. It may take an hour, or it may not happen for days, but I wanted to be as far away as possible before Sarnia was blown into the stratosphere.

I knew where I could find gas for the boat, so I steered down river toward Corunna. It was then that I afforded myself my first 'big picture' look at the nightscape around me. Fires raged out of control, through most of the city and alarms bled together and rose like a chorus of insanity. Fuck, man—I was Dante, floating up the river Styx without a coin.

Next stop: Hell

CHAPTER 7

Ohio River, Pennsylvania, USA
Lucia

The boat was stocked—Jason was wealthy, so we could have lived in comfort on the boat for days. "Comfort" was a word that would fade from the vocabulary of the remaining humans—I was sure of it. Fred was able to drive the boat, so I took his cell phone and climbed down below to call my parents. I kept replaying this song in my head—their joy when I told them I was Okay—Oh-kay! Oh-kay! An inevitable word, hollowed out by a virus, but I still had hope. They never answered. Instead, my father had changed his voice mail message:

If you are listening to this message, we want you to know how much we love you. Do not come back here. It isn't safe. They're trying to break in now, so we haven't much time. We knew we couldn't make it out of here, so rather than have those things eat us… oh, God! We're going to kill ourselves. Do not come back, please; get to safety. We love you.

And then my mother's sobbing voice. *We love you so much, honey. Just run; go west. They're saying Western Canada is still safe. Please…*

I heard a pounding.

We have the gun. It will be quick. We love you.

And then there was nothing but my teeth against the carpet as I screamed silently until I remembered to breathe. I held the floor and the floor held me. The boat lolled in the water. The pain was unbearable. I shed my furry costume and went above to find Fred as I choked on my own spit and tears.

"My parents are dead."

"How do you know?"

"They killed themselves—they left the message on their voice mail."

"Couldn't they make a run for it?"

"My father can't walk and my mum is waiting for a lung transplant, so she can't run. They were doomed. The creatures were already there."

I noticed I had referred to them in the present tense, and it made me cry even harder. Fred put his arm around me as snot and tears streamed out of me onto his FedEx shirt.

We could see people along the shore—normal people doing normal things. Word hadn't spread yet. The people in Pittsburgh were either too dead or too busy trying to survive to call. More than likely, all phone calls out of the city had been blocked. There was a rumor on the Internet that is what happened in Baltimore when the virus got out of control—all of the phones stopped working. I imagine I only heard my parents' message because I the call somehow bypassed the central system.

My crying slowed as I tried to calm down. "Do you know how far it is before we reach a lock?"

"I have no idea. I've never been up the river this far on a boat."

"Do you think they can swim?"

"The zombies? Nah. I don't think they can. They aren't coordinated enough from what I've seen."

I peered into the water at the rotting wildlife floating past us. The top of the water was littered with decaying rats and unidentifiable furred mammals. "This river's going to be a dead end for us. We can sleep on the boat, but if the virus spreads faster than we travel, it will be too hard for us to get to a vehicle. Plus we need to outrun roadblocks and the panicking crowd."

"So you think we should abandon ship?"

"Yeah. I hate to do it, but I think it's our best chance. And we should do it before nightfall so we can still see any infected people."

"I agree. Okay, go down below and see if there is anything else we can scavenge from this place. We'll take everything, if we can. Let's keep going for a while, and when we pick a spot, I'll steal us a vehicle while you stay on the boat. We'll transfer as much stuff from the boat to the vehicle and take off. We're going to have to take turns driving for a while until we can get far enough ahead of the virus that we don't have to drive 24/7."

"I can do that. I can drive."

"Good. First thing we take are the guns, then fuel, water, and food—in that order. Got it?"

"Yes."

"Then say it back to me—in what order?"

"Guns, fuel, water, food."

"Right. Now get ready, because I'm stopping at the best opportunity."

*

Transferring from the boat to land was easier than we expected. Fred found a UPS truck idling in front of a business that he stole and then drove down the boat portage where he had docked us at. We took everything, even things we thought we wouldn't need, because we didn't know what the future held. As Fred drove, I slit open boxes addressed to such pleasant addresses as "Cherry Lane" and "Arbuckle Farms Road". Some of the items would be useful, but most of it was just shit. Along some deserted road, we tossed out boxes and packing material, but nonsense such as cookie jars and Bibles had the potential to be weapons or firewood. We knew we'd need the room to stock up on food and fuel when we could find it, but I was determined to keep everything we could until we were desperate for space.

*

Somewhere in Ohio, Fred and I agreed we wouldn't tell each other much about our lives so it would hurt less if one of us died. He joked that we could just make up new pasts and that he could call me 'Giuseppe', because he thought that is what I was yelling from under my squirrel head as I ran from the hotel. I told him it was a combination of "Get!" and "Help me!", but the foam head stifled and skewed the sound.

I kept the squirrel suit, but only because it was bite-proof. Besides the boy shorts and white tank top I wore under my costume, it was the only thing I had left that was mine.

Each town was more stupid than the next. People mowed lawns and businesses accepted credit cards. No one knew what was coming, and they trusted the government to keep them safe.

Newspapers were still being printed and the infection map showed that the United States was being cinched into a V—I kept thinking: vagina, vestibule, viper—as the virus stalled at the Mississippi River and the Rocky Mountains. We heard that the Air Force had vaporized all of the bridges across the Mississippi two days before the virus reached there, but three days after we'd already crossed it in Minneapolis. But even Vs can fill in from the bottom, and upwards from Texas, the infected zone crept.

*

I liked Minnesota. It was flat enough so we could see for miles, and I saw one lone cow standing in a field. In my mind, I named him 'Worthington' and would return to his black and white spotted memory as a sign of hope. The fall was kind to us, and most days were sunny, and the nights weren't too terribly cold.

When it rained, we took turns getting naked and bathing ourselves with designer shampoo and Egyptian cotton wash cloths someone had ordered from Macy's. One of us was always on lookout. We learned that we'd only survive if we kept our guard up.

By this time, our UPS truck was a cross-country treasure chest. We had cleaned out two pharmacies in South Dakota and I had been collecting things at hardware stores to make a homemade flame thrower. I had a nice supply of chemicals, wood screws, and other materials to make pipe bombs. Best of all were the four sticks of dynamite we found at an abandoned granite quarry. Amazingly, the GPS on the truck still worked. The satellites suspended in Earth's orbit never blinked at our plight. We were guided down back roads, and we avoided cities. It wasn't until we crossed into Montana that the virus reached us from the south.

CHAPTER 8

Dublin, Ireland
Paul

One of the three at my back asked, "Is she dead?" I turned to see which one the idiot was.

"Her head is all over the street. What the fuck do you think?"

"Shit! Sorry… I'm not… Fuck it. I don't know." He was babbling. After what we'd been through, I couldn't blame him. What the fuck was his name? Gary! Yeah, Gary. Maybe I was a bit harsh on him, but fuck it—the woman's brains were decorating the road. My only thought was for the lad, Brian. Shit-fuck, had he seen his mother jump, fall? Which was it? Had she jumped or fallen? A stray thought slid under the door into my brain… pushed?

I ran towards the main entrance, my heart thumping in my chest, my mind doing somersaults, trying to find a reason for what I'd just seen. At the main door, I stopped and my blood froze.

Like I said: forgiveness and regret mean nothing to the dead.

"Who was last out?" I demanded, whirling around to face my three neighbours. They all looked at each other. I spotted Gary's eyes drop and his face go pale.

"You left the fucking door open!" We all stood aghast, looking at the front door, slightly ajar.

"Jesus! I'm sure I closed it. I must have!" he said.

I shook my head in disgust, turned on my heel and ran. Jesus, what if little Brian had run downstairs to get to his mammy? How long would a nine year old kid last on these streets?

"You're a fuckin' idiot," I called over my shoulder.

I passed the deserted lobby and headed for the stairs. *That fuckin' stink*, I thought to myself as I took the steps two at a time. I would never get it out of my nostrils. My heart was racing now; how things had turned all of a sudden. An hour ago, we were all relatively safe, just sitting it out, waiting for it to all end, or for the rescue services to get their act together and come to rescue us. Now, five of us were dead. At least I assumed they were dead. Mrs. Watson certainly was, and surely the four men left behind on Talbot Street were, too—or, God help them, infected and turned into zombies. Fuck! What a nightmare.

I still had the axe in my hand and the bottle of pills stuffed into a pocket. I'd dropped most of the bags I carried back in the pharmacy, except one sports bag I had on my back. I was pretty sure the whiskey was in there. I was going to slaughter that bottle sometime soon. What a disaster! Half of the foraging party was left behind, presumed dead, and bugger all supplies to show for it. I decided there and then, there was no way I was setting foot outside the door again. Even if I had to barricade myself into my own apartment, well, fuck it, so be it.

Who was going to look after little Brian now? Why the hell had his mother taken a high dive off the balcony? It was easy to imagine the pressure getting to her. Fuck, we were all on the verge of snapping. There did not seem to be a Mr. Watson; at least I'd never seen him. What were the chances he was still alive somewhere? Fuck all.

I burst into the corridor and felt the stench in the back of my throat. I wondered if it was coming from my clothes. That bastard zombie in the pharmacy was probably all over my jacket without me even noticing. I slowed down as I noticed Mrs. Watson's door was open. Her apartment was at the end of the corridor, three doors down from mine. I'm not sure why, but I felt nervous—kind of cold and clammy. The smell didn't help. I started to wonder if I was imagining it.

Just then, I felt something grab my shoulder. I jumped and swung around with the axe, ready to strike.

"Jesus Christ, you fucking bollocks!" It took a huge amount of effort to stay the axe from splitting Gary in half.

"Sorry, man. I'm really getting creeped out. What the fuck are we going to do?"

This fuckwit was really starting to get on my nerves. There's always one—always one sniveling little shit who brings everybody down. Funny enough, I thought it would have been me.

Then I heard a muffled groan coming from Mrs. Watson's apartment.

"Brian? I have your medicine." I crept down the corridor.

"That fucking smell is gross. It's like somebody died in here," Gary said. I swung around and glared at him. Oh shit! More urgently this time, I said, "Brian!" That poor kid had been through so much. I felt so incapable. The sight of his mother floating through the air would not leave my head. I could feel Gary on my shoulder as I inched towards the room.

I peered around the door, and the stench nearly knocked me over. I saw him straight away. The poor little fella had his back to me as he looked out of the window. My heart went to him. I knew what was out there, what was lying broken on the rain-soaked, cobble-locked street.

"Brian, come away from the window," I said, as gently as I could.

The little boy turned slowly. I had an image of a group of kids knocking on my door collecting sweets for the Halloween party—cute little things all dressed up in their handmade costumes. Trick or treat!

"Oh fuck, this is not good," Gary whimpered from behind me. Yeah, no shit, Sherlock.

Brian snarled a junior version of the zombie theme tune, a sort of low moan from the back of the throat. His little face had the sunken cheeks and dark eyes of the infected, and blood dripped from his bottom lip, down his chin. That's when I caught sight of the body behind him. It looked like Lisa from the next floor. How many times had I drooled over her and the cute little skirts she wore? It always felt as if she were teasing me… she had this way of smiling. Not anymore.

This explained why Mrs. Watson was lying with her skull decorating the footpath below the window. Imagine seeing your only child turned into a flesh craving zombie. Jesus, he'd probably tried to eat her.

I gripped the axe tightly. This whole thing was so fucked up. It was hard not to imagine that God or some greater source had just gotten fed up with us and decided to flush us out of existence. Surely they could have picked a kinder way. I was going to say more humane, but inflicting the maximum amount of suffering has always been the human way.

"Don't make me do this," I said. I searched his milk-white, empty eyes for any trace of the child who had once been there; the poor sick child who had problems breathing. I had his pills in my pocket. My vision was getting blurred from tears forming in my eyes.

"Oh shit, shit, shit," Gary said rapidly behind me. "Here he comes!"

I swear to God, I was going to bury that axe in Gary's head any minute.

How could I have been so bloody stupid? The open door, the smell, and I, like a moron, go charging in. I suppose watching your friends being eaten alive will do that to you.

Brian started to run towards me. It was probably the fastest his ill body had ever run in his whole life. *It's not him, it's not him,* I repeated in my head. His face was a mask of twisted hate and hunger, a grotesque parody of a little boy. Why could I not get past the Halloween costume? This was no holiday, there would be no party at the end of it all, just survival.

Closing my eyes, I swung the axe. His neck was at just the right height for my weapon to complete a perfect arc. The momentum of his legs kept his body going until it crashed into the wall behind me. His head flew through the air, spinning like a comet traversing the night sky, with hair and blood for a disintegrating tail. Gary retched and then puked behind me. I couldn't move as I contemplated what I had just done. Images of Mrs. Watson and her ill son, Brian, walking down the corridor, smiling a greeting to me as they passed, flooded my memory banks. He had never been able to play football with the other kids, or rip around a playground, whooping with laughter. His life expectancy was probably not that great anyway. I wiped the tears from my cheeks and the snot from my nose before turning my back on Mrs. Watson and her son.

"You left the fuckin' door open," I spat at Gary, pushing him out of my way.

Life is shit.

CHAPTER 9

Omaha, Nebraska, USA
Sharon

His name was Tate, and he was a Spectacled Sun Bear who had a fondness for muskmelons. However, right now, he was doing his level best to take a bite out of anything that got within, well, biting range.

In the early 70's, the zoo had set up an enclosure for a colony of prairie dogs. Unfortunately, no one thought to line the bottom of the exhibit with cement, and the little buggers dug their way out.

They quickly spread along the hillside on the north end of the zoo. As they seemed content to stay there, the directors decided to let them have free rein, along with the peacocks that prowled around showing off their vivid plumage and loudly shouting 'pee-oor!'.

Three days ago, a groundskeeper found a dead rat near one of the prairie dog mounds. I examined the rat, and it tested positive for the Hauksson virus. By that time the following day, we had lost 50% of the prairie dog population. Two days later when I showed up for work, I was told there were only a dozen of them left alive out of a population of nearly a thousand.

I had gone to the board of directors and asked them to close the zoo before we had an animal-to-human event. They balked. I hinted at possible lawsuits from the families of the infected. The zoo was closed an hour later.

Beneath the zoo was a vast labyrinth of tunnels and cages. We put every animal we could in those cages and monitored them all for signs of infection. Tate started presenting symptoms right after lunchtime that same day. A few hours later, he was in full-on rage mode.

We were in the process of moving him as far away from the other animals as we could. One of the interns, Mindy, had the lead pole with a lasso on the end around his neck, while two animal handlers prepared the containment cage. It was small, about three feet wide and three feet high, and cramped. It had wheels so that we could move it easily and was only open on one end. As I said, not real pleasant, but I didn't think Tate was concerned with comfort.

We finally managed to wrangle him in and close the door. The ground must have been wet. Mindy slipped and fell against the cage, and Tate bit her. Hard.

She screamed and fell back, holding her arm while blood trickled through her fingers. I stopped and exhaled, trying not to let panic show on my face. Thanks to my press release about a virulent strain of rabies, no one here knew about the effects the Hauksson virus had on humans.

Another intern rushed towards Mindy, intent upon helping her. "Don't touch her!" I shouted. I hoped that the edge of panic I heard in my voice was not as evident to everyone else as it was to me.

"Mindy," I said, kneeling down next to her. I had the first aid kit with me and snapped on a pair of latex gloves. "I'm not sure what type of effects this virus will have on you, but we need to put you in quarantine." I felt horrible, I had just looked her in the eye and lied, while Tate screamed and roared in his cage.

Pressing gauze to her arm, I examined the wound, and swabbed it for samples that I put in secure cases. "I am going to put you in the birthing room. You'll be more comfortable there." The zoo had the privilege of housing several severely endangered species. It was our goal to breed them whenever possible. A small, cement, windowless room that was kept warm and quiet was where we put the expectant mothers when they were due to give birth.

The room only had one door, but was riddled with cameras at various heights along the wall so that we could keep watch. The outer room was filled with medical equipment, including a surgical suite, just in case. I knew Mindy was going to die, but I was determined to learn as much as I could with the opportunity I now had.

I led her to the room and encouraged her to go inside. Locking the door behind me, I went to the control panel and spoke into the microphone. "Mindy, can you hear me?" I asked. She nodded. I had left the first aid kit with her. She was seated on the floor amidst a bed of hay, bandaging her arm. She was calm because I was calm. The guards looked at me and nodded. We had an understanding. When things went bad, they would deal with it. The two animal handlers left, completely unaware of the seriousness of Mindy's bite.

"Mindy, I am going to slide a tray of electrodes through the door. I want you to apply them and then talk to me about what you are feeling. Let me know if you start to experience pain or anything." She nodded and swiped a hand across her mouth—she was drooling.

Tate screamed in his cage and thrashed about. I put the cameras on 'record' and went to tend to the sun bear. He was going to die; I knew that. There was no point in making him suffer. I walked over to the cabinet where we kept the medicines and prepared an anesthetic syringe. The dose was four times the regular amount and would prove fatal. Instead of dying in pain, he would just go to sleep and never wake up.

I had a dart gun that I put the syringe in. After loading it, I fired it into the cage, striking Tate in the large vein in his neck. He groaned and clawed at the dart, but couldn't get it out. He calmed almost immediately, a few minutes later, he blinked his sad golden eyes at me, and died.

I swallowed and fought back the tears that welled and blurred my vision. But all thoughts of Tate left when I heard a crash from the birthing room. Mindy had thrown the metal first aid kit at the door and was pounding on the walls with such force that she left bloody handprints behind.

As I had requested, she talked her way through the symptoms, but not for very long. She had lost all ability to speak at eleven minutes, thirty seconds. Now, fifteen minutes after the bite, she was drooling profusely, and was extremely violent.

The electrodes sent signals to the machines that were monitoring her heart, blood pressure, and brain activity. Her brain stem was lit up like the 4th of July, and the monitors showed activity that was not generally found in a human brain. Her blood pressure was steadily climbing into dangerous levels, while her heart rate pounded away at over 180 beats per minute.

I made sure that the main computer was tracking the information that was coming from the monitors and that the cameras were still recording. Thankfully, they were digital, so running out of film was not an issue. There were nine cameras built into the walls. I could not watch them all at the moment, but I would be able to review the footage later.

Mindy raged on, banging her head against the wall and slamming the medical case around. Twenty-three minutes and seventeen seconds into the event, Mindy's heart exploded, and she died.

"Time of death, 16:43," I said into the recorder. "Cause of death, heart failure induced by Hauksson virus." I sighed and sat down. "Now we wait," I said to no one. The guards assigned to me never spoke. I had grown used to that. There were three rotations of them. This was the second group. One looked much like the other, and I had long since given up trying to get to know them.

While Mindy lay dead, I let the monitors and camera keep recording and documenting. In the meantime, I walked over to Tate and took samples of his spinal fluid. I even drilled a hole in his skull and took brain samples.

It had been a month since my visit from the CDC and the various Powers That Be. From that point on, I had been trying to figure out a virus that could resurrect the dead. I knew what it was doing and how it was doing it; I just couldn't figure out how it was possible for it to do what it did. A single-celled organism simply should not have that kind of ability.

I needed to know what allowed the virus to animate a dead brain. Was there a chemical that it released? In that time of hyper brain activity, was the virus synthesizing a new type of chemical that it would use for resurrection?

The scans only looked for what you told them to. If there was an unknown chemical that was released, I could not get the scans to test for it if they did not have a sample of what to look for—which meant that I would have to search for some unknown molecule that was likely hidden behind or within a normally occurring one. I needed a chromatograph. With that machine I could separate my samples into their chemical components and identify each one.

I leaned back in my chair and closed my eyes. I had been working non-stop since I found out about all of this, and I was exhausted. I must have fallen asleep, as a bleep on the monitors woke me. According to the clock on the wall it had been more than three hours since Mindy died. The underground catacombs echoed with the sounds of slumbering animals along with the occasional grumble from the nocturnal ones. My two guards stood by the door, faces impassive, but eyes alert.

I leaned forward and peered at the monitors. She hadn't moved yet, but the EKG was registering activity. As I watched, a finger twitched, a foot wiggled, and seconds later, Mindy sat up. No heartbeat, no respiration, and only minimal brain activity, but she was up and moving.

I swallowed and tried to tamp down the panic that I was feeling. Up until this point, part of me didn't really believe it. Now that I had seen it with my own eyes, there was no denying it.

I let the machines monitor for a few moments longer. She wasn't really doing anything but wandering around the room. I suspected that she was just reacting to lack of stimuli. I broadcast a few animal sounds, and she turned towards them. She lifted her face and sniffed the air. The lack of expression was eerie, but it told me what I wanted to know—she was hunting.

I didn't have an animal that I was willing to sacrifice, but I was pretty sure what she would do if I did. The virus wanted to spread; she would bite anything that moved. I didn't need to see that to know it.

I sighed and nodded to one of the guards. He slid open a small window in the door. She reacted instantly, running towards the door with amazing speed and growling low in her throat. The Bengal tiger down the corridor heard her and snarled threateningly. They were reacting to her.

She crammed her arms through the slot, scraping off skin and exposing muscle and tendons to get to the guard. He stepped back, bent to see through the opening, and fired.

She fell to the ground in a heap with a single hole in the middle of her forehead. A few moments later, I unlocked the door, and we entered. As I had done with Tate, I took samples of her spinal fluid and brain stem.

One of the guards made a call. A short while later a team arrived. They zipped Mindy up inside a black body bag, disinfected the birthing room and containment cage with bleach, and left. Mindy's family would be told that she was taken to a military quarantine facility where she would receive the absolute best care. Unfortunately, due to the infectious nature of the disease, there could be no visitors.

Three weeks later, 90% of the zoo's animal population was dead, and the Military was about to call for a nation-wide retreat.

CHAPTER 10

Sarnia, Ontario, Canada
Gerry

I coasted up to the dock in Corunna just as the engine stalled out. The sudden absence of noise sent a shiver up my spine, causing me to wonder who (or what) had heard my approach. The boat's fuel tank was empty, so I was pretty much committed. There were forty-five gallon drums of fuel behind the harbourmaster's office. Every kid in Corunna who'd ever siphoned gas knew about it. I hopped off as the boat bumped along the wharf and tied it down. For better or worse, I was home. For gas. For food. For Carmen.

Carmen wasn't a 'who'—she was my motorcycle, and I wasn't leaving town without her. Sunrise was an hour before, but the combined haze from the belching smokestacks of the Valley and unchecked burning houses had choked the sky, lending it the hues of a bruise. The streets were deserted, at least as far as I could tell, and the clock tower across from the now burning Provincial Police Station offered the only heartbeat my small hamlet could muster.

I'd planned on walking, taking a route through backyards and side streets to reach my house, but I found a discarded bicycle on a nearby front yard and pedaled for home. The shotgun had to be left behind, but I tucked a pair of .45s into my belt and teetered off down the street. I spied movement here and there, or thought I did, but after the attack by the woman back at the jail, I didn't stop to investigate.

Funny how loud the wind is when the bustle of civilization isn't there to drown it out. Every so often a whisper, a cry for help, a moan, a prayer, would reach me, but what could I do? I mean, other than feel like shit for being afraid? I was lucky to be alive as it was. No use tempting Fate.

I dumped the bike half a block from home and hoofed it the rest of the way. I felt like I was being watched, and travelling down the center of the street on a children's bike left me feeling vulnerable. While cutting through a neighbor's back yard, I came face to face with an infected woman caught in a clothesline. She'd somehow gotten the wire wrapped around her neck, and it dug in, cutting into her flesh as she flailed and jerked. She ceased struggling upon sensing my presence. I say 'sense' because sight would have been impossible. One eye-socket was a bloody cave, and the other eyeball hung from its stalk and bounced against her ruined cheek. My bowels turned to ice as her head tilted and she sniffed the air.

I gasped and raised my gun, and she pounced. She pounced and bounced back. I shakily lowered my gun as she lunged for me again and again. I stood mesmerized by the sheer tenacity of those infected with the virus. I pitied her, I feared and loathed what she'd become, but I was held rapt. I shook my head and turned away. With no voice box to moan out any sort of alarm, she was no threat to me. And soon, unless the line broke, she'd decapitate herself with the clothesline. I didn't relish seeing that happen, so I left her behind.

Many houses on my block looked to have either been looted or had windows smashed, and mine was no exception. My front door stood wide open, and the bay window had been smashed from the inside, but whoever had done it had long since vanished.

I pulled a .45 and wasted no time entering the house. The feeling that eyes were following me grew with each minute spent in the open. The kitchen pantry had been ransacked; most of what remained had been trampled during what seemed to be a bloody struggle. Blood streaked the walls and floors leading to the rear of my bungalow. Fuck pillows, fuck the clothes. If one of those things was back there, I wasn't going to fight them for my teddy bear. No blood marred the landing leading to the basement, but there was only one way up and down. No way was I going down there.

From the front hall closet, I pulled my old hockey bag down from a shelf. I dumped the contents onto the floor so I could load up supplies and strap it to Carmen for the ride back to the boat. As an afterthought, I tossed the gloves, elbow pads, shin guards, and five rolls of hockey tape back into the bag. You never know, right? I hoisted the bag and headed for the garage.

Because it looked cool, and for no other reason, I kept a machete on a hook beside the door leading from the kitchen to the garage. I transferred the .45 to my left hand, snatched the machete from its hook, and switched on the garage light. I expected to see her gone, stolen by someone before I got here, but no. She was there, and my leathers were draped over the saddle seat.

I stepped into the garage, but faltered at a thump from behind me, somewhere at the back of the house. No thought required here: *get the fuck out* didn't need to be translated for me. I rushed over to Carmen and sped through suiting up, leaving the chaps hanging off me instead of taking the time to zip them up, then threw my jacket on. From the bottom of one saddlebag, I pulled a bungee strap, wrapped it around the hockey bag, and hooked it to the back rest on the 'bitch' seat.

Another thump and groan from inside the house told me I should hurry the fuck up and get gone. Without knowing what I'd find when I raised the garage door, I took the time to walk the bike through a five-point turn so it was facing out, then fired it up.

Stupid idea, really. I still had to get off the bike and open the door, so all I did was announce myself to whatever was inside the house. Also, the automatic door opener was beside the door to the kitchen. Yeah. It was pretty fucking dumb. I slid off the bike and ran for the garage door button. I was still halfway across the garage from the switch when a man lurched through the kitchen door. I think it might've been my neighbor, Randy, but there was too much of the face missing to say for sure. One arm was outstretched, fingers clutching the air before him, the other hung from his shoulder by a few tendons and torn muscle. Then it came for me.

I can't say what came over me right then. Maybe it was the fact that it had defiled my house. It might have been because I finally snapped and found insanity easier to deal with. Or maybe I was just tired of running—of being afraid—but I screamed and charged at it with my machete raised. My first swipe took the outstretched hand off at the wrist, and the backhand stroke buried the machete three-quarters of the way through its throat. I pulled, but couldn't dislodge the blade, so I kicked the body away from me and pulled both .45s. Standing above the… I don't know what, but no longer human… I stood unafraid for the first time since the week before. The creature wriggled and tried to reach me, but I stepped forward and pinned it under my boot.

I took a deep breath and pointed both guns at its head. The sickly-sweet, coppery aroma of gore and fetid flesh from the body at my feet filled my lungs, and I retched, but held onto my lunch long enough to finish him off. Looking back, I'd have to say this was a defining moment for me. It was the moment I stopped pitying them for what they lost, for what they were in life, and began to hate them for the virus they'd become. Without remorse, I fired twice—once from each gun, one bullet for each eye—and it stopped struggling.

I moved both guns to my left hand as I pried my machete from its throat. Once freed, I wiped it on the creature's pant leg and slid it through my belt.

I felt liberated, like I'd passed some sort of test. I strolled over and punched the garage door opener. Above the whine of the opener's motor, a chorus of groans reached me from out on the driveway. No wonder I had the feeling earlier that I wasn't alone.

"Fuck." I turned to the body on the floor and shook my head. "Why didn't you tell me you brought friends?"

Because I had to keep my hands free to shift and throttle, I wouldn't be able to shoot while riding. Whatever I was going to do, I had to do it fast. The door was rising, and a few had already turned toward the noise. I walked over and settled into Carmen's seat, her rumbling purr soothing me as I braced my forearms on the handlebar, both .45s trained on the closest of the infected. I tensed as I silently counted the roaming band of infected: one, two, three, four… twelve in all. By the time the door chugged to a stop at its zenith, all twelve had turned and were lurching, stumbling or crawling in my direction.

I wasn't much of a praying sort, never really put much stock in any sort of faith, but I was quickly finding a reason to toss a Hail Mary to the man upstairs. Hypocrite that I am, with a prayer on my lips, I dropped the closest gurgler and shifted my aim to the next before the body hit the concrete. The second one fell before I could shoot it, a fibreglass, feather-tipped arrow protruding from its forehead. Then another was felled by an arrow. And another, and another, until all twelve lay bleeding out the small amount of blood left in their bodies.

'Dumbfounded' was a pretty light word to describe the utterly fucked-up nature of my current situation, but I was speechless. A pear-shaped wedge of shrubbery separated itself from my evergreen hedge and moved up my driveway. Once it was closer, I noticed its sneakers. I lowered my guns and squinted in an attempt to see who it was under the mesh camouflage.

The shrub waved a crossbow at me as it approached, and said, "Hi, Mr. Johnston. Are you bitten or anything?"

"Justin? Is that you?"

The camo shrub raised the crossbow. “I said, ‘Are you bitten?’ ”

Sure, his voice may have cracked when he said it, but the crossbow pointed at my head caused me to bench any attitude. Before I could answer, four more bush-people materialized from elsewhere in the yard, all of them holding a crossbow, and every one of them trained on me.

A bundle of branches from near the foot of the driveway loosed a bolt that shattered a beer bottle on the work bench to my left, then yelled, “You better answer his fucking question, mister. We got places to be and they don’t include pissing around with your wannabe biker ass.”

“No!” I said, raising my arms. “No bites, no blood, no snotty nose. I just came for my bike and I’m gone.” I turned to the pear-shaped one again. “Justin? Where’s your mom ’n dad?”

Justin pulled the leafy hood from his head and tucked it into his belt. “Don’t know where my dad is, Mr. Johnston, but my mom is… well, she’s just gone.”

Another shrub spoke up, “He means she had to be put down.”

“Total fucking zombie,” chimed in another evergreen.

Justin spun around. “Shut up, dicksmack.”

“Yeah, fucker. That was his mom.” said the fourth bush, who’d been plucking the bolts from the corpses and wiping them down with a cloth.

The one who leveled the insult yanked his head covering off and threw it at Justin. “And how’s that different than my mom? Or his,” he pointed at shrub number two. “Or his?” he nodded toward the arrow cleaner. “Fuck you, Justin. You’re only in charge ’cuz Tagger made you patrol leader.”

“Justin,” I said. “How long have you guys been out here?”

Justin stuck a finger in the air. “Hang on.” He produced a walkie talkie from beneath his green smock and keyed the mic. “Unit Three checking in. Over.”

The walkie crackled, then a voice came through. "Go ahead, Three. Over."

Justin nodded reassuringly in my direction. Into the mic, he said, "Section Four clear: no casualties, twelve enemy re-kills. We'll be returning one heavy. Over."

"One heavy?" came the reply. "You mean that douchebag who stole my fucking bike? Over."

Justin shrugged. "Come on, Tagger. He didn't know it was yours. Over."

"I don't give a fuck. Let him fend for his fucking self. Over."

"Tagger, don't be a dick. I deliver his paper. Over"

"Not anymore, you don't. Leave him there. Over.

"He's the only one who knows how to start that boat. Over." Justin wiped his brow and winked at me, his face pink and soaked with sweat.

Boat? I thought. "Hey! You guys aren't planning on stealing my boat, are you?" I wasn't even going to mention the crossbows or their Marine-like stealth killing. If I tried to understand it, my head might have exploded.

Justin snorted. "It's a police boat, Mister…"

"Gerry. Call me Gerry."

"Fine," he said. "It's a police boat, Gerry. Last time I checked, you weren't a cop."

"Yeah," I said, "but I got the keys. That makes it mine. If you kids wanna come with, you better get your shit and meet me at the dock."

"What's the hurry?" Justin said. "We've cleared the whole town."

"Apparently you haven't taken a look downriver. If that horde heading this way doesn't mow you down, the Valley's gonna go up any time now."

"Go up?"

"Yeah," I said. "As in blow up. There'll be a crater big enough to park the moon in."

"No shit?"

I nodded and started weaving Carmen around the scattered bodies in the driveway. Before taking off, I stopped at the foot of the driveway. "I'm getting out of here. You wanna come? Get your asses down to the dock by noon." I checked my watch. "That's an hour from now. I'm not waiting, so don't think about it for too long."

I dropped Carmen into first and peeled away from the curb. Justin was already shouting evacuation orders before I turned the corner.

Totally fucking surreal. I was saved from certain death by a pack of kids with crossbows. All I have to say right about here is one thing: Thank God for first-person shooter games and the crazy little bastards who spent days at a time playing them. It seemed the children really are our future. Well, at least my future.

Tagger was waiting for me when I got to the boat. My shotgun lay across his lap and the keys for the boat swung from his finger.

Tagger was a kid named Kyle who worked the midnight shift at Tim Horton's. I sure hope he was better at shooting than he was at making coffee. I remember always thinking they'd hired a retard at Timmy's to cover some sort of hiring spread. Who knew?

I rolled Carmen out onto the dock and dropped the kickstand. By the time I slid off, he had the shotgun pointed at my chest. It wasn't loaded. The only shells for it were in a pouch on my belt.

"Let me guess," I said, pulling one of the .45s from my belt. "You must be Tagger."

"I'll blow your head off, mister! Stop and put that gun down." He backed up and stumbled over one of the cabin chairs.

I stepped aboard and strode over and slapped him. With the .45 nudging his forehead, I leaned into his face and said, "Gimme my fucking keys, dickhead."

"You'll take off on us! I wasn't gonna shoot you."

"Yeah, I know. The gun you have isn't loaded."

"Huh? Yes it is. I loaded it myself."

"With what? I have the shells for it in my pocket."

"Mister, I brought that gun with me. Your shotgun is over there."

I followed his finger to the spot I'd left my shotgun. It was still there. My heart skipped a beat and dizziness swept through me like a fever. He could've shot me!

Fuck!

I lowered the .45 and held out my hand for him to shake it. "Sorry, kid. Calm down now. I won't leave anybody behind. Honest."

He hesitated, but took my hand. "You stole my bike."

"Get over it, kid. There's a whole world of bikes out there for you now."

"Yeah, I suppose. I'm gonna check on the guys." Tagger turned and keyed the walkie's mic: "All units, sound off ETA."

"Unit One: On schedule and nearing the final stop before heading back to the dock. ETA three minutes. Over."

"Unit Two. We had to fall back to second rally point. That dude wasn't kidding about the zombies heading our way. They're fucking legion, man. New orders? Over."

Tagger keyed before Unit Three could check in. "Unit Two, scrub your objective and get back here. We got a hog to load." He grinned up at me, hoping for a smile at his play on words. I humoured him with a grin. "Unit Three?"

"Unit Three: all packages en route. Leaving the grocery store and heading for the dock. ETA six minutes. Over."

I checked my watch. I was impressed. These kids had rounded up supplies in less than forty minutes. Now all we had to do was load them and Carmen onto the boat, load the extra fuel, and then get the hell out of Dodge before the cattle came charging through.

Altogether, there were sixteen warm bodies (and one Carmen) with me to push-off from Corunna's dock. Our plan was simple: we'd set out for an island not touched by the disease and hide out there until things settled down… if they ever settled down. Until then, I was Lord High Fucking Commander. I'd made that fact glaringly clear by telling them that anyone who thought differently could stay there and wait for the next boat.

I throttled the boat up to a nice cruising speed and headed north toward open water. To the west, a bloated orange sun sunk obliviously toward the horizon, and to the east my home town, a polarized mask of calm and chaos, lay dead.

CHAPTER 11

Anaconda, Montana, USA
Lucia

There were natural things, and there were unnatural things. Zombies chasing us had become a natural thing; the vibration of terror was normal, and bullet rationing was a necessity. A zombie in a wheelchair was an unnatural thing. Somehow, it still knew how to wheel towards me, but it couldn't figure out how to get up on the curb.

Smelling something besides the rot of cadavers as flesh sloughed off of bones became a rarity, and the luminescence of an albino zombie I saw in Bismuth was like watching the aurora borealis of zombies lurching towards me. I was so consumed by the color that I almost didn't see one of the fast zombies barreling towards me. One shot knocked his head back, and he dropped. I returned to watch the albino zombie coming closer to me. He walked heel to toe, with his hips popping foreword with each step. I had learned my lesson—I didn't let him get too close. I blew his brushstroke purpleness into a million blood stars.

We collided with the red zone when we reached Montana. It folded in on us from the south long enough to slow us down until it waved over us from the west as well. If the population hadn't been so sparse to begin with, we would have been dead. Fred and I had all but stopped looting homes and businesses—it was just too risky. Hunger made me change my mind after I was on my third day of eating canned mushrooms. I had already inventoried all of the food I failed to pick up along the way, and was starting down my wish list of dinners my mum would never cook for me again. When I got too hungry, I'd ask Fred to tell me about his life, even though I was breaking one of our rules. He had season Penguin tickets and I made him promise that if life ever returned to normal, he'd take me to some of the games.

"I'll take you, Giuseppe."

"If your seats are shitty, I'm warning you, I'll just drink the whole time."

"My seats aren't shitty," he smiled at me.

"Yeah? That's what all the guys say." I winked at him. "Don't worry, I'm a cheap date—two beers and I'm drunk."

"That's not cheap there…it'll still cost me almost twenty bucks."

"Hey, this squirrel's worth it."

"Oh yeah? Do I have to own a furry suit to hang out with you?"

"Nah, I'm not one of them. I was just going to observe the freak parade."

"Suuure." Fred winked at me and I rolled my eyes.

*

We scouted out a gas station that sat along a deserted road without much around it. Three zombies paced the lot, but we didn't see signs of others. We decided we would shoot the three shufflers and grab what we needed. Fred was a better shot than I was, but I hesitated less. He would serve as lookout as I donned my squirrel costume and went in search of food. I had kept the costume because it was bite-proof, as far as I could tell, but it wasn't tested after the incident in Pittsburgh. I moved so slowly in it, but if surprised, my chances of survival were increased.

Fred picked the three zombies off and we remained locked in the truck, waiting for signs of more of them. We didn't have a silencer, so the shot echoed far. There was no movement. We both emerged from the truck—Fred with his rifle poised up, ready to shoot, and me in my squirrel costume. We walked into the store together and I took my squirrel head off and started gathering things—chips, soda and crackers. There wasn't any water left, but plenty of gum and beef jerky. The loaves of bread were green with mold, but juice waited for my eager hands in sealed containers.

Fred lowered his rifle as I collected items. He leaned against the counter, "Well, this is turning out better than I expected."

A glass bottle of grape juice slipped from my paws as a zombie stood up from behind the counter and grabbed for Fred. He scurried out of the way, but dropped the rifle and fell as the zombie climbed over the countertop and rolled beside him. I ran for the gun, but a zombie emerged out of the back and came after me. He was dragging his mangled right leg behind him, and it slowed him down. I slipped in the grape juice and fell to the floor. I scrambled to get up as the zombie opened his toothless mouth and emitted a rabid growl from deep within his decaying lungs.

Fred fended the other zombie off with the butt of his rifle, now secure in his hands, as he tried to maneuver into a position so he could fire it. I pulled my paw gloves off and pulled myself along the tile floor with my hands. The zombie reached for my legs as my fingernails grated the tile, desperate for traction. We were like writhing worms drying in the sun—two zombies, a man, and a she-squirrel—frantic for what evaded us.

I didn't yell for Fred. I didn't want to distract him. He had to get the gun faced in the right direction. I kicked at the zombie's snapping jaws, but the blows were softened by my plush feet. I started throwing anything I could reach at him—donuts, bags of chips, and the moldy bread. The zombie clamped down on my pleather toe and bit, nearly crushing my bones. I heard the rifle shoot and saw that Fred had been able to stand up and kill the zombie he was fighting.

The zombie chewing my costume tore a chunk of it off. His face rose up and I could see his mouthful of white stuffing. Fred blasted a hole into his head.

"Not so fucking tasty, am I, motherfucker?" I yelled.

"Are you okay?" Fred was panting.

"I'm okay."

"Did you get bit?"

"No. Did you?"

"No. What about your foot?"

"He only got the costume. Listen, once we get in the truck you can check me over if you'd like, but can you help me get up so we can get the fuck out of here?"

"Yeah." Fred lifted me up from under my arms like he was picking up a child. "Now gather what you can, fast, and let's go."

I wouldn't bring anything that might have gotten zombie blood sprayed on it, which didn't leave much. I had already put the beef jerky in the bag, so we had that and a few other things. Several miles down the road, in an open clearing, we stopped and cleaned ourselves off with gauze soaked in rubbing alcohol. After that, we were ravenous. Our mouths were stuffed with several different varieties of snack food at one time.

I spoke, but it was inaudible because my mouth was full.

"What did you say?"

I swallowed, "I said, 'I hate coconut.', but, you know, this tastes delicious." I shoved a raspberry snowball snack cake into my mouth. Fred smiled and nodded his head as he chewed. "It's kinda stale though. I miss TastyKakes…they were never stale." I took a drink of warm soda. "That sucked back there."

"You aren't a-kiddin' me."

"Are you sure you're okay? That zombie was really on you."

"Pfft, I'm fine."

"No scratches?"

"No, no scratches."

"What next?"

"I dunno. We should look for signs of other people. We haven't seen anyone for days."

"I agree. I saw signs for a town up ahead—you wanna try there?"

"How big is the town?"

"I dunno." I ripped beef jerky off with my teeth and chewed.

"What's it called?"

"Anaconda."

"Sounds like a fucking resort for reptiles."

"Yeah, don't even make me think about zombie snakes." I shivered. "Let's do it before it gets too close to nightfall."

"Okay."

Anaconda had lots of zombies, but the infection must have been there for a while because they moved so slowly that they seemed to be stopped most of the time. As we drove through the streets, we didn't even need to run them over. For the most part, we could just drive around them. We picked a street and started looting. I left the protection of my squirrel costume in the truck in exchange for a gun on each hip, and a machete strapped to my back.

Early on, we encountered a school. The playground was fenced in and about fifteen zombie children paced around. I walked up to the fence and they gathered to me, like when I'd visit the pet store and place my finger on the glass aquarium full of goldfish. The children moved as I moved—from left to right, and back again. I walked away and they emitted these low gravely hisses.

"Fuck off, you little piss-ants. I didn't like kids when they were alive, and I sure the fuck don't like you now."

"Lucia, stop messing with them," Fred scolded.

We tried not to shoot. Shooting only drew the other dead towards us, as if smelling like fresh meat wasn't alluring enough.

We were methodical in our raids: grab a few items, slash until a zombie's head was separated from its body, and move on. We checked houses in the town instead of the stores. Most of the stores we'd visited lately had already been raided. The only real chance of finding things was by searching homes. We checked garages for cans of gasoline, kitchens for food and drinks, and everywhere possible for guns and ammunition.

After hours of looting, my arms hurt. I was ready to stop. We were locked back up in the truck when a zombie woman approached my window, slowly. She startled me, but I knew I was safe inside. Her nose was gone, replaced by two pear shaped holes on the front of her face. Her dress looked like it had brown flowers on it, but it was just a pleasing pattern of dried blood splats. She opened her mouth and gurgled something as she cocked her head to the side.

"Can I help you, ma'am?" I said.

She tilted her head to the other side and responded with a growl-coo. Her eyeball was loose in its socket and it jiggled around a little.

"You want to eat me for a snack?" I said, my voice bouncing back off of the glass.

She straightened her head and released a slow growl that sounded almost happy.

"Lucia, will you stop talking to the fucking zombies?" Fred started the truck and pulled away from the zombie woman.

"What? She was talking back. And besides, that's going to be me one day—the smart zombie."

"Don't say things like that." Fred gave me a look that warned me not to speak of my death because that might imply he too was dead, or at the very least, alone.

"You know—I liked those zombies… well, except for the creepy little kids. They were easy to kill, and there weren't swarms of them. We should go back and loot again tomorrow. Maybe we'll just drive around for the night or park somewhere. What do you think?"

"I think that's a good idea."

CHAPTER 12

Dublin, Ireland
Paul

What a mess. Despair crept over me like a hooded cowl, threatening to trap me in the depths of its dark hood. I wondered if there was any hope at all. Was there anywhere in the world left untouched by this evil curse? I was looking out of the window of my own apartment at the street below. Maybe Mrs. Watson had the right idea. I wondered if she had finally found peace. Was she reunited with little Brian in some better place? I doubted it.

I opened my bag and took out the bottle of Jack Daniels. Was there ever a better time to get roaring drunk? I brought the bottle to my lips, savouring the peaty aroma as I took a mouthful of the whiskey, grimacing as it slid down my throat, burning all the way to my stomach, searching for the cold empty spot inside me that once housed my soul. Then I heard the screams.

"Jesus! Can you hear that? They're all over the building." Gary burst through the door. I looked up at him and then back at the bottle in my hand. With regret, I screwed the cap back on.

"Well fuck this for a game of soldiers," I said, picking up the axe.

I stepped out into the corridor, with Gary right behind me. The screams were louder out there. It was hard to tell where they were coming from, or even who was making them.

"What are we going to do?" Gary asked. I felt like telling him to go fuck himself, to ask him how the fuck should I know? Right at that moment I just wanted to find a dark corner of the world where I could be alone, to drink my bottle of whiskey and forget any of this was happening.

Instead, I started to walk. I headed for the stairs. In a way, I think I'd finally snapped. Having to kill the kid had pushed me over the edge. Our sanctuary was no longer safe; it had been compromised by a gobshite.

"Where are you going?" Gobshite followed me down the stairs.

I just ignored the cunt. I closed my ears to the pleas for help from my neighbours, their screams and cries. I headed down the three flights of stairs, the axe in one hand, the whiskey in the other. Some part of me was hoping I'd run straight into a pack of zombies at each turn, to put an end to it once and for all. I wished I'd had the guts of Mrs. Watson. I wished I'd had the balls to throw myself off the building.

I stepped outside into the street and paused at Mrs. Watson's body. I lifted the bottle of Jack Daniels to my lips and took a slug as I gazed upon the broken shell of a woman I knew briefly. Another scream pierced the air.

I turned my face to the sky and closed my eyes. I could feel the rain landing little kisses on my skin. It felt good, refreshing, clean. It saddened me to think I would most likely not feel the heat of the sun on my face again. I drank once more. The bottle glugged as I felt the amber liquid warm me all the way down. It had been a while since I'd last had a drink; I could feel it going to my head already. I was sorely tempted to finish the bottle and find some kind of peace, or at least oblivion.

My brief respite from the real world was shattered as the now familiar smell of rotting flesh drifted in the air, then the terror-inducing low growl. I turned towards the building and saw a zombie framed by the doorway. I contemplated standing there with arms spread and letting him take me. I took another drink, one last swig before flinging the bottle down the road. It shattered with a loud smash echoing in the deserted street.

Bollocks to this.

"Okay, Fuck-face, time to earn your dinner." I took three strides while he ran at me. Rotting, filthy hands with black, claw-like nails reached for me. I drove the axe into his skull, wrenched it out and, with a swing that could have graced any ancient battlefield, took his head off.

Two more lurched into the lobby. I didn't hesitate. Like a warrior of old, reveling in the heat of battle, I was on them, my fireman's axe hacking into them before they had time to respond. Death was no longer a fear for me; I welcomed it.

Kicking in apartment doors, I hunted them down, killing them in a frenzy of violence, until I ended up back in my own apartment. I surprised one in the living room. "Get off my fucking couch!" Before it had time to respond, I attacked it with a fury coming from somewhere deep inside of me, a strength I would never have guessed I possessed.

I realised they were all over the building, and even if I could root them all out, the stink of the place would render it uninhabitable. I walked into the kitchen and turned on the gas cooker. I contemplated sticking my head in the oven and ending it all there and then. That would be the easy way out. *What's wrong with easy?*

This was my home, all I'd known most of my adult life. My parents were long gone. I had a brother living in Germany, and a sister in America. I hadn't heard from either of them since the outbreak. I suppose I had already assumed the worst and did not expect to ever see them again. I was slowly coming to realise the world was fucked. There would be no rescue. Who was left to save us?

I walked from the room and paused.

Fuck it all.

I flicked a match over my shoulder.

CHAPTER 13

Omaha, Nebraska, USA
Sharon

I hadn't eaten breakfast yet, so the only thing I had to throw up was green stomach bile. For a moment, I starred at the garish stain on the hallway carpet and considered cleaning it up. But in the end, I decided that I had bigger things to worry about than my security deposit.

Jenny lay sprawled in the hallway. I watched her, waiting to see if she was going to move, though I knew she wouldn't. On unsteady legs I rose, walked around behind her, held the muzzle of the gun near the base of her skull, and fired. I wasn't taking any chances.

I then stepped over her and walked into the apartment. At some point, Jenny had gone outside and been bit; the wound on her arm attested to that. And judging by the large stain of necrotic fluid on the living room carpet, she had died there. Lividity had set in, the accumulating blood giving the backs of her legs a bluish cast. It was safe to say she died late last night. I was guessing that she resurrected about the time the Stealth was making its way down the Missouri river, leaving a trail of destruction in its wake.

"Parker?" I called out. I heard a whimper from the bedroom and followed it. He had locked himself in the bathroom. She had tried her best to get to him, judging by the bloody handprints all over the white wood.

I tried the knob, but it was locked. It had one of those wimpy locks that you could pick with a hair pin. I didn't want to do that; I wanted him to come to me. The poor kid was likely traumatized enough as it was.

"Parker, it's me, Sharon," I said, being careful not to touch the blood. "Can you hear me?" I heard him whimper, but at least he wasn't screaming.

"Listen, little guy, I know you are scared, but we really need to leave. Can you unlock the door for me and come out? It's okay, I promise. Nothing is going to hurt you." I prayed to God that wouldn't prove to be a lie.

I kept glancing back towards Jenny. Mindy had been my only experience with a zombie, and she had been behind concrete walls. I knew Jenny wasn't getting up, but my nerves were on end. I could not get my brain to accept that she wouldn't rise.

I heard the lock click, and the door creaked open. Huge doe-brown eyes below a mop of blond hair peered at me through the crack. "Aunt Sharon?" he whispered.

"Yes," I said. "It's me." I held my arms out. He threw open the door and flung himself at me. While I held him, I checked for bites or scratches and sighed in relief when I didn't find any.

"Listen, Parker, I know you're scared. I am too," I said, and it was true. "But we need to leave. I need you to be brave right now. And I promise that when we get to where we are going, we can both break down and have a good cry. Okay?" He sniffled and looked up. He had turned eight on his last birthday and was in the second grade.

I smiled and wiped away his tears. I then took his hand and led him into his room. "We are going on a trip. I'm going to pack some clothes for you. Grab a few things that you want, but don't get carried away. Alright?" He nodded. I closed the door to his room, just in case.

My family regularly vacationed at Lake McArthur in British Columbia, Canada. The lodge was a large two story affair made out of timber and stone that had weathered the winds of time for more than a hundred years. It sat next to a lake that lapped serenely against a shore strewn with pebbles. The outbreak had begun in Greenland, but had moved out. The population was heading south, which meant the best place to be was North. I suspected that the coming cold weather would slow the walking dead down.

With the military retreating, I had little doubt that they would come for me. I had no desire to be locked on a base as their pet biologist. If I was going to leave, I needed to do it now.

Parker's Thomas the Tank clock showed the time as 6:45 A.M. I found his brightly colored suitcase and threw in jeans, long sleeve shirts, pajamas, and all his underwear, cramming as much in as I could, until the seams bulged.

He had his backpack filled with his DS, an iPod, and some favorite trains. In his arms was a worn Paddington bear that I had brought to the hospital the night he was born. I choked back a sob when I saw it. I had killed his mother, and the Lord only knew where his dad was. With that thought in mind, I took one of his crayons and wrote on the wall:

Jamie, I have Parker. Going to Lake McArthur. I have my cell and Jenny's cell. Call me if you can, come there if you can. Sharon

Then I wrote my cell number under it just in case he didn't have it. I had laid the gun on top of a high dresser while I packed. I found that now and eased open the door. "Stay here," I said, and walked slowly out into the main room. Jenny was still lying there. I breathed a sigh of relief when I saw her.

I turned and took Parker's hand making sure he stayed behind me. Jenny's purse was hanging on the closet door handle. I found her phone and left the rest. On a table nearby was their wedding album. I took it along with a small album full of Parker's baby pictures. I didn't really have the room for any of it, but the poor kid was an orphan. He deserved to have some memories of his family in happier times.

"Parker," I said kneeling before him, "stay here." I then pulled a blanket off the back of the sofa and covered Jenny up. I didn't want him to see his mom that way. When I shot the base of her skull, the bullet exited through her face. It wasn't a nice image for him to be left with of his mother.

He whimpered when he saw her lying there. I hugged him to me and walked quickly past her. I keyed open the service elevator, locked the doors so they wouldn't close, and put the suitcase and his backpack inside. I then took him into my apartment, shut the door behind me, and locked it. Jenny might not be getting back up, but I wasn't about to be surprised by another zombie.

I had packed for the lodge so many times, it didn't take me long. Jeans, hiking boots, sweaters, sweatshirts, underwear. I sighed when I looked at all the clothes I'd be leaving behind. I didn't have kids, so I bought expensive shoes. But a $600 pair of Manolo Blahniks would not be useful in the wilds of Canada.

The one frivolous concession I made was my jewelry. They were sparkly; I liked them. It was enough of an explanation for me, and my jewelry box was small, easy to cram into the bottom of my suitcase.

After taking a few more things from my bathroom, I put my suitcase in the elevator as well. My gun case along with all my ammunition went in there too. As I was standing there trying to think of what else I needed, I happened to look at Rob's door. I knew he had weapons, and I had the key to his apartment.

The closet in his bedroom was filled with cases. The shotguns I set aside, as the shells were buckshot and wouldn't kill a zombie. They would only pepper it with holes, not penetrate the skull. I looked to see if he had shotgun slugs—if he did I'd take them. He didn't, so they stayed. He did have three handguns. I took them all. A huge .357 Magnum that I could barely hold, along with two others that I left in their cases.

Standing up against the back of his closet was a soft, zippered nylon case. I unzipped it and sat back on my heels in awe. It was a high-powered rifle with a holographic scope, which gave it the potential for deadly accuracy. I had no idea how to use it. But I was pretty certain I could manage it.

He also had a box of Meals Ready to Eat, or MREs. It was a full case with fifty high-calorie meals. The lodge should have food, but I didn't want to rely on that, and we'd need something to eat along the way. It was normally a few days' drive. But with things the way they were, there was no telling how long it would take.

The elevator was quickly filling up. After one last look around, I was content I had what I needed. There was a fire extinguisher on the wall along with an ax. I grabbed the ax, just for good measure, unlocked the elevator doors, and descended to the parking garage.

I had a small Audi TT that, if I was honest, I would admit I bought because I liked the headlights. When the doors opened, the garage was quiet. The guard had left, leaving the place feeling like a tomb. I grimaced—not a good analogy in light of things.

My car was off to the left; to my right was Mr. Kowalski's 1965 Mustang. It was a Fastback and black as sin. He was its only owner and spent every spare moment tending to it. And even still, I doubt he ever got it out of first gear.

I looked at his car, looked at mine, glanced at a massive white Suburban, and considered that if I was about to commit grand theft auto, I should be practical. Again, I locked the elevators doors open, took Parker's hand, and walked over to the guard shack. There was a spare key for everyone's car, just in case. As they were usually secured, no one had an issue with it.

Two hits of my ax opened the small box, revealing rows and rows of shiny keys. I had mine; I took the ones for the

Suburban and the Mustang. As I walked over to the cars, I tossed the keys to the Suburban on its hood and opened the trunk to the Mustang.

I couldn't get the MRE box to fit in the trunk, so I settled for opening it and dumping the loose meals in. My suitcase and Parker's, along with most of the weapons, followed. I settled Parker along with his pillow and blanket in the back seat. My Glock, its case, and some ammunition went on the passenger seat.

I slid inside, enjoying the smell of well-oiled leather, and started the car. It rumbled to life with a growl, and despite myself I smiled. I backed out, drove over to the entrance of the garage, and keyed in my code.

As the door cycled up, it seemed as though the very gates of Hell had opened.

CHAPTER 14

Lake Huron, Canada
Gerry

'Dead in the water' wasn't a phrase I'd care to experience. The police boat was a throaty V-8, but still a single screw, so slow and steady would have to do. Overloaded as we were, conservation needed to be our main concern.

To save fuel, I kept the boat at about twenty knots and hugged the shallows of the American shoreline. Staying away from the choppy waves of the lake's open water would save us from continuously needing to stop and refuel. Eventually, though, we'd run out and need to stop somewhere. I'd followed the yearly sailing race to Mackinaw Island a few times, so I had an idea of how far our current supply of fuel would carry us.

Because I'd eventually need to sleep and didn't want to drop anchor when I did, I decided to teach three of the kids how to steer, set the cruise control, and start the engine. Not like it was rocket surgery, but better cautious than dead... or to end up as one of those things out there.

It wasn't long after leaving the dock in Corunna that we came across our first floating zombies; poor fucks wearing life jackets who'd sought refuge in the water after being bitten, then died of the infection and reanimated while floating down the river. They bobbed and moaned like some freaky nightmare Grimm version of a waterlogged Siren, so they were easy to spot, but hard to kill. We approached the first few, believing them to be survivors, but after an infected nearly dragged one of the teens into the water with it, we steered clear of anything in a life jacket.

Aside from the occasional bobber, for the past week I'd had nothing but water, water, and more fucking water to keep me company. The kids avoided me for the most part, and kept at the tasks Kyle (my self-appointed First Mate) had laid out for them, so I'd had plenty of time to try and put things into perspective. There were certain realities I—or I should say all of us, I guess—would have to face. The most glaringly apparent was that our home and everyone we knew were gone. If the virus or one of the infected didn't get them, the explosion that rocked the horizon at 7:02 this morning sent them on a bullet train to the afterlife. Even from our position nearly 200 kilometers away, the resulting aftershock nearly capsized the boat. I couldn't describe the explosion or its fiery aftermath if I tried. One minute there were clouds and a hazy outline of land, then the next it all suddenly burst into a wall of flame. Sarnia had been wiped from the face of the Earth. Family, friends, the tree in Canatara Park where I scratched a heart and the name of my first crush: all gone.

As tough as the kids wanted me to think they were, I heard them at night—maybe not all, but enough—crying quietly into their makeshift pillows, or waking up screaming from nightmares. I covered my ears and left them to their demons. I had enough of my own to deal with. I could never confess to being an overly sensitive man, but the night of the explosion, after most of the kids had turned in and I relieved the two who remained on night watch, I cried. Off in the distance, carried out over the water by prevailing winds, the gurgling moans of the dead kept me alert enough to stay awake all night, and were loud enough to cover my grief.

*

On day six, we emptied the second-to-last barrel of fuel into the boat's main tank. It was time to make a decision. Cheboygan was an hour up the coast. I remember spending a few days there once as a teen, on my first trip to Mackinaw. And I knew of a good spot to go ashore for fuel—dock-side pumps used by fishermen working for the local fisheries. The inlet used to get there was tricky to find after so long—like I said, I was a teen the last time I came this way—but we found it.

Kyle (a.k.a. Tagger) was barking order before we'd even sighted the dock.

"All right! Listen up, you screwheads. This is gonna be a four-dude mission. T-Rex, Bogus D, you two scout the perimeter. Top Gun, Fish342, you take the dock. If we need to remote start the pump, this area needs to be secure. You dudes get me?"

Four heads bobbed in affirmation. T-Rex said, "Righteous"; Top Gun and Fish said, "Yes sir"; and Bogus D said, "Dude".

These kids said 'dude' an awful lot.

T-Rex thrust his hand up. "Radios, sir?"

Kyle shook his head. "Won't need 'em, dude. Stay within the zone while Fish gets shit going."

"Wait," I said. "I should be the one to go start the pump if needed."

Kyle raised an eyebrow. "So you know which buttons to push to activate the pump?"

"Well, not exactly, but I could figure it out."

"Nu-uh, Captain. You gotta stay with the boat." Over his shoulder, he said, "Tell the captain what you did before, Fish."

Fish lifted his face from where he was busy priming his crossbow. "I worked for my dad down at the gas station."

Kyle smiled. "We got this shit, trust me. Dude, you're looking at the clan that's plastered every wannabe paintball team in Southwestern Ontario. You didn't think we were just a bunch of Halo-playing couch potatoes, did you?"

I shook my head. “No, I never thought that.” Even though I really, really did think that.

“Look, man, this raid’s gotta happen. You said yourself we’re almost out of fuel.”

He was right. It was either raid or we’d be drifting. Not something I’d care to do in water populated by the aforementioned ‘bobbers’, but I had a bad feeling.

My asshole was clenched tight enough to crack diamonds, but I had to give in. “Yes, we are almost empty. I just feel like a dick about sending, you know, you guys out there.”

Kyle’s eyes narrowed. “Don’t you mean ‘you kids’?”

“No, really.”

“Fucking right you don’t. ’Cause we’re not.”

And then the boat was bumping along the tires tied to the side of the dock. The mission was going down whether I wanted them to go or not. I nodded.

Show time.

Kyle whistled, and T-Rex and Bogus hopped from the boat. They hit the dock running, followed by Fish and Top Gun, who stopped long enough to tie us off. As soon as they’d taken their positions, Kyle jumped off and snatched the fuel hose from the pump. He tossed the nozzle end onto the boat, and another boy (whose name escaped me) snatched it up and stuffed it into one of the barrels on deck.

When Kyle flipped the lever to activate the pump, the coinciding motorized hum brought a rare grin to his pimpled cheeks. “Fucking beautiful, man.” He gave a thumbs-up to Fish, who passed the good news along.

“Yeah, B.A.,” I said as relief flooded through me, “I love it when a plan comes together.” Relief or not, I kept the rifle’s scope to my eye, scanning the tree line, the buildings, and the parking lot, but nothing so far except a few dead animals near the dock.

Justin, my paperboy, tapped my shoulder. “Who’s B.A.?”

"Never mind. It was a show long before your time." To Kyle, I said, "Call your crew back to the boat. We can keep watch from here."

Kyle turned toward the boys on the dock. "Why? We won't be full for another few minutes. What about snacks and shit? We're growing boys, ya know. If there was anything nasty out there, it would've come at them already."

Without waiting for an answer, he raised his voice and called out, "Fish, take T-Rex and Top Gun and search those squats for some eats. Bogus, you keep an eye."

Bogus nodded and stood his ground while the other three headed for the first of the two small buildings. Top Gun reached the door first. He nodded, waved at us, and shouldered his crossbow as he entered.

My arms began to ache from staring through the scope for so long. I lowered the rifle in time to see movement at the opposite end of the parking lot, near an abandoned pickup truck.

"Kyle, get 'em back here. There's something over there!" I raised the rifle and searched, but couldn't find anything. Just as I was about to tell Kyle to forget it, a head appeared from the other side of the pickup. Without thinking, I fired. The side window blew out of the truck, but missed the target.

"Abort! Abort!" Kyle took off running toward the end of the pier, his shotgun bouncing on a strap over his shoulder. "Bogus, get back to the boat. I'll cover you."

The drooler that had been behind the pickup lunged toward Bogus, and I trailed it, trying to get a good shot. My first shot missed. I fired again and struck its shoulder, spinning it, but it kept coming. Bogus dropped to one knee and aimed his crossbow at the creature as it gained on him. His arrow struck the monster in the throat, staggering it. Onward it rushed, and Bogus turned to run for the boat. I aimed, but he was covering my shot. Kyle swore and yelled for Bogus to drop, but the drooler fell upon him near the open door to the building the other three had entered.

Kyle stood and ran toward Bogus. It was too late. We all knew it. The thing had already taken a chunk out of his leg, but I understood his rage. "Bogus!" I dropped the rifle, pulled both 45s, and followed him.

My first thought was that Kyle meant to save Bogus, but he veered away and headed for the building. "Fish," he screamed. "Get your asses the fuck—"

Before he could finish, T-Rex fell through the door, grappling with a female gurgler. Kyle stepped forward and shot the girl in the face.

I pushed past him and entered the one-room building. The room was dark, but I found T-Rex near the entrance, his throat torn out, and missing half of one forearm. Blood flowed from his wounds, but slowly; he was already dead. I found the light switch, and immediately wished I hadn't. Across the room was the fattest man I'd ever seen, alive or dead, advancing toward a form huddled up in a corner of the room. Two arrow shafts protruded from the top of its scalp, but hadn't been enough to stop it.

"Fish!" I yelled. "When I shoot, you run back to the boat, got it?"

Fish lifted his face at hearing my voice. He'd been crying, but hope lit up his eyes at seeing me. He rolled sideways and prepared to run. I took that as my cue to shoot. I hit it five times, but only one was a headshot. It blew the skin off the top of its head, exposing a steel plate.

My mouth fell open. Not fair! I opened fire on the creature, blowing bits of it off while I screamed for Fish to run. When Fish shot past me, I turned and darted out the door. Fish collided with Kyle at the entrance, and I tripped over both of them. Fucking moron was gonna get me killed. I rolled to my feet and shoved the teens ahead of me. The fat gurgler, though holier than before, was still very much in the game. It fell out the door and found its feet as we reached the dock.

Kyle spun around and raised his shotgun. "I got this. You get him aboard."

"Like fuck you 'got this'." I grabbed him by the hair and dragged him, kicking and screaming, back to the boat.

"You," I pointed to the closest teen, "get someone to help you with the ropes. You," I said to another, "gimme that gas nozzle and shove this fucking boat off."

Fish was already on the boat, probably somewhere below deck, but Kyle stood before me, rubbing his scalp like a chastised child. I pushed him toward the boat and he didn't protest. His shoulders slumped as he slid over onto the deck. I cast the boat off with a push from one foot, then turned to face the four-hundred pound gurgler that had killed two of my people. While I fished through my pocket for my lighter, I doused the dock with gasoline. Halfway out on the dock, the gurgler stopped and sniffed the air. Thinking back to my time in the cell, I remembered Jack doing the same thing. This thing couldn't smell me over the gas.

From the boat, now about five feet from the dock, Kyle whispered, "Forget it, dude. It's not worth it."

"No. Fuck that. I'm not leaving 'til that fat prick is dead… again. Whatever. Just shut up and keep the boat about six feet away."

I took a breath, released it, and stomped my foot on the dock. The creature's head snapped up, and it lurched forward. Each time it growled, greenish slime oozed through the bullet holes in its neck. There was no need to wait 'til the last second. This thing was committed. It wanted my ass. When it got close enough to douse it, I sprayed it down and lit the stream with the lighter. Before it could crash into me, I ran and jumped for the boat, covering the distance with no trouble.

I thought the creature would follow me and fall into the water, but it stood at the edge of the dock, flames eating it pound by pound, sniffing at the air.

I had to turn away before I puked. "Alright," I said. "Get this tug moving."

"Wait," Kyle said.

I spun around, ready to hit him, but saw he had my rifle raised and aimed at something near the dock, to the left of the burning gurgler. It was T-Rex. Or what was left of him. He'd… come back.

Kyle turned to me and we shared a look. Neither of us said a word, but a lot was said. The pain he felt had stitched itself into his face like a mask.

I nodded grimly, biting back an insult. "Do it," I said, and left him to deal with it on his own. Call me callous, but I blamed him for those three deaths. Arrogance and inexperience can't cancel out the utter stupidity he showed by sending them after snacks.

I don't know if it was some sort of self-imposed penance, but once we were back on track, heading north toward Mackinaw, Kyle came to me and begged to take the night watch by himself. I let him. Maybe I felt sorry for him. He was just a kid, after all. I fucked up plenty when I was a teen.

Long after the rest of the kids were sleeping, crying, or both, I stood in the shadows at the aft of the boat, watching Kyle. Out under the stars, curled up in a tight ball, he sobbed quietly into a clenched fist.

The kid steering the boat (Jamberman, I think his name was), well, he ignored Kyle as best he could, but every once in a while he'd glance over, then hang his head.

I needed to take care of this before the pain sunk too deep, before it spread to the rest of the kids. We were gonna be on the water together for fuck knows how long, and I didn't want to have to worry about him or any other angst-riddled teen losing their shit and shooting everybody in their sleep. I left Kyle and tiptoed below deck. The duffel I was looking for was easy to find.

I'd hidden it so the kids wouldn't find the weed I'd taken from the police lock-up.

Mine means mine.

I lifted a tightly packed brick from the bag, then grinned and shook my head. I didn't have any rolling papers, and finding papers on a police boat seemed a little far-fetched. However, one fact that found its way onto every report card sent home from school said 'Gerry has a very creative mind'.

It had been years since I'd smoked weed, but a bong took less time to fashion that I thought it would. Half an hour later, pop bottle/duct tape/toilet brush bong in hand, I walked out and sat down across from Kyle. He nodded and swiped the back of his hand across his eyes.

"I was awake," he said. "I was just thinking."

"I know. That's not why I'm here." I produced the brick of weed and the bong. "I come bearing gifts," I said (lamely, if I do say so myself).

After inspecting the bong I'd constructed, he shook his head. "I got papers if you need 'em. That doesn't even look like it'd work."

"Oh," I said, and dropped the bong into the water. "Yeah, papers would be much better."

We didn't smoke the whole brick, but sure made a healthy dent in one end. Sometime during the fourth or tenth joint, Kyle finally relaxed. We talked about a lot of things. To be honest, I don't remember most of it, but one thing I do recall saying to him was this: very soon, we were gonna need to find somewhere to land. As safe as it seemed out in the water, we were at the mercy of our stomachs, water shortage, the fuel tanks, and a thousand other things I couldn't think of at the time, but would kill us dead all the same.

I don't remember which one of us brought it up, but we started talking about Thunder Bay and the many national parks surrounding it.

The next morning, I was still thinking about it. I looked up the population density of Thunder Bay's surrounding parks. It was something like one person for every five-hundred kilometers or some shit. I liked those odds. Besides, the kids were starting to get a little ripe. I couldn't speak for them, but I'd have been hard pressed to remember the last time I was near a bar of soap.

Later on that day, I called everybody up on deck and let them vote. I don't know what would've happened if they voted against Thunder Bay, but I'm glad I didn't have to make an executive decision. The final tally was fourteen for, one against. I never found out who voted against the idea, but didn't really care. We had a destination. That meant something to strive for. An end was in sight.

CHAPTER 15

Anaconda, Montana, USA
Lucia

We almost never slept, but were always moving, like gravity's peculiar pull on river water. My body was used to the vibrating hum of the truck and the isolated quietness didn't help me to sleep. Fred couldn't sleep either. He kept sighing and moving around. After two hours, I asked him if he wanted to drive instead.

"No. You said you wanted to go back and loot more tomorrow."

"Yeah, but there will always be places to loot."

"Go to sleep, Lucia."

"I can't sleep."

"Try. You need to be alert for tomorrow."

"Okay," I whispered.

I closed my eyes and decided I wouldn't open them again until morning, no matter if I slept or not. The creatures moved less at night, and we were relatively safe locked in the truck. I concentrated on an even pattern of breathing until I fell asleep and woke up before dawn, freezing.

I nudged Fred, who jumped as he was startled awake.

"Dawn is coming, and I'm cold. Turn the truck on."

Fred obliged me and we sat idling for a few minutes before we took turns peeing. Sometimes we pulled along the road, sometimes we peed in bottles in the back and tossed them out the window. Whenever we had been sitting, we always took the cautionary route and used bottles. We were never sure if a zombie was lying under the truck, waiting for us when we got out, or if they'd climbed up on the roof, ready to pounce. These were the scenarios I had come up with in my head, but so far, paranoia had served me well.

We re-entered Anaconda and passed a Wal-Mart.

"Wanna try it?" Fred asked.

"There's no point. They're usually full of zombies and already looted. How about over there?" I pointed to a trailer park across the street.

"Looks good to me," Fred said as he pulled in. We slowly crept up and down the roads, scouting for large groups of zombies or signs of life. It was deserted.

"It seems quiet."

"Yeah, it does. Maybe the zombies are migrating south naturally because winter is coming."

"I wish." I rolled my eyes.

"Are you suiting up, or going stealth?"

"Stealth. Have gun, will travel."

"That's my girl."

Fred stopped the truck and we armed ourselves quickly. I followed his lead into the first trailer. We made sure it was empty and began rummaging for items. I found Ramen noodles and wooden matches. Fred found toilet paper and two bottles of Gatorade. The next two houses were fails except for five gallons of gasoline in a can under the one car port.

"Hey, hey, look at this." Fred pointed to the number on the side, "Number sixty-nine. It's gotta be lucky."

"I hope."

We cleared the house and started our hunt.

"Wahoo! Candy galore," Fred chimed as he emptied the contents of a cabinet into his backpack.

I opened the fridge, "Gah!" I had to pull my shirt up over my nose. "Nothing in there we want."

"Hey, look at this," Fred said as he handed me a piece of paper.

"What is it?"

"It was just lying there. They're coordinates for some sort of camp or safe house."

"Lake McArthur? Where the fuck is that?"

"It says British Columbia."

"What do you think?"

"I don't know; let's take it with us."

I shoved the note in my backpack, "I'm gonna check the bedroom for a gun."

"Okay."

Under the bed, in the closet, and in the nightstand drawers were always the most likely places people hid guns. This person had none. In the nightstand drawer was miscellaneous junk. I pulled a photo album out from the drawer. I leafed through it and quickly shoved it into my backpack. *If we're inviting ourselves to someone's safe house, it might help to have an offering when we get there.*

"Lucia," Fred called in a hushed voice.

I tossed a few more things into my bag, zipped it up, and raced into the living room. Fred was peeking out the curtain. "We have company."

"They can smell us, huh?"

"Yeah, they look slow. They're probably hungry as fuck."

"What do we do?"

"There's about ten of them, maybe more. We either run for it, or one of us can run while the other person waits here and brings the truck closer."

The thought of being stuck in the house alone pounded fear in my head. "We go together. Did you lock your door?"

"No, did you?"

"I don't remember."

"Fuck, Lucia."

"I'm sorry."

"It's okay. Get your gun ready. Okay, on the count of three, we go—straight for the truck and don't stop for anything, got it?"

I nodded my head and buckled the strap to my backpack around my waist.

"One… two… three…"

We bolted out the door. I almost pushed past Fred as I ran. The truck was only about fifty feet from me, but between me and it stood a sorry excuse for a zombie. Her flesh was pulled off of the crown of her scalp and all she was left with was a mud flap of bleach-fried hair. Her femur was exposed and so were her toe bones.

I ran at her, my arm stretched outward, pistol in my hand, and I fired at her head. Two shots landed in her face as she fell backwards. With a shot of adrenaline, I leaped over her collapsed body and pounded onward to the truck, glancing over my shoulder at Fred. Two zombies were closing in on him, so I stopped and shot at one. I missed, but it drew its attention to me as it veered away from Fred and headed in my direction.

"Dear motherfucking Jesus in Heaven please let my fucking door be unlocked," I prayed the runner's prayer over and over again.

I reached the door and it opened up immediately. I jumped inside, slammed the door shut and locked it, waiting for Fred. He was seconds behind, but the zombies were closing in on him. I checked my side view mirror, and it was clear. I opened the door and leaned out, taking aim at the closest zombie. He dropped like a log in front of the other zombie and tripped him.

As the zombie fell, he reached his arms out for Fred, but just missed scraping the backpack with his bone-protruding fingers. Fred was locked in the truck, finally, panting and sweating. I was crying and I didn't even realize it.

He looked at me, but didn't say anything. He started the truck and we drove off. When we were down the highway a few miles, he stopped the truck and rested his head on the steering wheel.

"Is this what it's always going to be like for us?" he asked.

"I don't know."

"I can't keep doing this."

"Don't give up on me. I can't do this alone."

Fred looked at me. "Maybe we should just end it."

I shook my head, "Don't talk like that."

We were quiet. The world was quiet.

"We have that camp," I whispered.

"It's probably full of zombies."

"We can try."

Fred looked at me and grabbed my hand. "Thank you—for back there. You were great." He smiled at me, even though I knew he was forcing the smile. "Lucia, if you want to try that camp, I'll go along with the idea."

I smiled. "I have hope."

"You may be the only person alive on the planet that has that."

CHAPTER 16

Dublin, Ireland
Paul

So I ran. I ran from fear and pain, from the shame at what I'd done, from the exhilaration, and sheer bloody joy I'd felt while rampaging through the apartment block. How I had given in to the rage, ignoring all consequences. I ran from the image of Mrs. Watson diving from the balcony of her apartment and dashing her brains on the cobbles in front of me. From the memory of little Brian charging me, his face a mask of torment and hunger, right before I took his head off. Most of all, I ran because I didn't know what else to do. I ran without thought or conviction, not knowing nor caring in which direction I fled.

Rain poured down from a grim sky, soaking the streets in a torrential downpour. No amount of cleansing from the heavens could wash clean my sins now. My soul, like the overhead clouds, had darkened that day. Pavements and roads may be scrubbed, but the real foulness lies in our hearts and our deeds. Perhaps what was happening to the world really was God's vengeance, a plague right out of the pages from the Old Testament. There were enough around the globe who claimed it so. They, like almost everybody else, were most likely either dead or dead walking. What does that say about God's justice? If you believed in that sort of shite.

I ran until I thought my heart would burst, and then I ran some more. The utter devastation of the city began to sink in as I skirted around abandoned and crashed cars, jumped over smashed glass and all manner of debris blocking the streets. We'd really had our heads firmly stuck in the sand, my fellow residents and I. How could we have been so innocent to believe a rescue might come? There was nothing or no one left. Maybe a few pockets of misguided souls, like us, were scattered here and there. But from what I was witnessing as I ran through the deserted streets, the end really was here.

Dublin was once a home to one and a half million people, which meant one and a half million potential living-dead cannibals running out of snacks. It occurred to me then that I was likely the tastiest thing on the menu for miles. I still had Robbie's axe in my hand; somehow it wasn't that much of a comfort. So, running blindly through the zombie-infested streets of a ghost town was not a particularly clever thing to do? Who'd have thought it? Yet one more moronic thing to add to my never-to-do-again list.

I almost literally ran into the first one as I rounded a corner. It was lurching along, minding its own business, and probably looking for a relative to gnaw on when I came into his life. It brightened him no end; I can't say the feeling was mutual. That is, until I buried the axe in his head. It was becoming instinctive, and I was becoming adept at using it. Its legs buckled, and it collapsed to the floor while I wrenched the axe free from its shattered skull.

There's never only one though. Soon I was doing more than just running because I didn't know what else to do, I was running because I was fucking terrified. I was beginning to attract quite the crowd. One or two I could handle, but any more than that and they were likely to swamp me. I remembered the woman who ran past my window being chased down by a mob of the infected. Not a great memory while running for my life. She had stumbled, and they were on her in seconds. I'll bet she was having a right good laugh at me at that moment, Mr. Hide-in-the-Shadows while she gets her head ripped off.

I needed a plan, but for some reason they tend not to form in the midst of blind terror. I stuck with the old one and just ran. I was afraid to look back and see how many there were, petrified that if I did I'd slow down, or worse, stumble and trip.

Running into the courtyard of a block of council flats seemed like a plan at the time—that was until I realised there was only one way in and one way out. I was in, and a little over half a dozen walking corpses were blocking the out. There were four men, two women, and two kids. They truly were hideous—their exposed skin rotted, their faces a mask of demonic possession. I noticed one of the women had one arm missing from the elbow; it didn't seem to bother her.

Fear welled inside me like a physical knot forming in my stomach and rising all the way to my throat. I fought for calm. It was a fight I was never going to win as I tried to snatch oxygen into my lungs in ragged, sharp breaths.

"Over here, mister." A girl stepped out of a darkened stairwell leading to the upper stories of the block. I didn't wait for a second invitation, and neither did the pack. I was running towards her from one direction; they were coming from another like she was the point of an arrow. As I drew closer, she raised her arms and I heard two loud cracks. Two of the infected dropped.

Bam! Bam! Two more fell. Holy shit! She had a gun… and knew how to use it, too. She took out the two remaining adults before any of them got within spitting distance of her. The two kids were nearly on her then. Lucky for her, I was there.

I took out the snarling eight-year-old and six-year-old with the axe.

"Holy fuck! Thanks!" I panted.

The girl grinned. She was pretty—about nineteen, I reckoned. She had long blonde hair. Her roots needed doing, but what can you do? She was wearing a denim skirt, white blouse, and a pair of brown Ugg boots.

"It's really great to see somebody. I haven't seen a single soul except them things in over a week. I'm Ciara, by the way."

"You have no idea how happy I am to see you. Paul. Nice to meet you, Ciara." I flashed her my best smile.

"Do ya want ta come in for somethin' to eat?" She asked. "I have a campin' stove and some tins o' stew up in me flat."

"That sounds really great," I answered. In fact I couldn't think of a single thing I'd rather do. Well, that and just curl up somewhere and sleep for a month. The adrenaline rush was ebbing away, and I felt absolutely dead tired.

"Where did you get the gun?" I asked. I looked around the courtyard. Graffiti adorned all the walls—not even artistic graffiti, just ugly scribbles. A lot of the flats had their windows and doors boarded up. Unsavoury tenants evicted by the council, probably. One even had black scorch marks on the wall around the wooden hoardings. Nice area.

"Oh, it's me boyfriend's," she answered.

"Oh yeah? Is he…" What do you say? Is he still around, or is he wandering the streets looking to eat someone?

"He's across the road in the playground. His name's Martin," she said.

"Oh right, so there's a few of you here, then?" I wondered why they didn't move to a nicer and more secure location.

"I have a little baby upstairs. Me son, we called him Liam."

"Just the three of you then?" What must it be like to have a baby now, I wondered. What a nightmare. Poor kids.

"Nah, just me and Liam."

"And Martin," I added.

She looked at me, then, in a curious way, a sort of smile flickered at the corner of her mouth. "Come on," she said and walked to the entrance of the courtyard. I followed, keeping a close eye on the infected we'd just taken out. I wasn't in the mood for any more surprises. "Over there, see?" She pointed across the road at a small playground fenced off by some metal railings. Inside, strolling around in a circle, his feet crunching on broken beer bottles and what looked suspiciously like discarded syringes, was a hoodie-wearing, tracksuit-clad young man. I say 'young man' to be nice.

"Here, Martin!" She called out. Martin looked up and growled. He ran to the railing and started shaking it, all the while baring his dirty, black and yellow teeth.

"Oh, sweet divine Jesus," I muttered.

"That's him there," she said. I wasn't sure, but I thought I could detect pride or maybe satisfaction in her voice.

"Ciara," I began, "he's infected. You can't help him." It wasn't an easy thing to say, but then I assumed it was not an easy thing for her to put her boyfriend down.

"Wha', are ya mad? He fuckin' deserves everthin' he gets. He's a prick!"

I took a step back, unable to hide the shock from my face.

She walked into the centre of the road and started shouting at Martin. "I hope ya bleedin' rot in there, ya prick! I hope yer fuckin' eyes drop out and yer bollocks falls off!"

"Eh, Ciara…"

Then she shot him in the leg. It made no difference to him; he just kept clawing at the railing.

"Prick!"

"Maybe we should go inside," I suggested, wondering if I should just start running again and get the fuck out of there.

"Sorry. I'm sorry. You must think I'm mental," she said.

Noooo, the thought never crossed my mind.

"I had a baby for him," she said, "and then the little bollocks got me kid brother hooked on smack, and all the other kids around here."

"Okay, come on, let's get inside." I glanced over my shoulder at Martin; he was trying to bite through the fence but only succeeded in leaving half his gums smeared on the metal. I ushered her into the courtyard as quickly as I could. God alone knew what sort of attention that little show had attracted.

When we got to the stairwell, she took me by the hand and led me up the steps. I don't know why, but somehow I got the feeling I was not the first strange man to be guided by her up those stairs. The flat was cramped and full of clutter. A baby's crib sat on legs in the middle of the sitting room floor. The place stank. I really was not getting a comfortable feeling about her or her home. She made straight for the cot and picked up a small bundle covered in a blue blanket.

"Here, will you hold him while I get the stove on? I have some tea if you'd like some."

"Sure, that'd be cool." I took the baby from her.

It was only seconds, and another time I would have been quicker, smarter. But I was exhausted, traumatised even. I just wasn't thinking straight. That is, until I felt something on my hand. I looked down. The toothless baby had its gums wrapped around my finger; I could even feel its teeth under the skin that hadn't come down yet. Its milky white eyes were sunk into a grey rotting face.

"Shit Fuck!" I yelled as I flung the baby from me. It hit the wall with a thud. "Jesus fucking Christ!" I screamed, examining my hand. The skin wasn't broken. At least I didn't think so.

I ran into the bathroom and attacked the cabinet. I pulled out a bottle of disinfectant and poured it over my hand. *Much good that will do,* I thought. Fucking hell, gummed to death. What a way to go.

"Ciara, your fucking baby is infected!" I roared from the bathroom, praying it hadn't broken the skin. *Please don't let me get killed by an infant fucking zombie.* I looked over my shoulder and saw her in the living room. She had the baby in her arms. "Nooo, Ciara!" I ran in and then stopped, totally horrified.

She unbuttoned her shirt and pulled out a plump breast. She offered the nipple to the baby, which he latched onto with relish. "Hush little baby don't say a word," she began to sing. I was dumbstruck. She looked up and saw me standing there. She had a manic, wild look in her eyes, part ecstasy, part agony. She flinched as the baby suckled, I could see her milk mixed with blood flowing down her breast and his chin. "Paul's going to live with us now," she said to the baby.

He is in his fucking shite. I didn't say it out loud though. I pulled the axe from my belt.

"We can do business later if you like," she said to me, "I won't even charge you. You can have it whenever you like for free."

"Eh..."

"Papa's gonna buy you a mockingbird."

New plan. I ran outside. The trapped drug dealer in the playground looked up at me and snarled. He'd broken half his teeth on the fence since I'd last seen him, and a good part of the skin on his face had disintegrated.

"Hey, Martin," I yelled across the road. "Your kid has your eyes."

CHAPTER 17

Omaha, Nebraska, USA
Sharon

Car alarms blared as smoke rose from the rubble of the I-80 bridge. Frantic people ran from buildings to cars, packing whatever belongings they could fit into their vehicles.

Martial Law had been declared three weeks ago, a curfew was imposed, and armored personnel carriers had rumbled down city streets that had previously only seen harried commuters. But now those military vehicles were gone, even the local police were absent.

We all knew what blowing the bridges meant—a retreat had been called, it was obvious to even the most casual observer. They had fallen back behind the electrified fences of Offutt, closed the blast proof doors of NORAD, and hunkered down in Texas and South Dakota. It was now every man for himself, those of a giving sort now found themselves ruthlessly concerned with only the welfare of loved ones.

As I left the underground parking garage, the Mustang growled with impatience to go faster. I intended to give it ample opportunity, but for now I needed to be careful more than fast.

Even after all that had happened, the population still thought it was best to head south. What they thought they would find down there, other than the sun baked sands of Mexico, was beyond me.

An epidemic was spreading, a congregation of people was exactly what it needed, and exactly what I intended to avoid.

Taking the back streets, I managed to get to the zoo in record time. Everyone was on the highways and interstates… something else I planned to avoid.

I keyed in my access code; the paneled gate slowly opened, revealing the desolation of a once thriving wildlife preserve. As I drove along, I saw great gaping holes cut in the massive aviary. Someone had released the birds. The virus seemed to be contained to mammals, so we had not bothered to quarantine any of the other species. A flock of brightly colored parrots flew across my field of vision. With winter coming, I prayed they had the sense to fly south. Right about then, that was all I had to offer most things—prayer.

The research facility was secured access with underground parking. Again, I entered my code; the door slowly rose. It was quiet and empty, save those vehicles the zoo owned. Everyone had left. I expected as much. Still, I grabbed my Glock and Parker's hand—better safe than sorry.

I had been allocated my own secured lab in order to work on the Hauksson virus. Of course I could not call it that without having to explain things I wasn't supposed to talk about. So, I had dubbed it 'Project Z' and left it at that. For all they knew, I was working on a vicious new strain of rabies. Given my background, it fit perfectly, and very few people even bothered to take notice.

With Parker in tow, I moved quickly to the lab, swiped my card, and made sure the door closed behind me. I had two laptops that I was using for the project. Each one was locked away at night in a safe to ensure that nothing was stolen.

I zippered both of them inside a padded nylon case and set them aside. The lodge had an ancient desktop PC that we could use in case someone forgot their computer, or, in my case, when I dropped mine in the lake one summer. The old PC, when compared to the laptops, was like comparing a tricycle to a Ferrari.

I found the steel case that I had been given and loaded it full of my samples, along with the iPad, my hand written notes and theorems, and latched the case closed.

The Mustang's trunk was getting full, but I had intentionally left room for my research. There was no way I was leaving it behind. I paused and looked at the microscope on the counter. It was state of the art, and I loved it, but it was big, unwieldy, and bolted to the counter. With a sigh I reminded myself that I knew I wouldn't be able to take it. I wasn't happy about it though.

Reaching towards a cabinet above me, I found a wooden case. Inside it was an older, manual microscope. No fancy interfaces, no digital dial, just crank knobs. I had purchased it long ago, wistfully imaging all the hands that touched it and the things it must have seen. It was coming with me.

The door hissed opened behind me. I didn't even turn, just pointed the gun. "What the hell, Red!"

I turned and met the rounded eyes of Jack. "What the hell, indeed," I said. "It's probably not the best time to be sneaking up on people, Jack."

"I wasn't sneaking," he grumbled.

"What are you doing here?" I asked, and went back to packing.

"I figured this was the safest place. It's secured; there is food and water," he said. I had to admit, he was pretty accurate. Even still, I wasn't staying.

"You are the one that released the birds."

"Yes," he said taking on a defensive tone.

I held up a hand to forestall whatever explanation he was about to give. "Look, I would have done it too." And I would have. I felt sorry for the marine animals locked in their tanks. There was nowhere to release them to. It bothered me that I could not help them. It was the same with the reptiles, but we had a lot of very dangerous snakes. I simply could not loose such things on the public. Besides, it was getting colder; they likely wouldn't survive the winter anyway. Ruthlessly, I shoved the thoughts aside, forcing myself to realize that I couldn't save everything. Best to just concentrate on what I could, which is what all the research was for.

I found a small cart on wheels and loaded it up with the cases. With one last look around, I headed for the door.

"Where are you going?" he asked, following after me.

"North," I mumbled, swiping my card to open the door. Quickly, I made my way to the car and unlocked the trunk.

"Hey, I didn't know you had a kid," he said, observantly noticing Parker.

"I don't."

"Then where did you get him?"

"Wal-Mart," I replied.

"Okay. Is this your car?"

"It is now," I replied as I packed the truck with the cases. I had to move the MREs about and cram them between the cases, making sure nothing would slide around. I opened the door and told Parker to climb inside.

"Take me with you," Jack said in a rush.

"What?" I paused to look at him with a frown on my face. "Why? I thought you were staying here."

He fidgeted for a moment and then blurted out, "I don't want to be alone." It was an honest answer and I had to give him credit for voicing it. The thought of being alone with Parker at the lodge was frightening. I had to admit that it would nice to have another adult around, even if it was just Jack.

"Are you packed? Because, Jack, I am not waiting for you. I am leaving now, get your crap and get out here. One bag, bring only what you have to, and only your warmest clothes. It's cold where we are going."

He beamed at me. "I'll be back in five minutes!" And then he ran off. And God help, but if he took six minutes, I was leaving without him.

A few minutes later, he ran out of the building like he was being chased. I unlocked the door, and he climbed inside. "I opened the cages," he said.

I knew there were several of the large cats that had not become sick. The remainder of the bears had proven to be healthy as well. I nodded and said nothing. To my amazement, he had only one small duffel bag.

"Can you shoot?" I asked.

"Yeah, my dad was a Marine. He wasn't really happy when I decided to become 'zookeeper', as he called it." Jack was actually an exotic animal veterinarian, and quite a skilled one at that.

"That's good, but listen to me, if you put me or the kid in danger, I'll shoot you myself." I knew I was being harsh and I didn't care. The time for pleasantries had passed.

"Don't worry; I'll pull my own weight. We can take turns driving." I sighed and calmed down a bit. I'd have to think about the driving though. When running for my life, I preferred not to be a passenger. But for now, I needed to get gas. I suspected that most of the stations were being overrun with panicked travelers. Thankfully, the zoo had a few gas pumps for the work trucks and lawn mowers. I drove over to one and got out to fill up.

"I'm gonna run inside the shop, get us some drinks, and snacks," he said.

"Jack, wait." I walked around to the trunk and took out the .357. It was too big for my hand, but he was taller, over six feet. It would work better for him. "Just in case," I said, handing him the weapon after I made sure it was loaded.

He nodded and trotted off to the snack shop. I filled up the tank and climbed back in. Jack returned a minute later carrying a cooler and several canvas bags bearing the zoo's logo.

"I filled the cooler with soda, water, and juice for the little guy," he said. I slid into the driver's seat and put the cooler on the floor behind the passenger seat. It meant that Jack could not scoot his chair back but there wasn't much I could do about it.

The Mustang wasn't a big car; we had to make use of what room we had.

"I snagged as much as I could carry in the way of chips, candy and sandwiches. They were refrigerated still, so we should be safe eating them," he said as he climbed in and slammed his door with the resounding thud that only Detroit steel had. Then he reached into a bag and pulled out a bunch of stuffed toy animals and handed them to Parker, who grinned and reached for the furry critters. For just a moment, that haunted look left his eyes.

I turned towards Jack and smiled. He shrugged. "I figured he would like them."

"That was very nice…" My next words were cut off by a frantic scream. We both looked up to see a woman running towards us; she was being chased by two of the groundskeepers, who were now zombies.

"Parker, lie down and cover up," I said as I started the engine. There wasn't a lot to do except pray that she got to us before they did. I didn't want to accidentally run her over, so I kept the car still. Unless I planned to shoot through the windshield I couldn't get a clear shot. They were right behind her, and I didn't want to risk hitting her. Jack opened the door, jumped out and shouted at her to run faster.

Panicked and not thinking clearly, she slowed down and looked behind her, giving them valuable seconds. She stumbled, but didn't fall, sacrificing more seconds. She recovered, ran towards us as fast as she could, and flung herself on the hood of the car, her hands smacking against the metal.

"Shit," I whispered. Jack was reaching for her just as they grabbed her and dragged her off, ripping into her as they fell to the ground. "Get in!" I shouted at Jack. Putting the car in reverse I hit the gas before he even fully closed his door. I backed up about twenty feet, rolled the window down and aimed.

She looked towards me for just a moment and blinked, long and slow. Then she nodded and closed her eyes. I took the shot and ended her misery. Swallowing down the taste of bile, I cranked the window back up and drove off. I suppose I should have shot the zombies also, but I didn't want to waste the bullets.

A flash of orange streaked across my rear-view mirror. It was Bruce, a massive Siberian tiger. He had been wild caught as a means to introduce a new bloodline into the captive breeding program. Bruce knew what it was to be free and hunt for his meals. I saw him scent the zombies, no doubt smelling the rot over the lure of fresh blood. He hissed, baring his teeth, and ran in the other direction, disappearing into the gloom of the surroundings woods.

Nebraska was about to see its first Siberian winter.

CHAPTER 18

Thunder Bay, Ontario, Canada
Gerry

Almost four weeks after leaving home, we found our first survivor. Well, sort of. I guess you could say his voice found *us*.

"... The kings of the earth, and the great men, and the rich men, and the chief captains, and the mighty men, and every bondman, and every free man, hid themselves in the dens and in the rocks of the mountains; and said to the mountains and rocks, fall on us, and hide us from the face of him that sitteth upon the throne, and from the wrath of the Lamb: For the great day of his wrath is come; and who shall be able to stand? Revelation, six point one-five."

The voice coming over the boat's radio droned on, broken sporadically by spikes of static. His tone, gravelly and thin, was mesmerizing. All the kids had come up to hear. Aside from its overall gloom and doom-type jabber, what made this signal different from the multitude of pleas and babbling we'd heard over the past three weeks of our journey was that it wasn't a recording like the rest. The speaker was alive and well and living somewhere near Thunder Bay. We'd found a survivor.

"Hello?" I couldn't think of anything else to say, like breaker-one-niner or whatever, so I removed my thumb from the mic and waited for him to answer.

"Is there someone there, please?" the man said, then cleared his throat. "My name is Micah and I am the shepherd."

Kyle piped up: "Ask if he's heard anything—you know, about all this stuff."

Several other boys joined in, all with their own questions, but I held up my hand. "Everybody shut up and relax, let me talk to this fella and see what's what."

Static. "Are you there?"

"Yes, Micah, we're here. Are there any of those things where you are?"

"Those things?"

"Yeah," I said. "Infected people; you know."

"Ah, you mean the resurrected. No... we have none among our community."

"Community? Are you telling me you're in a city or something?"

Micah chuckled. "You could say that. We are The Coven of the Lamb; we have been chosen to usher in a new dawn."

I exchanged glances with the boys surrounding me. Their eyes mirrored my own feelings: this guy was a fucking lunatic.

I keyed the mic, "Say, Micah, is there anyone else we could talk to, you know, someone who might give us directions to your, ah, community?"

"I am the shepherd. It is my caste. Jonas hands down our assignments."

"I see. Can you give me a sec, Micah? I need to confer with my crew."

"Crew, you say? How many are your number? We will welcome you into the fold."

How many are your number? Was this guy for real? Who spoke like that, anyway? I didn't answer him; he creeped me out.

The boys were looking to me to make a decision here, but I had a bad feeling. Maybe it was because we'd been so long on the water without another soul around, or maybe I saw freaks and geeks where there was only safety.

Kyle shrugged, "Well, what do you think?"

The reality of the situation was that we were low on stores, fuel, and morale, and it was beginning to show. Everybody was edgy, but why shouldn't they be? Everyone they'd ever known who wasn't in this small radio room was dead. Yes, Micah seemed a little crazy—OK, a lot crazy—but it's possible that religion was the crutch he used to make it through, to keep him alive in these mad times.

"What I think doesn't matter, Kyle. We need to vote on this. Do we go find this guy and his people, or do we keep on and try to find our way further on? I mean, you all heard him. He gives me the heebie-jeebies, but he says it's safe where he is. Alright, a show of hands—who says we go find the creepy old guy?"

The vote was unanimous.

"Micah, are you still with me?"

"I am."

"Whereabouts are you?" I said, smiling as the boys whooped with laughter. "We thought we might stop by for a visit."

"I can give you coordinates to a dock near our camp. There will be people sent to greet you upon arriving. How many are you in number?"

"Six," I said. It probably wasn't best starting any relationship out with a lie, but his insistence on knowing our number bothered me.

The rest of the kids all left the small room, off doing whatever teenaged hormone factories did when they were excited about something, but Kyle stayed behind.

After I signed off with Micah, the old preacher returned to his sermon, "On the tide of dead, the chosen will rise above the swell, and the ignorant wail en mass under the might of Heavenly Judgement. Even as the final darkness blankets the sky and extinguishes the stars of Heaven, The Coven of the Lamb lights the way to the future. I am the shepherd, I am the way—"

I didn't know how Kyle felt about the preacher, but I was getting tired of hearing his voice. I switched off the radio and switched on the navigation system. I punched the coordinates into the boat's computer. We could be there in under an hour.

"Just think, Kyle, the next meal you eat could be at a real table, with real people."

Kyle nodded. "Sounds good to me. Say, why did you lie to that old guy? Seemed like a harmless coot to me. He even made me think of the pastor at my church. Are you some kind of atheist or something?"

"Or something. But that's not it. To be honest, I don't know what it is." I didn't want to alarm Kyle for no reason, so I deflected his concern, "Don't worry about it; it's probably nothing. Why don't you help the rest of those mongrels gear up with some bed rolls and supplies? I don't want us showing up empty handed."

Kyle nodded and stood to leave.

Before he left the room, I said, "And it wouldn't be remiss for you guys to clean up a bit, scrub some of that stink off. We wouldn't want them to think we were some kind of savages, would we?"

*

Before arriving, I had all but five of the boys go below deck. I'd told the man six, and that's what they'd see when we got there. If things went well, I'd call them up on deck and we could all have a good laugh about it later on over dinner. My father never imparted any sage advice to me, but I sometimes pretend he did. A saying my fictional guru father would have approved of is: fortune favours the prepared.

I really hoped my gut was wrong.

The dock the old preacher had given us the coordinates to was lined with boats of all shapes and sizes. He'd apparently been at this shepherding gig for a while. I idled the engine down, but instead of coasting in close to the boats surrounding the small dock, I let us drift past. The old man said there would be someone here to meet us, but unless they were aboard one of the boats tied off to the dock, his welcoming party wasn't here. Maybe we were early. Hell, maybe they were late. It's even possible—and very likely, regardless of the assurances of the old preacher to the contrary—that whoever was supposed to meet us could have met up with a herd of infected. Whatever it was didn't calm the queasy feeling building up in my guts. I also couldn't shake the feeling that we were being watched.

"Justin," I whispered to my former paperboy, "grab the binoculars for me, would you?"

"Sorry, Mr. Johnston. They got lost in the water back near the last place we fueled up."

"Fine, then hand me that rifle—the one with the scope."

I swept the rifle across the tree line, pausing occasionally to adjust the sight. It was impossible to hear anything over the boat's rumbling idle, so I killed the engine and continued searching the forest. After a few minutes, I began to feel silly for thinking there was anything out there watching us. Just as I was about to call off my scan, I picked up a tiny movement on the branch of a tree. Then I saw them. Lined up like a murder of crows, ten or more green-clad people, all with weapons pointed at our boat.

My heart lurched, but I held my panic in check. If I moved too fast, those people might shoot.

I let my arm holding the rifle drop to my side. "Man, do I feel stupid," I said, louder than needed. "Let's dock and go see what's keeping our new friends."

As casually as I could muster, I fired up the boat and slowly turned in toward the tangle of boats.

Kyle was grinning, but he could sense there was something wrong. "Everything all right, Gerry?"

"Couldn't be better, my man." When my back was to the shore, I dropped my voice to a whisper, "Go tell everyone to grab a weapon, but don't move too fast. When I punch it, shoot the fuck out of that tree line. Got it?"

The colour drained from his face, and I could tell it was taking all the control he had to keep the smile stretched across his face. "You know we don't have enough fuel to get very far, right?"

For the sake of our watchers in the trees, I laughed and slapped him lightly on the back, then said, "I know. We're fucked. But we passed a dock a few miles down the coast. That's where I'm heading."

"*If* we make it away from here."

"Yeah, if. Now stop being a pessimist and do your job."

I waited until he'd walked from one boy to the next, telling them what was expected of them, then I cranked the wheel and slammed the throttle open.

As plans go, it wasn't a very sound one, but it's not like there was time to make up a good one. When the boat lurched forward, the boys all tumbled to the deck. Seconds later, bullets rained down from the trees, cutting a swath across the bow and tearing holes in the motor. I left the steering wheel, grabbed the first gun I could find, and joined the boys at the bow as they returned fire for fire. All around us splinters of fibreglass and wood flew, the boys both below deck and above screamed, cordite and fear filled my nostrils, and bullets tore the boat apart.

But we were alive.

The dock shrunk into the distance, but the gunfire kept up (at least on our end) until I yelled for the boys to stop. After checking everyone over, I was relieved to see that the worst of the injuries were splinters from the torn-up decking. Apparently the preacher's buddies were shit shots. Good to know. We, on the other hand, capped at least two of the fuckers. Hoo-ah.

The motor coughed and sputtered, sending smoke billowing out in our wake. We'd be lucky to make it back to the dock I'd seen on the way in. As bad as that sounded, I couldn't keep the grin from my face. Some of the boys were crying, some blanched as they stared a thousand yards away, some were grinning back, but they'd all held the line and done what needed doing. I felt like a proud father. "I'd play paintball with you little bastards any day. Good job."

One of the boys—Simon (a.k.a. thepieman), I think—said, "What are we gonna do now? We're almost out of fuel."

Kyle jumped in, "Don't worry about that, Si. From the sounds coming out of the engine compartment, it's gonna die long before we run out of fuel."

Off in the distance, still only a speck on the horizon, was our destination. "Hey." I pointed. "Things are looking up. There's our dock, right where I said it was."

And then the engine caught fire.

CHAPTER 19

Montana, United States/Canadian Border
Lucia

We felt lucky in unlucky times. Just after crossing out of Anaconda, we found a zombie-free, barely looted gas station. We stocked up on gas, food, and water. We figured we had enough gas strapped to the roof of the truck to make it to British Columbia.

"You know... we could stop looting and just make everything last until we get there," I said.

Fred smiled; cherry rope licorices dangled from his mouth. I was staring at him when I saw the grin leave his face. I turned my head and looked out onto the road. Up ahead, a tree lay across the highway, blocking our way.

"What is that? A tree fell?"

"No. It has to be looters; the tree has been cut."

"Stop and turn around."

Fred slowed to a stop and a man stepped out onto the road with a shotgun.

"Fred, please leave."

"I can't. He'll blow a hole in our radiator. Let's just see what he wants."

The man approached the truck, his gun pointed at us, and mine at him. Fred rolled his window down a little bit and the man stopped.

"Where ya goin'?" the man called out.

"Canada," Fred answered.

"Yer' in Canada."

We both knew that wasn't true.

"How can I help you?" Fred asked.

"Oh, we'll just take everything you got," the man said in a calm, matter o' fact way. Five more men emerged from the woods with guns pointed at us.

"How about we give you half of what we have and you let us go on our way?" Fred asked.

I looked at the other men with guns pointed at me, but I refused to lower mine.

The man didn't hesitate. In a flat tone, he retorted, "Yep. I said everything. That includes the truck… and the girl."

My face twitched.

"We have lots of gas and food and water. You can have all of it, just let us be."

"There won't be any bargaining today. Just come on out of the truck and we'll take care of the rest."

Fred put his hand on his door handle.

"Don't you fucking dare, Fred. Get your fucking hand off of that door." I murmured through my teeth.

"Lucia, we're surrounded. Put your gun down."

"Don't fucking do it. I'm not putting my gun down. Zombies, I'm afraid of— men, I'm not."

"Don't be afraid, ma'am; we'll treat you good here."

"Don't get out," I whispered as I opened my door. "Tell your men to stand back, or I'm not putting my gun down," I yelled.

I had it ready—my rigged toilet bomb had sat on the floor next to me for weeks, regularly refreshed. Inside of a two liter bottle was a bed of aluminum nails with a smaller bottle inside filled with toilet bowl cleaner. I held the bottle still between my two feet as I reached down slowly and tightened the lid. I opened my door wider, keeping my gun aimed at the man closest to the truck. The other men had backed away, as directed, waiting for further instructions. I stepped out of the truck, grabbing the bottle as I exited. I gave it one good shake and the hydrochloric acid in the cleaning fluid splashed onto the aluminum. Instantly, the bottle started to expand with the gas from the two compounds mixing. I threw it like a bowling ball towards the group of men and jumped back into the truck. Within seconds, it exploded. The sound cracked through the woods, spitting out the nails like shrapnel. Fred threw the truck into reverse. The man nearest to us aimed and fired.

Fred turned the truck around and we barreled down the highway.

"Fuck, that was close," I said.

Fred scowled.

"What's wrong?"

"I'm fucking hit, Lucy."

Fred's shirt was turning red at his gut.

"We gotta pull over."

"Nah, it's not that bad, we need to put some mileage between us and those rednecks."

"Let me drive then."

"I'll be okay, just sit tight."

I jumped in the back and started sorting through our stuff. I found our stash of medicine, dumped a small pill into my hand, and climbed back up to Fred. I opened a bottle of water, pushed the pill into his mouth, and held the bottle of water to his lips. He drank.

"What was that?"

"A roxy."

"Fuck, Lucia. It's gonna make me puke."

"It's the best thing we have for pain."

I returned to the back and laid out every blanket and towel we had, making a bed for Fred. I started ripping open gauze and then returned to the front.

"As soon as you think it's safe to pull over, I need to look at that wound."

"Just a few more miles. I don't think they followed us."

"I don't think so either. How is it?"

Fred looked at me. "Painful as fuck."

He was sweating and pale. After several minutes, he stopped along a desolate road.

"Can you climb into the back?"

"I think so." Fred winced. He stood up and I saw the blood had puddled on his seat.

He lay on the makeshift bed and I lifted his shirt, pressing gauze to the wound. The edges were burnt and the hole gurgled blood like a tipped-over bottle of wine. It was worse than I thought.

"Fred, whatever the bullet hit, if it doesn't get fixed, you're going to die."

"Perfect. Just find me a doctor."

I pulled my lips into my mouth and bit them. "There's no doctor."

"A veterinarian?" Fred joked weakly.

My eyes overflowed with tears.

"Tell me you've been to vet school, Lucy, and that FurCon business was just about your love for animals."

I was crying silently. "I can't tell you that," I whispered.

Fred turned his head and stared at the wall of the truck. I felt guilty, like if I had only just cooperated, this wouldn't have happened.

"Don't think what you're thinking, Lucy. Those men would have killed me, no matter what we did. If they didn't kick me out of camp without weapons or food, I would have died getting you out of there anyway."

"I—I worked in an ER once as an intern. I was pre-med. I could try...if I found the right things."

Fred looked at me, "What do you mean?"

I inhaled deeply. "The blood—it's coming out too fast. If the bullet hit a minor artery, at best, you have a few hours to live.

I—in no way—am skilled or trained to open you up, but it might be the only chance you have."

"Do it!" Fred smiled. "I trust you; just do whatever you can."

"It's only if I can find everything, and even then, you might get an infection and die anyway. Or what if you need intubated? I can't do that."

"It's better than my other option," Fred smiled.

"We'll have to find a hospital…"

"No, the hospitals are too full of the infected. You'd never make it in and out alive."

I grimaced at the thought. "I got it. In Anaconda, we passed a plastic surgery center. They would have everything we need. We have to go back."

"Can you go it alone?"

"I have to. Keep as much pressure on your wound as possible." I piled more gauze on the injury and pressed his hand on top of it. "Can you hold that there?"

"Yeah."

The drive back to Anaconda seemed quick, but once in town, I had trouble navigating around the burned-out vehicles as well as remembering exactly where I saw the plastic surgery center. Fred grunted when I drove over bumps. He was quiet as I pulled in front of our destination. Armed with two guns and an axe, I said, "I'll be back," and didn't give him the chance to say goodbye.

Like most of Anaconda, the place was quiet. I was greeted early on by a woman with an exposed chest cavity. Her left breast had a sagging void where the other side revealed a silicone implant. I wanted to stay as quiet as possible, so I separated her head from her body with two axe swings. Rotting flesh gave way easily and zombie bones seemed more brittle, thus more likely to snap when struck.

I located the operating room and began filling my backpack with bottles of saline, suture kits, sterilized tools, IVs, and at the end, I busted the lock off of the medicine locker and took what I sought most.

I exited the building to find a crowd limping towards our truck. Thankfully I had parked as close to the door as possible, so I had time to unlock my door and climb inside before they were too near.

"Lucia!" Fred exclaimed.

"I'm okay, but we have a herd of them coming this way."

"They can probably smell me more now."

Indeed, the entire cabin of the truck was thick with the scent of iron. I started the truck and pulled out as they approached.

"You're a lucky girl," Fred joked.

I didn't respond. I thought, *Lucky to be alive, or lucky to have not been eaten?* How fortunate I'd feel with a mortal wound right now.

I drove until I found a spot—chosen with consideration for the need of safety, but also the urgency of the situation. I parked, crawled in the back, and prepared the items I'd need. A list of instructions ran through my head, but I must have murmured part of it because Fred repeated, "Bevel up."

I smiled nervously. "Yes, bevel up. I won't lie, this will hurt. I've started an IV before, but I'm not very good at it. Okay? Here I go."

Bevel up, thirty degree angle, the length of the needle back from my desired position. Don't blow the vein… Okay. There's the flash. I'm in. Holy fuck! I'm in! Now, cath in, needle out. Tape it down. Flush it. Heparin. Where the fuck is the Heparin? Wait, there. Oh, I bet that burns. Heparin burns. I remember the burn from before… Okay, start the saline drip.

"How's that? Do you feel it? It's just saline, but I'm going to start the medicine now that will put you to sleep."

"It was fine. You did a good job so it barely hurt."

I tried not to cry. "What if I kill you?"

"Impossible to kill a dead man. Remember that." Fred's color was completely gone now and his words slipped out of him weakly.

I hung the bag of Versed on one of the truck's interior hooks and connected it to the saline. "I'll try to remember that. When I open this line up, you'll fall to sleep."

"I'm ready. But, Lucy…"

"Yes?"

"I believe in you. Even if I don't live, you can do this on your own."

"Ssshh. Neither of us is dying today." I opened the line and let the Versed drip into the saline that flowed into his vein. I wasn't sure how fast I should set the drip rate, but I started slow, knowing I could increase it as I went along. With a slight exhale, Fred closed his eyes and began to sleep.

I was alone. *I could just keep him asleep—keep him comfortable until the end,* I thought as I held the scalpel above his abdomen. I shook the thought away.

Six inches, vertical, running the incision along the outside of the wound. Three inches downward, and to the left. Counting ribs… one, two, three, four—it must be the spleen. Oh, fuck, I hope it's not the stomach. If it's the stomach, I know he'll die. Flush it out with saline. Fuck, why didn't I open the bottle? There's so much blood. Okay, here we go. Oh, fuck, what if this goes back the whole way to his spine? No, he moved back here. Okay, find it. Separate the abdominal walls. Careful! Follow the direction of the muscle fibers… like filleting beef, but it's not a cow. Fuck me! Don't think that. Okay. Is that it? Yes, it has to be! The bullet! Get the tweezer thingies. Slowly, slowly, pull it out. Fucking evil thing! Oh, that's the spleen. The bullet had blasted a hole through one of the branches of the splenic artery. It's pumping out blood. Fuck, clamp both ends. Shit! Now what? Do I tie them shut, or do I tie them together? Thinkthinkthink. Hurry. Okay, tie them shut. It isn't that big. I know I can't repair it. What was I thinking? Even mediocre surgeons wouldn't attempt it, not to mention my fucksquat operating skills.

I reached for the suture kit and just started sewing. When I was done, I flushed the abdominal cavity out. The water was more pink than red this time.

Did I do it? I hope! I think I did. The bleeding's stopped. Okay, I got to get him closed back up. I'll do it in layers. Fucksmacks, what if there's an infection? No, close it. I'll open him back up if I have to and wick it out. I'll just close it.

In my head, I hummed… *loop, loop, pull; loop, loop, pull; snip…* for each single stitch that I made. Finally, he just had a neat black X of railroad stitches on his belly. *I'm a better seamstress than I am a surgeon.* I dressed the wound, took my gloves off, and felt for his pulse. It was still strong. *He probably needs a transfusion. But where could I get blood—refrigerated blood?* I gathered everything I could that was bloody—towels, gloves, and gauze. I put it into a plastic grocery bag and tossed it up front for me to get rid of as soon as possible. We were like a swimmer with a severed arm treading water in a shark-filled sea—they were bound to smell us. I slowed the drip on the Versed considerably and crawled up front, careful not to disturb Fred. I knew he needed to be kept still, but I had to move, or we'd be swarmed with zombies.

A half-mile down the road, I tossed the bloody bag out the window. I knew a zombie would find it eventually and suck the blood out of the cloth and gauze.

CHAPTER 20

Dublin, Ireland
Paul

The explosion had blown out all the windows on the third floor of my apartment block. An orange halo lit up the darkening sky over Dublin. Flames still billowed from the doomed building, visible from Ciara's flat, on a dreary, wet evening. I headed deeper into the City Centre, walking alongside the river Liffey. The green water snaked a course into Dublin Bay and out to the Irish Sea. I wondered, could I just get on a boat and head out with it? Go where though? Traffic blocked the quays—more cars, buses, and trucks abandoned. Where had all the owners gone? Surely not everyone was either dead or infected.

The adrenaline no longer pumped through me. My rage and desire for revenge had eased, and it was vengeance that drove me. I no longer saw the infected as ill people. They were zombies, they were the enemy, they wanted to fucking eat me. I wished I hadn't thrown away the JD.

One of them stepped off a bus ahead of me. It would have been comical if it had not been so serious, seeing this half rotted head peering out from a green bus, "Bren's Tours" emblazoned across the back. The tourists get uglier every year.

I didn't know how much longer I could do this shit for. Was this what the rest of my life was going to be like? Constantly on the run, fighting running battles every day, just to stay alive? Somebody once told me if they were going to die, they hoped it would be by drowning. They imagined once the initial struggle for air was over, it would be a pretty pleasant way to go, just sort of floating there, at peace. I don't know about that, but I will admit, leaping the wall and plunging into the river below did occur to me.

I decided not to die that day; maybe the next, but not that day. The zombie spotted me, or smelled me—whatever it is they do to find their food. I noticed it was moving slower than normal. I wondered, was it the rain or because it was getting dark? A second one followed it, filing off the bus. Oh good Jesus, it was the closest I'd come to laughing in weeks. The fucking thing was dressed up as a leprechaun; it even had the green top hat.

Maybe it was the costume, maybe I'd just had my fill of killing for one day, and the battle lust had abated. I suppose it was a kind of battle lust that had overcome me when I rampaged through the building. Once that red mist descended, it had to be fed. Christ, I probably would have lashed out at any of the other survivors had they got in my way. Maybe they had, I couldn't remember. I turned away from the two zombies and ran the other way. Looking over my shoulder, I could see them following, but not as fast as I'd seen them run down that woman outside my window, or as fast as they had attacked us back in the pharmacy.

I passed by an off-licence, I reckoned I'd have time before Darby O'Gill and his sidekick would catch up. If I was going to die, I was going to do it happy. I entered the ransacked shop. Looked like I wasn't the only one who fancied partying. I wasn't greedy; I only wanted one bottle. As I approached the counter, I noticed the cash register had been opened. Yeah, money will be real useful to whatever sap decided to empty it.

I don't know why I didn't spot it. Maybe I was becoming immune to the smell, maybe I was too focused on grabbing some booze. When he jumped up from behind the counter, I froze. Not so much at being taken by surprise by yet another zombie, it was recognising this one. I had to admit I'd seen him looking better. The flap of skin still hung down from his cheek, his clothes were splattered in his own blood and God only knew who else's. Robbie growled at me, his eyes full of hunger. I staggered back. Jesus! He was a big bastard; thank God they were all moving slower. Broken glass crunched under my feet. I didn't want to kill him. It was only a couple of hours since the ill-fated expedition, since we were bosom buddies. I told myself I would be doing him a kindness. It seemed harsh to do it with his own axe though.

As I backed away, I felt something grab my shoulder. I nearly jumped out of my skin.

"Shite on a fucking stick!" I jumped back from the leprechaun.

A leprechaun and a fireman. Seriously! The two of them came at me together. I grabbed a bottle of wine from a shelf and smashed it across Robbie's face. Did these things even feel pain, I wondered. It stopped him momentarily; he had a sort of dumb, shocked look on his deformed face. I used the time to spin around to the side of the leprechaun and hack at his neck… once, twice, third time wins the pot of gold.

"Jaysus, Robbie! This is gonna hurt me more than it hurts you." I drove the axe into his skull. I like to think he would have thanked me.

I knew there was at least one more around somewhere. I really did not have time to delay or get sentimental, but I'd just killed somebody I knew. I'll not say he was a friend; I didn't even like him that much. I'm not the religious sort, so saying a prayer seemed a bit pointless. I did pause for reflection though. The whole ordeal was making me feel weary, bone tired. I looked at my feet then and saw the green leprechaun hat. What a fucked up world.

I had a drink for Robbie; it seemed the right thing to do. It was ironic really, the building we both lived in was now a towering inferno. I could even see the smoke from where I was, and I was wandering about the city killing firemen.

I wondered if it was time to leave the town. That is, if I could even be bothered trying to keep myself alive. It struck me, surely out in the country there would be less of the infected, more space, and cleaner air. But then again, in the city there was much more access to essentials, like food and shit. Maybe I should just sit in a corner somewhere and let the world pass me by.

I headed outside; it was darker now. The city was a weird fucking place with no lights. I'd lived there all my life, knew every inch of it, but in the dark of night, with not a sound but my footsteps and my own breathing, knowing that around the next bend there might be a flesh eating zombie scared the living shite out of me.

I had nowhere to go. Where was safe? Every building, every vehicle could be harbouring a monster. I really did not fancy wandering around aimlessly in the dark. It was still raining, and the clouds would block out the light of the moon and stars. It was already getting hard to see. Nor did I fancy spending the night in the company of Robbie and king of the fucking little people.

In the end, the decision was made for me. As I dithered in the doorway, I was grabbed from behind and dragged back into the off-licence by strong arms. A black gloved hand covered my mouth, stifling my yell.

I finally realised I did not want to die.

CHAPTER 21

Sun Prairie, Montana, USA
Sharon

Mr. Kowalski had kept the Mustang in its original condition. It had a 289 V8 that wasn't fuel injected. So, it wouldn't beat much off the light, but it could run full out for long distances without blinking an eye.

The interstates were packed. A few drivers figured out the southbound lanes were gridlocked and took to driving south in the north lanes, which had generated some serious pile-ups. I decided it would be best to take as many of the smaller highways and local roads as I could.

"Aunt Sharon, what are these?" Parker asked, handing me a block of plastic. I laughed when I saw it.

"It's an old 8-track." As I said, the car was in original condition, including the 8-track player and AM-only radio. We had turned that off, as all it was broadcasting were civil service warnings.

A few weeks ago, the Internet started to go down. Sites began to crash or were really slow to load. As the pandemic spread, videos of zombies began to be posted on YouTube and on Facebook. It was no surprise that those sites were the first to go.

When garage doors began to open and close on their own, I realized that the government was jamming the signal. What they were broadcasting at such a low frequency that it messed with garage door openers, I didn't know. But I did know that it meant things were going really bad if they were taking such measures.

"What's an 8-track?"

"It's like a cassette; it plays music," I answered, slowing down to maneuver around a couple of abandoned vehicles.

"What's a cassette?" he asked.

I snorted; Jack laughed. "It has a tape in it, like VHS that you watch movies on in a VCR." When Parker still looked confused, I laughed outright.

"A VCR came before DVDs." As I drove past the cluster of vehicles, I could see a leg sticking out from under a mini-van. I didn't know if it was attached to anything... nor did I want to know.

"Do you mean like a Blu-Ray player?" Parker asked.

I looked at the 8-track in my hand, reading the label for the first time, "The Carpenters", and groaned. I showed it to Jack who, without blinking an eye, rolled down the window and tossed it out. The plastic shattered into a million colored specks, releasing a black ribbon that soon became entangled in the guard rail.

The others included the Statler Brothers and Glenn Campbell singing about being a lineman. I was growing tired of not having anything to listen to on the radio, but not tired enough to suffer through any of that, and so we littered a little more.

As we headed north along the river, we began to notice that the water levels were rising. The flood plains were filling up, almost reaching the small highway we were driving on. Eventually, the road ahead was completely flooded, and we had to stop.

"The plane this morning damaged the bridges. I bet they also blew Gavin's Point dam," I said as we surveyed the rising waters. The files I had been given said a zombie couldn't swim. How they knew that I shuddered to think, but it certainly fit. The virus could manage basic locomotion. Swimming would require far too much coordination.

"What do we do?" Jack asked.

It was around noon. We had been heading north on Highway 81, and were just outside Yankton, South Dakota. I had hoped to cross the state line, head up to I-90, and take it west from there. But the river stopped us, and the bridge had been damaged as well; I chided myself for not thinking of that possibility.

I ran my hand through my hair and walked around to the trunk. There was an atlas along with the spare tire and jack. I grabbed it and flipped it open to Nebraska. "If we follow some of the small county roads and a couple of the gravel back roads, I can still get us to I-90," I said, trailing my finger along the proposed route. "It will just take about twice as long."

"Well, it's not like we're in a hurry," Jack said, ripping open an MRE for Parker.

"No, we're not," I agreed, and climbed back in the car.

A few hours later, we stopped to get fuel at a small gas station. My mom had managed several of these stations. I knew how to turn the pumps on; it was just a matter of if there was any gas left. Thankfully, there was.

Fueled up and replenished with snacks, I let Parker have what he wanted from the store to play with. He took some coloring books and markers and settled himself once more amongst his bed of pillows and blankets in the back seat.

Jack took a turn driving, and despite my best intentions, I fell asleep. As night was falling, I woke up to the feeling of the car slowing down.

"We are running low on gas again," he said, pulling into a small town whose weathered sign showed it to be Vivian, South Dakota, population 119. And judging by the desolation and smoldering remains of vehicles, I thought that would be an overestimation.

We had figured out a routine with gassing the car: pull up to the pump, lock the doors, one person got the gas, the other kept watch. And with that plan, we were on the road and driving within minutes, leaving Vivian and its eerie stillness behind.

Jack and I took turns driving, sleeping in shifts. Every so often we would pull over, let the car cool down, and stretch our legs. We stopped to admire the scenic beauty of the badlands and have a lunch of MREs.

After two days of driving and backtracking through small side roads when the interstate was blocked, we had finally made it to Montana and were on our way north on Highway 15.

It was then, in a little town named Sun Prairie, I met my first "thinker." We had fueled the car. Jack took Parker to the bathroom, and I was collecting some things to eat. He stumbled out of the back room, and the tag on his shirt dubbed him Vincent. Before I could stop myself, I had said his name out loud.

He paused, narrowed his eyes, and grunted. He had a huge bite mark taken out of his left bicep. It looked fresh, and still oozed blood.

I moved to the left; he mimicked me. I stepped to the right, he did also. "Can you understand me?" When he took a few steps towards me, I brought my gun up, and he stopped. I frowned; obviously he knew what a gun was. No other zombie that I had seen was concerned with guns.

I was on the verge of asking more questions when his head exploded. The sound of gunshot echoed in the store, making my ears ring.

"For fucks sake, Red!" Jack yelled. "What were you planning on doing, dancing with it?"

"But Jack, it understood me. It was thinking," I said, feeling both embarrassed and fascinated at the same time.

"The only thing he was thinking about was taking a bite out of you. These things are dangerous. You know better than that." He was right, I did, but the discovery that Vincent represented had overwhelmed my better judgment. I should have shot him when I saw him, not asked him questions.

"You want to collect a sample, don't you?" he asked.

"Yes, I really do," I said grinning.

"Well, go on then, just be careful." I smiled even broader and opened a box of sandwich bags. I carefully picked up some pieces of Vincent's brain that had been blown all over the floor and packed them in a small thermos that I filled with ice. Jack then kept watch while I re-filled our cooler and supplies.

While I was settling Parker, I heard a scream that made my blood run cold. I slammed the door shut and turned around to see Jack wrestling with a zombie that had its jaws locked onto his neck.

As I watched, in those torturously slow seconds, Jack brought his gun up and fired once into the zombie's head. He fell to the floor in a rotting, maggot ridden heap. I slowly walked into the store. Not once did I break eye contact with Jack.

"Sharon," he said, gasping in pain; it was the first time he had ever called me by my actual name. "I know I've been an ass, but please, don't let me be a zombie." I started crying then. Just last week I could not stand this man. Now he was a fellow survivor and a connection to my old, safe life. I didn't want to lose him.

"Jack…" I whispered, reaching towards him.

"No!" He shouted and jerked away so forcefully that he slipped in his own blood and fell. "There isn't much time; I can already feel it burning in my veins. Please…" he said as his heart pumped his life's blood out through the gaping hole in his neck.

"You are a good man, Jack," I said, wiping away my tears with a trembling hand. "I wish I had come to know that man sooner," and then I took aim and fired twice. He fell to the floor with a meaty thud. I clasped a hand over my mouth to keep back the animal moan of pain that threatened. When I turned, I saw Parker in the window, his palms pressed to the glass and eyes wide. I looked away, unable to bear what I saw in that little face. I left the .357 with Jack—it was his gun.

Eighteen hours later, I turned down the road that led to the lodge. When I saw it standing there, perfect and untouched, I laughed. And if that laughter held a trace of hysteria, I chose to ignore it.

CHAPTER 22

Thunder Bay, Ontario, Canada
Gerry

The fire in the engine compartment was tragic but manageable. The flames died after we emptied the contents of two fire extinguishers onto it. Even so, the fire had done a fair bit of damage, and smoke still billowed up into the sky like a beacon.

The engine laboured louder and louder, choked, and then sputtered to a stop. Angled as we were, we'd be able to coast into the docks, but then what? We'd be legging it from now on until a vehicle could be found. I tossed an empty fire extinguisher over the side, into the water, and cursed under my breath.

"Kyle!"

Kyle popped his head up through the door that led below deck. His face was blood-splattered and pale, and tears streaked the grime on his cheeks. "Y-yeah?"

"Did anybody get hit back there?"

"Jester. He's dead."

"Who?"

"Marcus. He got it in the throat. They tried to stop the blood, but there was just too much. By the time I got there…"

"It's shitty, Kyle, but you gotta stow what you're feeling. The boys need you. *I* need you. Are you with me?"

Kyle stared wide-eyed at the blood on his hands, but nodded. "I'm with you."

"Good. Any injuries?" Seeing Kyle crying broke my heart, and I felt like shit for sounding callous, but we needed to keep it together or we were fucked.

"Yeah, lots, but the only bad one was Noname—I mean Tim. He took a bullet through his arm. Kelly tied it off and got the blood stopped."

"Kelly? Who's Kelly?"

"Her mom is… her mom was a nurse. She took a first aid course."

"There's a girl on this boat?"

"Huh?"

"Never mind. Just get everyone taken care of, and wrap up Marcus' body in a sheet and get someone to help you bring it up here. I need everyone else who isn't hurt up on deck, and tell them to bring only crossbows."

"Are you expecting any of those preacher's fuckers to come back?"

"No, not them, something else. Look," I pointed at the dock our boat was coasting toward. Two figured lumbered in a meandering gait, while another with no legs crawled, grasping at the smoke as it swirled past. They must've smelled the fire and come to see what was cooking.

Kyle came to stand beside me, "Are those things wearing combat gear?"

I hefted my rifle and peered through the scope. "Yeah, RCMP is stenciled across the back of that one's flak jacket. They were cops."

"Too bad we don't have a high-powered, silenced sniper rifle."

"A what?"

"A silenced rifle."

I shook my head. "Shit."

"Shit, what?"

"I mean 'shit'. We *do* have one. It's under the seat near the captain's chair. At the time I didn't know what it was, but thought it was damned impressive looking."

"Oh."

While Kyle left to gather those who were able to shoot, I hurriedly ran and grabbed the case from the seat, then stared dumbly at the many separate components. "Kyle!"

"Yeah, boss?"

"I don't know how this goes together, and we're almost at the dock."

By this time, seven of the kids had come up on deck, all carrying crossbows. They lined up and took aim at the creatures who were now no more than fifty yards away. Smoke drifted from the engine, shrouding the figures of the three dead in a haze.

Kyle picked up the stock and barrel, slid them together, and twisted until there was a click. "I think I can get this. Take my crossbow and help them. I'll be right there."

Still too far away to fire with any sort of effectiveness, we waited. Forty, thirty, twenty yards. I raised my arm. "OK, wait for my signal, then fire. Head shots only, ladies."

As soon as the words were out of my mouth, all seven of them fired. Most struck their targets ineffectually in the chest or legs. They reloaded and fired again, then again. I was going to have to work on their listening skills. The two standing infected resembled a pair of pin cushions, but neither seemed hurt. All but one of my own shots went wide, and I wasn't aiming for the one I actually hit. So far, the crossbows were doing no good, but at least they were quiet and kept the kids focused on something besides Marcus.

Kyle tapped my shoulder. "Got it," he said, and handed me the sniper rifle.

I immediately raised it, thumbed the double safety, chambered a round, aimed, and fired. The concussion took me back a step, and the noise was deafening.

Through the scope, I watched as the monster's head disappeared. The body jerked for a few seconds before collapsing.

My eardrums felt like they'd exploded along with the thing's head. "I thought you said this fucking gun was quiet!" I yelled.

"You didn't let me finish. I was gonna say 'all we gotta do now is screw on the silencer'."

I rubbed my shoulder where the rifle had kicked me. "Well. Now I know that."

He took the rifle and held it while I threaded the silencer onto the muzzle. It was heavy. No wonder he said it was a two-man job.

From behind me, one of the teens said, "Got 'em!" Then another whooped and said, "Me too."

Less than a minute later, our boat bumped unguided along the side of the dock, splitting through the hull and tearing up a few boards from the dock's surface. It wasn't pretty, but we made it.

Two of the boys jumped from the boat and tied us off while another three walked over to the dead and shot another arrow into the head of each, just to be sure. So much for the infected. We didn't need the sniper rifle after all.

Before any of the teens could take off and get themselves hurt, I called for everyone to gather around so we could work out what to do next.

"All right, we're here. It ain't perfect, but it is what it is, and we gotta make do. Here's what's gonna happen: the three injured kids are to remain here at the boat, along with another couple who'll act as sentries. The rest of us will offload enough shit to sleep the night away from the boat, 'cause we sure as shit don't wanna be close to this boat when those ambushing green boys come this way looking for us. Then we'll come back for the injured.

While Kyle supervised the offloading of supplies, I searched my motorcycle for bullet holes. One smashed mirror and a hole in the front fender. Not bad. Using the boat's hydraulic hoist (which still worked, thank God) I maneuvered the motorcycle over to the dock, then rolled it a short distance away into the bushes.

For better or worse, this was our jump-off point.

I pulled the bike into the bushes and covered it with a few branches. Before leaving, I boarded the boat and climbed down into the cabin. Marcus's body had been wrapped in a sheet and placed in a sleeping bag that was then tied closed. Sorrow aside, the kids still had their wits about them. We didn't know whether the disease was confined to those bitten, or everyone who dies. It was safer to not take chances.

I took in the three wounded, then the two left to keep watch. They were terrified, and I didn't blame them. I was scared shitless. To Kelly—who, with her short-cropped hair and grimy face, I still couldn't tell apart from the boys—I said, "You're doing great, kiddo. You guys keep an eye out for those green boys and the dead, and we'll hump it back here as soon as we find a safe spot to squat for the night. You cool?"

"Totally."

The boy I'd told to stay with her—I couldn't remember his name, but thought it was Jake—said, "Yeah, we got this." His gaze drifted to the lumpy sleeping bag. "Are you gonna take that outside, or…"

"Yeah," I said. A lump rose in my throat. This kid was tough. They all were. As gently as I could, I picked up the bundled sleeping bag. "Marcus was a good guy. We'll have a service later on, when we settle in at camp."

*

I guessed the preacher's camp was west, somewhere not far from the dock where the green boys had opened fire from the trees, so I led the group in-country to the east. After fifteen minutes of walking, we'd seen nothing alive—no birds, no squirrels, nada—which did nothing to quell the nagging sensation we were being watched. Each footfall, cough, or whisper from our group seemed amplified, and I thought the green boys would have to be deaf to not hear us clomping through the forest.

And then I heard something that froze my heart and stopped me in my tracks: gunfire. We all dropped, not knowing where it was coming from, only that it wasn't close by. Then it hit me, and I felt like I'd puke.

"Oh my god," I whispered. "The boat. They found the boat. Kyle, keep 'em safe. I'm going back."

"Nuh-uh, fuck that. We should all go. Those are our friends back there." He started forward, and I pushed him back.

"No, you'll fucking listen to me and keep still. I'll take one person with me. Justin, tuck in your dick and grab your gun. The rest of you—Kyle's in charge so listen to him, unless he tells you to head back to the boat. You see more dead than you can count on one hand, you run like hell in the other direction."

Loaded down as he was, Justin did well to keep up with me. We slowed about twenty yards from the tree line, and I crouched and crept forward. The gunfire had died out a couple minutes before we arrived, but I could hear people speaking.

I parted the leaves of the bush I was using for cover and raised my head. I counted four of the green-clad gunmen. Two joked near the end of the dock, and the others led four teens from the boat at gunpoint. All four had their hands tied behind their backs, and a rope tethered them together like a line of cattle. A quick scan revealed the other sentry lying sprawled near the edge of the dock, his blood pooling around his mid-section. He was dead, and I might as well have killed him myself.

At the sound of a twig snapping behind me, without turning, I said, "They got 'em, Justin."

Justin didn't answer. Even as I spun, reaching for the gun tucked into my waistband, one hand clamped over mine, and another over my mouth. Strong arms lifted me and flipped me onto my stomach.

Then a mouth was at my ear, "Stand down, we're not here to hurt you."

I struggled and nearly broke free, but a second shape stepped up and dropped a knee into the small of my back, then twisted my arm up behind my back to my shoulder blade.

"OK, we're in a bit of a time crunch, so I'm gonna take my hand off your mouth and let you up—but only if I get your word you won't cause a fuss. We golden?"

I nodded. What other choice did I have?

As soon as the man relaxed his grip and let me up, I twisted and lunged at him, hitting him in the jaw. He fell back and I jumped on him, throwing wild punches as I fell.

Before I could call out, the butt of a rifle struck me in the face, stunning me and knocking me backward. When it fell again, the lights went out.

*

I awoke upside-down, my head bouncing against the back end of the man carrying me. My head throbbed with each step he took. They'd tied my hands, but not my feet, and I'd been gagged. There were two of them, both wearing police tactical gear with the letters RCMP stenciled across the back.

"Mfff ffft ffft."

"Gerry? Are you OK?" Justin's face appeared before mine. He hadn't been tied or gagged. He tugged on the sleeve of the man carrying me, "Can I take his gag off now?"

The burly man stopped and shrugged me from his shoulders. I fell clumsily to the ground and rolled over. The man turned, pulled a knife and cut the gag from my mouth. He bent and stuck a thick finger in my face, "One fucking word and I'll cut your tongue out this time, got it?"

Then the other man stepped around his partner, "No you won't." He extended a gloved hand and I took it. After he pulled me to my feet, he cut the ropes from my wrists.

To me, he said, "I'm sorry for the rough stuff, but you'd have given up our position to the men who took your friends."

"Yeah," I said, "about that: why the fuck didn't you do something back there?"

The man shook his head. "I'm sorry about that, but the four you saw at the boat weren't alone. They were part of a larger party. If we'd have engaged them, we'd be food right now."

"Food?"

"Yes. They eat people."

"That crazy preacher lured us to that dock to eat us? What the fuck?"

"Preacher? Oh, you mean Randall's lieutenant, Micah. Yeah, there've been other boats hijacked. You're the first people we've gotten to before them." He slapped me on the back. This is a lucky day for both of us. Let's go catch up with the rest of your people. They should be just up here with the rest of our team. I had them rounded up as well."

I grabbed the cop's shoulder and spun him to face me. "Let me tell you something, buddy: if your people hurt any of my kids, I'll fuck you up. Got it?"

"Jenks," he said. "My name is Jenks, and the gorilla over there is Thompson. Your kids'll be fine. My guys might've put a little scare into 'em, but that's all. I told 'em no rough stuff."

After a few minutes, Jenks raised a hand to stop us, then turned with a finger on his lips. He pointed to a pile of gear heaped in the center of the clearing, "That yours?"

I recognized the sleeping bags. "Yeah, that's ours. But where the hell—"

Jenks tugged a gun from his holster and swept the tree line. "Shh! You hear that? Sounds like moans."

Thompson raised his shotgun and crept forward. "Yeah, it's coming from all around us."

The trees were thick, but the infected would make enough noise for you to hear them coming fifty metres away. This was something else. I reached for my gun, then realized it wasn't there.

I poked Thompson. "Hey, gimme my guns back."

Without pausing his scan of the forest, he took one hand from his gun long enough to reach into his flak jacket and retrieve both my .45s.

As I thumbed both safeties, Justin placed a trembling hand on my arm. "Gerry."

"Kinda busy, sport."

"Look up."

So I did. There, bound and gagged and hanging upside-down twenty feet off the ground, were four men dressed in the same gear as Jenks and his partner.

Jenks took a step toward the pile of gear in the center of the clearing, and two arrows hit the ground inches from his front foot. He froze, but didn't lower his gun.

From somewhere to our left, a familiar voice said, "Drop your weapons, dicks. We got you surrounded."

"Kyle?"

First Kyle stood, crossbow trained on Jenks' chest, then the rest of the boys followed suit. Not one of them had been more than ten feet from us, and we didn't even hear them.

Kyle glanced at me, then Justin, then he searched behind us. "Where's everybody else? Still back at the boat?"

I shook my head. "They took them." I glared at Jenks as I went on. "There were too many of them."

Kyle lowered his crossbow and blinked. "You let those pricks take them?"

"I'm sorry, Kyle. I was kinda busy being knocked out."

Justin nodded. "It's true. The big guy there pounded the crap out of him."

Jenks stepped between us. "Enough. Where's my team?"

Kyle pulled a knife and held it out to Jenks. "They're over your fucking head, pig. Feel free to cut them down yourself." He dropped the knife in the dirt and turned toward me, then turned back. "Oh, and FYI, they went down like a pack of bitches. I think the short one peed himself when we strung them up."

*

While Jenks and Thompson cut the rest of their team down and untied them, I filled the boys in on what happened at the beach with the green boys, and then with Jenks and his partner. While we spoke, one of the boys dug into a pack and handed out food. The kids all huddled around the police officers, and I took Jenks aside to see if he could shed a little light on The Coven of the Lamb and their people.

After Jenks took his helmet off and used it as a stool, I said, "We mean to get our kids back. What do you know about these creeps who took them?"

Jenks took a swig from a bottle of water and then dumped the rest over his head. "I know a lot about Randall's people. But what I know doesn't mean shit anymore. Things have changed… *they've changed.*"

"And how come you guys are out here in the sticks, anyway?"

"We were part of a larger detachment, here gathering intel on the Coven's activities. When the infection hit, most of us stayed. Since all this shit started, we've dwindled from fifteen to the six you see before you. Two days ago we lost our captain and two others."

"Yeah, and I think we found them this morning."

Jenks nodded. "You did. I saw their bodies near the dock. I'm sorry about that. We were out tracking them when I saw your boat go past the first time."

Micah's radio sermon came back in a flash, and a shiver ran through me. "So they're a cult?"

"Yeah, they've been here for years, but only hit our radar after a few hikers went missing last year. We were getting ready to wrap things up and start making busts, but then everything went to hell and the dead started walking. After that, Randall and his people began to get bold. No more hikers for them. They took an old school bus into the closest town—Freemont, I think—and snatched a bunch of people right off the street. We didn't know what they wanted them for at the time, but knew it wasn't anything good."

"Why didn't you try to help them?"

Jenks chuckled grimly. "We were kinda busy, mister, what with staving off an army of the dead and all. Not everyone had a boat to keep them safe."

"Yeah, but you're cops. You had to help, right?"

"Once things quieted down, we did. A few weeks go by and we find out they're keeping slaves, so our captain has us rush in for the rescue."

"How many did you get out?"

"None. There was no one to save. They were all dead."

"And you let them get away with it?"

"Let? Shit, those of us who made it back out were lucky. We lost five men that day for nothing."

"So, what," I said, "these people they took were used as some kinda human sacrifice?"

"No. You already know what they were doing with them. I told you at the water."

I flashed on the faces of the kids I'd left on the boat, then to what Jenks had said earlier about them luring us to the other dock. "Oh, no." Panic rose within me, but I stopped it from taking over.

Jenks held my gaze for a moment before speaking. "I'm sorry."

"Sorry for what?"

"I know why you've been asking me all these questions, and I know what you plan to do, but I'm not gonna let you do it."

"You don't know shit," I said. "I'm not leaving those kids to die. You try and stop us and maybe I'll make sure the boys leave you in the tree this time."

A grin suddenly split the RCMP officer's face. "Yeah, that was kinda funny. And I also know you weren't going to be talked out of this, but I had to try."

"Yeah? So what are you gonna do about it?"

"We're going with you."

"That's a relief."

Jenks snorted. "You won't think so when it goes down. This is gonna be a horror show, Gerry. Their compound is big, but it's not the only one. There's another one to the west about ten kilometres."

"Kyle!"

Kyle leaned out from behind the bulky frame of one of the police officers, "Yeah, boss?"

"Get the boys ready, we're going to war."

CHAPTER 23

South Central British Columbia, Canada
Lucia

The zombie fairy woke me up. A small zombie girl appeared to be about eight years old and was dressed in a pink fairy costume that looked like the hem had been dipped in blood. Her sheer wings were embellished with glitter and atop her head sat a princess crown, but she had lost her wand somewhere along the feed. She gasped in cougar hisses as she jumped at the truck window. After I shook the initial startle off, I almost laughed as I pulled away.

Fred moaned when the truck jerked to a start. When he woke up in the night, he complained pain, but stable. He said I saved him, but I knew my botched job could give way and he was guaranteed an infection of some sort. The surgery increased his chances of surviving, but they still were far from good. I'd switched his IV to antibiotics. I wasn't sure what hadn't expired or gone bad, so I opted for the Cleocin, pulled the internal plug inside of the IV, causing the powdered medicine to cascade down into the saline, and then shook it until it dissolved. Most hospitals and physicians' offices had switched to digital versions of the Physician's Desk Reference years ago, so I had no way of checking dosages on any of the medications. I knew I could probably find an out-dated copy in some second-hand thrift store, but I wasn't about to stop and search. The IVs I'd given Fred were a risk I was willing to take to save his life, but since he'd been awake, I'd switched him to oral pain killers.

I was determined to do two things: drive until we made it to Lake McArthur, and get out of the truck as little as possible. I would only fill the gas tank in wide-open spaces and I'd do so as quickly as possible. Tasks that were frightening with two people were now terrifying on my own.

I started taking some of the speed I'd looted from the pharmacies. Adipex and other stimulants, like medication for ADD, kept me awake as I rolled miles under and beyond. After just two days of being awake, my eyes felt parched with the need for rest. My muscles ached, and I was cranky. Tired people make mistakes. I knew this.

Canada was barren of towns for the most part. I had no choice but to fill the gas tank in a wooded area—it was all we had passed for hours. I was strictly avoiding any populated area and the main highways.

*

They came out of the woods—a dozen of them at first, approaching me from the front of the truck, near the door I so desperately sought. I ran. Like a scared kitten, I climbed a tree, but poorly. My rifle was slung around my shoulder and I struggled to get traction on the bark. The wood chips took bites out of my skin as I clawed my way to the first branch large enough to hold my weight. Zombies had already reached the tree, but their attempts to climb were even more poorly executed than my own.

I stood on the branch and stretched to the next highest one up. I almost lost my balance as my abdomen swayed outward, but I was saved by my fingertips digging under the bark. I climbed higher and straddled a large branch. My legs locked around it at the ankles, and my thighs squeezed with all of the strength they could.

I positioned my rifle and began picking them off. The smell made me gag and vomit burst into my mouth, which I gladly spewed on the crowd below. A group had surrounded the truck, pawing at it, moaning and scratching at the metal. I had kept the doors locked, so Fred was safe—for now.

One emerged from the woods, its intestines trailing out of its ass, but the loop of entrails had caught on an old log. The monster whimpered grimly as it realized its predicament, but knew not how to free itself. I considered ending its misery, because, after all, it was a human of sorts. I shook off the idea since I only had so many bullets, and returned to shooting the zombies below me.

The kick of the rifle wasn't forceful, but I still worried about falling. The monsters below me were easy enough to kill with one shot. Those by the truck took longer. I didn't want to shoot the truck, and I didn't want to waste bullets. Despite this, I knew I had to hurry. It was getting dark in the forest, and as time passed, more and more zombie crept from the shadows of the trees.

When there were just four left near the truck, I decided to run for it. They weren't the super-fast zombies, but they weren't the slow ones either. Mid-threat feeders were still dangerous. I climbed out on the lowest tree limb and jumped down, trying to avoid the pile of dead zombies skewed at the base of the tree. I fell when I landed, but I had expected as much. I regained my footing and ran. Two of the zombies walked towards me and I picked them off with head shots. Another waited for me near the front, but the last one kept scratching at the truck. I couldn't shoot the one closest to me because I might hit the truck. I circled him—a grandfatherly looking man with suspenders over his bloodied flannel shirt, and he reached for me. I got a good angle on the shot, and I took it. One bullet in the head, and he didn't drop. This startled me. I put three quick ones into his neck until it separated from the stem of his body with a cracking sound, and gooey strings of connective tissue stretched between the two. He dropped and I turned my attention to the final zombie humping the truck.

She was wearing one blue slipper and a robe. She turned to look at me and I saw she was missing the bottom half of her jaw. *No wonder she moved so slowly...she probably hasn't been able to feed for a long time,* I thought. I got close enough so I wouldn't miss, and I popped two bullets into her forehead.

I heard a growl and turned around. Standing in the middle of the road, about fifty feet away, was the mother-bubba of all obese zombie women. I ran around to the side of the truck and frantically searched my pocket for the truck key. She thundered towards me; her enormous tits and belly rolls waved up and down with each bounding step she took.

The door opened. I looked up and saw Fred. He had crawled forward and unlocked the door. I jumped inside and slammed the door shut as soon as my pursuer collided with the truck. No law of physics could explain how she would have been able to stop the motion of that ocean of blubber, so I realized a collision was inevitable.

She was angry! It was as though her bucket of fresh-meat limbs had just been taken away from her. She threw herself at the truck, denting the metal inward.

"Get the fuck out of here, Lucia!"

"I'm trying!" My hands shook so bad that I couldn't fit the key into the ignition. She charged the truck again, bounced off and fell backwards this time. I fit the key in and started the truck. I backed up so we didn't run over the moose-sized zombie. She continued to chase us, but gave up after a while. I turned the truck around and headed back the road we'd already traveled.

"Thank you, Fred."

"Don't mention it. I heard them clawing at the truck, but there wasn't anything I could do."

"It's okay. I need to be more careful. Oh, shit!"

"What's wrong?"

"I pissed my pants!"

CHAPTER 24

Dublin, Ireland
Paul

"Can I trust you to keep your mouth shut?" a muffled voice asked. I nodded; there wasn't much else I could do. "Have you been bitten?" I shook my head. "You sure?" I felt the grip around me tighten. I shook my head, vigorously. "Okay, I'm going to let you go now. Turn around really slowly." I did.

Standing in front of me was a sight almost scarier than the fucking zombies. Whoever he was, he was dressed from head to toe in black. On his head was a black helmet, black goggles, and what looked like a gas mask covered his face. On his body he wore black body armour, and underneath was black military gear. He had pistols, knives, shells, bullets, and what looked suspiciously like grenades strapped to him. In his arms he carried an assault rifle.

"Jesus! What the fuck is that?" I said, pointing at his weapon.

"Steyr AUG A3," he said.

"Huh?"

"It's a gun," he said. I couldn't see his face, but I could imagine the expression.

Suddenly, he brought the rifle up. I froze, with my jaw hanging open. A blast of automatic gunfire ripped through the quiet of the night. I turned to see a crumpled mess lying in the doorway—the leprechaun's mate. I exhaled a loud sigh of relief; I thought he was going to shoot me.

"Have you fired a gun before?" he asked me.

I shook my head. I was going to ask him if paintballing counted, but didn't think he'd appreciate the joke.

"Here," he said pulling a shotgun from a holster on his back. "Hold this end, point it this way. And try not to shoot yourself, or me."

I took the shotgun from him and pumped it. Now we're fuckin' talkin'!

"Okay, follow me, stay low, and stay close to the wall. They'll be moving slower now because of the drop in temperature, but they are still dangerous. Do not let them get close. Do not get their blood on you, especially your eyes, nose, mouth."

I decided it was probably not a good idea to tell him about my mad axe frenzy.

"Wait!" I said. "Who the hell are you?"

"Army Ranger Wing," he said.

My heart leapt—the Army! Not just ordinary Army either—Special Forces. Was this the rescue? Was it possible that life could somehow return to normal, or at least one where we returned to the top of the food chain? I wanted to ask him, but he seemed preoccupied. It was at least nice to have someone in charge.

We crept out into the night.

"Where are we going?" I whispered, as we hugged the wall on Burgh Quay. He stopped then and answered. His voice sounded agitated or impatient—it was hard to tell.

"Dáil Éireann," he said.

The Irish House of Parliament? What the hell were we going there for, I wondered? Did we even have a government anymore? We turned the corner into Westmoreland Street and froze. The street was wide enough for four lanes of traffic but it was still filled with zombies. There were hundreds of them—milling around slowly, thankfully—but they were there, dark shapes emitting a collective low drone. My blood froze.

"We're gonna need more guns," I said.

He brought his fingers up to where his lips would be behind the mask, then spoke into some sort of communication device. I didn't think anything worked anymore, but I suppose if shit did, the Army would have it. Then I heard a rumble.

Bright lights lit up the street as an engine roared to life. My soldier put his hand on my chest and pushed me back against the wall. With the street now illuminated by spotlights, I could see clearly just how many there were. I shuddered involuntarily; how the hell were we going to get through them? I needn't have worried.

Two loud explosions erupted in the middle of the street, sending bits of zombie spiraling through the air. This was followed by the thunderous crack of automatic gunfire.

"Holy shit, what the fuck is that?"

"Mowag Piranha," he answered.

"A fucking tank!" I wanted to scream and jump for joy—a fucking tank.

"An armoured personnel carrier," he corrected me.

It rolled into view, gunfire from a manned turret on top cutting zombies in half. Any that got in the way were simply driven over. The zombies scattered in every direction, including ours. The soldier started cutting them down with short blasts from the Steyr. I joined in, discharging and pumping the shotgun. Zombies exploded in front of me. I'm not sure how well I would have coped had they been running at their full speed, but with them lumbering like geriatrics in a nursing home, it was almost kind of fun.

He spoke into his collar again, and the turret ceased fire.

"Go!" he said, pushing me forward. We both ran towards the armoured car. A hatch opened at the front, and I clambered up. As I turned I saw a zombie reaching for the soldier and grabbing his shoulder. He stumbled and fell; the zombie landed on top of him. I couldn't fire the shotgun or I'd probably hit him, I jumped back down, dropping the gun. I still had the axe.

He was face down with the weight of the zombie on top of him. The thing was trying to bite him but seemed to be having problems with the body armour. Two more soldiers spilled out of the hatch. They were shouting and roaring, probably telling me to get out of the way. I was deaf to their words. All I could see was the monster trying to eat the first man who had brought me some hope, the first positive thought I'd had in weeks. I slid the axe from my belt.

Everything slowed down for me. I was overcome with a sort of euphoria, a sadistic joy to feel the weight of the axe in my hand. When I looked back on it later, it sort of scared me. Freaked me a little to think how comfortable, how right it felt. How easy it was to become a killer. I hacked at the zombie with the axe, each swing cutting deep cuts into its neck. It squealed each time—a pitiful sob. I'm not sure if it was from the blows or because I was denying it a meal.

The two soldiers kicked it off and helped their colleague up, and all four of us dove into the hatch. Inside the armoured car, I sat opposite the soldier. He pulled off his helmet and mask, and our eyes met. I could see the fear in his. The muscles in his cheek twitched; his hands shook. He nodded to me, an unspoken thanks.

"Were you bitten?" somebody barked at him. He shook his head.

"Are you sure you're clean?"

"Yeah, I'm sure," he answered. He looked away from me then, leaving both of us with our own thoughts. I wondered where his had gone.

CHAPTER 25

Lake McArthur, British Columbia, Canada
Sharon

Let no one say, and say it to your shame, that all was beauty here until you came, declared a wooden sign that had been nailed to the door of the lodge. At some point it had been affixed to a post and set into the ground. I could only imagine that as the caretakers fled, this was their last act of stewardship, a plea to any future tenants.

Dawn painted the sky crimson, the hue reflecting in the lake, giving it the impression that the waters had been turned to blood. It was an unsettling thought, and one I tried to stamp down as hard as I could.

I left Parker in the car, loaded my guns, and walked in. The door was closed, but unlocked. A very anxious hour later, I had checked every room, closet, and peered under every bed; the lodge was clear. I then walked around the building, closing the shutters over the windows, and making sure that the back door was securely locked.

A shed, just behind the property, housed a four-wheeler with a trailer attached to it, along with two generators that had been covered with tarps. They were on wheels, so I hauled them inside the lodge for safekeeping. For now we had power, but I didn't know how long that would last. I'd feel silly if the generators were stolen because I hadn't secured them. The keys to the four-wheeler were in the ignition. I pocketed those and closed the doors behind me.

The black Mustang sat next to an old, yellow bus that was used to shuttle passengers from the parking area, twenty minutes away, to the lodge. I shoved open the door and checked the bus too, making sure nothing was lurking in there. It was clear, and like before, the keys were in the ignition. I imagined that theft wasn't a big issue up here, and it was likely that was where the keys were normally kept, but I wasn't taking any chances. I didn't know how to drive a bus, but that didn't mean I couldn't use it. As I walked back to the lodge, I jingled. I was starting to feel like a janitor with all my keys.

I unloaded the car, hauled in some firewood, and settled Parker on the sofa before the fire. I had tried to leave him in one of the rooms upstairs, but he would not let me out of his sight. So, while I worked setting up our new home, he played his DS. The tinkling sounds of Mario Cart actually helped to dull the horrors of the past few days by adding a touch of normalcy.

The lodge had been empty for several months. The milk had soured, and the bread had gone moldy. I breathed a sigh of relief when I opened the freezer to see it crammed full of frozen meat. Rummaging around in the cabinets, I found a crock-pot and put one of the small roasts in it, along with an onion from the cupboard, a few potatoes that had not rotted, and a handful of herbs that just said 'meat rub'. It smelled good, so I figured it would be safe.

The pantry was stocked with canned goods, jars of homemade jams, sauces, and vegetables that the lodge had evidentially grown in the garden out back. The shed with the generators had been full of gardening implements. I presumed it had been the groundskeeper's shed, and that was what the four-wheeler and trailer were for. I had snagged everything with a sharp edge on it and brought it inside. I preferred to have anything that could be used as a weapon under my control. Hell, I probably would have brought the quad-runner in if I could have figured out a way to fit it through the door.

The lower level of the lodge was situated around a common room that had a massive fireplace with a collection of mismatched sofas and chairs gathered around it. Along the side of the lodge, overlooking the lake, was a long dining hall. I appropriated one end to set up my equipment.

The reception area had a desk, an ancient PC, and filing cabinets. I put the generators and tools in there and closed the door. The kitchen ran along the length of the back of the lodge, and despite its rustic feel, it was rather modern. A huge refrigerator, a massive deep-freeze, stainless steel counter tops, and a double oven filled every available space. A beat up wooden table with four chairs sat in the middle of the room and was where Parker and I would have our meals.

Upstairs there were eight bedrooms, each with two twin beds. Another seating area that faced a balcony was at one end, while the restrooms were at the other. The bathrooms had been shared by the guests, and to my delight, they both had an antique claw-footed tub. I paused for a moment to stare wistfully at one, envisioning sinking up to my nose in bubbles while the warm water eased away my aching muscles and tired mind. Perhaps after Parker went to sleep, I told myself.

As the smell of roasting meat filled the kitchen, I went through the refrigerator. I poured the clabbered milk down the sink, grateful that there was still running water. The rotten vegetables and moldy bread, I tossed out back. I couldn't eat it, but perhaps whatever wildlife was left in the area would appreciate the meal. Raccoons would eat the vegetables, and the birds could use the bread. I tore it up into little pieces to make it easier for them.

Opposite the dining hall was the boiler room. A sink with a toilet sat along one wall, an industrial washer and dryer set lined the other, while an enormous hot water heater sat at the end next to the boiler. I grabbed some matches, lit the pilot light with a whoosh, and flipped the switch. Not long after, warm air began to flow out of the vents. I did the same with the hot water heater, nearly crying at the notion of a hot shower.

Walking back across the lodge, I paused to cover up Parker, who had fallen fast asleep. Tucking the blanket in around him, it struck me just how much he looked like Jenny. A lump formed in my throat that made swallowing difficult. I forced my tumultuous emotions down, swiped away stubborn tears, walked over to my work area, and powered on the computers. There was no Internet access up here, but my phone would serve as a Wi-Fi hotspot for as long as my cell phone company was operational. I would just need to make sure it stayed charged up.

I unrolled the charging pad and put my iPod, Parker's iPod and DS on it, along with my phone. The iPad and my Kindle could be plugged into an outlet, so I did. I had found a small dorm room refrigerator in the office that the staff had used for their lunches, and wheeled it into the dining hall. This is where I put all my samples from Tate, Mindy, and my newly acquired ones from Vincent. Thinking of Vincent led to thoughts of Jack, and the tears that I had been fighting finally broke free. I laid my head down on my folded arms and surrendered.

I cried until my eyes felt like sandpaper, and my nose became stuffed. With my complexion, I was sure my face was covered with red blotches, but I didn't care. I had shot the best friend I ever had, drove like a bat out of hell across the country, and killed a man that had been an ass most of the time I knew him, only to find out too late how good and kind he was. Misery and heartache piled on top of each other until I collapsed under their weight. My mind, having met its saturation point, shut down, and I slept.

CHAPTER 26

Thunder Bay, Ontario, Canada
Gerry

Screams pealed through the trees and froze me in my tracks. After a beat, I pointed south with my rifle. There was no turning back now; the first team had made contact somewhere near the beach. We'd split up into three units, and the first team had been discovered long before we thought they would… but it changed nothing. They were the diversion, and doing a fine job judging by the heightened activity inside the compound. With any luck they'd made it close enough to draw most of the fire.

I thumbed off my safety and nodded over my shoulder to my team; it was Go Time. Every nerve in my body vibrated and I'd never felt more alive. Fear clenched my gut in an icy fist, but purpose kept me moving. Once upon a time, a guidance counsellor told me I was best suited for, well, not much of anything more than saying 'yessir', but he was wrong. I was built for this shit. I was a vengeful scythe, tearing through blood and bone with steel and lead. God help the unlucky motherfuckers who made the mistake of crossing my path. I made a promise to those kids and I planned on keeping it.

My group was smallest, since we wouldn't be engaging with the cultists unless discovered. We would sneak over the wall next to the poorly guarded north entrance, near the only brick building in the compound—what appeared to be a kitchen if my guess was right. With me were three of the older boys: Justin, Cory, and Simon, and one of the cops, Jenks. Most of the firepower had been distributed between the other two teams. We'd need to be quick and couldn't afford to weigh ourselves down with too much gear. Hopefully we wouldn't need guns for more than intimidation anyway.

Just then, a shimmer of movement to the west caught my eye. "Gimme your binoculars," I whispered.

Justin handed them to me and poked his head up. "What? You see something?"

I hoped I was wrong, but when I focused on the tree line beyond the compound's perimeter, it seemed as though the forest were alive and slouching toward the lights pooling at the western entrance to the camp.

"Fuck."

"What?"

"Nothing, Squirt. We gotta boogie. I hope you brought your running shoes."

Jenks had binoculars of his own, and was shaking his head as he took in the meandering dead. "Wait. We need to call this off. Those things down there will kill us all."

"Not happening, Slick. We go. You wanna stay here, stay here, but give us your guns."

"Look," Jenks said, "I get it, really, but I count at least twenty-five of them, and that's just the ones I can see from here. That's more than enough to give us a bad day. I'm not afraid of dying, but not for nothing."

"Don't look at it like that, then. Think of those beasties out there as Team Four. Those Cultist pricks will be too busy beating back the dribblers on the west wall to pay attention to little old us."

Jenks hoisted the binoculars to his eyes and studied the movement in the camp for a moment. Still facing away, he said, "You're a real bastard, you know that?"

I nodded. "Time's wasting. Let's go."

To the group, I said, "OK, everybody buddy up. It's full-on run from here to the east wall. If you get separated from the group, head there and wait 'til it's not safe to do so anymore. Do not—and I want to make sure you understand me, 'cause I'm dead fucking serious—do not fire your weapons unless you find yourself cornered. Nobody's supposed to know we're coming in this way. Our single goal is to find our missing friends. That means only engage if your life depends upon it. Got it?"

I was met by blank stares, all except for the cop, who knew we were in for a world of shit, and that everything I said was gonna go out the window as soon as we were hip-deep in crazies.

He said, "You take Justin and I'll keep an eye on the other three."

I knew what he was feeling because I felt it too. These were kids playing at being soldiers. But the sad reality was that there was no Option B. We all fought or we all died, simple as that.

I shrugged. "Fine. Watch your back."

He gave a thumbs up and waved Simon and Cory to follow him. Before melting into the forest, he whispered, "See you on the other side." Then they took off running.

"Justin."

"Yeah, boss?"

"If we meet up with anything, you keep running and let me take care of it, OK?"

"Yeah, right." He snorted, which sounded like it could have meant anything from 'fuck you' to 'I'm bored', and then he bolted for the trees. "Last one there eats farts."

For a chubby kid, Justin was surprisingly fleet of foot. He almost lost me once. When I caught up, he was creeping along the shadows of the north gate's overhang with his crossbow pointed at someone—or something—I couldn't see. Then he froze.

"Justin," I hissed.

He was a statue of concentration. He either didn't hear me or chose not to.

"Justin! Wait for me."

He loosed a bolt, and a shadowed form fell from a tree near the wall. "Gotcha, dickweed," he said to the darkness. "Betcha didn't think I knew you were there." He nodded. "Yeah, that's what I thought."

I raised my gun and scanned the trees as I stalked over to where he stood at the now deserted gate. "Goddammit, Justin, I fucking told you to stay with me."

He smiled innocently as he reloaded the crossbow. "You eat farts," he said, then ducked through the gate into the compound.

I took a deep breath, and then followed. Once inside, I immediately understood why there'd been only one guard at this gate. The entire western wall was aflame and partially collapsed. The dead had breached the compound and even now poured through the cracks like water.

I whistled for Justin's attention, then pointed to a brick building standing in the center of the compound, "Jenks says that's the kitchen. That's our destination."

"Why?"

"Cause that's where the radio tower is." I pointed. "See the antenna? We take out their eyes and ears and they're fucked."

As I spoke, two green-robed figures appeared, running in the direction of the kitchen. One toted a long pole similar to a dog-catcher's, and the other carried a weighted sack and a flashlight.

Justin looked up at me. "Now what?"

"Nothing changes. Wait ten seconds, then hustle your ass."

Before he could stand, I grabbed Justin by the arm and slid the bowie knife from my belt. "Boy, if I see your ass in front of me, I'm gonna drive this knife into your tubbiness, capiche?"

His eyes widened, but then he smiled and held an arm out for me to take the lead—like it was his to hand over in the first place, the little puke.

We covered the distance quickly while staying alert to anyone or *thing* that might come at us from the rear. For the time being, it seemed we'd gone unnoticed. The door through which the two figures had entered was nothing more than a blanket tacked over the opening. I parted the cloth and peered into the gloom. There were no windows in the main room, so the only light was the tiny amount that slipped past me as the blanket parted. Unless they'd clicked the flashlight off, the two we'd followed in were gone, possibly upstairs to the radio tower, or another room on the main floor. I held the cloth back and Justin entered. The smell that met me was rancid. Justin doubled over and vomited. My stomach lurched, and I swallowed several times in an effort to choke it back.

"It's black as Satan's heart in here. Stay with me for a sec while our eyes adjust." "Not a problem, Boss. It stinks like a fucking abattoir in here. What if those two come back?"

I tapped his crossbow with the blade of my knife. "Follow my lead."

"Is… is this where they, you know…?"

My body was racked by a momentary shiver, and my breath caught in my throat. "Yeah." I didn't feel the need to elaborate. The cops had filled us all in as to the local culinary habits.

Barely audible above our breathing and shuffled steps, there came a subtle scratch-scratch from what I guessed to be the floor. *Rats*, I thought. Given the nature of the activities carried out in this place, there was a strong possibility we were surrounded by them.

I peered into the darkness. My eyes had adjusted, but it was still impossible to see further than a few feet. "OK," I said, "start edging forward 'til you hit a table. I think I saw one from the doorway when the light was shining in. I'll watch your back."

Justin took two steps forward, and then he disappeared as the ground beneath our feet collapsed. His arm shot up, and I caught him before the hole he'd slipped into took him. Through the gloom I could just make out the circumference of the hole.

Above the hoarse urgency of Justin's whispered pleas to pull him out, a tortured moan tore through the silence. The ground at my feet crumbled, and I scrambled backward, dragging Justin's flailing body with me.

He fell on me, then rolled away and immediately began to hyper-ventilate. "It didn't get me it didn't get me it didn't get me… I'm OK I'm OK I'm—"

I hugged him close and clamped my hand over his mouth. "Shut the fuck up, kid. You're safe. I got you."

Then the two green-clad people walked into the room, their flashlight illuminating a point on the floor between them as they chatted quietly, oblivious to the two of us, standing not more than four feet from them. When the light reached our feet they stopped, and one raised the flashlight up to see our faces.

I stepped away from Justin and raised a hand, palm out. "We're not here to make trouble. We just want our friends back." I eased my other hand toward the small of my back, for a pistol.

The taller of the two turned in the direction they'd come, cupped his hands around his mouth, and yelled, "Micah!"

Justin lifted his arm and put a bolt through the man's face, pinning him to the wall. Before the second could call out or run, I lunged forward and punched the robed figure in the general area of the head, but missed, connecting instead with their throat.

The cultist emitted a winded squeak and crumpled to the floor. I stepped over and grabbed a handful of robe with one hand, then slapped the other over the fallen figure's mouth.

Justin retrieved the dropped flashlight and shined it on our captive. It was a woman.

I pulled her close enough that my lips grazed her ear. “You make a sound and I’ll cut your fucking nose off. Blink if you understand.”

Her body remained rigid, her countenance defiant, but she nodded, and blinked once.

From through the door and up a narrow set of stairs, a familiar voice wafted down, “What is it, child?”

Justin stepped past and shined the light on the opening at the top of the stairs. “Hey, man, that sounds like that dude.”

Barely checked rage coursed through me like lightning. I steadied myself, loosened my grip on the woman so I wouldn’t accidentally snap her neck, and said, “Yeah, it looks like we’ve found our host. Let’s go thank him for the invite.”

“What about her? We don’t have any rope or nothing.”

“No problem. I have a plan.”

I turned to the woman and placed the point of my knife under her chin. “You,” I said to her. “Strip.”

She flinched from the knife, but complied. She opened the robe and let it fall to the floor.

“Holy shit,” Justin said. “She’s buck-ass naked, dude.”

The woman’s venomous stare never left my face. Over my shoulder, I whispered, “Keep it in your pants, sport. She’d probably bite it off and toss it to that thing in the pit.”

I turned back to her, looked down, said, “Nice tits,” then head-butted her in the face. I didn’t miss this time. She fell unconscious to the floor.

The creature in the pit moaned, and the scratching returned, more furious than before—as though it planned to dig a tunnel to escape.

“Should I put an arrow in that thing?”

I shook my head. “We’ll get it on the way out, after we deal with that fuck upstairs.”

“Yeah? How we gonna do that, walk right up there and say hi?”

“Nope. I got something better in mind.”

I snagged up the woman's robe and tossed it to him, then pulled the robe from the still-twitching corpse of her partner.

After donning the robe, I palmed my knife and nodded toward the ladder. "Let's go see the preacher. I feel the need for a confession."

"Are we gonna leave her like that, with her boobies hanging out and shit?"

"Kid, your sense of chivalry's seriously fucked up. If it'll make you feel better, we'll cover her up on the way down, when we wax that walking bug farm."

Without checking to see if he followed, I grabbed the railing and hoisted myself up the steep staircase. He bumped into my back when I stopped at the top to poke my head up for a look. The room had been set up for double-duty; a ham radio occupied most of a table pushed up against one wall, while the three remaining walls were open to the night. At each opening, a mounted gun rested. Two sat idle, while the third was manned by a similarly robed man. He swung the gun back and forth, sputtering out sound effects, but didn't fire a shot.

After everything I'd witnessed over the past month, this man's lunacy didn't faze me.

Aside from the sound effect gunner, a spindly, ancient man hunched over a map spread out upon the small space left on the table. *Micah.* There was no doubt in my mind.

Justin popped his head past me to see, and I pointed to his chest, then to the old man at the table. "But don't you dare kill him. I got plans for his ass and they don't include a quick death."

No sooner had the words left my mouth than Justin bolted past me and clocked Micah over the head with the butt-end of his crossbow.

Micah shrieked, and the gunner turned just as I reached him. I reared back with my knife hand, ready to plunge it into the man's chest, but he grabbed my wrist and twisted my arm backwards. Then a fist the size of a Christmas ham struck me in the center of the chest, knocking the wind out of me. As I dropped to my knees, the stuttering gunner, who I thought was standing already, stood, his head brushing the ceiling.

The giant bellowed, palmed me out of the way, and rushed across the room, screaming, "You mussent! You mussent! You mussent hurt him!"

Justin must've been as surprised as me, because he squawked, dove sideways, and fired a panicked shot. The bolt sailed past and stuck in the floor between my feet. Justin swung the crossbow, but the man tore it from his hands and snatched him up in a bear hug.

Above Justin's throaty wails and the screams and gunfire out in the compound, the giant chanted a run-on loop of, "You mussent! You mussent!"

I frantically tugged at the cord of the robe, freed a .45 from my waistband, and ran across the room. I put the gun to the bellowing freak's head and yelled for him to let go. Instead of dropping Justin, he swung around and pushed Justin at me. We fell to the floor, but I kept my hold on the gun.

The big man lumbered forward, towering above us. In the instant before he dove, the light caught his face, and I realized why he'd been dry-shooting the gun at the window. He was mentally challenged. Fear and pity for this man welled and warred within me for an agonizing second. And then my eyes fell to his necklace. A string of fingers of all shapes, sizes, and varying states of decay jiggled as he flexed to pounce. Before I could lose my nerve or my mind, I aimed true and shot him between the eyes. When his body hit the floor, the room shook and plaster fell from the ceiling.

Justin sat up and kicked at the man's leg. Then, as he rubbed his side, he said, "I got mine. Why couldn't you get yours?"

I let out a breath I didn't know I was holding, and chuckled. Not because it was funny—this situation was anything but comic. I laughed because it was safer than crying. If I started crying, I'd likely never stop.

I picked up my knife and stepped in front of the unconscious preacher.

"He's out. I clocked him a good one," Justin said. "Which brings me back to my question: why didn't you take your guy out before he tried to make me his girlfriend?"

"Fine," I shot back. "Next time you take the giant retard and I'll take the feeble old man. For now, why don't you go down and tie up that woman, then watch the door while I ask the preacher a few questions."

Justin blushed, but nodded. "Fair enough. But what if she wakes up?"

"Then you can swap phone numbers and see if she'll add you on Facebook. Now get the fuck down there!"

I waited until Justin was at the bottom of the stairs, then patted Micah down for weapons. He had none. He was still alive—his chest stirred with each breath—but the kid must have done a pretty good number on him. I shook him and he slumped, so I loaded up and slapped him as hard as I could. His head rocked back and hit the radio, and his eyes shot open.

Before he could call out, I slapped him again.

"Shhh," I said, and slid the flat of my blade down his cheek, resting the point just to the left of his adam's apple. "We haven't been formally introduced. You must be Micah. My name's Gerry and I've been dying to meet you."

"Sinner. You'll burn for what you've done." He pointed his bony finger at the dead giant. "Brother Adam was an innocent lamb, and you slaughtered him."

"Fuck you. Your innocent lamb is wearing a necklace made of human fingers." My blade bit into his neck and blood dribbled down and pooled in the bony crevasse above his collar bone. His eyes widened, but a sneer turned his lip.

I pulled the knife away and wiped it on his robe. "Do you know why I'm here?"

"To infect the minds of the young and bring ruin upon the righteous?"

"No," I said. "As fun as that sounds—no." I laid the knife across his throat and pressed until blood seeped around the blade. "Where are my friends?"

"Martyr me and another will rise up to take my place."

He may have been nothing more than a twisted old bag of sticks, but Micah had balls. I stepped back from him and nodded out the window.

"You know," I said. "From here it looks like there won't be any *Chosen* left alive to fill your shoes, fuckwad. I grasped his ear and squeezed until he screamed. "Tell me where my friends are, or I start taking souvenirs."

He shook his head and I let go. "Please. We meant your people no harm. You brought it upon yourself." As he spoke, his hand crept along the desk behind him, moving so slowly I almost didn't notice. There were books, a map, and a few papers, but no weapons. All the same, it was better to be safe than sorry. I let him get his hand to the center of the desk, then I plunged my knife into it. His scream was both immediate and ear-piercing. I stepped back and clapped my hands over my ears.

When his cries died down, I noticed two things: he was giggling as tears streamed down his cheeks, and the gunfire outside had all but ceased.

My mind reeled. The infected must have broken through. I ran to the window to see, but smoke from several fires close by lay like a blanket over the compound. I strained to hear, but Micah's cackling drowned out all but the closest noises.

"They're all dead, sinner, and now God's army of resurrected come for you. Reap your reward, for Hell is where you are headed."

I ignored him and strode to the staircase. "Justin!"

No answer. *Fuck.*

"Justin! Get your lumpy ass up here."

Still no answer. Thankfully, Micah had lost steam and stopped giggling. His eyes remained on me, but at least he'd shut up for the time being. I walked to the west facing window and peered out into the smoky haze. Sporadic movement caught my eye, but was gone before I could discern what or who it was. I thought about calling out the window, but realized that would be the best way to give myself away if things had gone bad and the dead were all that was left. Or worse, Micah's people.

Just as panic mode kicked in and I began mentally counting bullets I may or may not have fired, a noise from downstairs caused the breath to catch in my lungs. A stair creaked and I pulled both .45s.

When Micah spoke, I nearly shot him—I was that spooked.

"The tide rises, fool." His eyes shone with the single-minded purpose of the insane. "We are the eternal wave that shapes the shore," he said. Then his eyes rolled back as he passed out.

"Chickenshit," I said. "You're not even gonna be awake when they chew your shit off."

"Fuck it." I walked to the stairs to meet whatever came with dignity. The stairwell was dark, but two shapes climbed toward me. "Friend or foe," I said. "Speak now or moan and die twice."

"Whoa! Gerry! It's me, Kyle."

"And me," came Justin's familiar voice. "Kyle wanted to come see the woman with the tits."

My head bubbled over with questions. "Where is everybody? Are the infected gone? Did you—"

Kyle cut me off. "We got them out, and all the dead things are gone."

"But—"

Kyle wiped grime from his face, then smiled. "Come see. It's the coolest thing."

I was so confused I thought my brain would shut down, but I nodded. "Yeah, OK. I guess I can come back and finish playing with Micah later."

"Yeah," Justin said. "There are so many of them."

"So many of what?"

But they were already down the stairs and out the door. I spared one more look at Micah, then followed the departed boys down the stairs.

CHAPTER 27

Yoho National Park, Canada
Lucia

"Why did the zombie cross the road?"

"I don't know, Lucy. To eat you?"

"No, because he wanted a UPS truck to pop his brains out of his skull."

The truck jumped as we ran over a zombie. Fred grabbed his side and winced.

"Sorry," I tossed over my shoulder. "I didn't like the way that one was looking at me.

I cracked my neck from side to side. I hurt from being awake for so many days.

"We're not too far from the McArthur camp."

"I hope they have valet service and a wheelchair handy."

"I'm hoping for cocktail hour—short on the tail, and long on the cock," I quipped.

Fred laughed, "You should have asked me before I was shot, Lucy."

I popped another Adipex in my mouth and washed it down with piss-warm water. "Oh yeah? You should have asked me before I was a month into developing my eau du shower-less scent." In the review mirror, I looked him in the eyes, winked, and laughed. I leaned my head to look at the sky—it was gunmetal gray. "I hope it doesn't snow. When does it start snowing in Canada?"

"I don't think it ever stops snowing in Canada."

I could see something up ahead—it was black—perhaps a wrecked vehicle. "Hey, Fred, I'm coming up on something."

"What is it?" He strained to lean forward to look.

I squinted as we neared. "It's some sort of military gathering."

"Zombie infested?"

"I can't tell, but they're not moving like zombies… no, it's the fucking Army or something. What should I do?"

"Slow up and look."

"It's a helicopter and a bunch of guys in riot gear. They don't look infected. Maybe they can help!" I was excited.

"Lucia, be careful," Fred warned.

"Someone's waving me down. I'm stopping."

A soldier approached the truck with his gun pointed. "Are you infected?"

"Nope! No infection here," I smiled.

Another soldier came alongside the other door, "What about the man in the back? Is he infected?"

"No, he was shot."

"Are you sure he wasn't infected?"

"He was shot days ago. He's not showing any signs of infection."

Their guns were still pointed at me. "Get out of the vehicle."

I listened. I eased myself out of the truck slowly. "My friend can't move. Please, don't make him get out. Do you have a medic? Someone can check him. Please." I was pleading, and I shivered without my squirrel suit on. I only wore a tank top and shorts in case I had to slip the suit on quickly, and the air attacked my bare limbs. Desperate times made me feel even more naked.

An older soldier came towards us, "Put your guns down and let's get the back of this truck opened up."

"Yes, Captain," they responded in an echo.

They threw open the back of the truck and looked at Fred.

"What happened to you?" the Captain asked.

"Some fucking redneck shot me in Montana."

"Looters?" The Captain scratched the stubble on his chin.

"Yes, and rapists too, apparently," I said with disdain.

The Captain glanced at me, "Hmph. Okay, I'll get someone to look at you." He moved around the side of the truck and yelled, "Murphy! Get your kit and look at this man."

Another soldier reached into the helicopter and trotted over with a bag in his hand. I was smiling. Help was a freedom I hadn't tasted in weeks.

"I—I had to operate on him. The bullet ruptured one of his splenic arteries."

"Are you a doctor?"

"No, I did an internship in an ER and was pre-med. That's it."

Murphy examined Fred. "I can't tell exactly what you did, but the site isn't infected. How long ago did you operate?"

"Two days, nearly three."

"And the bleeding stopped?"

"Yes."

Murphy shrugged. "Okay, I'm just going to take some vitals."

Murphy talked to Fred as I approached the Captain. "Are you going to rescue us?"

"We weren't scouting for civilians and we aren't on a rescue mission for them. We needed to land for some repairs, but we're headed for the Pacific coast."

"Can you take us with you?"

"Miss, I'd consider it, but we're already lifting thirteen people in an eleven-person Black Hawk. I'm not even sure we'll make it at the capacity we're at with the fuel we have left."

I put my hand on his arm, "Would you please… please just try fourteen people?"

The Captain looked me up and down. I was a mess, but wasn't below sucking my way out of the situation. "How much do you weigh?"

"Not me, Sir, my friend. He wouldn't have a chance without me. If you can take just one of us, please, let it be him."

"You'd be alone then." The Captain was still eyeing me.

"I'm alone anyways. He can't help me." I bit my lower lip. "We heard there's a safe camp up at Lake McArthur. I'll keep heading there if you can take him. Maybe I'll find others. Please, I have a chance, but he doesn't."

The Captain turned from me and walked back to the UPS truck, "Murphy!"

"Yes, Sir!"

"How's that man holding out?"

Murphy ran over to us, "He'll live, Sir, if he doesn't get an infection in that wound. He's in good health besides the gunshot, so he has a decent chance."

The Captain looked at me, "What's your friend's name?"

"Fred, Sir," I said, continuing to unknowingly copying the 'sir' the others had called him.

"Fred!" The Captain called into the back of the truck.

Fred lifted his head. "Yes?"

"How much you think you weigh?"

"Uh…maybe about 170."

"Hmph!" The Captain walked over to the helicopter. "Okay, we need to unload! Let's get rid of anything else unnecessary—we're taking on a wounded civilian."

I hugged the Captain and started crying, "Thank you, thank you so much. I'm sorry; I know I probably smell, but thank you."

I pulled back and the Captain patted me on the arm. I wiped my tears.

"Get the stretcher ready once you are done; we'll load him in first. Whatever gear the girl can use, load in the truck for her."

I ran to the truck and crawled in the back with Fred, "They're taking you with them." I smiled.

"Me? What about you?"

"Just you."

"Lucy, NO!"

"Fred, stop. It has to be this way. You'd never make it without me and they shouldn't even fit one of us. It has to be you."

Fred started crying. I sat near him and gently lifted his head onto my lap.

"Sshh…don't cry."

"Lucia, I'm so worried about you."

"Don't worry," I smiled, "I promise—no more talking to zombies. And besides, I'm almost there."

"I'll come back for you."

"Don't do anything foolish. If you get to safety, stay there. I'll be okay, and you'll know exactly where to find me if this thing ever ends."

I started stroking his hair and two soldiers arrived with a stretcher.

"We're ready to take him now, Ma'am."

I leaned forward and kissed Fred upside-down. He grabbed my hand and squeezed it.

"Not goodbye…" he said.

"No." I bit my lower lip so I wouldn't cry.

I moved as they transferred him to the stretcher. I watched them load him into the helicopter and stack items into my truck. The Captain approached me.

"Lake McArthur, eh?"

"Yep."

"You'd best avoid Calgary—take 93 North."

"Will do."

"Captain, I—I was wearing a squirrel costume when I was first attacked and the zombies couldn't bite through it."

"Oh yeah?"

"Yes, I'm a materials chemist at a place called MLCP Technologies in Pittsburgh. We do R&D for the Department of Defense—bullet proof, stab proof, and fire proof fabric, mostly. I had lined my squirrel costume with some of the material we manufactured at our facility—it seems like the zombies can't puncture it with their teeth. I know it's probably similar to what you're wearing now, but ours was silicone based, treated with an anti-viral chemical, and intended for biological warfare. Maybe if someone can remote access our files they can use what we were making to produce bite-proof suits for people."

"Good to know, thanks. I'll pass the information along."

I nervously smiled and backed away as the Captain returned to directing his men. I gave them a friendly smile, anxious that they might change their mind and offload Fred. The helicopter took off, kicking dirt and loose grass all over me. I quickly sought refuge in my truck, double checking that the doors were locked. I was awake now, and somehow, less frightened than I had been in weeks.

CHAPTER 28

Dublin, Ireland
Paul

A harsh *caw-caw* from behind made me duck down just as a huge black bird swooped over my head, landing on a corpse in front of me. I watched the crow with disgust as it pecked at the face of the body, pulling out an eyeball with its sharp, evil beak. All around me a low mist, no higher than my knees, covered the soft, marshy ground I stood on. I had the axe in my hand; it felt more like an extension of me than a weapon or tool.

I heard my name on the wind—the soft, gentle voice of a woman called to me. I squinted into the distance and saw her standing on a hill. She had long, dark hair that fell over her shoulders, down to her elbows. She wore a simple, ankle-length dress, belted at the waist. The only thing of beauty left in a desolate world, she raised her arm and beckoned to me. The crow regarded me curiously before returning to its gruesome meal.

I knew then I had to go to her; to reach her meant sanctuary. I stepped forward onto the wet, spongy ground. Almost immediately, dark shapes rose from the mist—grotesque undead creatures risen up from their eternal slumber. The first one ran at me: a childlike demon yelling a high-pitched wail. My axe came up before the creature could touch me; its head spun in the air.

A woman cried then—it was Mrs. Watson. She cradled the headless body of her little son, Brian. Her mournful weeping carried across the marsh.

"You did this," she said sadly. One side of her skull was smashed in; half her face was missing. She rocked back and forth with the boy in her lap.

"I…" I was lost for words. I looked up to the woman on the hill; she was beckoning urgently, but her words were drowned out by the sobs of Mrs. Watson.

"You did this," she repeated. "You left the door open."

"No! It wasn't me."

Another shape appeared in my path. It was Robbie, his whole cheek hung down off his jaw now, and one eye was missing. I realised it had been his body the crow feasted on.

"You killed me! You left me to die."

"No! What could I do?" I looked up to the girl on the hill again. I could see her face now; she really was beautiful. Somehow she looked familiar, like I'd known her all my life, and yet I knew I had never seen her before. I had to reach her; she needed me to reach her. All around me the rotting corpses of everybody I ever knew gathered, pulling and clawing at me with skeletal hands. They started to drag me down. The girl on the hill reached for me with outstretched arms. Tears rolled down her cheeks. I knew she wanted to help, but could not reach me. I had to go to her. The weight of the dead was too much for me. I screamed as they pulled me down into the mist.

"Hey!"

My eyes snapped open. I was disoriented as I took in my surroundings. I was sitting in a plush leather armchair; all around me books lined the walls of an expensive room.

"Shit," I said.

"You Okay?" the soldier asked.

"I must have fallen asleep, I was dreaming."

"Yeah, we noticed," he grinned. "Half the north side of Zombieland heard you screaming."

"Christ, I'm sorry." I remembered now, we'd made it back to government buildings. I was ushered inside and led into the plush surroundings I woke up in. I had even been fed a hot meal. I must have dozed off.

"Don't worry about it; I think we're all entitled to a few bad dreams lately. I'm Sean, by the way." He offered a hand.

The memory of the girl stood out vividly in my mind. She was not somebody I knew or had ever met before, and yet in the dream she felt so familiar. I couldn't help wonder, would I ever meet a girl like that again?

"Paul," I said, taking his hand.

"That was a brave thing you did, Paul, coming back for me. I won't forget it."

"Meh," I waved away his thanks, embarrassed by it, to be honest.

"Fuck sake, seeing you go at that big bastard zombie with the axe had me shittin' meself," another soldier quipped.

There were three other soldiers besides Sean in the room. They all looked a lot more human and friendlier without the goggles and masks. They all chuckled at the joke.

The door swung open, and all the soldiers snapped to attention. I slowly stood up when I recognised the man who entered the room. Flanked by an older soldier who screamed authority in his every fibre was Patrick Ryan, The Taoiseach or Prime Minister of Ireland.

"So, this is the stray you picked up?"

"Yes, Taoiseach," Sean answered.

"Lucky for you these men found you," The Taoiseach addressed me.

"By all accounts, he was doing alright for himself." The officer smiled before releasing the soldiers with a nod.

"Well, he's stuck with us now, and we're stuck with him. I just wish we could've rescued a whole lot more," Ryan said. I was struck by the genuine remorse in his voice.

Another man entered the room, this time a civilian—at least he was dressed in a normal business suit.

"The plane is on the tarmac, Taoiseach, ready to go whenever you are," the man said. He did a double take when he saw me, noticing me for the first time.

"Hmmm, we can't go anywhere until Professor Tompkins gets here." He tapped his chin nervously.

"Plane?" I asked. "Are we going somewhere?"

CHAPTER 29

Field, British Columbia, Canada
Sharon

Dawn broke through my window, finding me sprawled out on my narrow bed, with Parker snoring on his. I rose, stretched, closed the door behind me, and went to stand on the small balcony.

The new light shimmered off the clear waters of Lake McArthur and ignited a fire within the ice crystals that blanketed the ground with fine powder. It had been a week since our arrival at the lodge, and winter would be arriving soon. Once it started snowing in earnest, we would be stuck here until the thaw. This served to remind me that I needed to get some supplies.

The road to the lodge was limited access, closed to public traffic. Every time I had come to the lodge, I had parked in the town of Field and took the shuttle bus. Field was a small town of less than 200 people. I had spent many hours there playing tourist. I'd go there first. If I didn't find what I needed, then I'd drive to Golden.

Hours later, Parker was coloring on the floor before the fire with all of his trains lined up around him, while I was in the kitchen cleaning up. I had found some yeast packets, and after several abysmal failures, I managed to get bread to rise. Now, the comforting smell of baking wafted through the lodge.

A few days ago, while searching the shed, I happened across a bin full of bird seed. I filled all the feeders near the garden and scattered some seed on the ground. Not long after, the first small birds appeared. From then on, the flock had grown, but I had not seen a single mammal since I arrived. A few random prints in the snow gave evidence that there were some around. In the middle of a national park, there should be a thriving population. Instead, much like my zoo, the mammals had been the hardest hit.

I sat at the old table and flipped through the book that I found with Rob's rifle. Apparently, it was an AR-15. I was reading about the holographic scope when I caught movement out of the corner of my eye.

A white-tailed rabbit burst from the densely packed trees of the forest into the clearing, scattering the birds that were pecking at the seed. A woman emerged from the same spot, running faster than her state of decomposition should allow. Two small children ran along after her. A young girl with long brown hair, now hopelessly snarled, was missing her left arm below the elbow. Her twin, a boy, followed after her at a slower pace. His shirt had once been bright yellow, and bore the smiling face of SpongeBob, but was now stained dark brown. His intestines flowed from beneath the shirt, leaving a rusty stain in the snow as they trailed behind him.

I swallowed hard and walked into the common room. "Parker, I am going to practice shooting the rifle, so just stay in here. Okay?"

He looked up, nodded, and went back to his illustration. I let the kitchen door swing shut behind me, walked over to the sink, and eased the window open. The lodge was elevated, so the window was about eight feet off the ground. The mother zombie was closing in on the rabbit. She lunged, caught him, and ripped him in half, spraying scarlet drops everywhere. His pained scream scattered the birds from their new perch in the trees with a rush of feathers and snow.

I took aim, flipped the switch to burst, and fired. A barrage of bullets left the gun in quick succession. I was not prepared for the force of the gun and grunted as it recoiled against my shoulder.

To my amazement, the mother's head exploded in a shower of bone and brain. Her children didn't even pause in their feeding frenzy. I then flipped the switch to single shot, looked through the scope at the girl, and fired again. She fell forward on top of her mother, while her brother snarled and gnawed on a rabbit ear. I took a deep breath, trying to swallow the taste of bile, and fired. The little boy, who couldn't have been much older than Parker, joined his mother and sister in death for the final time.

With shaking hands, I closed the window and pulled the shade. The gruesome family was several hundred yards away. Now that I wasn't looking through the scope, I was amazed at how far away they really were. I'd have to do something about them at some point. I didn't want dead bodies around, but for right now, there was no way I was going near them.

*

"Well, Sharon, how hard can it be?" I asked myself the following morning as I inserted the key into the bus's ignition. I needed supplies, and while I had grown deeply attached to the Mustang, it wasn't the best vehicle for a supply run. I had in mind to clean out a store; I needed room to do that. The bus was my best bet.

Parker was seated behind me; I could see him peering at me in the big mirror overhead. "Ready?" I asked. He grinned and nodded; I smiled and turned the key. The bus had been sitting for a while and protested at the notion of having to move. But after some coaxing, the engine finally turned over and rumbled to life. With my map next to me, I trundled down the dirt road with the sound of overhanging branches scraping the roof.

The Trans-Canada highway was eerily quiet. A deer crossing sign warning drivers to use caution seemed like a cruel reminder of how much the world had changed.

When the outbreak began to spread, the press release that I had written said it was a new strain of rabies. No matter how virulent we warned them it was, it still seemed innocuous enough, so the citizenry remained calm. When the infected began to die, and resurrect rumors spread no matter how hard the government tried to squash them.

Not long after, the exodus began; people headed south, packing up their families and possessions. Unbeknownst to them, a violent stowaway had accompanied them—the Hauksson virus—and the epidemic spread.

Viruses are simple organisms. They cannot survive on their own, and so need a host. Its sole purpose is to replicate and spread. The Hauksson virus triggered hunger. That caused the resurrected to bite, which allowed the virus to spread via the infected saliva. The process is technically called shedding, and is the final stage in the viral life cycle.

I had no notion of what the lifecycle of this virus was. I had to believe that, like any other, it would follow that same stages: infect, replicate, spread, and die. My suspicion was confirmed as I drove. I passed zombies lying on the side of the road, dead—for good this time.

I needed to know how long the virus lived in a host, and wondered how I could manage to acquire such knowledge. Ideally, I could have kept Mindy in her cell until the virus ran its course, but even in the name of science I could not do it to her. She had been someone's daughter, sister, lover. I had not known her well, but as a human being I owed her more consideration than that. Still, the scientist in me grumbled about it.

The Kicking Horse River meandered along the highway. When the spring thaw came, the river would swell and rafters would brave the white waters by the dozens. But for now, it was calm and docile, its fury restrained for the winter. I drove over the bridge and rumbled into town.

Field was quiet. Most of the cars were gone, but a few still lined the streets. I pulled the bus up on the curb before the Pig Truffle General Store.

"Parker, I am going to go check it out. You stay here. Keep the doors locked. If you see anyone, call me on the radio." He nodded, his eyes huge, and his hands dug into my arm.

"I'll be okay," I said, hugging him to me. Reaching into my bag, I fished out one of the two-way radios that I had found in Rob's closet. "You can talk to me whenever you want."

"Okay," he said, his lip trembling. I knew he was trying his best to be brave, and I lamented that fact that this was his new reality. I had grown up with two older brothers tormenting me, and no matter how much I had complained, it had been a good childhood. Would he spend his life running? What kind of life was that I wondered as I closed the door behind me, listening for him to pull the latch that locked it.

I had the rifle slung over my back and the Glock in a holster on my leg. I caught the reflection of myself in the store window and grimaced. I was a zoologist for crying out loud, and here I was, about to empty a store into a giant yellow bus amidst the zombie apocalypse. "How craptastic is that?" I muttered under my breath as I opened the door to the store.

A small silver bell chimed. I reached up and silenced it. I considered taking it down, but it would be a good warning should anything enter. There were four aisles. I walked across the front, aiming the rifle down each one as I passed. Once I was content that nothing lurked in the aisles, I made my way back to the storage room. Peering in, I switched on the overhead, flooding the room with light. It was one large room that served as an office, an employee break room, and a small stock room. A door to the back was the only exit. I made sure it was locked. I didn't want anything sneaking up on me.

With a great sigh of relief, I allowed myself a small moment to rejoice that the store was empty and still fairly well stocked. Grabbing an armload of empty boxes, I made my way down the aisles that had the medicines in them. There were no prescriptions, but over the counter meds would always come in handy. I tossed in bandages, disinfectants, and every other kind of medicine that might be used.

Slinging the rifle over my back, I hauled the boxes to the bus. Parker opened the door, and I slid the box in. He grabbed it, closed and locked the door, and shoved the box to the back of the bus. I had him slide down a window, then I started throwing in bags of toilet paper, paper towels, and blankets. I found several stuffed animals and tossed them at him, just to see him smile.

Around noon, I paused to have lunch on the bus. I'd managed to make a huge dent in the store and was proud of my accomplishment. I didn't realize until I sat down how foolish it was to stop. My aching muscles screamed in protest and rebelled when I tried to stand up.

I had to ignore the pain and work on. I wanted to be out of there by 5pm so that I could be back at the lodge by dark. I'd unload the next day.

I was packing canned goods into a box in the back of the store when I heard Parker on the radio.

"Sharon?"

"What's wrong?" I asked, walking over to the window.

"I heard something. It sounded like an engine."

I looked down the street and didn't see anything. "What kind of engine?"

"It sounded like Rob's motorcycle." Rob was a pilot; he liked fast cars, fast women, and motorcycles. I knew he had a massive Harley that he'd take Parker for a ride on, but he also had a faster Ducati that was basically an engine with a seat on it.

I had grown used to handling the dead; I wasn't prepared to deal with the living. I was a lone woman with a child. I didn't know who the owner of the engine was; I planned to keep it that way.

"Okay, I'm almost finished. I think it's time to go." I had several boxes of clothes waiting to be loaded on to the bus. Most were tourist items bearing the logo of Yoho National Park and 'Welcome to Canada'. It would be cold this winter. I wasn't going to leave them behind. I could care less if they fit. This was no time to be particular.

I had just loaded the last box and was shutting the emergency door on the back of the bus when I heard the sound of gunfire ricocheting in the mountains. I ducked and hid next to the bus's wheel, waiting. With my heart beating fast, I ran to the front door and jumped in; I cursed under my breath as I tried to start the bus. When it finally roared to life, I released a shuddering breath. I hit the gas a little too hard and bounced off the curb, knocking over a quaint mailbox carved to look just like the store.

On the way out of town, I saw two zombies dead on the road. They had not been there before, and judging by the spray of blood and muck, these were newly killed.

"That man is naked, Sharon," Parker said, pulling my attention from the zombies. He pointed towards the river. Along the bank sat a motorcycle, but that is not what dropped my jaw and had my foot hitting the brake. There was a man, hip deep in the water, furiously scrubbing himself.

CHAPTER 30

Thunder Bay, Ontario, Canada
Gerry

With very few exceptions, Man is a social animal, and during dark times there is strength to be had in numbers. I don't mean strength of arms, or even the strong versus the weak. Strength is found in setting aside former petty prejudices, fears and hatred, and standing shoulder-to-shoulder to preserve a humanity that doesn't see colour, station, or religion as a means of entrance into the club. We need each other. We nourish each other.

When Kyle told me there was something wonderful, something I just *had* to see, there were tears in his eyes. In the center of the cultists' compound there was a large forest-green tent, similar in size and shape to a three-ring circus tent. That, he said, was our destination. Even before arriving I saw them. Aside from the boys and the small group of police officers, several men and women bustled back and forth. Some tended to the wounded, while others carried weapons or dragged robed prisoners toward the circus tent.

Call me a pessimist, but my hands never strayed far from my shoulder rig.

"Where did all these people come from? Did some of the cultists switch sides when they saw they were gonna lose?"

Kyle grinned and shook his head. "No, man. Everyone you see right now was a prisoner. If I hadn't stumbled upon them in that tent, we'd all be puddles of maggot soup right now. The deadies would've totally kicked our shit in."

Two unfamiliar men flanked the tent's opening, both armed with rifles. I stopped Kyle and pulled him aside before nearing the tent. "How can you tell the difference?"

"Check out their right hands. The prisoners were all branded when they were picked up."

"Like cattle? Holy fuck." Then it struck me. Cattle is exactly what these people had been in the eyes of the Coven.

I nodded to the pair on the way into the tent. "Fellas. How's it going?"

Neither answered, but their eyes had a certain look; they were alive with questions, with anguish, with fear. I remembered the look well. At first, back when this all started, I used to see it each time I looked in the mirror. Not so much anymore, though.

I'd found a way to eat the pain, but my solution wasn't theirs. As much as I wished I could say something uplifting, maybe pat 'em on the back or whatnot, I couldn't. That's not me. I had no answers for them.

Not everyone was like that. Inside the tent there were groups of people, some smiling, some huddled in whispered conversation, and some who simply wandered about in a daze. At the center of the tent, where the ring would be if it were a circus tent, was a twenty-by-twenty cage. Inside the cage sat thirteen robed men and women, hands tied behind their backs.

I pointed to the cage. "Is that all of 'em?"

"Yeah, 'cept for that old guy you stuck to the table up in that radio tower."

"That old guy was Micah, the asshole who lured us here. There was a girl too. Justin tied her up beside the pit with their leader in it."

Kyle spit on the ground. "You should've killed him."

"The thought crossed my mind." And it still did. Whatever fate had in store for the rest of them, Micah was a dead man.

Kyle pointed out a portly, balding man in a soiled business suit. "That dude over there seems to be calling the shots for these people. Says he's been here for almost a month. And get this: he's putting a meeting together to see what to do with them."

"Already? Shit, they've only been free for, what, an hour?"

"Yup, everybody not fixing the walls or watching the gates is going to be there."

As Kyle spoke, I watched a man run in from outside the tent, then head for the old, bald guy Kyle said was running the show. I joined them so I could hear what the man had to say.

"What's up?" I said.

The man who'd run in turned to me and nodded. "They got away in a school bus."

"Who did?"

I didn't realize how close we were to the cage until a voice from behind me spoke up. One of the cultists stood no more than three feet from me, glaring at us.

He said, "Randall. He has risen, and he shall rain down his anger upon you."

"Shit," I said, then turned to the man who'd seen the bus. "What did the people look like? Can you describe them?"

He got as far as "One was a skinny old guy," when I stopped him.

At my back, the cultist spoke again, this time loud enough for all to hear. "Micah delivers Randall into the arms of our brothers and sisters. Your day of atonement will come soon."

I turned, a return quip already primed to deliver, when my eyes fell to a necklace dangling between the open flaps of his robe. I was prepared for the fingers, the toes, the ears, but at the very center—a sort of jewel to set any necklace off—was a tiny severed hand. Words turned to ash in my throat and rage froze my heart.

The cultist followed my gaze to his chest. He plucked at the tiny hand and chuckled. "The little ones are so very tender," he said, and the group within the cell roared with laughter.

My stomach churned, but when it subsided enough that I could speak without puking, I reached through the bars and grabbed a handful of the man's robe. He shrieked when I yanked him close.

His eyes were round with fear, but he spoke evenly. "You'll die for this."

"Maybe," I said, as I slid a gun from my shoulder rig, "but I'm content with the knowledge that you won't be there when it happens." Then I placed the gun under his chin and blew his brains out through the top of his head.

Everyone screamed. The two guards ran into the tent with their guns raised, and the fat man in the soiled suit held his hands out to me, palms out, and pleaded with me to put the gun away. All this happened in the few seconds it took for the corpse to stop jerking after it hit the floor.

The fat man waved the guards back outside, then turned to me. "Please. Hasn't there been enough violence? How many more need to die before this madness ends?"

"About twelve," I said. "Give or take." I pointed the gun at his chest and told him to take his people and go.

The man's jowls jiggled as he shook his head. "I won't stand for this."

"Then you'll die for it," I said. "These animals aren't leaving this tent alive."

"But—"

"But nothing. Get out."

Kyle stepped between us, and I lowered my gun. "C'mon, Gerry. We're gonna have a meeting to see what to do with them. Killing those *things* is one thing, but this, this is…"

"Murder?" I said.

"Yeah, and maybe one day they'll be OK to leave the cage." The look in his eyes told me he didn't believe it, but what else was he supposed to say? He was only human.

Most of the rest of the people had already run from the tent. All that remained were Kyle, a couple more kids I hadn't seen in the tent 'til then, and the ad hoc mayor fat man.

Kyle bowed his head, then turned and ushered the last few people out of the tent. The fat man shook his head as tears streaked his face, but he didn't say another word. Once the tent flap fell I turned to the captives in the cage and pulled a second gun. They huddled at the rear, crying and pushing each other out of the way as they pressed themselves up against the bars. It was then that I hesitated. This was wrong. What they did was wrong, but didn't change the fact that what I was about to do was kill twelve unarmed people.

I turned to leave and Jenks, the cop I'd last seen out in the forest before we attacked, stepped into the tent, an assault rifle in his hands.

"It's OK," I mumbled, defeated. "I'm not gonna do it."

He stepped forward and placed a hand on my shoulder. "I didn't come here to stop you."

"You didn't?"

"No. Some of them may not get it, but I do. This is righteous. There's no place for the Coven's people here. They gave up that right."

He spoke the truth. I took a deep breath, nodded, and then we raised our weapons, took aim and fired. The cultists screamed as bullets tore into their flesh, but I screamed louder as their dying image seared itself onto my soul twelve times over. This was the new world order.

Once he'd spent all of his rounds, Jenks stumbled a few feet away, doubled over and vomited. My stomach churned, my throat was raw from screaming, my heart raced, and a cold sweat sent shivers through my body. On unsteady legs, I turned from him, from the tangle of blood-drenched corpses within the cage, and left the tent without uttering a word.

The camp was deathly quiet. People milled about, but no one looked my way, and the very forest seemed to be holding its breath. Kyle, Justin, and a few of 'my boys' stood near the building where I'd found Micah earlier, their expressions bleak but stoic.

Before I could speak, Kelly, the kid I formerly thought was a boy but was actually a girl, ran forward and hugged me. I waited a few seconds, then untangled myself from her and stepped back. A large X had been branded into the back of her right hand. I instantly hated myself a little less for what I'd just done.

Kyle pulled Kelly away and told her to go help at the gate. After she was out of earshot, he said, "Look, I'm sorry. We all are."

"Save it," I said. "I'm leaving."

"Where are you going?"

"I'm going to go get my bike, then go after Micah."

"Then what?"

"Then I don't know. Maybe I'll head out west... go to California or fucking Disneyland. I dunno."

"They'll get over it, Gerry. It'll just take some time, that's all."

"I know, kid. You take care of these little bastards."

Before leaving, I turned to Justin, who was hunched over, staring at his own feet. "You were a shitty paperboy."

He wiped his nose and smiled up at me. "Yeah, and you never gave me a Christmas tip, you cheap prick."

For a brief moment I forgot about the blood, the killing, the pain, and saw what we'd accomplished. I smiled back. "You killed a giant."

He looked past me, at the tent where the cultists had died. "So did you."

*

Hope was a word I thought to be dead. After more than a month of seeing nothing but the dead and dying, then the evils of the Coven of the Lamb, I dared to think we had a chance to survive. Well, not 'we' in the sense that I'd be included, but I chose my path knowing full well what the consequences would be.

Jenks had been right: there was no room for the cultists if those people hoped to stand a chance at surviving. I also knew there was no place for me there after doing what I did.

The walk back to the boat seemed to take no time at all. I pulled my motorcycle from the bushes, and loaded it down with as much food and ammo as I could carry. Then I went back for a couple of tightly packed bricks of weed. Given the nightmares that lay ahead, I'd need something to take the edge off.

As I was stuffing the bricks into the already overstuffed saddlebags, a sound from the forest jolted me to attention. In one fluid motion, I turned, kneeled and had both .45s in my hands. I held my breath and waited for the sound to come again so I'd know where to aim.

"If you're alive," I called out, "you better speak the fuck up or I'm gonna shoot your ass."

Still a ways off in the woods, Jenks's voice reached me. "It's me. I'm alone."

I relaxed and slid both guns back into their holsters. When he stepped out into the light, I was immediately struck by how pale he was.

"You look like shit, Jenks."

"Thanks."

I threw my leg over my bike and thumbed the starter. "If you're here to talk me into going back, you're wasting your time."

"No. I came because I don't want to be around them when it happens."

"Uh-uh. They need you. You're a cop. Wait… when *what* happens?"

He shook his head as he rolled up his shirt sleeve. A chunk of flesh had been torn from his forearm, and the surrounding area was black and swollen.

I didn't have much time to think about it when he came to the tent, but it all made sense as I watched him on the beach. Killing those cultists was his final act of bravery.

When I pulled my eyes away from the wound, I searched his face for tell-tale signs of infection. He was pale and his eyes were blood-shot, but his nose hadn't started running like the others I'd seen.

"When?" I said.

"Not long after we separated during the assault on the compound."

"So, what, you came here for me to kill you? I mean, it's shitty what happened to you, don't get me wrong. I just don't see what I can do for you."

"You can get me away from here so I don't end up hurting any of those people, and we can finish what we started. There are still a couple of those cultists left, right?"

As much as I cringed at the idea of having him behind me on the bike, I owed him. "Fine," I said. "Get on. But if you so much as sneeze in my ear, I'm dumping you."

I followed the beach to the path leading to the compound, then skirted around and took the fork heading west. With the added gear and an extra body, the bike was as easy to wrangle as a T-Rex, but I kept it between the lines.

We spotted a rusted, yellow school bus about fifteen kilometers from the compound. From the looks of it, whoever was driving had lost control, jumped the shallow ditch alongside the road, and struck a tree. The windshield had been broken outward, with most of the shatterproof glass lying on the smoking remains of the hood. Copious amounts of blood covered the driver's seat and the side window, and a trail of gore ran up the aisle where something—likely the driver—had been dragged toward the rear of the bus.

"Keep an eye outside," I said to Jenks. "I'm gonna see what's back there."

When I reached the back of the bus the rear emergency door swung freely. The trail led from the bus and back up the road in the direction we'd come. Funny I didn't notice the blood on the road until right then.

"Gerry!"

I jumped down and circled around the bus. "Yeah?"

Jenks stood in the center of the road, binoculars to his eyes. "We've got company… a lot of it."

"Infected?"

"Yeah." He spit on the ground at his feet, then swiped his arm across his nose. "And they're chasing a friend of ours. Have a look."

He held out the binoculars, but I shook my head. "No thanks. I'll take your word for it."

"Oh yeah," he said. "The infection. Sorry."

I cupped my hands against the sun, but could only make out a slender shape, followed by numerous others, heading right up the center of the road.

"How many?" I said, unable to discern one shape from another at such a distance without binoculars.

"About thirty, but guess what?"

"What?"

"They're all wearing robes."

"And you're sure they're dead?"

Jenks sniffed in and then spat out a chunk of phlegm. "Pretty sure, yeah. When they get here, I'll ask them."

"What about the old guy, Micah?"

"No, he looks alive, at least for now."

"Good. With any luck they won't kill him until I get a chance to."

And then it hit me. Back in the compound I'd noticed a few of the bodies being dragged away were wearing robes, but were among the infected that had attacked the west wall.

"Jenks, you said before that the cultists had another compound to the west. Is it on this road?"

"Yeah. Up ahead about two klicks. Why?"

"Because we gotta lead them back to their compound, away from the survivors."

"Yeah, but they're already headed this way."

"For how long, Jenks? Think about it. Once they eat that old man, there's nothing except us in this direction. I don't know if they can sniff us out or not, but I can't take the chance that they'll turn around again, not when all those people back there are sitting ducks. We need to give them time to at least repair the walls."

"Fine," Jenks said. "But whatever you're planning, let's get to it. I'm not sure how much time I've got."

His eyes were red-rimmed, and pus leaked in twin trails down each cheek. I'd only ever been present once while a person went through what Jenks was dealing with, but instinct told me that the infection had nearly run its course. I wasn't 100% sure, but I gave him an hour, tops.

"Hold it together, buddy. I got a plan. All we need to do is get their attention. Then we can pick them off a few at a time as they come after us."

"Seriously?" Jenks turned away and coughed, then came up holding his head. "Jesus, my head feels like it's going to explode."

"You don't look so good. Maybe you should sit down. And what the hell do mean by 'Seriously'? It's a simple plan that can't fail."

"No. Too much can go wrong. What if I turn before we get most of them? What if the bike dies? What if more of them come at us from the other direction?"

"And you have a better idea?"

"Yeah," he said, as he shrugged out of his backpack and unzipped it. He set it on the ground for me to see the contents. Inside were six or seven paper-wrapped bricks, and what looked to my untrained, television-watching eyes as detonators.

I stepped back. "Is that what I think it is?"

He nodded. "Yep, there's enough C-4 to send a square mile of road into orbit."

"Shit," I said. "All I brought was a couple chunks of weed."

"You brought weed?"

"Never mind that. How do we set up the charges and get away before they go boom?"

"That's the part that sucks for me."

"Oh. What about me?"

Jenks favoured me with a sour grin. "What about you? You get on your horse and ride as far as possible before the weenie roast."

Instead of arguing, I asked him what he needed.

"All I need is something to spark a wire. One of the batteries from the bus will work."

While I salvaged a battery, Jenks plugged all of the detonators into the bundled C-4, then stuffed all but one wire back into the backpack. By the time we were all set to go, the herd of dead, still lumbering after the wily old man, were no more than a thousand yards off.

Before setting off, I twisted in my seat and smiled. "Jenks, I just want you to know it's been an honour—"

"Hurry. I'm dying."

His words hit me like a bolt of lightning. In my panicked state, I nearly dumped the bike, but righted it and sped off toward the approaching herd.

I stopped and let him off about 100 yards from the cluster of infected, then passed him the battery. He took it from me, set it and the backpack on the road, and then sat down to wait.

Instead of turning and riding away, I sped forward and skidded to a stop before Micah. He must've thought I'd come to save him, because there was a big ugly grin stretched across his wrinkled face. That was good.

"Thank you, oh thank you," he wheezed, now only a few scant steps ahead of the herd.

I smiled grimly. "My pleasure," I said. Then I pulled a gun from my waistband, aimed carefully, and shot him in the leg.

"Remember that tide you were talking about the first time we spoke? Well, get ready, 'cause it's about to wash over you and dig into spots you never knew you had. Fuck you and die."

I turned and sped away before his screams deafened me. I slowed as I passed Jenks, who stared blindly in my direction. He wasn't dead yet, but any second he would be.

"Goodbye, Jenks."

"Go!" he yelled, then erupted in a coughing fit.

I didn't need to be told twice. As I passed the abandoned compound to the west, an explosion rocked the eastern sky, followed by a blast of hot air on the back of my neck. I didn't look back. There was nothing left for me.

*

Manitoba, on through Saskatchewan, then Alberta and the Rockies: I rode until I couldn't stay awake, slept fitfully until the nightmares woke me, then I hit the road again. No matter how far or fast I went, there was no way I could outrun the faces of the cultists I'd butchered; or Jenks, the poor doomed bastard, who traded the last few seconds of his life for the lives of strangers who'd never know of his bravery.

All along the Trans-Canada Highway entire cities lay in smoking ruins, their streets choked with charred remains and refuse. An army of the undead spread their disease unchecked, one bite at a time, and moved on.

Soon, winter would come and I'd need to trade Carmen in for something with doors and a roof. I'd scavenged a snowsuit and full face helmet from a sporting goods shop in Saskatchewan, but not even they would keep the chill out once the snow fell.

At first, if I came across any infected, I'd stop, shoot them, and move on to another place to seek shelter. But each day it seemed less and less important to kill them, and easier to simply go around and circle back to the highway. I paused occasionally and watched from afar as they swarmed unchallenged through city streets. They were a force of nature.

I passed into British Columbia on a windy, sunless morning pregnant with the promise of an early snow. Low on fuel and food, I exited the highway at a town called 'Field'. I paused at the town limits and scanned the road ahead. The Welcome sign boasted a population of 700, but I'd wager that had changed to one—me. After sitting, waiting, watching for over five minutes, I saw a dog run across the road and dart into the bushes. Seconds later, three more dogs of varying sizes followed and disappeared into the same bushes. Close on their heels, but likely not quick enough to catch up, a lone zombie, moving slightly quicker than I'd seen any move yet, jogged after them.

Shit. The walking dead were one thing, but add a pack of hungry dogs to the mix and that equaled me getting the fuck out of town before *any* of them caught my scent. My fuel was low, but not so low that I couldn't make the next town or a nearby farm. I turned the bike around and headed toward the highway. As I rounded the last bend before the onramp, just above the throaty purr of my bike's engine, I heard dogs barking. I checked my mirrors to find that all four dogs were chasing me down the road, and had almost caught up. I stroked down a gear and punched the throttle, leaving them behind. After passing an abandoned car, I checked my mirrors and saw that they were gone—not just far behind, but gone altogether from the road. I twisted around in my seat to look, just in case they might've been somewhere the mirrors didn't reach, but saw nothing.

I faced forward just in time to spot a pair of zombies not more than ten feet ahead, one facing me and the other pointed in the direction of the lake that ran alongside the road. With no time to stop or dodge, I tucked my head down and throttled up. The first one struck the bike a glancing blow on the left, twisting the handlebars slightly, but I was able to hold on. For a brief instant I thought I'd miss the second one entirely, but then it turned into me as I dipped to slide past. When we collided, the top half of its body ripped free and hit my chest, knocking me off the bike.

I met the road with a bone jarring crunch, and my helmet cracked when it struck the pavement. All the while as I slid, the now legless zombie held on and slid with me, its teeth gnashing ineffectually at the snowsuit.

Once I stopped sliding, I freed myself from its grasp and kicked it away. Unable to see through the film of blood that covered the helmet's visor, I tore it off and scanned the area for more of the dead, or the dogs that must have given up their chase when they smelled the zombies ahead.

I don't know how, but the bike was lying atop the first zombie, after dragging it down the road far enough to smear most of the top of its head into the pavement like a maggoty meat eraser. That one was down for the count, but the remains of the second—the one that had ridden me to the ground—were still moving, if a little slowly on account of the lack of legs.

"Fucker," I grunted, then unzipped the snowsuit and pulled a .45. I stood and kicked the creature in the chest, then shot it six times in the face. The first shot killed it, the other five were for Carmen.

As I slid the gun back into its holster, I was struck by an odd, cold sensation on my back. I reached over my shoulder and realized that the back of the snowsuit was gone, having been ripped off during the accident. Worse than that was the fact that I was covered, head to toe, in zombie goo. Unsure of what the effects of being exposed to their blood might be, I panicked and peeled off my snowsuit, my leathers, even my underwear. Then I strapped on my guns, hopped the guard rail and ran for the lake to wash myself.

After checking my entire body and not finding a scratch—thank you, snow suit!—I dunked my head underwater, an act that caused the breath to freeze in my lungs as well as wake me up. I was in the middle of going over myself for the third time, scrubbing as best I could with my bare hands, when I heard a woman's voice.

"Are you infected?"

Woman's voice or not, I reached for my guns, fumbled and dropped one in the water, then turned to face her. Up until right then, shock must have kept me from thinking of the cold. As I lowered the gun toward the water so as not to spook the stranger, I shivered so hard I wasn't sure if I'd be able to shoot if I had to.

She was pretty. If she didn't have a rifle pointed at my chest, or I hadn't been standing up to my junk in freezing cold water, I probably would've tried to come up with something funny to say to break the tension. As it happened, I had nothing.

"Fu-fu—"

"Freezing?" she said.

"N-n-no," I said. "Fu-fu-fucking pricks muh-made me c-c-crash my b-bike."

"Are you… OK?" she asked.

"I-I think you can s-s-see for yourself that I'm f-fine."

She shrugged noncommittally, and nodded toward the idling bus. "I have clothes if you need them."

"Yes, please," I said, and waded toward the shore.

She turned away with a blush about as red as her hair, and nodded. "I'll pass them out to you. Wait there."

As she searched for clothes in the back of the bus, shots rang out from down the road. I ducked my head into the bus and yelled for the woman to come out. "You have friends around here?"

"No," she said, handing me a pile of clothes. "I thought I was hearing things. Were those shots just now?"

"Yeah, they came from up the road somewhere. You sure you don't have friends around here?" Not that I didn't trust her—she seemed nice enough—but trust wasn't something I was ever going hand out like candy ever again.

"You're the first person I've seen in a long time—well, except for Parker."

Another volley of shots rang out.

"I'm gonna go check it out. Care to come with?"

"Sure. It's on the way home anyway."

CHAPTER 31

The Dailey Farm, British Columbia, Canada
Lucia

I knew why people prayed. When I parked at night to sleep and heard things that used to be human moan in the dark, I prayed too. The flesh fell off of the bones of the older zombies. If they rubbed up against my truck, sometimes they left pieces of themselves on the hood. I didn't remove them. I'd wait until I was driving and the air would lift the decaying meat until it took flight and smacked against my windshield.

The child sitting on the yellow line on the middle of the road, snacking on someone's hand—not a severed hand—a hand torn off of a body—should have been my omen to turn around. The freshly-fed afoot was never a warming sight. If Fred had still been with me, he would have told me to turn around—to take another route. But he wasn't with me, so I made the decision to drive through the small Canadian town.

I hadn't planned on getting out of the truck—I didn't need to, but there were all of these flyers, and I wanted to read them. I stopped the truck near a telephone pole some were attached to. They were once rain-wet, but now wind-dried, leaves of newsprint with stories—human stories—of survival, and how the virus spread.

There were many different flyers, and I greedily collected them all by dashing from pole to pole. I carefully ripped them from the staples that they were attached with. They crinkled in my hand and I heard the moan. There were at least a dozen zombies swaying towards me, almost in a synchronized, rotting dance. I jumped into the truck, locked the door, threw the leaflets on the seat, and scrambled for my keys. They arrived at the truck by then, and more were coming. One eyeless woman licked the window with her green and black tongue. I gagged. They pawed at the truck, rocking it. I fumbled and dropped the keys. Even more moved towards the truck. I could hear one trying to climb onto the roof. I stuck the key in the ignition, turned it, and started to pull away. The truck hesitated against the crowd of bodies, but pushed through them with a lurch.

I was terrified. *That was a stupid mistake. You have to be more careful.* My heart raced and my body felt exhausted. I found my way out of town and turned back on the main road. After a few miles, I pulled over and looked at the leaflets.

The first was about two Canadian teens who were infected on their walk home from the mall. Upon discovering their state, their grandfather tethered them to a post in his basement and provided them with meat from the grocery store until they broke free one night and ate him. The lesson: don't keep zombies like pets. *Yeah, no freakin' kidding.*

The second was even more useful: zombies cannot swim. One woman lived on a raft in the middle of a large pond for nearly 36 hours as zombies tried to swim to her, but couldn't make it. They don't have the coordination to swim once the water is above their head. *Good to know instead of just guessing that's how it is.*

Some were pictures of missing people, now assumed dead. Others were pages filled with government notices—the same shit my local newspapers had said. There were lists of 'rumored' infection-free zones: islands in the South Pacific, Antarctica…all pipe dreams, as the infection had wrapped around the globe like the red cellophane on cinnamon candies.

I examined the directions for Lake McArthur again. I hadn't noticed it before, but it looked like the last leg of the trip included a road that might not be passable by a vehicle. *Fuck! Now what the fuck am I supposed to do?* The squirrel costume offered protection, but there was no way I could fight or run in that thing. I needed a dirt bike or something like that.

Up through the fields, a blonde haired woman came running towards the truck, waving her arms. "Help me. Please." I leaned back in my seat and paused. *Can she really see me?* Over the hill, behind her, a man in overalls chased her. Well, not a man *anymore*, but one of those things—and he was quick and fresh. I grabbed my rifle and got out of the truck. I took aim at him, but he was too far away. As he ran closer, I tapped off several shots before he collapsed. I was a bad aim. The woman had dropped to the grass after my first shot. She lay there, sobbing, covering her ears until I called to her to stand up. She rose slowly and approached me. I kept my gun pointed at her.

The whites of her eyes were already red and the snot flowed generously from her nose.

"Stop right there. You're infected."

The woman froze, "No, please, you don't understand. It's just allergies—fall allergies. I get them every year."

Yeah, the kind of allergies that eat your brain and then me. "You from around here?"

The woman relaxed and smiled, "Yeah, my name's Ginny. I live down the road—the first farmhouse on the left."

I kept my gun raised. "How many other people were living there, Ginny?"

"Just me and my husband, but that's who was chasing me. And we took in the neighbor girl."

"Is she infected too?"

"No, she's fine—just hides in the bedroom a lot."

"What's her name?"

"Katrina."

"You got food and stuff, Ginny?"

"Yeah, lots of it. I canned all summer—stuff from our garden. And I got a whole root cellar full of potatoes."

"Have you seen any zombies around lately?"

"Just one, two days ago, but my husband killed him—that's how he got infected—fighting that one."

"What about a dirt bike, Ginny? Did you guys own anything like that?"

" 'Did'? Yeah, we *do*." She laughed nervously and her head swayed a little bit. "It's over in the barn. Can you put that gun down, now, please?" A string of snot dangled from her chin. She didn't bother to wipe it away. "What's all of these questions aboot?" Her accent was noticeable.

"Do you know where Lake McArthur is?"

"Yeah, it's not too far from here." Ginny's fingers were twitching abnormally.

"Did your husband bite you or scratch you?"

"No. He never hurt me. He was sweet up until this morning."

JesusFuckingChrist. "Ginny, did you have sex with your husband after he fought off the zombie?"

Ginny switched her weight from one foot to the other while the snot yo-yo reacted according to the corresponding laws of physics. "He lays with me every night. We've been trying to have a baby ever since we got married."

"It's a fucking zombie apocalypse and you were trying to have a baby?" I yelled.

Ginny nodded and I noticed her eyes were pointed in different directions. I pulled the trigger. She was close enough that my aim was perfect. One shot in the head and she jerked backwards, falling to the ground.

I climbed into my truck and drove down the road to the first farm on the left. I wasn't far in before I came to a fallen tree across the road. My chest seized for a minute before I noticed the jagged end where it had naturally cracked. *This isn't the doing of rednecks in the woods; calm down.* It was small, so I was able to slowly creep up and over it. Just ahead of it was a large mud puddle. I smiled. I loved going through the mud when I was riding at home. But the mud puddle stirred, and from the bottom of it, a zombie sat up and looked at me. He looked surprised to see a truck—if a zombie could be surprised. I was startled, but quickly reached for my gun, wound my window down, and aimed it at him, firing several times to make sure he was dead. I shot into the water in different spots to see if anything else was in there, but nothing moved, so I wound my window up and went through the puddle. It was the lake of all puddles, and deep in the middle, so I maneuvered on the side and pulled through.

When I reached the farmhouse, I put on my squirrel suit and armed myself. Speed was my best bet, but I needed the suit's protection. The fact that zombies could be in the house scared the shit out of me, but I was prepared. I yelled Katrina's name, telling her to come out, but no one exited the house. I heard a groan and a peculiar zap. I walked around the side of the house. Far off in the field, I saw a zombie tangled in the wire cow fence. Part of it must have had current running through it, so every so many moves, the electric would snap. It was an open field and nothing stirred except for the rotting flesh bag bouncing like a marionette in the wires. He stuck his tongue out and the tip touched the electric fence, giving him a jolt. I watched curiously as he did it a few times, as though he liked it. He didn't even notice me until he caught my smell, sniffed the air, and strained to twist his head unnaturally in my direction. I shot him twice in the face and he slumped over, still hanging from the wires.

"Masochistic fuck."

I walked back to the farmhouse, my eyes scoping for even the slightest movement in the fields. I noticed the curtains in one of second floor windows fall back, as though someone had pushed them aside to look out. That was a good sign—zombies didn't move curtains to look out windows, they just punched through the glass or fell out of them.

My footsteps creaked as I crossed the wooden porch. I entered the house and scanned the area quickly.

"Katrina, I know you can hear me. If you aren't infected, now is the time to show yourself." There was no stir or sound of movement. "I'm not one of those things, but Ginny's not coming back, so if you don't leave with me, you'll be here by yourself."

To be cautious, I put my squirrel head on. I paused and listened. I didn't hear her footsteps, but she appeared at the top of the steps. She was about thirteen years old, dirty, and had the widest eyes that were emotionless, yet locked on me. "Why are you dressed like a squirrel?"

I lifted the squirrel head back off. "The suit is bite-proof."

"Where's Mr. Dailey?"

"Who is Mr. Dailey?"

"Ginny's husband. He owns this farm."

I swallowed. "He's not coming back either."

"Is he dead?"

"Yes."

"Twice-dead or just once-dead, walking around trying to eat us?"

"Twice-dead."

"Did you kill him?" Her voice was flat and her eyes scanned me up and down before locking with mine.

"Yes. Ginny too. She was infected."

"Good."

I blinked and looked away. "Is there anyone else in the house?"

"No. But sometime they come—the once-dead." She paused. "What's your name?"

"Lucia."

"Do you sleep in a tree like a real squirrel? That would be a good idea because the once-dead can't climb trees."

I laughed, "No, I just sleep in my truck. But my, you're a clever girl."

"I was top of my class before they ate each other. Now I'm the only person in my class."

I was growing impatient from being out of the truck so long and because the uppers had me on edge. "So, are you coming with me?"

"Depends. Are you some sort of freak?"

"No, I'm not."

"Then we probably won't get along. I had high hopes you know, what with the squirrel suit and all."

"I mean I'm not a threat." Being confronted with a snarky teenager made me feel old and my coolness meter bottomed out.

"I know you're not a threat. I'm not afraid of you."

I looked at her with a raised eyebrow, considering if I even *wanted* to put up with a mouthy teenager. "Listen, it's your choice. If you would rather have a go of it on your own, you can keep your root cellar full of potatoes."

I turned and began walking out of the door when she spoke, "It depends on where you're going."

"Lake McArthur. I heard there are some other survivors there."

"No one's at Lake McArthur. It closes early in the fall."

"I heard people were going to meet up there."

"Why? Winters are hard there. We should go south."

"The south is infected and the zombies move slower in the cold. It's worth a try. If not, we can come back here if you'd like."

Katrina looked at me. "I don't want to come back here." I need to get my stuff though."

"Okay. How about I help?"

Katrina nodded and I climbed the stairs. Once at the landing, she opened one of the doors. Stacked inside were dozens of make-shift weapons: knives were tied and duct taped to a hula-hoop, chunks of broken glass were glued to a baseball, and even an ice chipper had been sharpened to a point.

"Wow, what a collection." I picked up the baseball. "This won't kill a zombie, you know?"

"They aren't the only thing we have to worry about," Katrina replied.

I looked at her, "I found that out the hard way, too." She began gathering clothes, stuffing them into a backpack, and tossing weapons into a pile. "So, you like weapons?"

"They've been handy," she said curtly.

"I'm from Pennsylvania."

She stopped and looked at me, "I don't care."

"Fuck, sorry." I went quiet.

"Look, the last person who tried to 'rescue' me told me all about himself and when he got killed, it just made it harder."

"Oh, yeah... right."

"It's okay; I killed him with a rock. I smashed his zombie face in when he tried to eat me."

My eyes widened. "Shit."

"See that machete on my dresser?" She nodded her head towards her left.

"Yeah."

"That was for Mr. Dailey. I swore I heard him growl at dinner last night. I was ready for him."

"Yeah, he was a growler."

"I've killed lots of the once-dead. Maybe fifty so far. How about you?"

"I've lost count. There are a few rednecks in there that might have gotten taken out with my bomb." I lied to make myself look like a worthy travel companion.

"Cool. A bomb? Can you make them?"

"Pfft... yeah. Easy." I shrugged my shoulders.

"I had to smash lots of skulls to get out of my school. Lunch trays, a locker door, even a cheerleading trophy—everything's a weapon."

"Nice."

"It wasn't *nice*. I had that zombie goo-blood all over me. Fuck that place."

I realized that talking to this girl might make for long days at the lake. I sighed. "What about your family, Katrina?"

"Kitty. My name's Kitty. Only my grandmother called me Katrina…and that shit-for-brains Mrs. Dailey. But fuck, that woman could make some amazing blueberry pancakes. Anyways, my family's dead. All of them."

I glanced at Kitty and gave her a sad look, "Mine too. I'm sorry."

"I'm not. They would have eaten me. My fucktard brother brought the virus home—he snuck out to meet his girlfriend and got bit in the woods. I locked them all in the house and set it on fire. Burn, baby, burn. You know, even zombies scream? You think they can't feel pain, but they can if it hurts bad enough. I can still hear it in my head." Kitty continued to pack as she talked. "Don't think I'm some creepy fuck cuz I killed my family. They were once-dead. I sent them off to Heaven on a funeral pyre. Hey, aren't those song lyrics?"

"I—I don't know…"

A sickening groan was muffled, but distinctly came from outside. I ran to the window and peered out. Below, near the barn, a zombie slowly shuffled. A tree was blocking my shot. I had to go outside. "I'm going out to kill it."

"I'm coming with you." Kitty grabbed a boat oar with several knives fastened to the end.

"The hell you are. Stay here; lock the door."

"I'm not some fucking kid. I can kill zombies."

"I know. You told me, remember? It's just safer if one of us stays here. If I don't come back, make a run for the truck—extra keys are under the passenger seat. Can you fire a gun?"

"I haven't tried yet."

I rolled my eyes. I unsnapped a Glock nesting in my holster and laid it on the bed. "Just aim for the head and pull the trigger." *Great, a fucking pyro, mouthy teenager who can't shoot.*

I ran down the steps and slid part of the way because of my suit. I bolted through the front door and faced the barn. The moaner moved slowly. The air was cold and I figured between that and the hunger, it was impeding his gimp limp. Maybe it was the desire to live for someone else, but I boldly got closer to the zombie than I normally did, and fired. The shots were precise and he dropped, motionless.

Kitty slid the bedroom window open and yelled, "Lucia, there are three more coming around the side of the barn!"

Instinctively, I ran towards the house, but stopped when I remembered we'd have to leave eventually. I saw a shed with an old wooden ladder propped against the side. Three decaying adults moved in shrugs and shuffles around the south side of the barn. I skirmished up the ladder and pulled it onto the roof with me. Moving in my squirrel suit made every agile feat much more difficult.

After I had dropped those three and four more appeared, I regretted leaving the Glock with Kitty. Counting bullets in my head wasn't helping my aim and I kept missing, firing off into the field or hitting the side of the barn.

Between waves of the dead, I'd steal glances up at Kitty hanging from her bedroom window and shout things to her that she probably couldn't understand through the muffle of my squirrel head. I quickly unzipped my suit and pulled my last gun from my holster. I did the math—the number of bullets divided by the number of zombies...I'd have to be a near-perfect shot and hope more did not come.

They must have heard me, or saw me standing on the shed roof. A yellow school bus followed by a man on a motorcycle sped down the driveway. The man on the motorcycle aimed and took down three zombies before he even dismounted. A woman with a rifle exited the bus and thinned the rotting heard with her impressive aim. I saw a little boy in the bus window, jumping in delight over the giant squirrel standing on a shed roof. I could almost smell my own hope.

We finished killing the zombies and paused as if all synchronized in our wait to see if more came. When they didn't, I removed my squirrel head and smiled at all of them. No one smiled back. They had tired eyes and old eyes—like they had already seen too much.

"Hi, I'm Lucia, and I'm definitely *not* infected."

CHAPTER 32

The Dailey Farm, British Columbia, Canada
Sharon

The Canadian Rockies rose up around me. I could feel the chill in the air as the day began its descent into evening. The taste of gravel dust coated my tongue as I followed the cloud stirred up by Gerry's motorcycle down the dirt road, towards the sound of gunfire.

Normally, it was a good idea to head away from gunshots, but things were far from normal. When we heard the shots, neither of us questioned it, we just went. We went for the sake of the living that those bullets promised. Nothing else mattered— that was my new normal.

A tree had fallen, blocking the road. Gerry could get past it, but I wasn't sure the bus would. The log was old, cracked, and jagged on one end. With a mighty tug, he moved it a few feet, allowing me to get by. Up ahead, a depression in the road had filled with mud and water, and in the middle floated a zombie. He hadn't died when the virus ran its course. This one had been shot, several times by the look of it.

I crept the bus along the edge of the small pond with Gerry following behind me. Gunshots fired again; I sped up, hoping that we would be in time. The road curved, and there before me was a farm: big white Victorian farmhouse, barn, shed, squirrel. I blinked at the apparition. A giant squirrel stood on the roof of the shed shooting into a crowd of zombies.

A thousand questions flew through my mind, but my new normal allowed me to suspend all of that. Whoever was in that suit needed help. And for once, I was able to offer it.

"Stay here, Parker," I said as I grabbed the rifle and opened the door. Gerry rode up behind me, firing into the crowd as he drove past. I was about fifteen feet away from the herd and paused a moment until he passed in front of me. They heard the noise of the bike and the bus and turned as one. I took aim and fired. The scope on the rifle made it easy. Line them up, pull the trigger, and drop the bastards.

A few moments later, it was over save the sound of gunfire echoing in the mountains. When the smoke cleared, the three of us stood there for a second to make sure that was all of them. Nothing moved, even the birds had fallen quiet. I lowered the rifle and looked at the squirrel.

"Hi, I'm Lucia, and I'm definitely *not* infected," the woman said after yanking the head off her squirrel costume. I wasn't surprised to discover it was a women. I just couldn't see a grown man dressed like that, but then... I let the thought go as useless, and looked up at her.

"How do we know you aren't infected?" I asked. She could be hiding anything under that costume.

"The suit is bite-proof, and see, no snot," she said, tilting her head back. Gerry snorted and walked over to the ladder that had fallen down. He propped it back up so that she could climb off the roof.

"Are you the only one here?" I asked, taking a moment to truly look around. Zombies littered the ground, the stench of them growing by the minute.

"No, there's a girl," Lucia said. "Her name is Katrina. She's not infected either," she finished, anticipating my next question.

"Where is she?" I asked, popping the magazine on the rifle. I hadn't been able to count my bullets and wanted to make sure I wasn't running low. Satisfied I had enough left, I snapped it back in and looked up at the woman who called herself Lucia. She was looking at the rifle and then blinked at me. I shrugged. It was a big ass rifle, what was there to say?

"She's in the house," she said, answering my question.

"Gerry, you want to stay out here, guard the bus, and watch for us while we go look for the girl?"

"Yeah, I'll go check on the kid," he said, and wandered off towards the bus. The fact that I felt comfortable leaving him alone with Parker made me pause. *What was it about him that let me trust him,* I wondered, sparing him a glance over my shoulder. I had found him hip-deep in a freezing river. I knew nothing about him, where he came from, or who he had been.

In the end, we were survivors in a world that had gone to hell. I shrugged again and walked up the wooden steps to the front porch, my boots sounding on the planks. I hadn't decided what I was going do about Gerry. Up until this morning, it had been just Parker and I. Now it seemed I was acquiring more people as the minutes wore on.

I grabbed the old screen door; it opened with a creak. I stopped and looked at the woman. "You want to call for her?"

"Katrina!" she shouted up the stairs. I heard a door open, the sound of footsteps, and then a girl appeared. She had a gun and was aiming it at me.

"You plan on shooting me?" I asked, more than a little annoyed.

"That depends," she said. I eyed her, looking for any signs of the virus. I didn't see any. She was holding a Glock, and I could see the indicator sticking out a little, telling me she didn't have a round chambered. I was willing to bet it wasn't loaded either.

"Pointing an empty gun at someone is a good way to get yourself shot," I said. She didn't react much beyond a widening of her eyes, but it was enough to give her away. She was bluffing. She lowered the gun and blinked at me.

"It's okay. You can come down," Lucia said, talking to her like you would a frightened animal.

"I'm not staying. But if you are, we can help you burn the bodies. You don't want them out there rotting. There are other diseases that are just as deadly as the Hauksson," I said as I turned and walked out onto the porch.

Gerry was wiping down his guns while Parker sat on his motorcycle pretending to drive it and making sound effects as he did so. I grinned and walked towards them with the squirrel and Katrina following along behind me.

"I'm heading back up to the lodge. I have food, supplies, and clean beds. You are all welcome to come up there. But we need to leave soon if we do. And we need to find some food.

"Um… there's all kinds of food in the cellar," Katrina said. "Mrs. Dailey was a Quaker or something. She liked to can what she grew in her garden."

"Gerry, are you coming?" I asked, squinting up at him. I probably wouldn't have asked if it had just been he and I, but with the addition of Lucia and the girl, I felt much more at ease with the idea.

"Got nowhere else to be," he said as he snapped his rifle shut.

"Okay, Katrina—"

"Kitty," she said.

"What?" I asked.

"People call me Kitty."

"Okay, Kitty, why don't you show us this cellar, and let's load up what we can."

"I've got some supplies in the truck over there." Lucia indicated a UPS truck that was parked on the side of the house.

"Do you have any more room in there?" I asked.

"Yes, there is room."

"Great," I said. "The bus is getting full. Let's load up Lucia's truck with as much as we can. What doesn't fit we'll cram in the bus."

"There's a tack shed on the side of the barn. Mr. Dailey kept his guns in there," Kitty said, pointing to the far side of the barn.

"Come on, kid," Gerry said to Parker. "Let's go see what we can find." I watched them walk over to the shed and yank the doors opened. A couple of chickens wandered out; Parker squealed with delight.

"Hey, Gerry," I shouted. "Why don't you catch those birds and bring them along? Fresh eggs will be pretty nice once it starts getting cold." He had pulled his sunglasses down so that I couldn't see the look in his eyes or what he was thinking, but I could imagine. I grinned and wandered into the house as Parker gave an excited whoop and ran after a brown chicken that squawked loudly in protest.

Kitty giggled, but when I looked at her, she quickly stopped. I guess there was a rule about giggling during the zombie apocalypse.

Hours later, we had Lucia's truck filled, wall to wall, with boxes of glass jars. Mrs. Dailey was a very industrious woman. Thanks to her efforts, we had enough fruits and vegetables to last us the winter, if we were careful.

One last pass-through of the house confirmed that we had stripped it of anything that we thought might be useful. As we left, I pulled the door shut behind me and then paused. It seemed silly to lock the door, but habits die hard. This had been someone's home and, I hoped, there had been love here. There would be no funeral for the Daileys. No mourners or anyone to tend to their graves. This was all I had to offer. I clicked the door softly shut behind me.

Lucia and Kitty climbed inside the UPS truck as I wandered over to the bus. What hadn't fit in the truck went in the bus. Boxes of ammunition along with several rifles and shotguns were stacked in one of the back seats.

"Did you find any slugs, or do we only have cartridges for the shotguns?" I asked Gerry.

"A little of both," he said.

"Buckshot won't kill a zombie," I said, though I was sure he knew that.

"Yeah," he nodded.

"Then why take them?" I asked.

"Because I can't bring myself to leave them behind," he said.

It was a logical answer, so I let it go.

"I found some fishing gear and decided to take that too."

"That's good. There's a lake up there, I'm sure it's well stocked. And the virus doesn't affect fish. It should be safe to eat what we catch," I said, running a hand through my hair.

The sun was starting to set, bringing the already chilly temperature down a few degrees. I heard the rumble of the truck as it started, nodded once at Gerry, and climbed aboard the bus.

Parker hopped over the seat and sat next to a cage with the brown chicken in it. "Can I name it, Aunt Sharon?" he asked, grinning at the bird who was poking at the vinyl seat through the wires of her cage.

"I don't see why not," I said as I started the bus. There were two other cages in the seat behind him, one with a white hen, the other with a black rooster. As the bus rumbled to life, they squawked and complained. It struck me as funny, and I laughed. Parker grinned from ear to ear as the bus bounced its way back down the dirt road before a UPS truck driven by a squirrel and a girl named Kitty, followed by the throaty growl of a Harley.

I laughed again. This was my new normal, and I was glad to have it.

CHAPTER 33

Gerry

I'd never been what anyone would consider vigilant or gung-ho, but recent events had changed me in many ways. Maybe it was playing protector to a bunch of pubescent Rambos for over a month, but I immediately took to these people, felt responsible for them.

Then again, this could be my subconscious attempt at atonement for what I'd done to those cultists. Either way, I was here and had made the choice to stay with them. Another thing I'd never been was much of a thinker. I decided to not over think this… whatever this was… too much, and stay with them until I felt the need to move on.

While rummaging through the kitchen drawers, looking for batteries or bandages, or anything we might find useful, I found a pair of walkie-talkies and docking charger on the kitchen counter. I checked them and they worked, so I loaded it all into a garbage bag to take with us. Parker was with me when I found them, and before taking off for 'The Lake', as the redhead called it, he asked for one so we could keep in contact during the ride.

I'd showed him how to press the button to talk, then let it go to listen, and to not mix them up or he'd get nothing but static. The 'thumbs-up' and big grin he displayed brought tears to my eyes, and I couldn't explain why.

When I handed the receiver to him, he immediately clipped it to the front of his coat, keyed the mic, and said, "All's clear here, Gerry. I'm movin' out."

"Oh no," I'd told him. "You can never use real names over the air. That's how the bad guys know who's who."

"So what should we call each other?"

"Let me think on that and I'll get back to you before we take off for your mom's lake."

"Gross. She's not my mom. She's my aunt—aunt Sharon."

My heart sank. I didn't want to think about what might've happened to his parents. I shooed him off to help the teenager—Kat or Kitty, or something like that—with the boxes of preserves from the basement.

He'd nodded. "She's funny. She swears a lot." He keyed the mic, winked and whispered, "Ten-four, good buddy."

And then he was gone, racing like only a kid can, over to the girl. He'd arrived at her side in time for her to drop a box on her foot, kick the box, then scream, "Fuck this shit! Fuck it all to Hell!"

*

"This is the Big Ragoo, calling the Fonz, over."

I grinned and looked up at the rear window of the bus in front of me. Parker's nose was pressed up against it, fogging it over. He probably couldn't see me through the film, but I waved all the same.

Since leaving the farm—Kitty and the squirrel in the UPS truck, Sharon and 'the Big Ragoo' in the bus, and me on Old Faithful—Parker had kept me apprised of the situation as he saw it from inside the bus. His chicken was apparently in the middle of some sort of coup, trying to escape its cage by eating its way through the vinyl seat.

I keyed my mic, "This is Fonzie, over. What is it this time, Big Ragoo? Did one of the birds lay an egg? Over."

"Uh-uh, over. My chicken's a guy chicken. Over"

"Then what is it?"

"You didn't say over. Over."

When he said that, I thought of Justin and his comrades. One of them had said that same thing as they stood in the driveway in their coveralls. I spared a thought for them as I throttled to catch up to the bus. I honked, and Parker drew a lopsided smiley face in the steam on the window.

I keyed my mic, "Sorry. What's up? Over."

"Huh? Oh, yeah. You said to let you know if I saw anything, over."

"OK," I said. "What did you see?"

He didn't answer, and I grew alarmed. "Parker? Are you there, little buddy?"

"You still didn't say over. Over."

I chuckled. "OK, you got me there. What is it? Over."

"Doggies. I saw doggies. Over."

My heart raced but I fought to remain calm. It would do me no good spooking the kid. I checked my mirrors, saw nothing right away, but then a blur shot across the dirt road about five-hundred yards back.

"There," Parker screamed gleefully into the walkie-talkie. "Did you see it?"

"Big Ragoo," I said, remaining as calm as possible, knowing that any second a dog might dive from the trees and attack. "I need you to keep your cool and do something for me… something important. Over."

"Sure. What?"

"Give the radio to your aunt for a sec. I just need to tell her something. Over."

"Hehe, I forgot to say over and you didn't catch me. Over."

"Good one, Big Ragoo, now can you hurry up and give Sharon the radio? Over."

The next voice I heard was Sharon's. She cut straight to the point.

"Is there something up?"

"Yes," I said. "Dogs. Wild ones."

"So?"

"Remember when you found me at the lake?"

She giggled. "Yes. Are you going to tell me dogs tore your clothes off?"

"No. They were chasing me, and I don't think they were looking to be scratched behind the ear."

There was a pause, then she said, "What should we do about it?"

"We? Nothing. You guys keep on toward your lake. I'll stay back here and deal with it so the kids don't see."

"No. We all go or we all stay," she stated firmly. "As tough as it will be for Parker to see, this is our reality now."

"No, you go on. There were only two, and I think they were poodles or some shit. Really, I'm good. I'll catch up to you after I put them out of my misery."

Sharon didn't say anything for a long time, but Parker had returned to the rear window and was clapping and pointing excitedly over my shoulder.

Just as I was about to key the mic to repeat myself, Sharon's voice came through: "Fine, but if you get eaten by poodles, I'm going to make jokes about it later on."

"If that happens you totally have my permission to dis me after death."

I slowed to a stop, hit the kickstand, and then swung my leg over the bike. Above the uneven chug of my engine, I heard them. They were close. I'd counted four of them back in Field, but these might not have even been the same dogs. For all I knew they could have ended up being fucking werewolves. Whatever they were, though, they weren't following us to the lodge. We had enough problems ahead without having to fend off a pack of dogs, like Grizzly Adams or some shit.

I don't know if it was boldness in the fact that they had me surrounded, or that they were so desperate they didn't care, but one by one they padded out onto the dirt road and stalked—yes, stalked—toward me. In all, at least from what appeared before me in the road, there were five mutts, a pair of tan-and-white cockers, and a wraith-thin German Shepherd. Great, the four I'd seen earlier had brought friends.

But so did I. And I also had a plan, sort of.

Before loading supplies into the UPS van back at the farm, I'd procured a few weapons and some ammo for the trip back to the lodge. Thank God one of them was the six-shot pump shotgun I hoisted from where it hung from the back of my bitch seat.

I scanned the surrounding trees until I found one with a low enough branch for me to hoist myself up, then took off toward it, firing over my shoulder as I ran. I made it there ahead of the dogs, but just barely. One of the cockers had latched onto my pant leg and it took a few shakes to kick it free.

Once situated, I swung the big shotgun over my shoulder and lowered it to fire. Four of the dogs exploded into piles of twitching, fuzzy sausage links, but three others scattered and ran. At the back of my mind, even as I chambered another round, my head-count came up one short. The Shepherd had disappeared. The three that had run away didn't run far. Hunger, combined with the promise of fresh meat, overpowered their flight instinct. I had only to wait for them to try to move in and eat the dead dogs below the tree, and—*boom*—they'd be soup.

"Here, boys," I whispered, as I lined up the closest one, one of the caramel cockers. "Come and get it: fresh, meaty Rover surprise. Yum-yum."

I was so engrossed in watching the smaller dogs slink toward me that I'd forgotten about the Shepherd, which hadn't chased me up the tree with the rest of them. I'd foolishly thought it was smart enough to take off when I first fired. As it turned out, not so much. Also, a fact I decided to remember if I lived through the ordeal, was that Shepherds, while they are big, heavy dogs, can jump like motherfuckers.

In my panicked state, I saw it lunge at the last second from the corner of my eye—a snarling, flying bear, soaring in to snatch me up and eat my guts for breakfast. It knocked me from the tree and lunged for my throat even before we struck the ground. Instinctively, I grabbed him by the upper front legs and twisted, so I'd land on top. When we hit the ground, I heard a snap as my elbow sunk deep into the fur at its neck. Before I could gain my feet, the remaining three dogs were on me, tugging ineffectually at my pants and leather coat. All three dogs were small and likely weakened from hunger and constantly having to outrun the deadies, so finishing them off was easy. The hard part would come later, after I fell asleep and dreamed of this.

Yes, these dogs would've eventually led the dead up the mountain to the lodge, but knowing that didn't stop the ache in my heart for killing them. Most of them wore tags; they'd been some kid's best friend. Then I thought of Parker and Kitty. I'd had no trouble with the dogs because I'd been able to shut myself away from the emotions that would've allowed them to kill me. I don't know much about greater good, but I think that's what this was. I filed the experience away in my head vault under 'Mercy Killing', then mentally slammed the drawer.

If there'd been any more dogs, I'm sure they would've already tried to take a chomp out of me, so I wiped any telltale signs of blood from my jacket and hopped back on my bike. In minutes, I was behind the bus. Sharon waved at me from her rear-view.

I honked and Parker appeared at the rear window. He pointed at his walkie-talkie, then at me, and shrugged. My hand went to my collar, but the radio was gone.

I thought back to the Shepherd and the crunch I'd heard when we landed. The radio had saved my life. When it lunged for my throat, it had latched onto the radio instead of me. I smiled, suddenly—but not for the first time—thinking there might just be someone up there in the sky watching over me.

I winked up at him, jabbed a thumb over my shoulder and returned his shrug. By the time we stopped I'd figure out a shiny enough lie for him.

When I spotted what must be the lodge up ahead, I saluted at him, then throttled up and passed the bus and UPS van. I thought it would be best if I took the lead. The term 'ladies first' was cool and all, but wasn't very practical during a zombie apocalypse.

CHAPTER 34

Lucia

I had two things going for me—the allure of my friendly squirrel suit, and my enthusiastic joy at seeing other humans. I assumed the group found those two qualities things they either couldn't repel, or couldn't escape. I gushed all over them like shit on a Velcro toilet seat. I forgot things like I was an outsider, and how just a week ago I had encountered humans that did not value my life.

I asked their names over and over again, not because I couldn't remember them, but it was a simple joy to encounter humans with names...humans with clear eyes, four limbs, and who didn't smell like a cadaver omelet. If they were a field of daisies, I was rolling all over them. I resisted hugging and kissing all of them. I even told them my name—my real name. I wanted to chatter and be chatted to, but Sharon was too sensible and organized to allow me to piss away our sunlight.

Even Parker helped to carry things into the house, although we hadn't even come close to unloading everything. The last trip between the trucks and the lodge was made when the sky was a dusky purple. My UPS truck and all of the items I'd been hoarding remained my only connection to comfort over the past few weeks. But now… now I'd have a *home.*

The lodge was beautiful—like a retreat I'd once visited in some buried part of my subconscious because I'd been performing duties on auto-pilot for too many days. The others tolerated my paranoia as I tested each window and door to make sure they were locked…then I searched every room. Once I felt safe, I settled down and started checking all of the people. We were all 'fine'.

Survivors didn't know how to be anything other than okay. Life was a slippery incline down from handling everything and at the bottom was the only option—being eaten alive. I suspected none of us had any choice but to keep climbing upwards over the past few weeks.

Sharon was upstairs, running a bubble bath in the Jacuzzi for Parker. "It's nice to hear a child laugh," I said. "I never thought I'd hear that again. The last kids I heard hissed and growled at me." Kitty's demeanor was drained as she slumped in her chair, listening to me. "I'm glad we have him."

"I'm not." She gave me a horrified look. "I mean, as bad as this world was, the one he'll grow up in is even worse. I want to cry for him."

"It makes staying alive that much more important," I said as I slowly stood up from the couch." I should help Gerry—he's trying to scrape dinner for five out of such an odd array of supplies."

"I guess I have to help?" Kitty asked as she reluctantly rose.

I jumped up and grabbed her arm. "Nonsense. Stay here and I'll help him."

She sat back down and I went into the back kitchen area. Gerry was frying potatoes and I smelled corn bread. "Well, damn! You can cook."

"Are you surprised?" he asked.

"No, just thankful as fuck. I wasn't sure what I'd find when I came back here. Want some help?"

"You're going to cook in that squirrel suit?"

"Seriously, you'll thank me. This fur is the only barrier between you and the smell of a girl that hasn't taken a shower in weeks. Baby wipes just don't get the job done, if you know what I mean."

Gerry laughed and handed me two apples. "Cut these up for the kids. I could only find two, so we'll let them have them. I don't know where everything's at in this kitchen, so there might be more apples."

"Ha! Don't let Kitty hear you calling her a kid. She's 13 going on 45," I said. Gerry chucked and nodded his head. "How long have you been here?"

"I'm new, just like you."

"Oh." My mouth watered as I cut the apples into neat sections. "So, you just met Sharon too?"

"Yep." He stirred the potatoes in the skillet and cracked the oven door to peek at the corn bread.

"I thought Sharon was your wife at first."

Gerry shook his head. "None of us are related. We've all lost our families."

"Yeah, me too. I mean—obviously. I'm alone, so..."

"You wanna set the table when you're done?"

"Sure!" I was thankful he changed the subject. We all wore our loss differently, but there was a familiarity to it that we could all sense.

*

I sat at the end of the table near Parker. I'd never seen a child awash with sadness more than him, so I insisted I was a squirrel and had to eat like one. He laughed when I held a potato slice with the tips of both of my hands and nibbled it. I stuffed my cheeks with cornbread and tried to hold a straight face. I looked down at Kitty, Sharon, and Gerry, my cheeks round and expanded, and said, "What?" They all laughed and I started to chew.

"Okay, seriously," I leaned across the table towards Parker, "I'm only half-squirrel. It's like my super-hero alter-ego. The other half of the time I'm just an ordinary person, so I'm not always going to pretend I'm a squirrel, okay?"

He nodded his head and giggled. I winked at him, "Our secret...sshhh."

So many questions were pounding at me to ask the group, but we settled on polite get-to-know-you conversation, carefully sidestepping our predicament and zombie talk while Parker was at the table. After dinner, Kitty took Parker off to play and we gathered in the main room to talk.

"I have a lot of supplies in my UPS truck. I'd like to carry all of it inside and I'm excited for you guys to see the stuff I have."

"The bus is pretty full, too." Sharon nodded.

"True," Gerry nodded his head at Sharon. "We can take turns tomorrow: two carriers, one lookout, and one person can stay inside with Parker."

I liked the idea of having a lookout. I was still terrified, even though I'd been alone for so long. There was safety in numbers—that was in the zombie guide book that I assumed none of us had ever read.

"I also think we should set up some sort of booby-traps around the lodge. Maybe some type of alert system or something. Not too long ago, I ran into a bunch of rednecks who had established some sort of camp and they were hostile."

"I encountered an interesting group like that as well," Gerry nodded.

Sharon's eyes widened. "How frightening! I assumed some of the population would turn out that way. I think the booby traps are a good idea."

"Maybe after we gather all of our supplies we can see what we have that's useful."

"We don't have many supplies left in the lodge, so I think it's a good idea," Sharon said. "I hear the kids quieting down. I think it's their bedtime."

Sharon slid to the edge of her seat, "How should we do this? Break off into rooms?"

"I don't know if I'll be able to sleep. This place is so big. Shouldn't we take turns being lookout?" I asked.

The group exchanged glances, and Gerry spoke up, "I'll take lookout for tonight and the rest of you can sleep."

"You'll be so tired for tomorrow though, Gerry," Sharon said.

"A nap in the morning, some coffee, and I'll be fine," he said.

Sharon raised her eyebrows, "Are you sure?"

"Yes, I'm sure. Now go off to bed."

I scratched my arm through my squirrel suit. "I can't sleep just yet. I'll stay awake with Gerry until I'm ready to sleep. Does it matter which bedroom I take?"

"Nope, any one is fine," Sharon said. "Parker and I are in the one to the left of the top of the stairs. I'll put Kitty in the end room beside ours because it has its own bathroom."

"Oh, I think she'll like that," I said.

We all said goodnight as Sharon went upstairs.

Gerry looked at me, "Well, I've been dying to make some of her coffee."

"Cool! I'll watch."

We stood up and I followed him into the kitchen. He pulled the coffee pot out, plugged it in, filled the pitcher with water, and then turned around and looked at me. I was wide-eyed, watching him, just as I said I would.

"Are you always this… alert?" he asked.

"Oh, no. I'm high on amphetamines," I said with a giant smile. "Don't worry, I'm not some drug addict. I've just been taking them to stay awake since I've been alone."

"You don't say," he laughed.

"I'm sure I'll crash soon. I haven't taken any since before I met you guys."

"That'll be one hell of a crash." He scooped coffee into the filter and shut the lid. His mug was ready in his hand when the machine stopped dripping the coffee into pot.

"Do you miss coffee?" I asked.

"Yes, I haven't had a cup in weeks." He held the full cup between his hands and took a cautious sip. "Do you want a cup?"

"No thanks. I don't need another thing that'll keep me awake."

"I bet. Wanna go back into the big room?"

"Yep!"

I followed him and stood in front of the fireplace. "It's so nice and warm. I feel like I've been cold for so long." I sat on the floor in the glow of the fire. "So, tell me about yourself."

*

I woke up, curled in a ball, with my hands under my head. The fire wasn't as big, but Gerry was still sitting in the same chair he had been in when I fell asleep. I quickly sat upright.

"What happened?" I asked.

Gerry looked up from his book. "You fell asleep exactly two minutes into my life story."

"I'm sorry."

"That's okay." He took a sip of his coffee.

"What are you reading?"

"*Still Life with Woodpecker.* Have you ever read it?"

"No." I squirmed around and combed my hair with my fingers. "Did I snore?"

Gerry smiled. "No."

"Now I know you're lying."

"Honest, you didn't snore, and if you did, I wouldn't have heard it over all of your farting."

"Gerry!" I made a scrunchy face and turned red.

"Calm down, I'm just kidding. You were as quiet as a squirrel rug."

I shot him a doubtful look.

"I swear. I nearly wiped my feet on you. You didn't make a sound."

*

Not long after I woke up, Gerry and I made breakfast. The others came downstairs just as we finished it. Sharon tried to hide her yawns, but we all noticed.

"I'd ask you how you slept, but I'm sure you'd say 'fine'," I said.

"How did you know?" she smiled.

"Because we'd all say that."

Parker insisted I eat my breakfast like a squirrel, and a large amount of crumbs collected in my fur.

"Are you the Super-Squirrel since you still have your suit on?" Parker asked.

I nodded my head and winked at him. "I'm almost never a real girl anymore."

"You know, you kinda smell," Parker said.

"Oh yeah, well that's one of my super powers." I glanced down the table at the others. "What? I'll shower as soon as I get a chance."

"Squirrels don't shower," laughed Parker.

"I know. Squirrels hate water, that's why I've been avoiding it. I'd rather just groom myself." I licked the back of my hand and pretended to stroke it down my hair a few times. "All better."

Parker leaned over the table a little bit and sniffed loudly. "I don't think that worked."

Parker giggled and I sighed. After we were done eating, we all rushed Gerry off to take a nap while I cleaned up, and Kitty and Sharon spent time with Parker.

*

Gerry and I decided to unload the vehicles while Kitty was lookout.

"We need to do this fast. You unload onto a pile and I'll carry it into the house." He gave the instructions as he checked around the yard.

"It's so quiet here," I said, looking around at the woods.

"Don't think about it. You'll just spook yourself. Ready?"

It had snowed a little the night before, and the wind was cold. My fur suit kept me warm, but not warm enough. It was too hard to unload things with my squirrel head on, so I had left it inside the lodge.

After lunch, when we returned outside to finish unloading, I could see three zombies pawing at the truck. I wondered if they could smell my scent from living in there and if they'd always gathered around previously-inhabited areas for that very reason. They moved slowly—like frozen zombies—and Gerry easily picked them off.

Sharon came out onto the porch, her rifle ready. He waved her away and yelled, "It was just a three-bullet problem."

She nodded her head and went back inside.

"Were you so fast because you are scared?" I teased him.

"No, my fucking balls retreated up inside of me once we came back out into the cold."

"Yeah, I'm missing that fireplace," I said.

"Me too," Kitty's teeth chattered, "so let's hurry the fuck up."

Everything was desolate and still. "I think the rumors that zombies don't like the cold are true," I said.

"Let's hope so." Kitty held the scope of the rifle to her eye and scanned the woods.

Even though she was still young, Kitty was strong. I smiled. *Safety in numbers,* I thought.

CHAPTER 35

Dublin, Ireland
Paul

William Boland, the Taoiseach's aide, handed me a glass of whiskey and took a seat opposite me. Everybody else had left the room, busy bees that they were.

"Single malt," he said. "Might as well enjoy the good stuff." He swirled the amber liquid in his own glass and tipped it back, savouring the flavour before swallowing.

"Thanks," I answered. It was very fine indeed. *Nothing but the best for these government pricks,* I thought.

"Okay, look, this is the story," he began. "Professor Tompkins, probably our top man in the field, at least the top man still alive, has been working in a secure laboratory underneath Trinity College. He and his team hope to find a vaccine in conjunction with other scientists around the world. They need to get their research to a facility in Canada. I can't go into details; I'm sure you can understand, but the Taoiseach and what's left of the government are relocating there. It's ironic really—many of the world's governments have finally come together, united in a common cause when it is probably too late."

I held up a hand. "What? The government are fucking off to Canada? What does that mean?"

He sighed and drank again. "Look, Ireland is finished as a country; we've lost all our towns and cities. There is a seat on the plane for you, if you want it."

This was all coming at me too fast. Finished? Canada? Only a couple of hours ago I was running for my life through the deserted streets of Dublin.

"Is all hope gone?" I asked.

"No," Boland answered. "We'll regroup, find a vaccine, and then hopefully try and rebuild.

"Jesus!"

"Some have gone already; more will follow."

"What about those left out there, what about the survivors?" I could feel my anger start to rise. "And why fucking Canada?"

"Look, I can't go into specifics. The infected move slower in the cold. That's why Captain O'Neill and his squad patrol at night, looking for survivors, foraging and protecting us. We are trying to find as many as we can."

"But what about the ones you don't find? Are you just going to abandon them?"

"As soon as Tompkins arrives we are leaving. You are welcome to be on that plane." He drained his glass and stood up.

I thought about Gary and the others—were they doomed? Maybe I should have thought about that before I burned the fucking building down. The least I could do was give Sean and his army chums the address and ask them to keep an eye out for the dozy gobshite.

"Make sure he doesn't leave any doors open," I said.

Sometime later, after several more whiskies and another nap, I got a nudge. It was Sean. "Paul, Professor Tompkins is here. We're taking you lot to the airport. Time to shift, bud."

The whole thing just felt surreal. I'd barely had time to catch my breath, and I was heading off to Canada, of all places.

"Sean?" I grabbed his arm, and he turned. "Is this it? Is this the end of us… everything… mankind?"

"Fucked if I know," he answered.

"What about you? Won't you be coming?" I asked.

"Not this time. We'll take you to the airport and then come back. There'll be other planes; we'll follow eventually. When I get there, we'll have a beer."

"I'm buying," I said. I was genuinely sad. I could not help but feel that the longer anybody stayed here, the more likely it was to be staying for good. Then again, was where we were going likely to be any better?

The door opened, and another soldier walked in. He was carrying something wrapped with a green cloth.

"We've got you a present," Sean said, taking the bundle from the other soldier. "You were so good with that thing on your belt, we thought this might serve a bit better." He handed it over to me.

"Holy shit!" My eyes widened. It was a replica double blade battle axe, complete with stainless steel head and wire wrapped handle. "This is bleedin' deadly," I said, giving a few experimental swings. I threw Robbie's fireman's axe away without a backward glance.

When we went outside, it was still dark. I could see shapes moving slowly around beyond the main gates of the courtyard. A shiver ran down my spine. *I'm leaving,* I thought, *but this is far from over.* Nothing got in the way of the armoured car; what it could not go around it went either through or over.

Professor Tompkins was a right narky prick, even becoming irritable with the Taoiseach. He also kept sneezing over our glorious leader. His rudeness was tolerated. I suppose you get away with more when you have the potential to save mankind.

When we arrived at the airport, the sun was starting to come up. The sky was turning a peculiar shade of orange. I probably would have thought it a nice view if it was not the end of the world. We drove straight up to the plane—a government Lear jet. I was going in style. I could hear the whirring of the engines the moment I stepped from the Mowag.

There were more Army milling around the runway. They had done a pretty good job of securing the area, for the moment at least. I could see, beyond a wire fence bordering the tarmac, hundreds of infected clambering against the barrier.

"Let's get this show on the road and the fuck outta here before they start getting active," a voice full of authority shouted.

Suited me. I was happy to get on that plane. As well as me, the Taoiseach and the scientist, there were several soldiers, Boland, and three of Tompkins' assistants. As I walked up the steps, I heard a crash from the rear of the plane. The scientists all stopped as Tompkins let out a roar.

"Bloody idiots!" he shouted, and gesticulated at a group of soldiers who had dropped a wooden crate they were loading into the cargo hold.

"It's okay, Professor, they'll have more and better equipment where we are going. What's important is what you carry in your briefcase," one of the assistants said to placate the narky git. It seemed to calm him, and with a grunt he carried on into the plane.

We were travelling in luxury: plush leather armchairs, tables between facing seats. I noticed for the first time that Tompkins had a brown leather satchel handcuffed to his wrist, similar to one an old school master would have carried his lunch into school in. At least, as far as I can remember, they only ever had their lunch in there. I suppose they may have held the odd book or two. He turned and caught me looking at his case. Our eyes met, and he shot me a look as if I'd just slid my hand up his girlfriend's skirt.

Prick.

"You really were in the right place at the right time." The Taoiseach smiled across at me. I nodded a grateful smile. *I'm still not going to vote for you, you wanker.* Tompkins sneezed again, followed by two of his assistants. Jesus, I survive a city full of zombies, and I'll die from the flu.

As the plane taxied down the runway, I suddenly looked up. "Shit!"

"What? What is it?" Boland looked around, his face wide with alarm.

"We forgot about the duty free," I said. Nobody laughed.

I looked out of the window at Dublin Bay and the surrounding countryside, the patchwork fields and tiny buildings dotted about, wondering, would I ever see it again? Was there even anybody I knew left alive? Once we went through the clouds, I tilted my chair back and fell into a restless sleep.

I dreamt somebody was screaming—a high pitched wail of terror and desperation. It was so realistic it jolted me out of my slumber. Funny enough, when I woke, the screaming had not stopped.

Oh shit!

The assistant who earlier had placated Tompkins was on his feet with his jaws buried into the neck of one of the soldiers. Suddenly there was pandemonium in the small plane; everybody was on their feet. The second soldier had his sidearm out and pumped several rounds into the head of the scientist; blood sprayed everywhere before he dropped. The soldier turned to his friend then and, without a second thought, put a bullet between his eyes.

The world had become a fucked up place.

I heard a snarl from behind. One scientist was baring his teeth in a grin of pure evil at me. He got a smack in the face from a battle axe for his trouble. The second scientist clambered up the wall of the plane and dropped behind me. The Taoiseach tried to fend him off with an arm. The zombie scientist took a chunk out of it.

One of the pilots opened the door of the cockpit to see what the trouble was. He took one look and slammed the door. I heard the lock sliding into place. *Bastard.*

The Taoiseach got a bullet in the head from the soldier.

"You shot the fuckin' Taoiseach!" I said—some guard he was. He did not have time to respond, as the scientist was on him.

I saw Boland unclip his seatbelt and make a run for the door.

"What are you doing?" I said in horror as his hand reached for the lever.

"I can't die like this!" He'd snapped, I realised. I did not know much about aerodynamics, or pretty much anything for that matter, but I'd seen enough James Bond movies to know that opening the door was not a good idea. I made a grab for him.

Too late.

At first, it was blind panic as I tried to swim through the air. It didn't work. Below me, a blanket of white and green kept coming up faster and faster.

Oh shit! Please don't let this hurt too much.

I spotted Boland ahead of me; the bastard had a parachute strapped to his back. I made myself into a dive-bomb and aimed for him. It wasn't much of a chance, but it was the only chance. I hit him hard, grabbed for his jacket, and clung on just as he pulled the cord.

Jesus Christ! I did not like that. I've never even liked roller-coasters. I was screaming my lungs out; my breath was just as quickly snatched by the rushing wind. After the initial rush of the chute opening and slowing our descent, my emotions calmed to simple blind terror. Strangely, Boland appeared very quiet, all things considered.

I realised my eyes had been closed the whole time. When I opened them, I was looking straight into Boland's face. He did not look well. *Who would blame him*, I thought. His glare was focused on me, but seemed uncomprehending, which was odd considering I was clinging onto him for dear bloody life, God only knew how many thousand feet in the air.

Then I saw the blood on his collar. Had he been shot? I craned my neck, slowly. Half his ear was… oh shit! The words tumbled through my head: bite, infected.

His eyes widened and his brow furrowed as if he were in great pain; a string of translucent snot, like a trailing egg-white, hung from his nose. A strangled sob escaped from his open mouth. For a moment I forgot where I was and jumped with fright—it was enough. My arms grabbed at fresh air; my legs tried to run like an old time cartoon.

We were just about to hit the trees. It was crash, bang, wallop as I fell through the forest canopy, hitting pretty much every branch on the way down. I lost sight of Boland as I struggled to grab hold of something, anything. I braced myself as best I could. This was going to hurt.

Strangely though, it didn't. The hard earth seemed to cushion my fall; more than that, it embraced me, drew me in. I had the strangest sensation of being wrapped in a damp, pungent blanket made of moss and soil and sodden leaves. I felt as if I were sinking into a mattress made of the softest feathers and being wrapped in a duvet smelling of spring and winter all rolled into one.

Then I was falling… falling through dark earth into a thick white sheet, solid, compact. Only the ice was not hard or freezing; it welcomed me, called to me. I saw a herd of woolly mammoths, their great shaggy hides shambling along trunk to tail, with the smallest one at the back. A great cat the size of a pony, with sabres for teeth, stalked the herd. The lead mammoth raised his trumpet and blew a long, low note of mourning into the air.

In a flash, the hunter and prey were gone. A huge lizard raised a heavy head into the air, rows of razor sharp teeth dripping red grinned at me as it bellowed its annoyance and frustration in my direction, before returning to rip at the side of a horned beast it had slain.

Finally, I was released by the frozen womb of the earth and left to lie next to a boiling cauldron of bubbling mud and molten rock. A myriad of colours danced before my vision, crawling from the primordial soup. Billions of single-celled creatures snaked towards me, all individual, all part of the collective. They inched up my arm, my legs, over my face. *Virus:* the word tumbled through my mind, echoing along the dark corridors of my subconscious. I'm infected.

No! I am the infection. I am the virus.

Then all went black.

CHAPTER 36

Lucia

"Let's dig a wide ditch surrounding the entire lodge, fill it with oil, and light it on fire. That'll keep the zombies away." Kitty nodded her head as she spoke. The overstuffed chair in the lodge had nearly swallowed her. At the rate she was sinking, in a few minutes, I'd be able to squint my eyes and just see a talking head mounted on a piece of furniture.

Sharon's neck snapped to her left as she looked at Kitty. "It's also likely that we'd burn the entire lodge down, as well as a sizable amount of Canadian wilderness.

"I'm just day dreaming," Kitty sighed.

"Sick of zombies?" Gerry chuckled.

"Ha! Can you tell?" Kitty shifted in the chair, but sank deeper. "Well, does anyone have any other ideas?"

"I have one." I spoke up suddenly and surprised myself with my own voice. "Maybe we should cut a hole in the roof and make a trap door, not only as an alternate escape route, but so that we can walk the roof to scout for zombies. I'm not sure if it's possible to do so and maintain the integrity of the roof's structure, but I for one would like an escape hatch."

"Sure, we can cut a hole in the roof—climb up through the attic and mount a ladder of some sorts. I saw some wood stacked in the shed that we could use, and a Sawzall is in the basement," Gerry said.

"Great idea..." Sharon paused. "I don't want to start a panic, but with all of the windows in the lodge, this place isn't really secure, even with the shutters. We should board up the ground floor windows from the inside as well. I think that is our first priority."

Everyone exchanged glances and nervously muttered their agreements at the same time.

Gerry sipped his coffee and then spoke, "Soon the ground will be frozen. With only four adults, I don't think we really have the time or the resources to spend digging pit traps. Besides, they'd only maim a zombie, and even the ones missing limbs will still crawl after us for some brain chow. We could string up tin cans and things like that around our perimeter so we could hear them approaching. That might be more effective. What we really need is some C4."

Kitty picked a copy of "Trout Stream Fishing" magazine off of the table next to her and fanned herself. "Yeah, some C4 and tacos would just about make my fucking day." Everyone looked at her and she shrugged.

I scratched myself under my squirrel suit again. "Before we start booby trapping the place, can I take a shower? I smell like squirrel funk."

"We noticed," Sharon laughed.

My eyes widened, "Hey, end of the world and all…"

"Yeah, you can shower, then you can help Gerry and me haul all of the lumber inside to board up the windows. Kitty can watch Parker, then two of us can secure the windows while the other two string cans together," Sharon said.

*

As I showered, I felt like I was scrubbing zombie soot off of my skin—the dirt from traveling for weeks with fear seeping out of me, and the collection of things baby wipes hadn't washed away. A year of showers wouldn't make me feel clean—I was certain of it. My hair sat in a lathery dollop on the top of my head and my entire body was covered in suds. I stood and let it soak in for a minute, laughing at the realization that I'd exchanged a squirrel costume for a soap suit. I rinsed myself off and emerged from the shower, now keenly aware of the scent wafting from my squirrel suit which lay crumpled on the bathroom floor where I had left it. I'd hand washed it a few times, but knew it was time to toss it into the washing machine, even if it did shrink.

After I dressed, I walked down the steps to find everyone already working on stringing the cans together.

"All ready?" Gerry asked.

"Yep!" I said.

Kitty locked herself and Parker inside of the lodge while Sharon and I took turns helping Gerry carry the lumber, alternating who kept watch for zombies. I nearly suggested the lookout was unnecessary when I heard a rustling in the woods. I took two steps to approach the noise, but retreated back to wait for it to come to me. "Gerry, Sharon… I hear something," I called over my shoulder. As they arrived, two female zombies emerged from behind a tall pine tree. The one in the lead was a dirty, blonde-haired girl with a large bite mark on her cheek. The matted hair nearest her face was colored red from blood. She wore a t-shirt that said, "Don't Mess With Texas", but her abdomen was partially exposed and tangled in her rib cage was the exceptionally long hair of a second obese zombie, thus creating a leash of sorts by which the first zombie led the second around like a dog.

Gerry stood behind me and exhaled. "Huh. I wonder how that happened?"

Sharon's voice dripped disgust. "They were probably in a feeding frenzy, fighting over a meal."

"Great. Ugly and her pet, Cerberus," I moaned, "just when I thought I'd seen it all."

Gerry raised his pistol and shot Cerberus first. Her backwards jerk released her as her hair ripped from the other's sweater. "Nice," I said. "That was easy; too bad they couldn't figure it out sooner. She must have been a dumb one."

Gerry shot the other zombie, but she didn't go down. She was still moving as though the other was still connected to her. Sharon raised her rifle and the woman's head popped open, stopping her abruptly.

"Damn," Gerry said, "some bitches never know when to die… again."

I coughed. "It was almost poetic how the one fucked the other one over, even after death. If she'd been smart enough to realize that, she could have survived."

Sharon shrugged, but turned her head towards another noise. An elderly woman darted from the woods. Her blonde hair swirled around her head, seeming to move in a circular pattern from all of the maggots eating at her scalp. Lodged in her teeth was a finger—it might have been hers, since one hand was missing.

"I got this one," Sharon laughed as she skillfully shot the woman in the head. Her body shuddered, and she made a bleating noise before falling sideways to the ground. "Problem solved."

Gerry stood over the body. "Fuck, this one was a regular old crypt-keeper pre-virus." He returned to the shed, and we followed him.

*

The drills Gerry found in the basement made securing the windows go faster than I expected. Kitty and Sharon talked as they strung metal utensils—since they'd run out of empty cans—to the twine. Although Gerry and I were involved in our project, we could hear them share stories of their lives before the virus. Kitty had a large family that was all dead. The pain vibrated in her voice as she recanted how they'd all been infected before she fled her home. I assumed the only reason she didn't break down and cry was because it was a story she'd told a thousand times over in her head each day since. Sharon recounted the scene where she rescued Parker, talking in a whisper so he couldn't hear her as he played upstairs. There was a pause when Sharon choked, just before ending her story.

Boarding the windows blocked the sunshine that made the lodge cheery. A gloom settled in as the last board went up, but no one spoke of it. The metal garland was stretched all over the floor in a zig-zag pattern as Kitty and Gerry took it outside, careful not to tangle the shiny garland. I followed them as lookout while Sharon remained behind to continue stringing items together. The plan changed once we realized how complicated it was for Kitty and Gerry to attach the twine around the trees in the most effective way. It was nearly dinner time before we moved on to snares and sharpened stick traps. Saplings were stretched across some of the wider spaces between trees, perched for a painful release if something triggered their traps. Gerry marked the traps by spray painting red X's on the surrounding trees.

Exhausted, the three of us welcomed the smell of food roasting in the oven as we entered the lodge. The conversation over dinner consisted of what we'd accomplished and stressing to Parker that he should never go outside by himself, but if something happened and he did, that he was to avoid the trees with red X's on them. Gerry estimated we'd need three more days of work to complete the booby traps he had planned, and then he'd saw the trap door in the roof.

"I think we worked well together today—all of us," I said.

"Yeah," Kitty said. "We're a good team. What are the chances of all of us coming together under such extreme circumstances, from different parts of the world, and none of us being assholes?"

Laughter erupted from everyone until a noise sounding like a table sliding across the floor in the basement made us all freeze in silence. Even Parker remained motionless, mid-chew, as we listened for more noise. It happened again. Gerry locked eyes with Kitty, nodded towards Parker, and then looked at the long staircase. Silently, Kitty rose from the table, placed her finger to her lips, and waved at the boy to follow her. They crept up the stairs. Once their door was shut and we heard the lock click, the three of us stood, our hands absently checked for the guns strapped to our bodies, and we huddled together to whisper.

"Lucia, did you forget to lock the basement door?" Gerry spat.

"No, I swear, I double-checked it."

"How could a zombie have manipulated the latches?" Sharon asked.

"They couldn't have. I'm certain of it," Gerry said. "Well, no zombie I've encountered could have."

"Me either," I said, and Sharon shook her head.

"Now what?" Sharon whispered.

"We go downstairs," Gerry said a little too matter-of-factually.

"Oh, hells to the no. I stole the last light bulb out of there yesterday. It's dark as fuck," I said.

"What other choice do we have?" Gerry replied.

A knock came at the door and we ceased breathing for a second. "There's your choice," Sharon said.

Kitty emerged from the room, stood on the balcony, and positioned herself with her rifle pointed at the basement door.

"Who's there?" Gerry bellowed, deepening his voice.

"Judd," an elderly voice answered, panting.

We exchanged glances and Gerry continued with the questioning, "How did you get in?"

"I used my key—I work here in the summers."

"Are you alone?"

"I sure the hell hope so. These damn lights don't work and I lost my flashlight a few miles back."

"Are you infected?"

"No. Are you?" Judd let out a small moan.

"If you aren't infected, then why are you making noises?"

"I'm havin' some chest pain. Could you let me in?"

Gerry looked at Sharon—she nodded. His eyes fell on Kitty, and she nodded as well. When he looked at me, I shrugged, and he shrugged back. He poised his gun at head level, unlocked the door, and opened it with one sudden sweep.

A small, gray-haired man collapsed onto the floor of the lodge. Kitty remained in her position as Gerry shut and locked the door. Sharon's gun was aimed at Judd's head, but we could tell the man was in pain. Clutching his chest, he started shaking.

"Kitty, grab a blanket and a pillow," I yelled. I dropped down beside him and felt for a pulse. I looked up at Gerry, "It's weak. He's so cold. He has hypothermia, I'm sure." Kitty bound down the stairs, placed a pillow under his head, and Sharon wrapped a blanket around his body.

"Judd, can you hear me?" His eyes rolled to meet my gaze. With one rattling exhale, Judd stopped shaking. I pressed my two fingers below the fourth and fifth button on his flannel shirt, pressed around to locate his sternum, and begin chest compressions.

*

We never learned Judd's story, or how it was that he came to our camp. I was certain that the stress of traveling on foot, undoubtedly running from zombies, the cold, and his age, all factored into his death. We took turns digging his grave, six feet proper, and held hands as we prayed together over the dirt mounded above him. Inside his wallet were pictures of what we assumed where his grandchildren, probably all dead now, credit cards, and one small white fortune from a fortune cookie. It said, "Time and patience are called for, many surprises await you!"

CHAPTER 37

Sharon

My front door slamming open and the sound of booted feet stomping on tile woke me with a start. Rough hands hauled me from the bed, and my arms were yanked behind my back. There were at least a dozen of them, wearing full body armor, their faces obscured by visored helmets and pointing very large weapons at me. It was all I saw in the seconds before the world went dark as a hood was pulled over my head. I grunted when one of the soldiers threw me over his shoulder, the padding of his armor digging into my stomach painfully.

Unceremoniously, they carried me down the service stairs, skipping the elevator. I heard a door open and knew from the smell of tires and old exhaust that we were in the parking garage. I tried to struggle, but the grip on me was bruising.

The overhead door trundled open, a jet screamed across the sky, rattling the windows as it went supersonic. I could hear panic as people screamed in terror and anger. Hands pounded on the vehicle we were in, demanding that we take them with us. Clipped voices on the radio told someone that "the package has been secured." Ruefully, I realized the package was me.

I don't know how long we drove—it could have been minutes or days—but eventually the vehicle slowed down, the sound of its brakes squeaking in my darkened world. I heard more voices, whispering this time—scared voices laced with fear. Something had gone wrong, I heard one of them say. "Out of control," said another. My heart began to race, recognizing their fear and responding to it.

A door opened, I was yanked out; my feet barely skimmed the ground as they dragged me along. I could feel the linoleum under my bare feet; it was cool and smooth. I shivered.

A door opened and then closed behind us with a solid thud. The sound of the lock being thrown let me know I'd not escape easily. But if they thought I'd just give in, they were wrong, my mind screamed.

The hood was removed, light blossomed, and for a moment, I was blind. Blinking furiously, my eyes finally adjusted. There were three men and two women, all decked out in their best uniforms. Not one of them was higher than a lieutenant. One of the women was a sergeant—the man next to her, a corporal. I knew what that meant; the chain of command was breaking down. The higher ranking officers were either dead or in hiding. Neither option was good.

"Why did you bring me here?" I demanded.

"You are all that is left," said the other woman. She was young, probably fresh out of the Air Force Academy. "In the entirety of the U.S., we have not one single scientist left."

I shrugged, "So, it's too late anyway. There is no cure. The virus has a 100% kill rate. If you get it, you die. All we can do is wait it out. Why did you bring me here?" I asked again as I worked the rope that bound my hands behind my back.

"You were on the list as essential," she said. Her name tag told me her last name was Ortiz.

"Okay, so here I am. Now what?" I asked. The rope loosened a bit; I had to clamp my mouth shut to keep from giving a shout of joy.

"We are all that is left. Those that went to NORAD have been infected. The virus rampaged through there. The base is dead. Fort Hood was taken over by a herd of zombies. We've not had communication from them for days. STRATCOM is all that remains of the U.S. government," Lt. Ortiz told me. She was doing her best to sound calm and in control, but I could see her hand tremble when she gestured. She was scared; they all were...kids playing at war games in a world that had gone to hell.

"I can't help you. I've studied the virus. It shouldn't be able to do what it does. There is no explanation for it. No cure. All that is left is to wait it out."

"Can you create a vaccine, a preventative?" the young corporal asked.

I shook my head. "I don't know." I paused as he wiped his hand across his face, leaving behind a trail of snot on his dress blues. I glanced at the lieutenant. She knew the state of her comrade.

"I guess you get to die here with us," she said and then smiled. The flesh on the side of her face slid off, revealing maggots that squirmed and writhed. The sergeant's arm loosened from its joint, hanging loose in her sleeve as an acrid black stain spread across her uniform.

The rope finally came free; I turned to run, but there was nowhere to go. Zombies crowded into the room—decaying faces of people that I knew and loved, and some I had never known. The lieutenant grabbed my hair and took a bite out of my cheek. Tears ran down my face as my screams were drowned out by the sound of the dead feasting.

*

I woke with a gasp, my heart racing. Yellow sunlight streamed through the window, displaying an azure sky beyond as I took deep breaths to calm myself. For the past three days, it had snowed. The temperature had not fallen enough to start a freeze, so we ended up with wet, heavy snow that bowed the branches of the trees that struggled to stand. This was the first day the sun had shown its face. After the darkness of my nightmare, I was glad to see it.

Swinging my feet to the floor, I stood and stretched aching muscles that were tense with stress, both from my dream and from this new world. I dressed and walked out into the hallway.

Peering over the railing, I could see Gerry prowling around, keeping watch. I waved, he nodded, and I went to check on Parker. My room was at the end of the hall; Parker had been sharing a room with me, but he and Kitty had bonded, and she was happy to have him share her room. This was a good thing, as Parker was determined to be in there with her, regardless.

Slowly, I cracked the door open. Parker's narrow bed was empty. Opening the door a bit more, I found Parker and Kitty snuggled up together in her bunk. She stirred and cracked open an eye at me. I raised a brow, silently asking her if she wanted me to put him back in his bunk. She shook her head, and closed her eyes, falling back asleep. I smiled and closed the door behind me.

Lucia's room was next. She had left the door open. The squirrel suit and head were spread out on the bunk she wasn't using. After several scrubbings, its fur stood on end, much like a cat that had fallen in a puddle, but the pong that had been coming off of it was reduced. I was amazed all over again that she had managed to live in that thing for so long and wondered if she felt exposed without it.

I heard the shower kick on and realized that it must be her. I'd wait my turn. In the meantime, I'd go relieve Gerry. He and Lucia split the night shift, seeming to enjoy one another's company and being awake at night.

I jogged down the stairs and went to the kitchen. I didn't drink coffee, but I did like the smell of it brewing, so I put a pot on for Gerry and Lucia. Kitty decided she liked coffee, and since I wasn't her mother, who was I to tell her no?

I had found a hunk of frozen bacon in the back of the freezer the day before and had stuck it in the fridge to thaw. I grabbed it out, unwrapped the tinfoil, and poked it, nearly cheering when I realized that I'd be able to cook it.

The lodge had a full restaurant and had been known for its Sunday brunches. So, we were well stocked with utensils. I found a cast-iron skillet, lit a burner on the stove with a whoosh, and added some bacon strips as the metal warmed up.

The door cracked open; Gerry's head appeared. "You making bacon?" he asked.

I grinned, "Yep, and if you go get me some eggs, I'll make those, too." He disappeared without answer, but I heard the door to the cellar open and his feet pounding down the stairs.

"It's all about the proper motivation," I said to myself as I turned the bacon, jumping back as the grease popped.

"There were only two," he said, depositing two large brown eggs on the counter. I held them up to the light. The first one was fine, but the second had clearly been fertilized. "Take this back down to Chuck, will you?" I asked, handing him back the egg. I'd let it hatch; it wouldn't hurt to increase their numbers a bit.

"The kid does know that bird's a hen, doesn't he?" Gerry asked, taking the egg.

"Yes, I explained it to him. He doesn't seem to care though," I said, and so we had a hen named Chuck.

There were some leftover eggs in the fridge; I cracked them and fried them along with the bacon.

"Bacon?" Lucia asked as she walked in the door. "And coffee. I think I may love you," she said, pouring herself a cup. I grinned and set the bacon strips on a paper towel. Kitty showed up a few minutes later, lured by the siren song of frying pork.

We ate, and for a moment it was good to pretend that everything was normal, and that my nightmare had been just that—a nightmare. Sadly, it wasn't, and part of me wondered what had happened to General Daniels and the rest.

After breakfast, Gerry, having been up all night, wandered up the stairs, and I went to check on my laptops. The snowstorm had caught us by surprise. One minute we were unloading the bus and the truck, and the next a howling wind had kicked up. For two days, a steady fall of snow had blanketed the landscape in a thick veil of white that was nearly two feet deep.

The sun glinting off the snow was blinding as I sat down at the table. One of the laptops was strictly for running tests. It was not connected to the Internet. That was because the hard drive was classified as 'top secret', and keeping it off the web would make it more secure… not that it mattered anymore. The other one could link directly to a satellite, and if there was a connection, no matter how weak, it would find it.

I powered it on and wondered how I could find weather information. We had gas and electricity, but that would only continue as long as the power plants were operational. With no one to run them, how long would it be before there was a failure?

It was much the same with satellites. They needed constant course corrections or would fall out of orbit. When that happened we'd lose what was left of the Internet and our cell phones would be rendered useless. We were about to be cast into the stone ages, and who knew how long it would take to regain the technological ground we had fought so hard for.

"Whatcha' doin'?" Kitty asked as she plunked herself down next to me.

"I'm trying to see if I can get access to a weather sat," I answered, gnawing my lip in concentration as I typed in lines of code. "I have a high level clearance, but I just don't know where to look." The satellites were the providence of NORAD, and while I didn't claim to have prophetic dreams, I did wonder if anyone was still alive there.

"Here, let me try," she said, inching closer.

I shrugged and gave her the laptop, "Be my guest." Her fingers flew over the keyboard, and I had to admit, I was impressed.

"Here, enter your code," she said, handing me the laptop. I typed in my access code, the screen changed, and there it was, North America as seen from space.

"That's fantastic!" I said, smiling at her. "If we can have some idea of what weather to expect, that will save us a lot of trouble." And suddenly the dark ages got a little brighter.

A light in the corner of the screen began to blink. "Looks like you've got some messages waiting," she said, indicating the light. "Are you gonna answer them?"

"What's the point?" I asked. "Whoever sent it is probably dead." She nodded and wandered off. I squinted at the little light and clicked on it. It was a message center, not e-mail, but direct computer communication. I shivered and remembered my dream. I had left Omaha for a reason. I didn't want to be anyone's pet biologist. And I figured I was so far down on the totem pole no one would miss me.

The message was sent three days ago from General Daniel's office and requested that I submit a report. I stared at it for a second before leaning back in my chair. I watched as water dripped off the roof from the melting snow and considered what I should do. "I'm not going to be hauled in to die," I said, and hit the delete button. I then went in and changed the laptop's privacy features and turned off the tracking function. The world that I had left was dead and gone. I had no plans to return to it.

Parker came in and threw his arms around my neck. "Aunt Sharon!" he yelled into my ear. I grimaced and hugged him back. "Chuck is gonna be a mom!" he shouted, jumping up and down with excitement.

"Well, congratulations," I said, and closed the laptop. As he led me down to the cellar to see Chuck's baby, I realized that all that mattered was this little group clinging to life in the wilds of Canada.

CHAPTER 38

Lucia

I sat back on my haunches and drew a stick figure in the snow with my index finger. It didn't seem right without some of its limbs missing. Arms and legs on the zombies weren't severed—they rotted off. Sometimes it reminded me of a pig roast I went to when I was a kid how the meat fell from of the bones—but zombie flesh was cooked off with bacterial decay. Sharon and I prepared to scout. I squinted in the sunlight as she walked around the side of the lodge, snapping the rubber strap on a slingshot.

"Where'd ya find that thing?" I yelled.

"Inside the gardening shed. Maybe it'll help us catch something for dinner."

"I refuse to eat roasted squirrel," I called as I smoothed out the snow, erasing the stick figure I'd drawn. Sharon's one eyebrow raised and she gave me a knowing look. "Okay, but if it's all we have, I'll eat the squirrel… not that I've seen a squirrel in a few months."

"We aren't that desperate yet, but it will probably come to that."

"Maybe we should make a net and drag it through the lake for fish. Couldn't we salt them or something so they'd keep over winter? Didn't the Indians do that?"

"We could make a net if we find enough rope, and yeah, we can salt them."

"Maybe Gerry was a Boy Scout. We could use some knotty fingers for that job. Hahaha… naughty fingers… get it?"

Sharon rolled her eyes at me and smiled, "Let's get going, I'm already cold."

I stood up and wiped my fingers off onto my squirrel suit. "Which way should we head?"

"I found a trail map inside the lodge office. I have a route charted out for us already and I left a copy for Gerry so he'd know which way we went."

"Cool, I'll follow you." Sharon started walking around the side of the lodge and we soon saw markers for the trail peeking out of the snow drifts. "Do you think Parker will be okay with Kitty and Gerry?"

"Yeah, he seems to like both of them, plus I asked him first and he seemed fine with it."

"I'm glad."

We were well into the woods when Sharon pointed at a white bird perched on a bough on a pine tree, pecking beneath its wing. "That's *a Patagioenas fasciata,* and it should have migrated south by now."

"Maybe it can sense the zombies are in the south."

"Yes, it's odd."

"I never liked birds," I said, and Sharon glanced at me quizzically. "But you learn to love what you have, especially if it's tasty." We both laughed.

The forest was quiet except for our feet crunching in the snow and the occasional chirping.

"That's a *Falcipennis canadensis.*"

"You can tell from the song?"

"Yes, it's a call to warn of predators."

"You're good."

"Thanks."

There weren't many targets Sharon missed with her slingshot, so she turned out to be quite the huntress. "Is there anything you aren't good at?" Sharon laughed at my remark. "I feel a kinship with all squirrels. Maybe if you keep hunting and kill enough birds, we can skip the squirrel soup this week. If we find a nice fat goose that forgot to fly south, that would be even better."

"Ah, goose would be nice." We paused. The trail's incline had been a steady climb up one of the nearby mountain sides. Sharon pulled out her binoculars and scanned the area.

"Thank you for letting all of us live with you."

"There's strength in numbers." Sharon arched her head around, looking for life in the trees.

"And weakness in the resource drain."

"I didn't think about that."

"I'm glad."

Sharon smiled at me. "We should be quiet."

"Oh, yeah… right."

Our sack held six pheasant-like birds I'd forget the name of by the time I would finish de-feathering them later that afternoon. We had found honey in the pantry that morning, so I renamed them *Honeitus tastyus* in my head as we quietly trekked up the trail while fantasizing about roasting them. *One more night of tiny bones,* I thought, when I heard a queer noise becoming louder as something mechanical approached in the sky. "Is that a plane?" I asked.

"If it is, it's going down." Sharon scanned the sky with the binoculars. "It's coming this way."

Soon, I was able to see it. Sharon lowered her binoculars and shielded the top of her eyes with her hand. "Can you see it?" I asked.

"Yes. It's smoking."

The plane almost looked as though it could hit us, but it fell with a groaning whistle and crashed at the base of the mountain. We looked at each other and began running down the trail.

When we reached the bottom, I stopped. "Shouldn't we go tell the others?"

"There's no time. What if someone's dying and we can save them? Let's stop and grab the quad and cart when we pass camp. It'll be faster."

Sharon paused for a second to look at the trail map, and then continued running until we reached the quad. I was still panting and sweating under my squirrel suit when we spotted the smoldering remains of the plane. We briefly scanned the wreckage, but only found *parts* of people—no one was whole or alive. Sharon drove farther out into the field, towards a whole body. *Surely this person's dead,* I thought.

It was a man, and he wasn't conscious. Sharon dropped to her knees on one side of him. She felt for a pulse and looked at me. "Holy Hell! He's still alive."

CHAPTER 39

Paul

When I opened my eyes, I was looking into the face of a girl. She was beautiful; long red hair hung loose as she examined me with blue eyes. I thought I was dreaming again; I thought the girl from my dream had come down from the hill, after all, to rescue me. *No, the girl in my dream had dark hair.*

"Holy Hell! He's still alive." She sounded different—American, I thought. Then I remembered the plane. Maybe I was dead; was this the face of an angel? It could well have been. Then I spotted the red dot hovering over my chest.

"If you are going to shoot him, shoot him in the head," another girl's voice said.

Maybe not Heaven so.

The pain came at me in waves, starting at the base of my skull and shooting darts all the way to my toes. I knew I wasn't dead for sure then. Dead couldn't hurt this much.

"I can't shoot him, Lucia; he might not be infected." A giant squirrel appeared over her shoulder. Maybe not dead, but transported to some seriously fucked up world where giant squirrels and angels hunted men. I began to wonder, had the bastards drugged my soup on the plane?

"He fell out of the sky, Sharon. No one could survive that unless they were infected." The squirrel was wary of strangers falling from the sky. I didn't blame her.

"I've seen too many people die. For once, just once, I'd like to try and save one." I could see the redhead's eyes moisten. I had no idea what that was all about, but it made her lower a big fuck-off rifle she had pointed at me. "Besides, what the hell was he doing in a plane in the first place?"

I tried to say something like, "please don't fucking shoot me," but no words would form; all that came out was a sort of low groan. Judging by the reaction from the redhead, who jumped back, swinging the rifle up again, it may have been ill-judged to make a zombie-like moan.

"I dropped my axe," I said, don't ask me why or where those words came from.

"What?" she asked, turning the gun back on me.

"I had an axe; I dropped it when I fell out of the plane."

"Where are you from? You don't sound like you're from around here."

"Dublin," I answered. I could do without the interrogation, but if it meant they weren't going to shoot me, I would play along.

"Ohio?"

"What?" It was my turn to look incredulous.

"Are you from Dublin, Ohio?" Sharon asked, as if she were talking to a five year old.

"No, Dublin, Dublin."

"He's from Ireland," the squirrel said, as she took off her head and shook loose long, dark hair. "You know? Shamrocks and shillelaghs?"

Sharon blushed then and looked down in embarrassment. "I… oh, yes, of course," she stuttered.

"Could I get a little help here? I think I might have broken something."

"Where are you hurt?" Sharon asked. "If you broke your back falling from that plane, we aren't going to be able to help you." Under her breath, she added, "We can barely help ourselves."

"Trust me, if my back is broken, it will be a kindness to put a bullet in my brain," I answered. I meant it, too. Life had become barely tolerable as it was.

"Maybe you should look at him, Lucia. You're the only one with any medical experience among us."

Lucia? I thought, that's a funny name for a squirrel.

"Alright, we can use the cart to bring him back to the lodge."

Sharon turned back to me, pointing the gun in my direction. "But so help me God, if you have so much as a nick or scratch, I will shoot you. I'll not put anyone in any unnecessary danger."

I nodded. I could tell she meant it by her unflinching glare.

I yelled as they bundled me onto the cart.

"Could you keep it down?" Lucia said as they heaved me up. "Do you want to alert every zombie from here to Golden?"

"Where are you hurt?" Sharon asked more gently.

"Everywhere," I answered, and meant it, too.

"You know, we probably shouldn't have moved him; we could make his injuries worse," Sharon said.

"You're right," Lucia answered. "But what other choice do we have?"

"Good Jaysus! There's a right bang off o' this cart. What where you using it for?"

"Collecting bodies," Lucia grinned. Sharon shrugged apologetically.

Then I heard a familiar groan and a ripping noise. Sharon turned, pointing the rifle left and right. I looked up.

Boland was hanging from the trees, suspended by the parachute. The silk ripped and he came crashing down.

"The fucking trees!" I roared, suddenly finding enough power in my arms to point.

Lucia dropped the cart with a jolt and swung towards the forest.

Bam! Bam! Bam! Boland's head exploded in a spray of blood.

"Have you got anything else to tell us?" They both rounded on me, furious expressions on their faces.

"Don't shoot me," I said. "It's been a really, really bad day."

*

Lucia, it turned out, was another looker when she stripped off the squirrel suit. I could have landed in a worse spot, I supposed. I felt I should ask for an explanation about the suit, but at that moment, I just could not bring myself around to it.

"What's going on?" A male voice asked, as he rushed down the steps of a holiday lodge to help with the cart.

He was given the highlights of my spectacular entrance and what had happened since.

"I'm not a doctor, you know?" Lucia protested as she craned her neck this way and that, looking me over.

"You're the closest we have to one," Gerry said. I wasn't sure I liked the grim line of his mouth.

"I better check him for any bite marks as well. I'm not too keen on waking up in the middle of the night with someone we brought into the lodge trying to eat me," she said. "Have you been in close proximity to any infected recently?"

"Eh… one or two," I admitted. I thought about lying, but fuck it, what was the point?

They had set up home in some sort of holiday lodge on a lake. The scenery was breathtaking, even if I didn't fully appreciate it at the time.

They brought me into their shelter and lay me on a sofa by the fire. The bedrooms were up a wooden flight of stairs and looked a step too far to carry a broken Irishman they'd found in the woods.

Night fell over the mountains, for me, it seemed blacker than ever.

CHAPTER 40

Lucia

Kitty was flashing her protective claws when we brought Paul back to the lodge. She told Parker to go to his room and lock the door, then made Gerry and I promise that we'd keep a watch over the newcomer all night, in case he spontaneously showed signs of infection. Later, after she dragged Parker into her room for bedtime, I could hear her sliding a dresser in front of her bedroom door.

Sharon sighed, "Teenagers… at least she's taken to him."

Gerry and I nodded.

"We'll be fine with him all night," I said to her. "Get some sleep."

"Are you sure you don't want me to watch over him tonight?" she asked.

"No, we'll be good." Gerry placed a hand on the gun in his holster.

"It's best if I'm here in case he wakes up. I have a pharmacy of drugs for his every ailment, and besides, I feel safer with Gerry than I do you." I tried to hide my laugh.

Sharon smacked my arm, "Hey!"

"I'm kidding!" I giggled.

Gerry started towards the kitchen as he bid Sharon goodnight. Halfway up the stairs, a muffled, "Goodnight, Sharon," came from behind Kitty's bedroom door.

I stood over the stranger. He kept slipping in and out of consciousness, mumbling words I couldn't understand. Gerry returned with two cups of coffee.

"Is there anything we can do for him?"

I shook my head. "Only time will tell us if he'll live or not."

"He could die?"

"Yes. There's no telling if he has internal bleeding or how bad his head injury is."

"Maybe we should move him to the other couch—it's not as comfortable. I like the one he's laying on. I'd hate for it to get the death taint on it."

I scrunched my face up in confusion. "What do you mean, 'death taint'?"

"Well, what if he dies and his bowels let loose? Or consider the bad mojo a dead leprechaun would bring."

I stared at Gerry and his stoic expression broke as he laughed.

"You fucker! I fell for that."

"Here, drink your coffee…it's going to be a long night."

CHAPTER 41

Paul

I woke to the aroma of food cooking; it filled the air around me, making my stomach rumble and mouth water. I opened my eyes one at a time. I was confused, disoriented, and really sore. It took a while for the events of the previous day to come back to me. Apparently I had not broken my neck in the fall, nor had I died and gone to Heaven. I wasn't sure if some higher being was looking out for me, or just taking the piss and having a really good laugh.

"Good morning. I'm making breakfast. Do you want some pancakes?" Sharon said. She was smiling, more of a sympathetic smile than an all-out happy-to-see-me-still-alive smile. She was the first thing I saw when I opened my eyes after the plane crash. And it had crashed, it had not registered with me the previous day, but the memory of it came back clearly. I thought she was an angel then… until she pointed a gun at my chest. Now she was making me fluffy American pancakes.

"Sure." My voice cracked as I answered.

I pushed myself into a sitting position; everywhere ached. I noticed some clean clothes had been left out for me. I held up a red plaid shirt.

"We going to cut down some trees?" I joked.

"Ha ha, very funny," she said. She did smile though, and it lit up her whole face. She disappeared then, back to the kitchen I supposed.

I dressed slowly and carefully; by the time I was done, she was back.

"There are pancakes with maple syrup and coffee in the dining room, or I can bring it in here to you if you prefer."

"No." I shook my head. Everything had turned to shit, there was nothing I could do about that, but I refused to be helpless in a fucked up world.

My head spun as I stood on shaky legs; I staggered and started to fall. Suddenly, Sharon was by my side, propping me up with her shoulder. She smelled really good up close. It occurred to me, as I stood there inhaling the scent of oranges and jasmine from her hair, how much of an idiot I must look. I was new here and didn't know what was what and who belonged to whom. There were five of them: one man, two women, and two kids. I wondered where they were and asked her as much.

"In the basement feeding our chickens," she said. "You don't have to do this now; take more time to recover." She was probably right, but I've always been a stubborn bastard.

"I want… need to do this," I answered. Funny enough, the more I moved, the less stiff and sore I felt.

I devoured the pancakes. I was starving, and they were really good.

"Do you carry a gun everywhere?" I asked. I had noticed the pistol in a holster on her hip earlier, but said nothing. It was an unusual and unsettling sight for me to see—my new landlady armed to the teeth.

"Yeah of course, these are turbulent times. Don't you?" She replied, brushing some stray strands of red hair from her face.

"Well, no, I…" Suddenly I felt defensive.

"You're a lucky man to have avoided contact with the infected."

"Eh…" I thought of my rampage through the apartment block with Robbie's axe, the panic on the plane, and watching Boland transform into a zombie as I clung to him while we fell through the air. "I've had some contact," I answered sheepishly.

"How have you defended yourself?" she asked.

"With an axe." For some reason, I started to feel guilty.

"An axe! Holy Hell! Are you insane? Do you know how the virus is transmitted? One drop of blood in your eye, an open cut… Mister, you need to keep the infected a lot farther away from you than the length of an axe."

"Oh."

"Have you ever fired a weapon before?" She looked exasperated.

"Sure." I sat up straighter. "Yesterday."

She shook her head and rolled her eyes skyward. She left the room, leaving me wondering if I was in trouble. She returned a few minutes later and held up a gun. She clicked in a clip and placed it in front of me.

"Here, this is for you. It's a Glock 22 and your new best friend. Finish up there and I'll give you your first lesson."

Slowly, I reached for the gun. I'm sure I grinned like a moron.

Stepping out into the fresh open air of Canada felt surreal. The previous day I had been cooped up in an apartment block in the middle of Dublin City Centre; now I was in a national park on the other side of the Atlantic Ocean. It was a bright, clear day with blue skies and sunshine and the bite of autumn in the air. Snow had fallen that night, leaving a light dusting of white on the tips of the towering evergreen trees and the soft earth beneath our feet.

"The weapon that you have is the full size version of what I have. Mine is a 27; yours is a 22. They are both .40 caliber and take the same ammunition. The difference is not only in the size, but in the clip." She popped the clip to show me. "This one will hold nine rounds; yours will hold fifteen. You will want to make sure you keep track of how many rounds you have fired. Okay?"

I nodded, indicating I understood. I wasn't sure if I should be impressed or scared to death of this woman—maybe a bit of both.

"Okay, hold it firmly, but not tight." She placed her hand over mine.

"We're talking about the gun, right?" I joked. She just rolled her eyes and ignored me.

"Anyway, a Glock doesn't have a thumb safety. Instead, the safety is built into the trigger. If you fire it, it's because you meant to. My dad told me that the first rule of weapon safety is: 'Never place your finger on the trigger unless the thing you are aiming at you mean to destroy.' Okay?"

I nodded again, testing the weight of the weapon in my hand. Survival was becoming a serious business, and I was getting a new education on how to live.

"I have a shoulder holster for this. It was too big for me, but it should fit you. You need to get used to having it with you at all times."

I searched for something clever to say, but nothing came. I was being taught how to fire a weapon in order to kill, by a beautiful redhead who smelled of oranges and jasmine, in the middle of miles and miles of Canadian woodland. What was there to say?

"The second thing he told me was, 'Always treat a weapon like it's loaded.' " She clicked the magazine back into my gun. She called it a weapon, I called it a gun.

"When I was taught to shoot, I was told to aim at the centre mass as that would disable any attacker. But with zombies, that won't work. Sometimes that won't even slow them down. The virus that animates them lives in the brain, and that is what you have to hit if you want to stop them, which means a head shot, every time." She took aim, fired, and hit a tree, sending down a dusting of snow.

"See if you can hit that tree, the one with the carving in it."

I spotted the one she meant. Somebody had carved their initials into the trunk: 'LT hearts JC.' LT had probably eaten JC by now, I thought grimly. I took aim and fired. It sent a jolt back up my arm and sounded like an explosion had gone off right by my ear. I missed.

"Good job," Sharon encouraged.

After I had emptied several clips, even hitting the tree once or twice, Sharon suggested we take a break.

"Don't forget the empty clips; we'll need to reload them," she said as I started to walk away. I turned back and gathered the discarded magazines.

"Come on, I'll show you how to take it apart and clean it. There are some cleaning kits up in the lodge. You wait here; I'll go get them."

There was a picnic bench looking over the lake. I gingerly swung one leg over the seat while Sharon sauntered back towards the lodge. I watched her all the way until she disappeared inside, wondering all the while what to make of this American girl who made pancakes and fired guns with a deadly accuracy.

The water looked so calm. At one time it would probably have teemed with life. Now an occasional bird swooped down—a rare enough sight to pause and watch.

"So what's your story, Irishman? Why were you on a plane weeks after all air traffic has been grounded?" she asked when she came back.

I had no secrets to keep. We refilled the clips with bullets as I told her all. She was easy to talk to and listened to my story. It felt therapeutic sharing the ordeals I'd been through with someone else who understood. I told her about the doomed expedition to the pharmacy, about Mrs. Watson's dive from the balcony. Sharon made all the right sympathetic noises, and she put her hand on my arm when I told her about Mrs. Watson's boy. But when I spoke about boarding the plane with the scientists, she suddenly became animated.

"Wait, you're sure they said they were researching the virus? You're certain?"

"I suppose, yeah, they were taking their research to a facility in Canada. One of them had a briefcase cuffed to his wrist. They were loading equipment onto the plane as well."

"Holy Hell, Paul! I didn't realise they were co-operating with European governments, but it makes sense. They would need all the help they could get now. I'm a zoologist, Paul. A few months ago, I was contracted by the US government to research the virus at my zoo in Nebraska. They said it was affecting the animals, so it made sense they would contact me. Of course, after I read the research I learned that it had spread to humans and killed off most of the population of Greenland. They still thought they could control it then. In fact, I was the one that wrote the PSA about the virus being a new strain of rabies." She paused as if to catch her breath. She met my eyes and looked away, but not before I saw tears glisten there. I remembered then, what seemed like a whole lifetime away, but was only a couple of months. People said it was only rabies. No one worried. It was the bird flu all over again, just another scare blown out of proportion.

Christ, I thought, *is she harbouring guilt because of this?* I wanted to say something, but what... I didn't know. She'd made me pancakes, picked me up after I fell out of a plane, and taught me how to shoot. Damn it, she was fucking hot! I didn't want her shouldering the blame for the death of humanity. But I didn't know what to say; always first in the line with a smart arse quip, but when something really needed to be said, there was nothing but a big empty space of silence.

She cleared her throat and carried on. "The case I have was cuffed to a lieutenant's wrist. This case that you saw, what did it look like?"

"It was just like an old school teacher's leather satchel, nothing special. At least I think so." To be honest I wasn't that clear on events since I boarded that plane.

"Do you remember what the guy looked like?"

"I remember him getting a bullet in the head as he took a chunk out of the Taoiseach's arm."

"Tea-shock?" She raised one eyebrow.

"Sorry, it's an Irish title for the Prime Minister."

"Whatever is on that plane, I want it. There are some basic tests that I can't do. I doubt any of the equipment survived the crash, but it is possible that they are further along than me in their tests. We have to get to that plane."

With that, she leapt up and went running, calling out the names of the others. I stood there scratching my head.

CHAPTER 42

Sharon

I was halfway to the lodge before I realized what I had done. Then I stopped, hung my head in shame, and cursed under my breath. With a deep sigh, I turned around and walked back to the table.

"Sorry," I said sheepishly. "I can get a little lost in my own head sometimes."

"It's okay," Paul said. He was standing there with a look on his face that seemed to be part confusion, part amusement.

"No. It's not okay, actually," I said gathering up the cleaning kit. "I got so excited about the prospect of furthering my research, I forgot myself. But that doesn't excuse the fact that I ran off and left you here like zombie bait."

His smile wilted a bit as he cast a nervous glance about. And truth be told, the noise we had made shooting would bring them.

"Left or right?" I asked, picking up the holster.

"What?"

"Are you left handed or right-handed?" He had fired the Glock with his right hand, but I wanted to make sure as I adjusted the holster.

"Oh, right-handed," he said.

I nodded and slipped the nylon straps over his arm, settling it on his left side so that he could draw it comfortably. I leaned in, reached behind him, and velcroed it in place. As I did so, I felt his hand brush my hair. I glanced up and paused at the look in his blue eyes. An eagle screamed overhead and then dove skillfully, snatching a silver scaled fish from the gleaming waters of the lake. I blinked, and the moment passed.

"You're left-handed?"

"No," I said, looking down at the Glock that I had strapped to my left thigh. "I write with my right hand, but I am left-eye dominate, so I shoot with my left hand. Otherwise, I'd have to cross my arm over my chest to sight it." I pointed my right hand like a gun and aimed to demonstrate what I meant. "It's just easier to shoot with my left." I shrugged.

We gathered up the kits and the rest of the cartridges. He rolled his shoulders. "I suppose I had better get used to it," he said. I nodded, and together we walked back to the lodge in companionable silence. He seemed like a good man, and I enjoyed listing to the way he spoke.

The door to the lodge was always locked. No matter what happened, when someone went out, another locked it behind them. That was the rule, and one we adhered to diligently. I knocked on the door and was greeted by Gerry chewing on a piece of jerky. I had taken it from the store out of necessity.

"I have no idea how you can eat that stuff," I said, shaking my head as I walked past him.

"What?" he asked. "Something wrong with jerky?" I just grinned and shut the door behind Paul when he entered.

"So how'd you do?" Gerry asked Paul, clapping him on the shoulder. Paul grimaced in pain.

"Not bad for a first time," I said, locking the door.

"Oh, that means you suck," Gerry said with a grin.

"Yeah, but you should see me with an axe," Paul said. I left them to work through their testosterone issues and headed towards the kitchen. I found Kitty and Parker sitting at the table playing checkers. Parker was winning, though I expect it was because Kitty was letting him.

"Where's Lucia?" I asked, grabbing a bottle of water from the fridge. I enjoyed the smell of coffee, but not the taste.

"She's downstairs looking for stuff," Kitty said.

"Stuff?" I asked. "What kind of stuff?" We kept the chickens in the cellar so that they wouldn't become zombie food, and they didn't seem to mind. It was a rough-hewn basement, uneven in most places, with a dirt floor. I figured it had been carved out after the lodge was built. For what, I couldn't guess. Over the years the owners had crammed it full of boxes.

"Dunno, she just said 'stuff'," Kitty said with a shrug. I closed the refrigerator and leaned against it to watch the two of them. My mind was running in circles with what Paul had said. The notion of more research and possibly finding out what really had started the pandemic would not leave me be. I had given up trying to find a cure. The virus was so aggressive that it would be almost impossible to administer any cure in those few seconds before the virus began to spread and replicate.

The idea of an immunization was one that I had been thinking about a lot lately, especially in that week when it was just Parker and I at the lodge. I had meant to do it before I left Omaha, but with the ensuing chaos, I hadn't had much time to actually work on it.

Immunizations are either active or passive. The active ones involved injecting the body with a low dose of the virus and then letting the body build up an immunity towards it. But the Haukkson virus was so aggressive that there really wasn't such a thing as a low dose. Even the slightest contact with the virus would eventually end with full onset and then death, so that idea was out.

However, the idea of a passive immunization was possible. It would involve synthesized elements, generally in the way of antibodies. I knew how to do it, but I didn't have any of the things that I needed to start that process.

"It sounded like a war-zone out there," Lucia said, as she walked into the kitchen carrying a box brimming with 'stuff'. She set it down on the counter with a *clink*, the kitchen door swinging shut behind her. "Did he actually hit anything?"

"He did a few times," I laughed. "But he held it right, and has a good stance. Plus he's pretty banged up. I think he will be fine once he gets some practice. And the Lord knows, he will have ample opportunity for that," I said before taking a deep drink of the cool water.

We had blown through a lot of rounds, but Rob had boxes and boxes of bullets. I had hundreds of rounds in the trunk of the Mustang. Even sharing that with Paul, we had enough to last a while, and if that ran out, I had the rifle. With most of the population dead, supplies weren't the issue. Like the farm where we picked up Kitty, we were free to take what we came across. The issue was just finding such caches. Things were pretty far flung up here.

I watched Lucia tinker around with some glass jars and bottles for a minute. When she pulled the tubing out of her back pocket, curiosity got the better of me. "What are you doing?" I asked, bemused.

"I'm a chemist," she said, and turned on the water to wash the grime off the bottles.

"Yes?" I said, drawing the one word out into a question.

"I'm going to make a distillation set."

"What are you going to distill?" I asked.

"I haven't figured that part out yet," she answered with a grin. I smiled and shook my head. Whatever she came up with, I was sure it would be interesting.

Paul and Gerry wandered into the kitchen. I stood there leaning against the freezer, looking at this group. None of us had seen another living human for days, and for all we knew, we were the last in all of Canada. These people were now my family, and for better or worse, I owed it to them to tell the truth.

"So, there is something I want to talk to everyone about," I said.

"Oh yeah?" Gerry asked, reaching past me to grab his coffee mug. I watched him refill his cup, enjoying the scent that wafted through the room. The homey smell lulled me and served to strengthen my resolve.

I took a deep breath to tell them, then stopped. "C'mon," I said, nodding my head towards the door. "Kitty, can you keep Parker in here for a moment?" I asked. She gave me a squinty eyed look that clearly said she didn't like being left out. I gave her a small smile, and she relented. I'd talk to her later.

I walked into the dining hall and found the iPad, then walked back to the fireplace where they had gathered. Paul had settled himself on the sofa where he had slept. Once he could manage the stairs, we'd move him to one of the rooms. Gerry was leaning on the fireplace, coffee in hand.

Lucia sat in one of the overstuffed chairs. I sat down on the end of the sofa by Paul, so that I was effectively between him and Lucia. It would be easier to show them what was on the tablet that way.

"You all know that I'm a zoologist, and I'm sure you've noticed my lab in the dining hall." They nodded. "But there is a lot that you don't know. So much that I'm not even sure where to start."

"Start at the beginning," Lucia said, offering me a kindly smile in encouragement, and so I did.

I pulled up the files on the Hauksson virus. "Patient zero was Malik Hauksson." I didn't worry about privacy or top secret files. The time for that had passed. I told them about the bite he took from the seal and what happened when he returned home.

"Greenland was quarantined less than a week later, but by then it was too late. People had flown to other countries. Norway was the next spot that the virus presented itself." It had become really quiet, and they listened with wide eyes. It occurred to me as I looked at them that I had taken my knowledge for granted. I had known for a while what was going on. How scary must it have been for them to know absolutely nothing?

I had the pictures of the carnage in Greenland. This group knew what death looked like. So, I concentrated on what they didn't know.

"By mid-July, the virus was confirmed on six continents. I had heard rumors, but I lived in Nebraska; it had not made it to us. Our government was keeping it pretty tight; they were jamming the video sharing and social networking sites. I spent most of my time at work and didn't pay much attention to it. That all changed in the beginning of August when I was paid a visit by the CDC and a group of military brass. They gave me the information that I am sharing with you."

"They were concerned about the mammals. They are carriers, and the government wanted a way to stop that. So it made sense they would contact me. At least that is what I thought then. I'm not sure what to think about it now." I paused, weighing my words.

Gerry had wandered over and sat in the other chair beside Lucia. They had spent the last few months running, and these were the first actual answers they had been given. I could see them absorbing the information like sponges.

"How did the virus get out of Greenland?" Gerry asked.

"I don't know," I said. "I was given limited information. Enough to do some tests and make some theories, but the hows and whys—I wasn't told."

"I do know that the Hauksson virus is fatal. There is no cure, and there is no immunity. If you get it, you die, and then you resurrect. But all the things that make you *you* don't. It's a necro-virus and its victims become zombies." My words hung in the air for a minute. They all knew this, but to have it voiced was a totally different matter.

"I came across some smart zombies," Lucia said. "What do you suppose that is all about?"

"Yes, I had an experience with that as well," I paused, recalling the thinker I had met. Jack had died that day. It wasn't a pleasant memory. I swallowed and continued. "The closest that I can figure is that there is some resistance to the virus. The person infected lives longer. Whether it has something to do with an RH factor, or just some sort of natural immunity, I don't know. I have samples from the thinker I met, but without some more lab equipment, there isn't a lot I can do with it." She nodded and leaned back in her chair. I could see her turning the information around in her head, processing it.

"Does that happen to those that don't get bit?" Paul asked. I turned to look at him.

"The virus is spread by bodily fluids. The portion of the brain that triggers salivation is targeted as a means to spread the virus. The virus also targets the part of the brain that makes the body think it's hungry, so the resurrected host is driven to eat, even though it doesn't really need it. It is just how the virus works.

"The virus is classified into two types. Type one is infection via a bite. The victim becomes hyper-aggressive and generally dies within four hours. Resurrection time seems to vary."

I flipped to the case files that showed the patients that had been studied. I then showed them the video of Mindy. They watched her come back to life. And even though they knew it was going to happen, they still gasped when she did. Gerry swore under his breath and stood. I watched him pace for a moment before I continued.

"Type two is infection via means other than a bite. For instance, if you get something in your eyes or mouth or through a cut, it takes much longer for the virus to incubate, but you will succumb eventually."

"Like Ginny Dailey," Kitty said quietly. I looked over at the kitchen door to see her standing there. Through the crack I could see Parker at the table coloring. I don't know how long she had been listening, but it didn't matter. She knew now, so I just nodded.

"But with regards to the thinker, I believe that when some people become infected, the virus can't take over as fast. I don't know if the incubation period is longer or what happens, but when they resurrect the virus has the ability to access some higher brain functions, which would imply an ability to learn. And I suspect they may retain some things that have become muscle memory. For how long, I don't know."

Gerry came and sat down across from me. "We were told it was just rabies."

I sighed. There it was—my worst fear voiced.

"You've done nothing wrong," Paul said, touching my shoulder gently. I smiled grimly, but didn't look up.

"It's a nice thought. I'm having trouble convincing myself of it though," I whispered.

"You were told it was rabies because I told them to say that," I said in a rush. "They had not alerted the public; something needed to be said. They wouldn't... couldn't... say what was really going on without a full scale panic. That would only have made it worse. But they did agree to the rabies story. So I wrote up the public service announcement, and they distributed it." I pulled a folded-up copy of it from my pocket and handed it to Lucia.

I looked up, expecting to see shock, horror, and recrimination on their faces. But that is not what I saw, and the lack of it affected me more than I thought it would.

Kitty looked over her shoulder and then came and perched on the coffee table in front of me. "Did you know what was going to happen?"

"No, I didn't," I said, looking at her intently. "They weren't going to alert the public at all. I thought at least this way there would be some sense of caution instilled. And then things went to hell so soon after that. I was being watched. There were guards stationed in the parking lot of my building. They drove me to work every day, and then drove me home. My personal computer was taken. I suspect my phone was monitored. There was no way I could tell anyone any of the things that were on those files." I swallowed back hot tears that threatened.

She nodded once abruptly. She hadn't told anyone what happened to her family or how she came to be on the farm. I wouldn't push her to do so now. We had all lost those we loved and done things that we never would have dreamed ourselves capable of. But we were adults, and no matter how grown up she acted, Kitty was still just a child. She should be chatting on the phone with her girlfriends about the boys at school. Yet here she was, stranded in the middle of a national park in the wilds of Canada with a group of strangers all just trying to survive.

"Would they have killed you if you told?" she asked quietly.

I took a deep breath and exhaled as I considered the idea. "I don't know. The day I left, the guards were gone. I didn't stick around long enough to find out why." I thought about Jenny and for the first time wondered how she came to be infected. How had the guards not noticed? Silence settled over the lodge as each of them processed what I had said.

"The plane I was on was headed to a research facility," Paul said. "They were clearing out of Europe. I saw them loading equipment and guns on the plane. One of the men had a case cuffed to his wrist."

"They've likely done a lot of what I haven't been able to. I'd like to review it and see if my theories are true. I don't know what I can do with it, but it seems a shame to just leave it lying out in the elements."

"There was a military presence on the plane?" Gerry asked Paul.

"Yeah." He said their name in Irish. We all blinked, and he grinned. "The Army Rangers."

Gerry whistled through his teeth. "So they'd have some serious weapons." Paul nodded.

I leaned back against the cushions and ran my hands through my hair. "In just a few months, the world has changed drastically. Approximately 90% of the population has contracted the virus. That means that there are over six billion people dead or undead." I paused there to let that number sink in.

"I'd like to know what the life span of this virus is. I've seen zombies that have died when the virus ran its course, so I know it has one. And I'd like to see if there is way to prevent a future outbreak."

"You are not looking for a cure?" Lucia asked.

"No," I said. There was no point in sugar coating it. "The virus is so aggressive, once it's contracted, there isn't much I can do. If I can figure out what causes the thinkers, maybe I can help those people before they die.

"Dead is dead," Paul said quietly.

"Yes," I sighed. "I'd like to see if I could synthesize some sort of immunization. But there is no way I can do that with the equipment that I have. I want to search the plane and see what was on there."

"That's some pretty sensitive equipment you'd be looking for. I doubt it survived the crash," Lucia said.

"I know," I said with a sigh. "But it's still worth a look. And then there is the research they've done."

"I'd rather have all the available weapons under our control," Gerry said.

"I agree completely," Lucia said. "So, when do we go, and who goes?"

"I'd like to go, but someone needs to stay with the kids," Paul said. Kitty flashed him a look at being referred to as a kid. "And, I'm pretty banged up from my fall. I can't go."

Gerry stood up. "Right, its only just now noon, let's go look."

"Look for a zombie with a brief case," Paul said.

Gerry snorted. "Hopefully the bastard hasn't eaten it."

CHAPTER 43

Lucia

Kitty had pushed the furniture to the sides in the great room. Parker sat on the steps, a dutiful student, as she showed him different moves with a machete in each hand.

"I call this one 'the McDeath', because Paul taught me it." Kitty began slashing both of her machetes forward, in a wheeling pattern. Her long, brown hair flicked from side to side.

Sharon was descending the stairs, "I hope Paul didn't show you with such vigor; he's still recovering."

Kitty stopped, arched one eyebrow and sashayed her head from side to side, "Look who's talking about vigor stunting recovery."

My eyes widened, but Sharon laughed, "Keep on training your prodigy, Sensei. You about ready, Lucia?"

I rose from the floor and picked my rifle up. "Yeah, Gerry is hooking up the trailer and bringing the quad around."

Kitty looked at Parker and continued, "Okay, I call this one 'the Cheerleader', because I killed a few with this move." She flattened her machetes and cut outward, in an X pattern.

Parker laughed, "Did you really kill cheerleader zombies?"

"Hell, yes. Your big sister's a lethal killing machine." Kitty laughed and stopped to tousle Parker's hair. "I had to mow down a pack of degenerate beauty queen wannabes to get out of my high school alive."

Sharon shook her head as we both laughed. Paul slowly descended the stairs. "What's so funny?"

Sharon and I looked at each other and she spoke, "Um… have fun babysitting."

"We'll be fine. But you guys…be careful."

"We will." Sharon nodded towards Kitty, "You wanna bar this door behind us?"

"Yep!" Kitty bounced over to us as we exited.

*

Charred documents and two bags of peanuts were the first things we looted from the plane wreckage. Burnt body parts were scattered around the crash site. We stepped over them and were careful not to touch them. Gerry whooped loudly when he found large cases of military weapons, still intact. He tossed them onto the cart and briefly examined them before snapping them closed and then he scanned the tree line with the scope of his rifle.

Sharon ran a few feet and stopped. "I thought I saw something shiny." She started kicking the snow around with her feet, then bent over and picked up an ax. High above her head, she held the ax and said, "Cool! Look at this!"

Gerry and I nodded in agreement, exclaiming how awesome it was. Sharon smiled and carried the weapon back to the cart. "I think this belonged to Paul."

"Is that it? Are we done?" Gerry asked. He seemed anxious to leave.

Sharon bit the bottom of her lip. "The briefcase is missing."

I removed my squirrel head so my words weren't muffled, "Maybe it burned."

Sharon shook her head, "No, I don't think so. Paul said it was handcuffed to the wrist of one of the passengers. The wreck was bad, but it didn't burn that hot. We'd have found a partially burned body with the handcuffs if that had happened."

Gerry pulled the zipper up further on his coat. "I've searched this field with the scope. I haven't seen any bodies and we didn't get any new snow, so I'd say it's in the forest somewhere."

"Do we go there?" I shot a look between the two of them, and then focused on the looming darkness amidst the gathered fir trees. I was scared.

Gerry shrugged. "I'll go if you guys think we need to."

Sharon sighed. "We really should try to get the briefcase."

"Why though?" I asked. "We don't have the equipment to formulate a cure. Without even the most basic of equipment, it's useless to us."

Sharon put her hands on the sides of her head and shifted her hat down. "But what if they were close to a cure and someone finds us? What if that's our only chance and it's lost in the woods just behind our camp all of this time? We should at least try… just once… before the heavy snows make it impossible."

"Let's walk in." Gerry nodded towards the woods. "We can be taken by surprise if we can't hear over the engine of the quad."

"Okay, I'm game." I put my squirrel head back on and swung my rifle strap over my shoulder. I was willing, but not eager.

Every fifty yards or so, Gerry paused to scan the tree line with his rifle's scope, and Sharon looked with her binoculars. I removed my squirrel head and cocked my ear towards the forest, listening.

"Guys, I see something." Sharon faced the east and focused her binoculars. "Here, look." She handed her binoculars to me as Gerry pointed his scope in the same direction.

Gerry chuckled. "It looks like a zombie stuck in the mud." He lowered his rifle, "Let's go see."

In a cove clearing free of trees, the torso of a zombie stuck out of the ground. As we approached, he didn't move. When we were close enough, I picked up a rock and threw it at his head. It bounced off dumbly, but his eyes didn't open.

Gerry threw his own rock, hitting him with more force. Still, the zombie didn't move. "Hmm… how can he be dead? I've seen plenty of zombie torsos still crawling around. His head's not injured."

"Maybe he was one of the smart ones and committed suicide." Sharon and Gerry looked at me. "You know, like Flipper did."

"What do you mean?" Gerry asked.

Sharon's mouth flattened into a line and she spoke. "She means that each breath for a dolphin is a decision. The main dolphin, Kathy, who played Flipper on the TV show, experienced depression and purposely stopped breathing, thus committing suicide."

"That's grim as fuck," Gerry said.

The zombie turned its head and we heard it crackle. "Oh," Sharon said, "not dead, just frozen. Good to know." She shot the moving torso through the head, and it flopped backwards. "Well, no handcuffs, so we have another zombie around here…somewhere." A moan erupted to our left; we all raised our weapons and walked towards it.

Navigating through the woods was difficult in my suit, and the fur was now slicked down from the wet snow. We moved in a triangular pattern, covering all sides. The jagged, rotting stump of a tree had impaled a zombie on his free-falling impact to the earth. He moaned and gnashed his teeth at us as we approached. His head kept darting forward as he futilely attempted to lurch his body towards us. Dangling from his wrist was the briefcase and it beat against the tree stump as he thrashed about.

"Well, aren't you quite the hors d'oeuvres, all toothpicked up in the forest?" I laughed at the zombie. "Hungry?"

He responded by trying to jerk his body loose. "Fuck this," Gerry said, and he killed him with one shot to the head.

"Nice aim," I said.

"Thanks." Gerry nodded once, in my direction. "I'm gonna try to shoot the handcuff so it breaks off of the zombie."

Sharon nodded and Gerry fired twice before the briefcase fell away from the decaying limb. He picked it up and handed it to Sharon. "Thanks. We can pop the locks open on this back at the lodge. For now, let's get out of here." She scanned the woods and we began trekking back.

The light of the clearing was just ahead when we heard a collective of zombie gnarls, growls, and moans. Gerry whispered, "Let's make a run for the quad. We'll have a clear shot in the field." Sharon nodded, and we started running.

Like objects slipping through the holes of a too-large sieve, the zombies pushed forward between the trees. We quickened our run and bolted for the field. The cold had slowed them down, but the zombies were closing on us. I could smell them as I was sure they could smell us.

Sharon and Gerry dashed ahead of me. The suit was slowing me down. I'd never worn it while running through the snow before. My padded foot caught on a rock and my body was thrown face-down onto the ground. My gun slipped out of my hand and landed a few feet from me. With the squirrel head on, I couldn't turn around and see the zombies, but I could hear their feet pounding towards me. I struggled to get up as one reached me. I screamed and fell as I kicked his knee backwards. All of the air in my lungs had been pressed out of my chest in shrieks and I prayed Gerry and Sharon could hear me. The zombie was on top of me and his teeth were fully exposed because so much flesh had rotted away from his face. I grabbed him by the wrists and held him off as my legs kicked at him. Over his shoulder, I could see other zombies staggering towards us. *So you were the fast one?* My squirrel head fell backwards, just as bullets whizzed overhead, one finding the zombie's forehead with a *thunk*. Gerry and Sharon stood over me, shooting at the horde moving through the forest. I rolled to my feet and picked up my gun to join them.

Slowly, we walked backwards as we inched out of the woods, laying waste to the zombies amongst the firs. Sharon arched her head upwards to search the sky. We all heard it: a helicopter was nearby, though we couldn't see it.

When nothing else moved, we stopped firing. As the last shots echoed through the forest, distinct pops came from the direction of camp. Gerry looked at us. "That came from camp. Let's hurry."

Again, we ran, but this time I didn't fall, and nothing followed us. My squirrel head was in one hand, my gun in the other. "Thank you," I breathed with each stride.

CHAPTER 44

Paul

"Paul?"

"Hi, Kitty. How's it goin'?"

She stood at the door to the kitchen. Somewhere in the background I could hear Parker making 'truck noises' and then bashing something off the furniture. It occurred to me I should probably tell him to stop. I had, after all, been left in charge while Sharon, Gerry, and Lucia took the quad and trailer to try and find the plane. I warned them there were likely to be some scientists and heavily armed soldiers looking to snack on them. At least the soldiers wouldn't use the weapons, just their hands and teeth. The horrors I'd witnessed in the past days made me shudder, as well as wonder how the fuck I was still alive.

So here I was: Mister Sensible Adult, the responsible one. Mister Banjaxed more like, left in charge of one small boy and a teenage girl, neither of which I had any experience of nor knew what I was supposed to do or say to. At least there would be no nappies involved, thank God for small mercies.

"What was it like?" she asked sheepishly.

"Eh… what was what like?" I had been savouring a cup of freshly brewed coffee. I put the mug down and raised an eyebrow at the petite girl. *Please don't let this be an awkward teenage question.* I so was not equipped for that sort of shit.

"Falling out of the plane," she said.

"Ohhhh," I doubt I hid the sigh of relief that came out. "Well, it was a bit like being a bird, but one who can't remember how to fly no matter how hard he flaps his wings, and then realises the ground is coming his way realllly fast."

She laughed. I wasn't joking.

"Wanna sit down?" I asked, not knowing what else to say. "Do you drink coffee?"

"Actually, I was wondering... could I bring Parker outside? There's still some snow on the ground; I thought it might be fun to build a snowman."

Normally that would be a perfectly reasonable request, only 'normal' was a word that no longer existed in the apocalypse dictionary. My hand strayed to the gun sitting snugly in a holster on my shoulder; it felt weird. Sharon had given me a shitload of shells; I think she thought I needed the practise.

"Sure, why not." I drained the mug and grabbed a heavy fleece lined jacket hanging on the back of the door. I had no idea whose it was, but I was pretty sure they would not be coming looking for it anytime soon.

I stepped outside gingerly; a thin coating of snow crunched under my boots. My back hurt, my legs hurt—in fact, everywhere hurt. I walked with a limp, rubbing an aching shoulder. I could almost taste the cold on my tongue. It wasn't like at home where the dampness hung in the air, chilling you to the bone; it was a cleaner, fresher kind of cold. Still bloody cold, mind.

It felt surreal to me, especially as I gazed at the rugged beauty of the park. Back home, a park was a small manicured green area. Here it was an untamed wilderness, a forest of towering trees that went on forever, and once upon a time even contained animals I would only ever see in a zoo. It was only days since I was sitting in my apartment, hoping to wait out the epidemic. In Ireland we called World War II 'the Emergency'; we have a funny way of understating things.

I heard Parker squeal with delight as Kitty flung a snowball at him. Who wouldn't smile at that?

"Don't stray anywhere you can't see the lodge," I yelled over. Kitty gave me the thumbs up as she ran in a circle around her smaller playmate. She was good with him. He was good for her, I supposed.

I slid the Glock from its holster and clicked a magazine home. Something made me think of Ciara then. I don't know if it was holding the gun in my hand or the noise of a child's laughter. She just wanted life to be normal, even if it was a shit life on the game with a drug dealing boyfriend. I pushed the memory aside and took aim at a tree.

I fired a few rounds, putting dents in the bark; I was getting better. At least the tree wasn't trying to eat me. I wondered if I would still hit it if it was moving towards me. I caught sight of a woodpile outside the door; I could see the handle of an axe with the head embedded in a log. It was still really hard to get my head around what had happened in the last few days... how immune I had become to death... to inflicting it so brutally. Okay, so the infected are already dead; there is nothing left of the person, just a reanimated body being controlled by a virus. Even so.

I killed the tree again... twice. And then I heard something in the air. Very faint, but growing gradually louder. At first I thought it was an insect buzzing, but it didn't quite fit. I realised then there were no other sounds.

"Kitty? Parker?" I limped over to where they had been playing snowballs. I could see a trail in the snow coming from the trees. I stood over a mound of tightly packed white snow.

"Kitty?"

The noise got louder, and in the distance I could see a black dot against a blue sky. My mouth dropped in disbelief. The way it was moving there was no way it was a bird.

Bloody hell, kids! I told her not to stray out of sight of the lodge; collecting snow in the darkened woods was not part of those instructions.

The dot got bigger really quickly, and it soon became apparent what it was. The swaying trees, the roar of the engines...

it was a helicopter. Not just a helicopter, a flying bloody fortress. I could see machine guns bristling, and rockets attached to the underside. It hovered just over the tree line, bending them towards me. The din of whining rotary blades drowned out my shouts and yells. I could see the white helmets of the pilots; surely to God they could see me in the open space behind the lodge. It passed overhead; I could see a manned machine gun sticking out of an open door at the side.

Why the fuck weren't they stopping? Maybe they would radio for help. It drifted away into the distance, gone as quickly as it had come. *Well bugger that!* I thought.

Then I heard a scream.

Oh fuck!

"Kitty?" I yelled, and looked into a dark forest; how many secrets would those trees tell if they could speak?

Then she burst from the darkness, half running, half stumbling with Parker in her arms. I could see tears streaming down her cheeks as she gulped down air. Then she tripped and fell.

A huge bastard of a zombie lurched out after her. I raised the gun and aimed—what if I missed? I could imagine the scene when the others got back. 'So how are the kids?' Oh fine, I shot Kitty and a zombie got Parker. Not good.

I took a deep breath; Kitty was scrambling to her feet and dragging Parker by the hand. *I can't do this,* I thought, but fired anyway. Bullseye! Well, under normal circumstances it would have been—I hit it in the chest.

"Fuck!"

I fired again and hit it between the eyes. Both kids ran to me. Kitty was sobbing, Parker was crying too, but I wasn't sure if it was because he had been chased from the woods by a zombie or because his teenage friend was, and he was just joining in.

"Okay, it's okay, I got him. Are you alright?" It only just occurred to me then what I might have to do. Oh dear God. "You weren't bitten, either of you?" Kitty shook her head vigorously.

"That's good," I said. *No shit.* "Let's get back up to the lodge and stay there for the rest of the day." *With all the doors and windows locked,* I silently added.

I put Parker down and realised Kitty had gone rigid and was staring over my shoulder.

"O…o…o…o…over…" She pointed with a shaking hand. "Over there!"

I turned around and followed her gaze. Melting from the trees, a line of zombies emerged from the darkness. And behind them, more, and behind them still more.

"Oh bollocks!"

I raised the gun and fired. *Bam! Bam! Bam!* Two of them crumpled to the floor; a third one spun around when I winged it.

Click… click… click. Fuck, I hadn't counted the rounds down.

"Run to the house!" I roared at the kids. Kitty grabbed Parker by the arm and dragged him towards the back door of the lodge. I rumbled about in my pocket for another clip, and it slid through my fingers.

It was cold, and the zombies moved slower when the temperature dropped, which was just as well, because I was an idiot. I bent down to pick up the fallen magazine and then heard Kitty scream. She was at the back door with Parker, but a zombie dressed in mechanic's overalls was shambling around the corner. There was no time to retrieve the clip, load it, and then take aim. I didn't trust myself to just fire wildly. I scooped up the ammunition and ran.

The kids were backing along the wall away from the mechanic, Kitty holding Parker defensively behind her. She had guts, that girl. As I ran past the woodpile, I yanked out the woodsman's axe.

"Hey, fuck face! Over here!" The mechanic turned and lost half his face.

A woman lurched around the corner after him, grinning evilly. A flap of her cheek hung loose, exposing her teeth. I swung the axe. The balance was off; the handle was longer than both the fireman's axe and the replica battle axe. Even so, it bit into her neck and only took two hacks to take off her head.

I swung around. The back yard was now full of zombies staggering towards us, driven by a burning desire to feed—their only instinct. All other forms of self-preservation were out the window. I wasn't mad keen on the idea, but the possibility of me becoming dinner was getting stronger.

"Quick! Inside," I yelled at the kids. I dropped the axe and slammed home the magazine. I let them run behind me and scramble in the backdoor, then I walked out to meet the undead host.

I stood my ground, legs apart, taking aim. "Bastards!"

At close range they were easy enough shots. Thankfully the icy conditions had them moving slower; even so there were enough to overwhelm me quickly enough. And the fuckers were relentless. I fired the last bullet from the clip, taking a grim satisfaction in the number of bodies lying in the mud and snow.

Still they came, hundreds. They poured from between the trees as if they were part of the forest. I thought this was meant to be a safe haven, for fuck sake. I couldn't help notice how fresh they all were, as if they had only just turned. What the hell was going on?

For some reason, an image of a sheep dog sprang to mind: a big fat, flying sheep dog with a fuckload of guns sticking out of it. Was the helicopter herding the zombies? And if so, why towards us? They probably didn't realise there was anyone here, I supposed.

I needed to get inside the lodge; there seemed to be no end to the walking dead shambling from the trees. It occurred to me then that maybe we should have run for a vehicle and just got the hell away. Too late.

They were coming up the other side of the yard now. I half limped, half shuffled in the back door… talk about a slow race. Kitty was there, sitting on a chair with Parker in her lap; I'm not sure who was clinging to whom. I rifled through a box of shells I'd left on the kitchen table and quickly reloaded the magazine. They were at the door now, their grotesque faces pushed up against the windows. Then we heard the sound of smashing glass.

"Upstairs! Go!" I shouted. They didn't have to be told twice.

We ran to the front of the house into the reception area. Three of the walking dead were shuffling through the main door. Shit! Had I left it open? It took six shots to put the three of them down, and then I flung myself at the door, slamming it shut. I felt something give in my back. Praying it wasn't something I'd done falling from the plane and now made much worse, I dragged myself towards the stairs.

"Come on! Please hurry," Kitty encouraged.

I half staggered, half crawled up onto the landing. Kitty was crying. This time though, I think they were tears of joy, or at least relief.

"I'm still alive, I'm still alive," I said. I didn't believe me.

Parker ran out from one of the rooms, grinning and pointing. I dragged myself up to the window. Coming up the trail on a quad was a giant squirrel, a redhead, and a bearded man, armed to the teeth.

CHAPTER 45

Gerry

At hearing the distinct, hollow pop-pop of a Glock, we took off in the direction of the camp. Soon enough we saw what Paul must have been firing at. Before us, all around us, and moving in on the lodge were dozens upon dozens of the walking dead. The entire mountainside was teeming with them. So far, none turned to face us as we bullied past on the quad.

The closer we came to the lodge, the thicker they crowded. After nearly striking three, and kicking two close enough to reach with an extended leg, I glanced over my shoulder to see if there might be an easier way to circle back around.

There wasn't. Our passage had been blocked by the dead, and they swarmed forward, filling the gaps between trees and all along the trail.

We'd spent a lot of ammo back at the wreckage, and had no more than thirty or forty shots between us. I yelled for Lucia to take over steering, and she clumsily edged forward and took over. I had to get to the weapons we'd taken from the plane. Their Army had some bad ass weapons, and we sure needed them right then. No sooner did I hand over the wheel, Lucia struck a zombie, jarring me enough that I nearly fell over the side.

"Fuck! Be careful," I said.

"Sorry," was her muffled reply. "It's tough as fuck to see. My eye holes are crooked."

"Just keep it straight for a minute," I said. "I gotta get to the back."

I ducked as a zombie hit the front left quarter panel of the quad, then skidded along the side. If I didn't know better, I'd have sworn she was aiming for them.

It was bumpy going, so I had Sharon hold my belt as I leaned into the trailer. I'd opened each crate before stowing them on the quad, so I had a general idea what I was looking for. I shoved a heavy crate aside and it fell off the back, the contents spilling out onto the snow. Ammo clips. Hopefully none of them were the ones needed for the bad boy I was searching for—the M249 Saw. In the destructive world of assault rifles, its specs sheet said, the Saw was a spiked wrecking ball. A grin split my face as I popped a lid and found it, along with six humongous, pie-shaped ammo clips.

I pulled it and a 3-pack of ammo clips from the box, then nodded at Sharon to pull me back. Before I had a chance to turn and face forward, a body flew up over the hood and knocked me backward onto the trailer. The body sailed past and disappeared into the snow kicked up in our wake. It was a good thing Sharon hadn't let go of my belt after pulling me up or I'd have been back there, making snow angels with the deadies.

Still holding my belt, Sharon crouched and shot at the closest of the dead. Three fell and five more crowded in. "I'm almost out," she said as she slammed home a fresh clip.

"Gerry!" Lucia yelled. "They're getting harder to miss, and some of them are turning this way."

"Give me a minute. I just need to load this gun."

Sharon looked at the Saw, then holstered her gun and reached for the rifle and ammo. She quickly studied it, then rolled the clip into place.

She shrugged and handed it back. "Beginner's luck. That's a powerful weapon. What size rounds does it use?"

I found the safety, flipped it, then said, "I dunno—big, I imagine." When my finger touched the trigger, a laser sight activated.

"Cool," I said, chambering a round. "You should probably keep holding onto me. This thing must kick like a fucking mule."

My first spray of bullets blew a zombie in half – lengthwise – and wiped out another seven or eight behind it. "Holy shit! Did you see that prick come apart?"

"Sorry," Sharon said, as she dropped two zombies that had turned toward the quad. "Little busy over here."

I flipped the gun on its side and found the switch to turn it from full auto to semi-automatic; no use wasting bullets. And there was no such thing as a bad shot from this gun. Whatever it hit vaporized, along with anything unlucky enough to be in its kill-zone.

Twenty, thirty, fifty of them fell, yet more and more stumbled out from between the trees. My heart sank as the lodge came into view. The building was surrounded, and a dozen or more lined the front porch.

To myself more than either Sharon or Lucia, I said, "Where the hell are they coming from?" I hadn't seen this many dead in the last three towns I passed *combined*, let alone *one* town. Their presence here was impossible… yet here they were.

Sharon dropped her Glock into the trailer, then reached out and stripped the pair of .45s from my shoulder rig. "I don't know," she said, "but they seem to be thinning out. There can't be more than seventy or eighty left."

She fired off three shots at a passing group, then clicked empty. "I'm out. I hope you have more bullets for these."

"I do, in the front pocket of my jeans, under my snow pants. I'm sorry. If I'd known the entire population of Deadie, Canada was coming for a visit, I'd have planned things a little different."

"Keep shooting," she said, then tugged up my coat and plunged her hand down my pants. "I'll get them myself."

I found it tough to concentrate with a woman's hand down my pants, but managed to keep it together long enough to cut the horde's numbers by over half, leaving no more than thirty in the clearing, and possibly another twenty out in the woods, hung up on one or more of our booby traps. Sharon pocketed a handful of shells, reloaded my .45s and joined me in taking out the closest of them.

Lucia struck one, then another, and then both her and Sharon ducked as a body bounced up and over the quad's stubby hood and over our heads.

Sharon checked to make sure it hadn't landed in the quad or trailer, then leaned over and yelled at Lucia, "Can you try to *not* hit every one?"

Lucia jumped when Sharon spoke, then nodded quickly. "Yeah, got it—miss a few. Sure thing. Or maybe you could tell them to stop getting in the fucking way."

The quad rocked as a zombie fell under the tires.

Over her shoulder, Lucia yelled, "That one wasn't my fault. Gerry, why don't you shoot some of these fuckers up here? I've already filled one pant leg with piss. I don't wanna drown in my own urine."

I faced forward and lined up the closest zombie in our path. The shot blew it in half as well as two others behind it. We ducked a shower of body parts as the quad bumped over their lower remains. After checking ourselves over for any spray or chunks, Sharon leaned over and punched my shoulder.

"Good God, Gerry. What part of 'transmitted through blood' did you not understand?"

"OK," I said. "So shooting forward wasn't the best idea."

I tapped Lucia on the shoulder as we entered the clearing surrounding the lodge. "Let me off near the lodge, then swing around and lure them toward the booby traps."

Lucia slowed, but before I could jump down, Sharon grasped my arm, then nodded toward the lodge. I nodded back, and she slid past me and hopped down from the quad. She shot a zombie standing between her and the lodge then ran up the steps, killing two more as she went.

"OK," I said to Lucia. "New plan. Get this thing moving while I find you a gun."

CHAPTER 46

Sharon

We managed to thin the herd out significantly. Bodies lay in piles like soldiers on some forgotten beach. Several more zombies were rolling around on the ground, still trying to get to us even though they lacked body parts. I had a theory about zombie parts.

When I was a little girl, I watched my grandmother wring the neck of a chicken. It flopped around the yard for well over an hour. She told me that if you damage the brain, the body won't do that, but it was a lot messier. I was horrified by both notions and refused to eat the chicken for dinner that night.

I suspected that it was much the same for zombies. Shoot the brain, the body dies. Cut the parts off, and the virus will still animate those parts for a short while after they are separated from the body. I hadn't tested my theory so far, and at the moment it wasn't my primary concern—getting to the lodge was. Paul was in there with the kids. I was praying they were okay. I would have run in there by now, but I couldn't leave Lucia and Gerry to face the undead horde alone.

The sound of gunfire ricocheted in the mountains like the rumble of distant thunder. I glanced over to Gerry and nodded towards the lodge. He nodded back. I jumped out of the trailer and ran knowing he'd keep watch and pick off anything that might come up behind me.

My boots sounded on the wood planks of the porch. Shattered glass was spread everywhere and glinted like diamonds in the late day sun. Three rotting corpses were piled before the front door. Dead for the second time, and for good. I slung my rifle onto my back and pulled out my handgun.

"Paul?" I shouted. "Can you hear me? Kitty?" I heard a grunt, then a crash and what sounded like pissed off Irishman. I grinned. If he was swearing, he wasn't dead.

"Paul?" I called again.

"Yeah?"

"Everyone okay?"

"Yes," he shouted back. I sighed in relief.

"I'm going to go around to the kitchen. Don't shoot me." I hopped off the porch and ran around to the back of the lodge. Gerry and Lucia were going from trap to trap, re-deading the corpses that didn't have the decency to stay dead.

The windows over the sink, those that we didn't board up because we thought they were too high to be a threat, were broken. A large woman had lodged herself in the frame. The hem of her dress flapped in the breeze, displaying her 'Tuesday' underwear to all of creation. I nudged her with the Glock. She didn't move.

The kitchen door was locked. I pounded on it. "Paul? Kitty?" I yelled. "Let me in." I heard more shuffling and then the sound of a bolt being thrown. Paul peered back at me though the crack.

"Are you bitten?" he asked.

"Nope. You?" I asked, scanning him for any signs of bites or scratches. He winced, but he had just fallen out of a plane. It was to be expected that he would be in pain. "You said the kids are okay," I said as I walked into the kitchen.

The woman hanging in the window may have once been pretty. It was hard to tell, as she didn't have a face. It was as though the skin had been peeled back, revealing putrid muscles and veins that would have pulsed with life. Now they stretched across her face like abandoned highways. Empty. A testament to life long gone. An eyeball hung from its stem, dripping fluid into the sink. I shuddered and looked away.

"The kids are fine. Locked in a room upstairs," he said as he closed the door behind me.

"I'm going to go check," I said. "You okay?" He nodded and waved me on. I turned and ran up the stairs to my room. The door was locked.

"Kitty? Parker?" I said. "You two okay?"

"Yeah, we're fine. No one's bitten." Kitty said. "Are you bit?" she asked.

"No," I said. I heard the door unlock, and then Parker launched himself at me, almost knocking me over. I hugged him close, enjoying the feel of him in my arms. I glanced up to see Kitty swipe a hand over her eye and looked away before she realized I saw.

The gunfire had dwindled down to just an occasional shot, but the feeling of unease was palpable. "I'm going to go check on Paul, Gerry, and Lucia…" I let my sentence trail off. I didn't want to pester her with questions. This was a new world, and the old rules were gone. She wanted to be an adult, had to be an adult, and I'd extend her the courtesy I'd give anyone else.

"We'll stay here," she said, seeing my need to keep them safe and my hesitation to ask her to hide. I nodded and walked away, hearing the sound of the door locking behind me. The tension in my shoulders eased a bit. *They're safe, for now,* I thought, and trotted down the stairs to see Lucia and Gerry coming in from the kitchen. Paul was sitting on the sofa. Lucia walked over to him. He said something to her about his back; she ran her hands down his spine, frowning, searching for the cause of whatever was bothering him.

"You left this in the cart," Gerry said, handing me the worn case that we had trekked out into the cold to find. I was on my way downstairs to get it and was glad that I didn't have to venture out in the killing fields that was once serene wilderness.

"Thank you," I said, taking the case from him. I had planned on picking the lock, but my adrenaline was still thrumming through me, and I didn't have the patience for it.

Wandering into the kitchen, I found a sharp knife and ran it along the seams of the leather, popping the threads of the stitching. The case I had been given was steel, and I wondered why they used leather to transport important materials. But like everything else, things had changed and this was likely the only case they had.

I couldn't stand being in the same room with Tuesday hanging in the window, so I walked back to the dining room where my laptops sat. I managed to work open a seam on the side of the case.

"Gerry?"

"Yeah?"

"Do you have a flashlight?" I couldn't see into the case and was hesitant to reach my hand in. I didn't know if the case was booby trapped, or I would have just dumped the contents out on the table.

He walked over and clicked on the light that he held in his hand. I pulled the seams apart. "Do you see anything in there?"

"Just papers and a flash drive," he said, shining the light around the corners of the case, just to make sure. I nodded and shook the case. A stack of clipped papers slid out, landing with a thud. I caught the cool metal of the thumb drive. The sun glinted off the shiny case. I wondered what secrets it guarded.

Lucia called to Gerry, and he walked away as the smell of coffee filled the air. I heard her say something about helping her get a body unstuck and assumed she meant Tuesday. I certainly didn't plan on using the kitchen until she was gone. But for now, the thrall of what I held in my hand captured me. All else faded away.

I powered on the laptop and inserted the flash drive in a USB port. A request for a security code popped up. I typed in mine and was relieved when it was accepted. The drive was huge and held over 100 gigs of memory. Thousands of files fanned out before me. It would take me days to read them all. I browsed through the headings, found one labeled "Darwin" and clicked on it.

Inside were journal entries from the research facility in Greenland. I started to skim through and then stopped, stunned by what I was reading. My breath left me in a rush as the origin of the virus was laid out before me.

They had found several seals that were exhibiting rabies-like symptoms. The animals were destroyed and samples tested. The virus was isolated and tests were run. They could not understand why the virus did not behave like they thought it should, and so they injected it into a couple of the lab monkeys and quarantined them.

The test animals began to exhibit symptoms later that night. A notation was made that only one tech was on duty as the wife of the other tech was in labor. A report from that technician said he fell asleep around 2 a.m. and awoke to several students who had broken into the lab to 'liberate' the animals. They shoved the tech into a closet and unlocked the cages of eight animals. I remembered the state that Tate had been in when he bit Mindy. Dread filled my heart as I read on, knowing what was about to happen.

Three of the students were brutally attacked. A fourth was so badly mauled that she died less than an hour later. The technician reported hearing screaming from outside the closet. He happened to have his phone with him and called Security. The research facility went into lockdown, and the students were detained.

I read an entry that said, "Female: age 18. Cause of death: brain aneurism." It listed her resurrection time as less than fifteen minutes after she died. The researcher noted that the body was still warm when she rose.

They had not been expecting that, as none of the test animals had resurrected. The technician, newly rescued from his closet, was her first victim. One of the security guards put her down, and the tech, whose name was never given, was put in a holding cell. They labeled him simply as 'Test Subject One'. The world's first captive zombie.

The students that orchestrated a rescue became prisoners themselves. The ones that had been attacked but not killed were treated and watched as symptoms progressed. And when they died, the researchers were prepared. Detailed notes were kept about each subject's death and subsequent resurrection.

I sat back, dumbfounded. I had been told that Malik Hauksson was Patient Zero, but that was not the case. They had these three students locked in their facility for well over a month before Hauksson went on the seal harvest. In their zeal to harness the virus, they didn't keep careful watch of the seal population or keep track of any animals that might be exhibiting symptoms. If they had, Hauksson would not have been bit, and the world would not have died.

"Son of a bitch," I whispered. I closed the file and went back to the index. There was a file named 'Rapture'; it was odd enough that it caught my interest. I clicked on it and found a list of names. Next to each one was a job description and an address. A third column indicated if they were living. Most of them weren't. As I scrolled down, I found my name. My hand began to shake.

The Rapture is a Christian term. It is supposed to happen during the second coming of Christ. A few will be taken, while others are left behind, I think it says. Clearly, this file was a list of people who were supposed to be secured. Where we were to be taken, I didn't know. But I did know that this list did not bode well for me.

I noticed that a few of the names had asterisks next to them. There was one next to mine. I hovered the cursor over that symbol and a note popped up. 'Location unknown, presumed living, liability'.

"Liability," I read out loud.

The light in the corner of my laptop that had started flashing when Kitty hacked into the weather system changed color and became solid green. I frowned and watched as a second cursor appeared on my screen. It began to select files and delete them.

"Oh, no…" I gasped, jumping up from the table.

I felt frantic and wanted to throw the laptops out the window like the bombs I perceived them to now be. "This is bad. Very bad."

CHAPTER 47

Paul

The cavalry came coasting over a snow clad hill on a quad bike. Parker was jumping up and down on the bed and laughing, I suspect, at the giant squirrel rider. Kitty and I looked at each other and grinned. The relief passing between us was palpable.

"You did good," I said as the sound of gunfire drowned out the groans of hundreds of the walking dead. She dropped her eyes and her cheeks reddened.

I hauled myself up at the sound of Sharon's voice calling to us. Before I could answer, I tripped on a discarded toy, which sent a spasm up my back. I fell against a bedside locker, and a vase fell to the floor and shattered.

"Paul?" Sharon called again.

"Yeah," was about as much as I could manage, grimacing with the pain.

"Everyone okay?"

"Yes." That was a lie. "Wait here," I said to Kitty and started for the door.

"Paul?"

"Yeah?" I said, turning.

"Is this what it's going to be like… forever and ever I mean?" Kitty was looking me straight in the eye; I could see her holding back the tears.

I didn't know what to say. She was a smart kid and had been through more than any person, let alone a teenager starting out in life, ought to. I wasn't sure what sort of reassurance she wanted from me. To lie? What was the truth anyway? I sure as fuck didn't know. The world we were headed into didn't have proms and sweet sixteen parties. There'd be no first dates to the movies and hanging out at the mall with her friends.

"I don't know, kiddo. We've survived so far, and I'll let you in on a little secret, so long as you swear not to tell anybody. I ain't Bear Grylls, so if I made it this far, you can be sure there are a hell of a lot others out there who did too. We'll find them or they'll find us, and together we'll form a community. So no, it won't always be like this."

I could hear footsteps on the porch below. "I'm going around to the kitchen. Don't shoot me," Sharon called up.

"I gotta…" I pointed downstairs; Kitty nodded and pulled Parker close to her. "Lock this door after me."

After I let Sharon in the back door, she ran up the stairs to check on the kids. I hobbled into the main living area and fell into a sofa. When Gerry and Lucia followed in, I could see Gerry was carrying Tompkins' leather satchel and a seriously big fucking gun. They'd found what they were looking for then. To be honest, I hadn't the energy to ask.

"You look like you're in pain," Lucia said. There was genuine concern on her face, which was kind of touching, considering we didn't know each other from Adam. Maybe that pile of shite I'd just said to Kitty wasn't that far off the mark. If enough people cared, maybe there could be life again.

"I don't think I'll be lining out for the Dubs this season," I said.

"Huh?"

"Doesn't matter." I half grinned, half grimaced.

"Let me take a look."

Sharon came back down the stairs and took the satchel from Gerry while I closed my eyes, letting the conversation wash over me. My mind wandered to home, rolling green hills, and girls dancing a jig at the crossroads… yeah right, bollocks to that. A post-apocalyptic city. The streets choked with abandoned cars, trucks and buses, where dead people walked around trying to eat live people. I'd never see it again; I knew that with complete certainty, and to be honest, I didn't want to. Again, I wondered if Mrs. Watson had the right idea when she flung herself from the apartment building. That seemed like such a long time away, a lifetime ago. That vision had haunted me every day since her graceful leap. It was beautiful in a macabre sort of way. I could nearly set it to music.

"Hey! That sounds like the helicopter we heard earlier," Gerry's words cut into the hellish vision of home I had been dwelling on.

"It passed over here earlier. I tried to get their attention, but they either didn't see me or ignored me, and then I got distracted by a zombie invasion."

"Sounds like it's coming back." Gerry hopped up and made for the back door. I followed a lot slower. Lucia took my elbow and dragged me out of the sofa. It made me giggle through the pain. Then I noticed the cut on her head.

"Hey, you're bleeding."

"Fuck!" She put her hand up to the cut, and the tips of her fingers came away red.

"Hey! You sons of bitches. Over here!" Gerry was jumping and waving. Lucia and I added our voices to the call when we made it outside. Everywhere I looked, dead people lay—dead people made proper dead this time.

"It's coming this way," Lucia said excitedly.

"It fucking is 'n all," I added.

"I guess they did notice you. It's hard to miss a jumping leprechaun," Gerry grinned.

"Yeah, hopefully there won't be another zombie horde leading the way this time."

"What do you mean?" Lucia asked.

"I dunno, I just had a stupid notion that the helicopter had somehow herded the last one towards us. Stupid, I know."

Lucia's eyebrows wrinkled in consternation. Sharon appeared at the door then. She was waving, but the sound of the helicopter drowned out the words. I waved back. Then the world went to hell in a hand basket.

The helicopter raked the yard with machine gun fire. A trail of turned up earth and snow railed past me. Twin tracks of gunfire punctured holes in the Mustang and exploded the tyres.

"Oh, Sharon'll be so pissed," Lucia said.

"I'll buy her a fucking new one. Run!" Gerry was the first to react to the situation. My brain was taking its time computing that our rescuers were trying to kill us. He returned fire with the heavy machine gun he'd salvaged from the plane, then ran towards the quad and snatched a green, metal case from the trailer.

We all ran in different directions. Headless chickens sprang to mind, certainly in my case as each way I ran was cut off by more gunfire. I eventually made it to the tree line and ducked down behind some cover.

The helicopter hovered a few feet above the yard, blowing a hurricane of wind and snow every which way as a squad of dark shapes jumped out one by one. The lead soldiers immediately began firing at everything. The house was riddled, glass smashed, and chunks of timber splintered in the air. The truck exploded in a hail of gunfire. Then from the far side of the yard, Gerry reappeared. It soon became evident what was in the green case he had snatched from the trailer. He dropped to one knee balancing an R.P.G. on one shoulder. Oh fuck. A rocket whistled through the air, and the helicopter turned into a ball of roaring flame. The blast sent a wave of heat in my direction, forcing me to duck and look away.

Soldiers flew through the air, many engulfed in flame. Most of those who survived the inferno searched out the source of the rocket. Fierce gunfire was coming from the far side of the lodge now. I remembered the Glock stowed at my shoulder. I took it out, and after a moment's hesitation, started firing.

I'd become pretty desensitised to the sight of blood and the letting of same, but this was different. Those soldiers, although they were trying to kill me, were living, breathing people. It was one thing to hack at one of the resurrected—they were already dead. It was another thing to shoot at the living. I got over it and stepped from the trees. I shot two of the soldiers before they even realised I was there. The heat around the wreckage was colossal. Thick black smoke drifted in a dark pillar to the heavens—Gerry's gift to the gods.

Gerry emerged from the smoke on the other side, and we met in the middle. There were still some soldiers moving around, but the fight was gone out of most of them. Even so, we backed towards the house, firing at any that showed signs of getting up. We made it onto the porch, and I saw Lucia was inside. She looked pretty banged up; the cut on her head was bleeding, and I noticed her limping. Then I saw a dark stain on the leg of her trousers. I opened my mouth to ask her if she was okay, but she shushed me with a gesture and made for the stairs.

Smoke from the blazing wreck was drifting over us and into the house, making it difficult to see or even breathe. Then I saw the dark shape of a soldier in the house. Bastard must have gone in the back door. I aimed the Glock and fired… Nothing. I really needed to start counting down the bullets. I ran in and intercepted him at the bottom of the stairs. A trail of blood led up the steps… Lucia's.

He fumbled for his sidearm when he saw me; I didn't wait. I stepped in, ignoring the pain in my back, and smashed him in the face with my fist. He went sprawling against a desk, scattering tourist leaflets all over the floor. He came up with a wicked looking knife in his hand.

I gulped in smoke-tainted air in ragged breaths. I never did understand what had happened to the world. Sharon had explained much of it to us, but to be honest, most of it went over my head. I still could not get my head around the idea that dead people were reanimating and trying to eat me. I did what I had to do to survive. I wasn't proud of a lot of the shit I'd done, nor was I ashamed. That's the way the world rolled now. The gun thing I was getting better at. I'd never even held one in my hand up until the previous couple of days. In time, I'm sure it would become the most natural thing in the world to be permanently carrying a firearm. But I grew up on the streets of Dublin, and having little shits come at me with knives was practically a hobby where I lived and did my thing.

The young soldier slashed at me with the knife. I grabbed his wrist and stepped in, snapped my head back and then buried my forehead into his face. I felt a crunch as his nose exploded in a spray of red. I jammed my knee between his legs with all the force I could muster. He crumpled to the floor and lay quivering

The knife dropped from his hand, and I picked it up. It was agony for me to bend down, but I did, and I rolled him onto his back. He was no longer a kid; he was not even human in my eyes. He was just a uniform with a gun. The world was fucked; the only rule now was to live. It no longer mattered how. My home was gone, overrun by flesh eating zombies. My family were either dead or walking dead. All I had were the people in this house, two American girls, a Canadian, and a couple of kids. They were my family now, and we were under attack. I knelt on the soldier's chest and dragged the blade across his throat.

I snatched up his gun and made for the stairs, each step shooting daggers down my back. I heard a crash that sounded suspiciously like a door being kicked in. Lucia was on the landing, she held her gun in both hands, taking aim. I could see her target, a soldier was framed by the open doorway of Sharon's room. I realised she'd frozen, it's no easy thing to kill a man, even one trying to kill you. I pushed past her and fired. A crimson spray painted the wall of the bedroom, and the soldier, first dropped to his knees, and then fell face forward.

Lucia looked at me with eyes wide. I heard screaming coming from the bedroom, but the words made no sense to me.

The thunderous roar of gunfire, from outside, had ceased, leaving only the sounds of sobbing washing over me. I felt dizzy, staggered back against the wall and slid down into a seated position on the floor. I had nothing left, my body would give me no more.

CHAPTER 48

Lucia

The cut at my hairline was bleeding into my left eye, blurring my vision. My ears rang from the sonic boom of the rocket launcher going off. The forest roared—now on fire, and I didn't know how long it would be until it spread to the lodge. I decided that if I could get to the roof through the hatch door we'd cut, I'd have a better aim at everyone on the ground—the soldiers and the once-dead. My hand was covered in wet blood and the gun kept slipping from my grasp. I fell against the doorway, my chest heaving as the smoke choked the air out of my lungs. Gerry and Paul retreated towards me, mowing down those that threatened us as they inched backwards.

I realized the door had been open when I got there. *Kitty... Parker... Sharon... were they still inside? Had anything or one gotten inside?* Snot choked in the back of my throat, and I struggled to yell for them, but nothing came. I shuffled towards the couch and grabbed a toss pillow. I wiped the blood from my eye and tried to blink the red away. I cleaned the blood from my hands and as what remained dried, my gun felt stuck to my grasp. The pillow was ruined. I dropped it on the floor. *At least it's my blood. Sharon will be mad. Maybe I can wash it before she sees.* I shook the thought away. There would be no lodge left by the time the fire burned itself out. *Maybe.*

Earlier, when I had fallen outside, one of the sharpened sticks we'd driven into the ground had imbedded into my thigh. Blood ran down my leg and filled my shoe. I shook my head—I knew one of us would eventually become hurt from the booby traps. *I'm glad it was me.*

The house was silent. I wanted to yell out for Sharon, but I knew better. As the cut on my head began to run into my eye again, I limped into the kitchen and my foot squished my blood between my toes with every step. A dish towel sat on the counter. I picked it up and pressed it against my head. Kitty's goth-bunny hat was on the table. I held the towel in place and pulled the hat down over it, securing it to my head.

Through the cracks in the boarded-up window, I could see Gerry and Paul had made it onto the deck of the porch. The seconds between their shots grew as their kill shot numbers increased.

The second step on the stairs sounded a loud, mewing creak. When I heard it, I knew someone was going upstairs. I grabbed my gun and slid alongside the wall until I could peek around the corner. A soldier was slowly climbing the stairs. I didn't have a clear shot. *Sharon could make that shot. Or Gerry, or Paul. Fuck! Probably even Kitty could.*

I watched as he disappeared up the stairs and turned the corner to walk down the hall. I crouched low and crept until I was at the bottom of the stairs. I climbed them slowly, skipping the second step altogether. I could hear him opening each door and checking the rooms. He had started in the back. If Sharon and the kids were in a room, it was at the closer end, and within seconds, he'd be there.

Paul was near the door now, and he shot a glance at me. I held my finger to my lips and pointed upstairs. Panic wiped across his face. I continued up the stairs as the soldier neared the end of his search. *You have to do it.*

He tried the door to Sharon's room. It was locked. *They are in there.* He stepped back to kick the door open and I bounded up the last four steps, two at a time. The lock broke and the door splintered open. I had a clear shot at his head, but I hesitated pulling the trigger. Paul pushed past me and fired. The man dropped, revealing Sharon, Kitty, and Parker in the bedroom.

Sharon stood ready with a shotgun aimed at the door. Kitty was huddled in a corner, her body covering Parker's. She moved aside and Parker jumped up.

"Daddy!"

CHAPTER 49

Sharon

When the fireball lit up the sky and the helicopter fell from the heavens, the percussion of the blast threw me backwards into the lodge. I landed hard on my elbow; pain danced up my arm, temporarily paralyzing it. My Glock skittered across the wood planks and slid under the couch.

I blinked for a few moments as the world danced away. A cloak of blessed peace settled upon me. The temptation to take comfort in its welcome embrace was strong. It would be so much easier to just let go of it all. The pain, the grief, the guilt.

This group of people had all shown up here just looking for a safe place. Unbeknownst to them, I had brought the war with me. The soldiers out there were here to either kill me or take me with them. And they didn't care who they had to murder to accomplish their mission. And just like that, I was pissed. Well and truly angry.

I fanned the heat of that flame and let it grow into an inferno that beat back the beckoning darkness. I took a deep breath and then coughed as my lungs filled with smoke. The forest was on fire. Hell had been loosed on earth.

Mankind was now an endangered species. We should be helping each other, not adding to the body count. And that too, pissed me off. My friends were outside fighting for their lives and ours. I'd not thank them by lying down and dying.

I stood; the room swayed as my vision swam. I reached up and touched my head; it came away sticky with blood. I'd lost a bit of skin, but the blood was not pulsing—that was a good sign. My rifle strap was tangled around me. I straightened it and went in search of my Glock. I could get another gun, but dammit, this one was mine and I wanted it.

I shoved the sofa out of the way. The brushed steel of the barrel gleamed at me. I grabbed it and ran upstairs. What was going on outside wouldn't swing one way or another with the addition of me.

If I thought that walking out there would satisfy the soldiers that had come for me, and if that would ensure that they would leave my friends alive, I would have. But they had been sent to kill, not retrieve. We would just be another group of people that had died during the zombie apocalypse…added to the tally that numbered in the billions.

I walked up the stairs towards my room and pounded on the door. "Kitty, Parker," I called. "It's me, Sharon. Let me in." The door opened, revealing Kitty holding my second handgun.

"You're gonna want to load that," I said, closing the door behind me. I yanked the trunk where I kept my weapons and spare ammunition out from under my bed. I found a set of headgear that protected the ears. Rob gave them to me to wear when I went to the firing range.

"Parker, under the bed," I said, tossing his pillow under there. My voice brooked no argument and he didn't offer any. I'd keep these kids safe with my last breath. It was all that mattered now. My life had been refined to this, and that is what I'd do. "Put these on," I said, handing him the headset. "Stay under there until I pull you out. Okay?" He nodded, his eyes huge and frightened.

Kitty had a small .22 revolver in her hand. I dug out the shells and showed her how to load it. Then I loaded my extra magazine, found some more ammunition for the rifle, and sat down on the bed.

I leaned back against the wall, rested the rifle on my knee, and sighted the door. If anything came through there, I'd take them out. I glanced over at Kitty. She looked back with grim resolve. I'll not draw comparisons with last stands, but this was ours. I could see by the look in her eyes that she intended to survive it. So did I.

The gunfire had slowed. I glanced out the window to see the blazing remains of Mr. Kowalski's prized possession. I grimaced— it was a shame. But I'd lament its loss later. I had more important things to consider right now.

I took a deep breath, steadying myself. Adrenaline was coursing through my veins, making my hands shake. I evened out my breathing, and focused. I heard glass break downstairs. They were in the lodge now, I realized. Footsteps sounded on the stairs; a board squeaked. That was the second stair from the bottom. It had a loose nail. I had planned to fix it.

The doorknob turned, painfully slow, meeting the resistance of the lock. A heartbeat, two, and then the door exploded inward. Kitty screamed.

I met the eyes of the man through the scope and gasped. He looked back; shock blossomed over his face when he recognized me.

"Holy fuck, Sharon," Jameson said, taking a step forward. I jumped off the bed, motioning Kitty to stay.

"Jamie?" I asked. I knew it was him, but the shock of it made me slow.

"Sharon you have to run and hide. The government is falling apart. The military is in control. General Daniels is dead, and the bastard that took his place didn't wait for the disease to kill him. They know you know what's on those files, and they aren't going to leave anyone alive who can jeopardize their grab for power.

"Why are you here?" I asked. "You work for Global Weather."

"I volunteered for this mission when I heard your name," he said, taking another step into the room. "We have to go, now." His voice was urgent.

"Jamie, I have Parker," I said, and then there was an explosion. Time slowed down. My breath was loud in my ears; my heart raced. Blood splattered across my face. Some of it got in my mouth. The taste of iron was heavy on my tongue. Jamie fell to the floor dead, and time resumed its course.

"Daddy!" Parker screamed and scooted out from under the bed. Kitty launched herself at him and pulled him to her before he could reach Jameson. I looked up to see Lucia standing in the doorway.

Her eyes widened when she realized who the assassin had been. Parker was on the floor sobbing so hard there was no sound. Kitty cried along with him, finally giving vent to the loss that she had endured. Paul appeared behind Lucia. He staggered back against the wall and slid to the floor, his body pushed beyond its limits.

"What happened?" Gerry asked as his presence filled the doorframe.

I bent down and picked up Parker, bringing Kitty with me.

"Are you all okay?" I asked, looking at them, searching for injuries. They nodded. Lucia's eyes were bright with tears. She was trying not to blink, but it was a losing battle. She nodded and closed her eyes, trying to hide the pain that this messed up world had visited upon us.

"We can't stay here. They'll keep coming," I said, looking at the body of my friend. Jamie had risked his life to come here and warn me. He didn't know I had his son; he was just trying to do the right thing. What he had told me about those who sought to control what was left of mankind wasn't a shock. I suspected that civilization would break down, but I didn't expect to become a target. As I stood there holding Kitty and feeling Parker's tiny body shake with sobs, my resolve grew. I had endangered them all trying to find those files. I knew I couldn't find a cure. And if I was honest, I knew I wasn't capable of synthesizing a vaccine. It had been a desperate hope of finding redemption on my part. It had been a fool's errand, but I'd not jeopardize them again.

We left the lodge that night under the cover of darkness. The UPS truck had not made it, but the bus had managed to escape any serious damage. We loaded up what supplies we could and headed north, leaving behind carnage. We didn't know where we were going or what awaited us once we got there, but that wasn't the point. We were together, and everyone was alive. Bandaged and bleeding from wounds that were both visible and unseen, but whole, and uninfected, we had all fought and killed for one another and if that wasn't family, then I didn't know what was.

* * *

It is said that to everything there is a season. A season to laugh and a season to weep, a season to heal and a season to kill. A season to live and a season to die. These are the stories of a group of survivors during the Season of the Dead.

ALSO AVAILABLE FROM SPORE PRESS

LYKAIA

by Sharon Van Orman
Co-Author of *Season of the Dead*

5 Stars on barnesandnoble.com
4.9 Stars on Amazon.com
4.65 Stars on GoodReads.com

"I'm afraid I won't be able to properly express my fascination with *LYKAIA*. It was such an awesome read I would definitely recommend it to all who'd love to spend some quality time with a really well-written book.

The main character, forensic pathologist Sophia Katsaros gets a phone call from Greece and finds out that her brothers have been missing for two months. She goes there to start an investigation of her own that might not end well for her.

This book has everything in it to satisfy a fastidious reader: really well thought-through plot line, fleshed out characters, tension, suspense, and more. I read the second half of the novel in one sitting, so riveting it was. I enjoyed Sharon's manner of writing. It is of the highest quality."

-Amazon Review

www.ingramcontent.com/pod-product-compliance
Lightning Source LLC
Chambersburg PA
CBHW021432240626
47153CB00001B/120

9780988192379